the doomspell trilogy

Praise for *The Doomspell* sequence

Part 1 – *The Doomspell*

'High fantasy, richly imagined and refreshingly well-written . . . an excellent novel.'   *Sunday Times*

'a great new voice in writing for children . . . an incredible world in which the reader will become totally absorbed.'   *The Bookseller*

'gripping . . . racy . . . [children] have been fighting to borrow it.'
                                                                           The Guardian

'a vivid world of magical possibilities'   *The Times*

Part 2 – *The Scent of Magic*

'McNish tells a rattling good tale, and his well-plotted narrative races through some excellent twists and turns to a spectacular climax.'
                                                                    The Daily Telegraph

'The language used is rich and evocative, full of visual and sensory imagery . . .'   *School Librarian*

'Continues the Doomspell story, but if anything the characterisations are deeper, the plot even more intriguing, and it is all carried off with a verve, pace and sheer passion for pure storytelling that make McNish's novels so compulsive.'   *Amazon*

'The writing is atmospheric and the plot gripping, as the children battle against awesome forces.'   *Good Book Guide*

Part 3 – *The Wizard's Promise*

'A fast-paced, gripping read.'   *Times Educational Supplement*

'breathtaking, swashbuckling stuff as the story relentlessly unfolds until it finally reaches its spectacular conclusion . . . the characters are believable; it is beautifully written, with page after page of powerful imagery . . . utterly compulsive and inventive.'
                                                                       Birmingham Post

Also by Cliff McNish

The Silver Child
Silver City

the
doomspell
trilogy

Cliff McNish

Orion
Children's Books

This omnibus edition first published in Great Britain in 2004
by Orion Children's Books
a division of the Orion Publishing Group Ltd
Orion House
5 Upper St Martin's Lane
London WC2H 9EA

Originally published as three separate volumes:
The Doomspell
First published in Great Britain in 2000 by Orion Children's Books
The Scent of Magic
First published in Great Britain in 2001 by Orion Children's Books
The Wizard's Promise
First published in Great Britain in 2002 by Orion Children's Books

A catalogue record for this book is available
from the British Library

Printed in Great Britain by
Clays Ltd, St Ives plc

ISBN 1 84255 102 7

www.orionbooks.co.uk

contents

the
doomspell

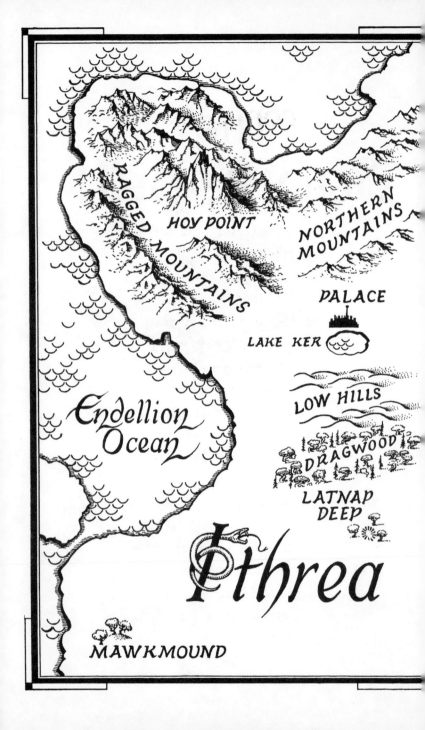

contents

For Rachel, of course

1

the witch

The Witch descended the dark steps of the Palace. It was a freezing night. Snow blew wildly in the sky and the wind howled like a starving wolf.

'What a delightful evening,' sighed the Witch happily.

Despite the bitter cold she wore only a thin black dress and her feet were bare. A snake clung passionately to her neck, occasionally blinking ruby-red eyes through the snow flurries.

The Witch walked effortlessly, relishing the crunch of ice against her toes, while a man alongside struggled to keep up. He was less than five feet tall and over five hundred years old. Bow-shaped creases either side of his eyes made them appear as if they had been gouged out and re-inserted many times. He shuffled down the steep Palace steps, only a big, flat nose and square chin exposed. His scraggy beard was neatly tucked under three scarves.

'Well, how do I look, Morpeth?' the Witch asked.

She flashed a pretty-woman face.

'It will convince the children,' he muttered. 'Why bother

to make yourself look nice, Dragwena? You don't normally care what they think.'

The Witch reverted to her normal appearance: blood-red skin, tattooed eyes, the four sets of teeth, two inside and two outside the writhing snake-mouth. Morpeth watched as the rows of teeth snapped at each other, fighting for the best eating position. A few purple-eyed, armoured spiders swarmed between the jaws, cleaning the remains of her last meal.

'Ah, but tonight a special child is arriving,' the Witch said. 'I don't want to frighten it too soon.'

Morpeth made his way down the remaining icy steps of the eye-tower. It was the highest point of the Palace, a thin column piercing the sky. Below, the other jagged Palace buildings huddled in the snow, their black stone poking up like beetle limbs. Morpeth placed one foot carefully in front of the next. He preferred not to slip – if he fell the Witch always waited until the last possible moment before rescuing him. Tonight he noticed Dragwena was unusually excited. She gently rolled the spiders on her tongue and laughed. It was an ugly laugh, shrill, inhuman – like the Witch herself. Through nostrils shaped like slashed tulip petals she sniffed the air eagerly.

'A perfect evening,' she said. 'Cold, darkness, and the wolves are out. Can't you smell them?'

Morpeth grunted, stamping his feet to keep warm. He could not smell or see the wolves, but he did not doubt Dragwena's word. Her bone-rimmed, triangular lids opened and stretched backwards under her cheekbones. Every detail of the night was always clear to the Witch.

'And the best of the evening is yet to come,' she sighed.

'Soon new children will be arriving. No doubt they will be the same as always – a little puzzled, yet grateful to receive our care. What will we do with them this time?' She grinned, and all four rows of teeth thrust forward menacingly. 'Shall we frighten them to death? What do you think, Morpeth?'

'Perhaps they'll be useless,' he replied. 'It is a long time since a special child arrived.'

'I think tonight will be different,' said the Witch. 'I have sensed this one for some time, growing in power on Earth. It is gifted.'

Morpeth did not reply. Although it was painful to spend any time in the Witch's company, tonight he wanted to be at her side. If a special child arrived he desired to know almost as much as she, but for different reasons.

They continued to descend the eye-tower. At the bottom a carriage awaited, led by two nervous black horses. The Witch usually flew to greet new children, but on a whim she had decided against it this evening.

Impatiently she watched Morpeth totter down the last few steps. So slow, she thought. So old. It would be enjoyable to kill him soon, when he was no longer useful.

Pushing Morpeth inside the carriage, she whispered a spell of panic to each horse and they bolted in terror towards the Gateway.

2

the cellar

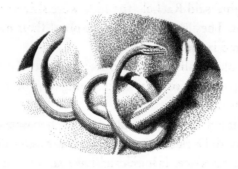

'What's the matter?' Eric asked, munching his cornflakes.

Rachel shrugged. 'You know.'

'The dream again?'

'Mm.' Rachel allowed her long black hair to dangle close to the breakfast milk, then flicked it at her brother.

'Leave off,' Eric said. He pressed his face close to Rachel, opened his mouth wide, and let milk and cornflakes dribble over his grinning lips.

'Oh, grow up,' said Rachel.

Eric laughed. 'Grow up like you? No thanks.'

Rachel ignored him, staring at her untouched plate.

'The dream changed last night,' she said. 'This time there were—'

'Kids,' Eric finished. 'I know. I saw them. In the snow behind the woman.'

Their mum stood nearby, stirring her coffee. 'Not that

again,' she sighed. 'Look Rachel, you began this dream rubbish. Now Eric's at it too. I wish you'd just drop the joke. It's not even funny.'

'Why don't you believe us?' Eric asked. 'We're both having the same dreams. *Exactly* the same dreams.'

'Last night,' said Rachel, 'the kids were shivering behind the woman. They had big creases around their eyes. They were covered in frost.'

'They looked half dead,' Eric said.

'Oh, stop it, both of you,' their mum warned. 'I'm fed up with all this nonsense.'

'I'm telling you, Mum,' said Eric. 'The woman in the dream's weird. Dark snow falls around her head. And she's got a snake-necklace. It looks right at you.'

'It's alive,' said Rachel.

'You've been practising this routine,' their mum said impatiently. 'I know you two. Do you think I'm daft? Get on with your breakfast.'

Rachel and Eric fell silent, finished eating and left the table. It was Saturday, so they could do what they liked. Eric trotted down to the cellar to play with his model aeroplanes. Rachel, deep in thought, went to her room to read, hoping it might take her mind off the dream. How could she convince her mum they were telling the truth? After a while she glanced up to see her mum standing hesitantly in the doorway. She might have been standing there for some time.

'Look, are you serious about this dream stuff?' she asked.

'Yes.'

Her mum glared. 'Really?'

Rachel glared back. 'Mum, I wouldn't make anything like this up. They're not like normal dreams.'

'If you're pulling my leg—'

'I'm not. I'm telling the truth.'

'Mm. All right.' Her mum rattled a bag. 'I'm going shopping. We'll talk about these dreams properly later. Where's your dad?'

'Have a guess, mum.'

'In the garage, fixing the car.'

'Again,' said Rachel.

They both laughed.

'Keep an eye on Eric for me, will you?' her mum asked.

Rachel nodded. 'OK, I'll check on him in a bit.'

Her mum left and Rachel turned back to the book, feeling much happier that someone apart from Eric was starting to take her half-seriously about the dreams. Outside a few cars zoomed by on the street. Some giggling kids ran past the house, setting off next door's dog. Dad cursed a couple of times from the garage – the typical Saturday morning sounds. Eventually Rachel yawned and went to find Eric. She made her way along the upstairs corridor – then stopped.

What she heard was not a usual Saturday morning sound. It was a scream.

Where from? Below her, yes. But not the kitchen, or the living room. 'Eric?' she called, listening carefully. There was definitely shouting. It came from the depths of the house. As she neared the cellar Rachel's shadow flickered orange against the wall. A fire?

'Get off!' Eric's voice roared. 'Someone help! What's holding me against . . . let go of me!'

Rachel reached the wide-open cellar door. She sniffed the air cautiously, peering down the steep flight of steps.

Inside there were no flames, but the entire cellar throbbed and blazed with crimson light. It was as if a great sunset had grown tired of the sky and burst into the house. Rachel shielded her eyes. On the wall at the back of the cellar a large black shape thrashed in mid air. She gasped, falling to her knees. Where was Eric? She could hear him panting. She followed the sounds and realized that the black shape *was* Eric. Both his feet flailed, his body pinned to the wall.

'Rachel!' he bawled, seeing her. 'Something's holding me. I can't get loose!'

She ran down the cellar steps. 'What is it?'

'I don't know! I'm stuck! I can't see it!' He thumped the wall behind him. 'C'mon, get me off!'

She grabbed Eric's wrists, pulling hard.

Then Rachel saw the claw.

It was an enormous black claw, the size of a dog. As Rachel watched it sliced through from the other side of the cellar wall. The claw gripped one of Eric's knees. It spread across his leg and yanked it through the bricks, outside the cellar.

'What's going on?' Eric wailed, noticing Rachel's wild expression. 'Can you see it? Don't just *stand* there!'

A second claw poked through the bricks. It encircled Eric's neck with three ragged green fingernails, wrenching his head completely through the wall.

Rachel leapt forward. She seized one of Eric's arms and heaved, inch by inch drawing his neck and face back into the cellar.

'Pull harder!' Eric's muffled voice yelled. 'Find something to fight it with!'

Rachel's eyes darted about for anything sharp. But whatever lurked beyond the cellar was not about to let Eric escape. The black claws again smashed through the wall. This time they stretched towards Rachel. As she backed away, the bony fingers hovered in front of her face and slapped her *hard.*

Rachel fell – and lost her grip on Eric.

Instantly, both claws tightened around his waist. They dragged Eric completely inside the wall. For a moment one of his arms shot back into the cellar, his nails scratching the floor as he tried to hold onto something, anything – before that was ripped away too.

Rachel staggered back, shaking violently. A loosened brick dropped near her feet, but there was no sign of the claws. She wiped a sleeve across her bleeding lip.

Get . . . Dad!

She retreated up the cellar steps, never taking her eyes off the wall. At the top she twisted and lunged for the door.

It slammed shut in her face.

Rachel reached for the handle, and yelped – it was too *hot* to touch.

Then, behind her, there was a ferocious rasping noise. The back wall heaved and tore open. Bricks burst like splintered teeth on the floor.

Rachel, shielding her hand with her jumper, tugged hard again.

'It's stuck tight!' she screamed, banging against the door. 'I can't open it. Dad! Dad!'

A blast of wind smashed her back. Rachel spun around. She saw that a *new* door was growing inside the back wall of the cellar. It was no ordinary door. It was luminous green, shaped like an eye, and slowly widening. A large black claw, the same giant fingers that had slapped her across the face, dragged it open.

Rachel heard dull thuds above her head.

'Dad!'

'Who's in there?' he said. 'What's all the racket about?'

'It's us – me and Eric! We're . . . something's trying to get in!'

'I can't hear what you're saying,' he bawled. 'What's that noise in there? What kind of game are you—'

'We're shut in! Dad, help us!'

He started pounding on the cellar door.

Immediately, as if sensing his presence, the wind slicing through the eye-door became a raging storm. It tore at Rachel's head, picking up all the cellar dirt, throwing it into her eyes. A wooden stool slithered across the floor. Eric's model aeroplanes spun crazily in the air, smashing over and over into the ceiling.

Rachel could barely breathe. The wind drove like fists, clogging her mouth and nose with dust. Dad could no longer be heard.

'Where are you?' she shrieked.

Suddenly, there was a splintering sound – an axe tearing into wood.

'Hold on!' Dad bellowed. 'I'm coming!'

Rachel felt herself being dragged backwards. She pushed her feet against the cellar steps for grip, clinging to the door frame with her fingertips. Dad's axe cut repeatedly through the door, but it was too solid to break down. He dropped the axe, thrusting his hand through a slash in the wood.

'Hold onto me, Rachel. Don't let go, no matter what happens!'

She caught his wrist. Then, blinking away the grit hurting her eyes, Rachel made herself look back. She saw that the eye-door now covered almost the entire back wall. Two claws stretched it open, and between the claws, filling the space, was a vast black creature with triangular green eyes. Hair all over its body bristled in the wind. On the tip of each hair a tiny serpent's head sprouted. The snake-heads seethed forward into the cellar, trying to bite Rachel's legs. Rachel tucked her knees in, kicking out, still clutching Dad's hand.

The creature within the eye-door was trying to push its way inside, but it was still too large to enter the cellar fully. Then, for the first time, a gaping mouth opened in the middle of the creature's head. Inside the mouth, between four sets of teeth, a dozen purple-eyed spiders rushed out. They crept along the body hairs towards her.

The mouth whispered, '*Rachel . . .*'

She screamed and, just for a second, let go of Dad's hand.

That second was all it took.

Immediately, the storm picked her up and yanked her through the eye-door.

The black creature lowered a shoulder to let her pass. It took a last look around the cellar. It sucked the spiders back into its mouth. The last image Rachel saw before she left this world was its huge shadow pass underneath and Dad smash down the main door with the axe, leaping through the air.

He was too late. With a final screech the cellar bricks reformed and the creature pulled the eye-door shut.

Rachel's dad ran into the cellar, beating his hands against the wall. Pieces of falling furniture crashed against his head. He ignored the pain and heaved the axe into the wall over and over. Eventually, when he had no strength left, he let the axe drop. The only damage to the wall was a few chipped bricks.

He stared furiously at the hand which had lost Rachel's, kicked the axe across the floor of the cellar, and wept.

3
BETWEEN
THE WORLDS

The moment she was sucked through the eye-door, Rachel found herself plummeting inside a vast, dark pit of emptiness. She covered her face, waiting to be crushed. Instead, she simply fell endlessly in the darkness, tumbling for several minutes, barely able to breathe as a freezing wind tore at her head.

Then, as if a cushion had been placed beneath her, Rachel came to an abrupt stop. Her body hung suspended in space, swaying gently. All around the air was still dark, but now Rachel noticed something even more densely black gripping her arm – the cellar creature. For a moment its triangular eyes, each the size of Rachel's face, held her in a fierce gaze. Then it pushed away, its immense shapeless body disappearing below.

As soon as the creature released her Rachel fell headlong again.

After several agonizing seconds she forced herself to stop screaming. Without consciously thinking about it she put her arms outward, cupping the darkness. Her spin slowly came under control, until she could tell she now only pointed one way – straight down, feet first. She thrust her shoes flat against the air below. *Slow down,* she thought, drilling into the air like a skier into a slope. She kept that idea alone in her mind, until the blasting cold air became a gust and the gust merely a light breeze rippling against her head and shoulders.

She concentrated, and said, 'Now, *stop.*'

As if the air around her had been waiting to hear this command all along, her body lurched to a dead halt.

Did I do that? Rachel wondered. How could I have done?

She told her body to turn slowly. Instantly it obeyed, revolving in a perfect circle, allowing her to peer around. Rachel gasped, bewildered. She lifted her hand. It stood so close to her face that she could feel her breath on it, but in the darkness it was invisible. Let me see it, she thought. Immediately, her hand gleamed dimly a few inches in front of her eyes. Rachel gazed in wonder, wriggling her fingers. 'The rest,' she said out loud, and her whole body lit up dully. Brighter, Rachel thought, and her body became a torch in the utter blackness around. '*Light up everything*,' Rachel shouted. She expected the space around her to burst into bright colours. Instead, all remained dark except for millions of dust motes shining close to her body, streaming upwards with the breeze.

She trembled. How could these incredible things be happening? She felt an exhilarating strength inside her, of powers strange and unrevealed, waiting to be used. What could it mean?

Rachel studied her surroundings. She hung inside a dark, fathomless silence. There were no walls or ceilings, no way to tell how far she had fallen or how far away the ground might be. Moist air from below streamed gently through her hair. Eric was nowhere to be seen. She tried calling – the breeze took her faint voice up and away. There were no other sounds.

Rachel's lip swelled where the claws had struck her in the cellar. A small drop of blood trickled down her chin and rolled off the end. Squinting, she could just make it out for a few seconds as it rapidly fell away.

There had to be a way to find Eric . . .

'Where is he?' she asked the darkness and immediately, below her feet, she saw a twisting blue dot. She *knew* that colour – Eric's jumper. 'Bring him to me!' she ordered – but this time her command was not obeyed. The blue colour merely dwindled, falling further away every second. The creature must be out there somewhere, Rachel knew, perhaps fixing its triangular eyes on Eric. Did he have her skills, or was he just tumbling over and over, terrified?

Fighting her fear to go downwards at all, towards the creature, Rachel knotted up all her courage and told herself to *dive* towards the faraway blue. Her stomach twisted. The next moment the wind whipped her head back and Rachel hurtled down. Faster, she told herself, and her body obeyed, the warm wind turning to frost against her face.

*

Ahead the blue shape loomed closer. Rachel swooped, using her arms like wings, and fell alongside Eric. She caught his spinning body and brought them both to a stop. Eric was unconscious. The fall, or fear of falling, or the wind driving out his breath, had made him faint. For a long time she hugged Eric until he awakened, and then she let him cry deeply into her shoulder, soothing him. For several minutes he lay cradled in her arms, while she murmured gentle words and sounds, allowing him to recover. At last he turned his face sheepishly towards her. A trail of sick hung from his mouth, plastering his neck.

He stared at her. 'You're . . . *shining*, Rachel. What's – happening?'

Rachel raised her eyebrows. 'I don't know, but while you've been out cold I've been experimenting. Watch this.' She focused her mind, turning her hair red, then yellow, then back to black.

'H-how'd you do that?' Eric stammered.

'Not sure,' Rachel said nervously. 'But I haven't found much I can't do.' She made her lips glint gold.

Eric blinked several times. 'Can I do it?'

'Try,' said Rachel. 'Just tell part of you to light up.'

Eric screwed up his eyes in concentration. His lips did not glow. He tried several more times, without effect. Eventually he gave up. 'What's going on?' he asked seriously. 'We're heading for the thing that dragged us in, aren't we?'

'No. We're just hovering here.' Rachel gingerly licked her sore lip. 'I suppose we should try to go down, though. We can't hang around here forever.'

'Don't go down, you idiot,' Eric said. 'Fly up, Rachel! Take us back to the cellar.'

Of course! Why hadn't she thought of that? Rachel clutched Eric and imagined them both cruising into Dad's arms. Nothing happened. She tried shoving herself up only a few feet. Still nothing.

'Great,' Eric moaned. 'I suppose that thing wants us to hang around.' He peered mournfully below. 'Did you see it? I know it was big.'

Rachel told him what happened in the cellar, missing out the part about the snake-hairs and spiders.

After a long silence Eric said, 'If it followed you down here, it's probably waiting at the bottom.'

'Maybe.'

'Definitely.'

'Mm.'

With no way to fly upward, Rachel allowed them to slowly descend. For a few minutes they both stared anxiously into the gloom, expecting the black claws to reach out of the dark.

'Hold on!' blurted Eric at last. He pointed to a weak spot of light below. 'There's something down there. It's coming towards us. Look!'

Rachel gazed in the direction of his finger, where a tiny grey patch, growing rapidly wider, formed beneath them.

Eric said, 'The thing's black, isn't it?'

Rachel nodded. 'With green eyes.'

'Maybe it's not black now.'

'It could be someone else dragged here with us.'

'Too big for that,' Eric said, matter-of-factly.

Rachel saw he was right. The grey object drew closer, spreading out to cover the whole space below. It was not another child. It was vast and featureless.

'It looks soft,' Rachel said. 'Don't you think so?'

Eric began kicking the air. 'We're going to hit it. That *thing's* down there! Stop us moving!'

Rachel tried to do so, but they just continued to drift towards the greyness. At last they fell so slowly that a feather would have passed them. A chill touched Rachel's skin, followed by a freezing gust of wind. The surrounding air was not only colder, but studded with points of winking light.

'They look like stars,' whispered Eric, gazing around. 'I'm sure they are. It must be night-time. We must be . . . we must be *outside.*'

No sooner had he said it than they landed, softly, on a blanket of snow.

A huge full moon, five times the size of Earth's moon, blazed coldly in the sky. Rachel looked intently for signs of danger. Strange, twisted trees encircled them. Each tree was covered in thick snow, making the branches appear to bow in welcome. The snow was grey, not white. Rachel held out her hands in astonishment to catch the wispy flakes falling from the sky. They dissolved, smearing a dark wetness across her fingers. All around the same grey-coloured snow smothered the ground.

Eric said, 'Blimey. Where on earth are we?'

'You are not on Earth at all,' said a voice behind them.

The children jumped. Kneeling in the snow and smiling at them was the woman from the dream. She had luminous green eyes, spangled with purple and sapphire streaks. Straight black hair cascaded over her shoulders, and around her graceful neck she wore an elaborate diamond necklace shaped like a snake. The snake had two large ruby-red eyes, and Rachel saw them blink.

Next to her sat a hunched, squat creature who looked like an ancient dwarf.

'Who . . . who are you?' Rachel asked the woman.

'My name is Dragwena,' the Witch replied. She indicated the man. 'And this is Morpeth, my servant. Welcome to the world of Ithrea, Rachel.'

Rachel blinked. 'How do you know my name?'

'Oh, I know many things,' said Dragwena. 'For instance, Eric is afraid of me. Why do you think that is?'

Rachel felt Eric hiding behind her legs.

'I don't like this,' he whispered. 'Something's wrong. Don't trust her.'

Rachel shushed him, but also felt wary. Could this really be the same woman from the dream? She noticed that the dwarf-man shivered in his snow boots, while the bare-footed Dragwena seemed at ease, unaffected by the cold.

'We fell down a dark tunnel,' Rachel said. 'A creature with black claws—'

'It's gone,' said Dragwena. 'I scared it off.'

'But how could you have done?' Rachel protested. 'I mean, it was huge, and—'

'Forget the black claws,' said Dragwena. 'Put these on.'

Morpeth offered Rachel and Eric warm coats, gloves and scarves. Rachel studied the clothes, knowing they had not been in the dwarf's hands a moment earlier. The clothes fitted both children perfectly. Rachel placed a fur-lined scarf around her neck. As soon as it touched her skin she felt the scarf tuck *itself* warmly around her shoulders.

She shivered, wondering what might happen next. Was

this a magic world? Could she use the powers she had discovered between the worlds here? Who was this woman? She glanced at Eric nestled against her hip, and saw fear in his eyes.

'We need to get back home,' Rachel said firmly.

'Never mind that,' said Dragwena. She glanced at Eric. 'What are your favourite sweets?'

'I don't like sweets,' he said suspiciously.

Dragwena smiled. 'Really?'

'Well . . .' His expression became confused. 'Jelly beans, maybe.'

Rachel's mind lurched. She knew Eric *never* ate jelly beans.

'I thought so,' said Dragwena. 'Look in your pockets.'

'Wait a minute,' Rachel complained. 'We want to go home. We're not hungry. Oh!—'

A green jelly bean crept from a pocket in Eric's new coat. It crawled across his sleeve and leapt onto the ground. Another blue bean followed. Within moments they scrabbled from the coats of both children, wriggling across the snow, trying to escape.

Dragwena's eyes sparkled. 'Don't let them get away!'

Eric, without understanding why, immediately found himself racing after the beans, stuffing them into his mouth.

Morpeth, standing close, groaned inwardly. He saw that the jelly beans were really armoured spiders, rushing to find their way back to Dragwena's mouth. The Witch had done what he expected, placing a spell on the children for her own enjoyment – and to test Rachel.

Eric grew increasingly frenzied in his efforts to find and eat the jelly beans. A spider with four serrated teeth crawled inside his mouth. He chewed it ravenously while searching the snow for others that might have crept away.

Rachel was just as fascinated by the jelly beans as Eric. She held one close to her lips. It wriggled its little body, longing for her to bite into the juicy head, but the expression of disgust on Morpeth's face made Rachel hesitate. Even so, she had an aching desire to eat the sweet. Rachel kept looking at the unhappy Morpeth, and at the woman, shaking with laughter, and at the jelly bean, begging to be eaten. At last, with an enormous effort, she flicked the bean into the air. It landed on the woman's dress and rushed towards her lips.

Dragwena plucked the sweet from her chin and held it towards Rachel. 'Don't you want to eat one?' she asked. 'They're delicious.'

'No,' Rachel murmured uncertainly. 'I mean, yes, I'd like to eat them. I mean, I don't like jelly beans . . . I mean—' She looked at Eric, busy scoffing the beans near her feet. 'I mean—' She tried to think of anything except the sweets. 'What we want is to go back home.' Eric ignored her. 'That's right, isn't it? We want to go back home now.'

'Oh, shut up Rachel,' Eric said, juice dribbling from his mouth. 'Don't listen to her, Dragwena.' He stuck out his tongue. 'Rachel's talking rubbish, as usual.'

Rachel stared in disbelief at Eric. A few moments ago he had been frightened of the woman. What had happened to change his mind? She gazed nervously at Dragwena and the dwarf, sensing a huge threat. Should she try to escape? But that would mean leaving Eric behind . . .

The Witch slowly uncoiled from her kneeling position. She stretched her limbs like a cat, pushing out her arms and legs until she stood over seven feet tall. Pressing her toes into the snow she floated, a few inches above the ground, towards Rachel.

'Let's take a good look at you,' Dragwena said. She traced a complex pattern with her fingers on Rachel's nose and eyelids. 'Mm. You are an intriguing child. I see now you are what I was expecting. *More* than I expected. Answer a question: Eric came through the wall first. How did you both arrive together?'

Rachel was seized by caution, but felt compelled to answer truthfully. 'I just flew to him. It was easy.'

Dragwena laughed. 'What else did you do easily?'

Rachel told her everything that had happened between the worlds. She could not stop herself. Every minute detail of the journey poured out.

At last Dragwena seemed satisfied. 'What came to you so effortlessly, no child has ever done before, Rachel. None. And thousands arrived before you. Thousands of *useless* children. Follow me.'

Again Rachel could not stop herself. She reached forward to accept Dragwena's frozen outstretched hands. Deep in her mind Rachel's instinct told her to resist, stay close to Eric and get them both away. Instead, she found herself linking arms casually with Dragwena. Morpeth took Eric's small hand and all four together followed a path in the snow as if they had journeyed as friends along it many times before.

The black horses and carriage awaited. Inside, Eric sat next to Morpeth, no longer complaining, hands neatly folded on his knees. Morpeth stared blankly ahead. Rachel hardly noticed either of them. Instead, she inched closer to

Dragwena, completely fascinated by her looks and voice and gestures. Rachel forgot about wanting to get back home. She forgot about home altogether. She could not take her eyes off the Witch.

Dragwena caught a few flakes of snow falling through the open carriage window.

'Shall we fly?'

Rachel nodded eagerly.

The Witch whispered to the great black horses. Instantly, their hooves reared into the air, heading towards the Palace.

4

ARRIVAL
at the palace

Rachel remembered nothing about the long cold flight in the carriage. During the journey the Witch held her tightly, firing questions. Rachel told Dragwena all about herself, secrets even her best friends did not know. She spoke about her school, her parents, her favourite colours. She told the woman about everything she loved and hated. Dragwena seemed especially interested in what she hated.

When the Witch had discovered all she wished to know, the snake-necklace slithered from her throat. It entwined Rachel's neck, rocking her head gently backwards and forwards until she fell into a deep trance – a state from which only the Witch could awaken her.

As Rachel slumbered the Witch fought to contain her excitement. This girl-child was even stronger than she had expected. She had learnt how to fly between the worlds. She had resisted the sweets, even when specially urged to eat one.

I wonder, Dragwena thought, if this girl is the one I have waited so long for? She sighed. How many other girls had been so promising at first, only to prove too feeble to master the difficult spells of Witchcraft? Perhaps, after all, Rachel was just another weak child . . .

The Witch brought the carriage to the ground, opened the windows and called softly to her wolves. Within moments they loped alongside, nipping the forelegs of the horses, sharing her enjoyment of the evening.

Dragwena relaxed, dropping the pretty-woman face. Her ear stubs collapsed inside her skull. Her face flushed blood-red and her eyelids stretched sideways, meeting at the back of her head, mastering every detail of the world with perfect clarity.

On impulse, the Witch kicked the driver from his seat. She held the reins and thrashed the horses mercilessly for several miles, her four sets of teeth flashing in the light of the enormous moon of Armath.

Eventually, the Witch pulled the terrified horses to an abrupt halt at the bottom of the Palace steps. Several small people, who looked like Morpeth, waited.

'Hurry, you fools!' Dragwena snapped impatiently. 'Take them up!'

'B-but, my Queen,' stammered one. 'The chamber is not ready for guests.' He glanced sharply at two others. They wrapped Rachel and Eric, both sleeping, in warm blankets and shuffled up the Palace stairway.

'Not ready!' snarled Dragwena. 'Whose fault is this, Leifrim? Yours?'

He gazed down.

'No, it's my fault,' said another – a red-haired creature with the face of a girl and the wrinkled eyes of an old woman. 'Punish me!'

'Be quiet, Fenagel!' Leifrim hissed.

The Witch laughed. 'Perhaps I should punish you both. Father *and* daughter. The father for idiocy, and the daughter for speaking at all.' She lifted her throat towards the moon. Instantly, Leifrim shot into the dark sky, suspended several hundred feet above.

'What should I do to your father?' the Witch asked Fenagel. 'Does this deserve a severe punishment or only a small one?'

'Please don't hurt him,' Fenagel pleaded. 'He was only trying to protect me. It was me who forgot. I'll do anything you want.'

'Child,' said Dragwena, 'you have nothing I want. In my kingdom only I am allowed to forget, and I never forget *anything.*'

Leifrim was thrown hard against a nearby tree, his knees snapping as he hit the ground. For a few moments Dragwena enjoyed watching him struggle to untangle his smashed legs. Then she raised her arms and sprang from the icy ground, soaring toward the lights of the eye-tower.

As soon as the Witch was out of sight Fenagel ran to her father. He lay at the bottom of the tree, moaning loudly.

'Shush, Dad,' she said. 'It's all right. She's gone.'

Another man, with a short pointed beard, immediately took charge. He inspected Leifrim's injuries and ordered three others to take him to a small wooden hut, where they tended his cuts and made splints to support his broken legs.

Fenagel glanced angrily at the bearded man. 'Couldn't you have done something to help him, Trimak? You're supposed to be our leader! All you do is talk about how we must protect each other from the Witch. But you just stood by, like the others. How could you?'

Trimak bowed his head. 'A direct attack on Dragwena will never work,' he said. 'Your father understands that. If I had done anything to try to stop the Witch he knows she would have killed me.'

Leifrim nodded and Fenagel tearfully held her father's hands.

Leifrim whispered through his pain, 'We cannot harm the Witch, but perhaps someone else can. Morpeth managed to send a message using the eagle Ronnocoden, before they left the Gateway. He says this new child Rachel resisted Dragwena. She would not eat the sweets the Witch offered. Can you believe that! I was so excited by the news I forgot to check on preparations. Stupid – Dragwena never tolerates failure.'

Fenagel stared at his ruined legs. 'This is all my fault . . .'

'Don't blame yourself,' said her father. 'No one avoids Dragwena's punishments for long.'

Trimak stepped forward. 'Are you saying this girl Rachel resisted, and Dragwena let her live?'

'Yes,' said Leifrim excitedly. 'Apparently even the hag

Witch herself was impressed. Rachel must be special.' He turned to Fenagel. 'Remember the child-hope I told you about?'

'The one who will come from the other world?' Fenagel asked. 'The dark child who'll take us back to Earth.' She half-grinned. 'Wasn't that just a story?'

'Shush!' Trimak hissed. 'Exactly. It's just an old story. Watch over your father.'

Trimak issued instructions for preparing a stretcher and left the hut.

It was, as always, bitterly cold outside. A storm brewed over the entire northern sky. In the west a few lonely stars shone down. Trimak sighed, willing their twinkling light to hold off the storm. Southwards, the vast cold moon of Armath stared balefully down, its scarred surface offering no comfort. I wonder, Trimak thought, how many centuries that moon has looked down on our planet? Had it ever witnessed even one successful attack on the Witch? Never, he knew. Never.

He took a path near the Palace steps and tramped back to his own home. Muranta, his wife, heated some soup over an open fire as he told her about the evening's events.

She shivered. 'Do you think this Rachel could be the child-hope?'

'I doubt it,' Trimak said dismissively. 'We have seen so many girls come and go. They always seem promising, but Dragwena either destroys them or turns their strength to her own advantage.' He caught Muranta's eye and said menacingly, 'I sense the Witch has waited a long time for this girl to arrive. Perhaps Rachel will turn out to be another Witch. Think about that! In any case, I hardly dare to believe this Rachel will be able to help us.'

But secretly he wondered.

5

spells

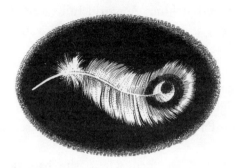

Rachel awoke late the next morning. She yawned loudly and dug her toes into luxuriously inviting sheets.

'Good morning, Rachel,' said a gruff voice.

She jumped up. 'Who's that?'

'Morpeth.'

Morpeth! Images crowded into Rachel's mind – the black claws in the cellar, meeting the snake-woman, and the dwarf. What had happened after this?

'Where am I?' Rachel demanded, trying to think clearly. 'Where is Eric? What have you done to him?'

'Your brother is safe,' said Morpeth. 'He's already had his breakfast and is playing nearby.' He pinched Rachel's toe. 'You, on the other hand, have overslept, sleepy-head.'

'Who is Eric playing with?' Rachel asked. 'Other children?'

'Of course! You are not the only children here. Our

29

world is full of children. He's playing hide-and-seek, I think.'

'In the snow?'

'Where better?' Morpeth laughed. 'Everything looks the same. Fantastic places to hide.'

Rachel stared at him. 'A world full of children? Why? Where do they all come from? Aren't there any . . . grown-ups?'

'I'll explain all that later,' Morpeth said. 'First let me welcome you again to the wonderful world of Ithrea.' He smiled brightly. 'You, our honoured visitor, are in Dragwena's Palace. Only special guests are given these rooms.'

Rachel studied the bed where she had slept. It was enormous, an ocean of scarlet sheets adorned with shimmering black serpents. Their ruby-red eyes all seemed to follow her.

'I'm not special,' said Rachel. 'I'm just like anyone else.' She examined the perfectly fitting pyjamas she wore. 'These aren't my pyjamas. Who—'

'A maid undressed you last night,' Morpeth told her.

'A maid?'

'You will have your own personal maid while you are with us. Her name is Fenagel.'

He looked across the room where a girl hovered awkwardly. Rachel saw she had the same strange bow-shaped wrinkles marring her eyes as Morpeth, making it impossible to tell her age. Neatly plaited red hair framed her thoughtful face.

Fenagel curtsied. 'At your service, miss.'

'I'm used to dressing myself,' said Rachel awkwardly.

'Dragwena says we should pamper you,' Morpeth told her. 'Fenagel will do anything you ask.'

'Anything you want!' gushed Fenagel. 'I'm not important, miss. I'm only a maid. Tell me what you need.'

Rachel did not know what to say. 'I don't . . . need anything. Don't call me miss. My name's Rachel.'

'Of course, miss – I mean, Rachel.'

'Time to get dressed,' Morpeth said. 'I'll wait for you in the Breakfast Room.'

'Do you know where my clothes are?' Rachel asked Fenagel, after he had gone.

'Oh Miss Rachel, you have lots to choose from. Come and have a look.'

Fenagel took Rachel into an area adjoining the bedroom. It was a wardrobe, but one so large that you could walk into the middle of it and still not see the walls at the other end. Everywhere Rachel looked, hanging on rails hundreds of feet long, there were clothes, thousands of them. And, as Rachel feasted her eyes, she found that all the garments turned towards *her*. Enticing dresses twisted to get her attention. A skirt flapped, showing everchanging colours, rippling with pleasure as Fenagel gently stroked its hem. Several jumpers nudged aside blouses and lines of shoes clumped into view. At a warning glance from Fenagel each pair stopped at a respectful distance and permitted dainty socks and tights and leggings to dance between them. Finally all the clothes surrounded Rachel, forming a neat circle, silently awaiting her decision.

Rachel stepped back, gazing in wonder. One bold white

dress studded with glittering gems suddenly launched itself through the air, pressing against her chest.

'Get off me!' Rachel shouted, throwing it down.

'No. No. Try it on,' Fenagel laughed, wagging a finger at a blouse trying to creep over Rachel's foot. 'The dress won't hurt you!'

'But how can clothes—'

'Oh, I don't know!' said Fenagel. 'Dragwena makes it all happen. Are you going to wear that dress or not?'

'Am I . . . allowed to wear anything I like?'

'Oh yes, Miss Rachel. They're all for you.'

Overcoming her nervousness, Rachel quickly tried on several outfits, dashing between the racks of clothing and the many huge mirrors in the room. Each item of clothing fitted perfectly. She was too excited to care how. The original white dress studded with gems had crept to a corner of the rack, pining, looking forlorn.

'Shall I wear you?' Rachel asked it, expecting the dress to say 'Yes!'

'It can't talk, but it wants you to!' cried Fenagel. 'Isn't it gorgeous?'

Rachel was tempted. Instead, thinking she might need to go out into the snow, she picked a thick white pullover, some black trousers and a pair of sturdy grey flat shoes. She tiptoed from the wardrobe, wondering if the shoes would show her the way to the Breakfast Room. Instead, Fenagel took her, but would not go inside.

'Aren't you coming?' asked Rachel.

'I'm not allowed in,' said Fenagel. 'I mean, I've already eaten. I mean – I mean I'll see you later, miss!' She ran rapidly back down the corridor, as if she could not wait to get away from whatever lay behind the door of the Breakfast Room.

Rachel composed herself and gently rapped on the entrance.

'Come in, Rachel,' said Morpeth.

The Breakfast Room disappointed her. It was small, no bigger than her kitchen at home, containing only a plain round table set with two chairs. There were no eager spoons or tantalizing packets of cereal begging for her attention. Rachel sat down opposite Morpeth and attempted a smile.

'I'm hungry,' he said. 'Are you?'

'Mmm.' Rachel realized she had not eaten for ages. This instantly reminded her of Eric. 'Has Eric had breakfast? Where is he? He'll be scared if he doesn't know where I am.'

Morpeth laughed. 'I just checked on him. He's having a great time building a snowman outside. Hasn't mentioned you once! You can join him whenever you like. Let's have some food first, eh? What would you like?'

'Have you got any cereal?'

'Yep. Every kind of cereal you can think of, plus toast, eggs, all that stuff, and things you probably rarely have for breakfast – like gigantic, mouth-watering chocolate sandwiches.'

'Then I'll have chocolate sandwiches!'

'Well,' said Morpeth, relaxing in the chair, 'they're not here as such. You see, in our world you just imagine what breakfast you want.'

Rachel was suspicious, but recalled the wardrobe.

'For example,' he said, 'today I want some eggs, and I'll have sausages with them in the shape of, let's see – in the shape of *teapots.*'

The next instant a plate of steaming hot scrambled eggs and sausages appeared on the table. Each sausage looked exactly like a tiny teapot, with a spout, a handle and a fat belly.

Rachel's eyes widened as Morpeth picked one up. It had a little lid, like a real teapot. He popped it in his mouth.

'Delicious,' he said. 'You have a try.'

'I-I can't do that,' gasped Rachel. 'How did you do it?'

'Have you forgotten the magic you used between the worlds?' said Morpeth. 'This should be an easy trick for a clever girl like you.' He gobbled the eggs with a fork appearing in his hand. 'You see, this world is different from the one you come from. There's magic everywhere.'

'Everywhere?'

'Absolutely,' said Morpeth. 'And it's all waiting to be used. Magic can't wait to be used! A bit of practice is all you need. All you have to do is know what you want and make it appear.' He leaned towards Rachel. 'Close your lids,' he said, 'and see those nice chocolate sandwiches on a plate in front of you. It will work. I promise.'

Rachel shut her eyes and pictured the sandwiches. She saw them cut into little triangles, with lots of soft dark brown chocolate oozing out of the sides. But when she opened her eyes the table was empty.

'I bet you thought of the sandwiches,' said Morpeth, 'but didn't imagine them on the table in front of you. Am I right?'

Rachel nodded.

'Go on,' he urged. 'Try again.'

Rachel did and blinked in amazement as a pair of chocolate butties waited to be eaten.

Morpeth studied them. 'Promising, but you forgot something.'

She followed his gaze and saw that the bread was a fuzzy grey.

'Ugh,' she said. 'They look horrible.'

'They're not bad,' he grunted, biting into a fresh cream cake. 'You forgot to decide what *colour* you wanted the bread. Do you want it to be white or brown – or even silver? You see, the magic doesn't know what colour bread you want. Only you do. Have another go.'

Rachel made the bread white and fluffy. No butter, she decided. Just lots of chocolate. This time the bread was appealing.

'Don't be nervous,' said Morpeth, chewing on a big toffee-apple. 'Try one.'

Rachel gingerly picked up one of the sandwiches and took a small bite.

'Yeuch!' She threw it on the table. 'It tastes disgusting!'

Morpeth laughed out loud, big wrinkles creasing around his cheeks and mouth.

'It's not funny,' Rachel said.

'Ah, but you forgot something else!'

'Did I? No, I'm sure—'

'You forgot to imagine what the sandwiches would *taste* like!'

'Oh.' Rachel realized he was right. She quickly pictured the taste of mingled bread and chocolate and nibbled the edge. This time it was perfect.

Morpeth picked up the other sandwich. 'Can I have a munch?'

Rachel nodded, wondering how he could eat so much.

He took a great bite and chewed it slowly.

'Lip-smackingly gorgeous,' he sighed. 'I couldn't have done better myself. Try something else. How about some fruit?'

Rachel put an orange in the middle of the table. She frowned, wondering what was odd about it.

'Look closely,' Morpeth said. 'You know what's wrong. You don't need me to tell you.'

Rachel stared at the orange. It was round. It was the proper colour. She made the orange revolve slowly, while Morpeth sat back watching her in fascination. Suddenly she knew what was wrong: it didn't have the little dimples all oranges have. It was smooth, like an apple. A moment later she had made the dimples appear.

Morpeth snatched the orange from the table and tried unsuccessfully to peel it.

'Oh, I forget to make the skin real,' said Rachel, annoyed with herself.

'It doesn't matter,' said Morpeth. 'Tell me what you think of my next trick.'

An apple appeared, sitting on top of the orange. Rachel placed a banana above the apple. Morpeth added a peach. Rachel dumped a pineapple on the peach. They continued until the pile of fruit was impossibly high, nudging the ceiling.

Rachel shook her head. 'Why don't they fall over?'

'Because we don't want them to!'

Morpeth excitedly squeezed four more bananas into the

pile, and together they built impossible towers of fruit growing upwards and sideways. On impulse, Rachel scattered the piles and made all the fruit float around their heads. Morpeth hid the bananas behind the pineapples and Rachel hurled the melons into the wall, splatting juices all over the floor.

At last, she gazed at the mess. 'I suppose we've got to clean this up.'

'We could,' said Morpeth. 'Or we can imagine it cleaned up!'

Rachel did. In an instant the room was exactly the way it had been when she entered it.

'Can I change the room as well?' asked Rachel, not wishing to stop.

'Change what you like,' Morpeth urged. 'Change everything!'

Rachel took her time. She imagined the bare room was a huge dining hall. She created cutlery and suspended chandelier lights from the ceiling. On the table she conjured up hundreds of plates, heaped with roast chicken and potatoes and sweet corn and Yorkshire pudding.

What else? she wondered, trying to keep all the plates of food in her mind. She imagined the entire room made of glass filled with fish. What, *exactly*, should the fish look like? Goldfish tails or little puppy-dog tails? Ugly mouths or pretty ones? Rachel decided on slender rouge-lipped fish – with dainty green earrings hanging from their gills.

When she glanced up the room was transformed. She sat in a transparent glasshouse where teeming fish swam through the air. But it was still a disappointment. The earrings of the fish had turned yellow. Rachel made them green again. A second later they turned back to yellow – as if something else was influencing them. Rachel sighed, noticing that all the lights and plates of food she wanted were missing. She had focused so hard on the fish that she had forgotten to keep them in her mind.

'Oh dear, I'm no good, am I?' she said.

Morpeth looked exhausted, almost falling from his chair.

'Are you all right?' asked Rachel, anxiously.

'I'm fine, I'm fine,' he muttered. 'I'm just a little tired, child-hope.' He stared at Rachel, his expression a mixture of surprise and – fear?

'What does that mean?' Rachel asked. '*Child-hope.*'

'Nothing,' Morpeth said quickly. 'Nothing at all.'

Rachel gazed disconsolately at the Breakfast Room, seeing all the faults of her magic. Nothing was as she originally imagined it any longer. Even the fish were starting to look jaded and insubstantial now that she was not concentrating entirely on them.

'I'm rubbish at this,' she said.

Morpeth watched a fish swim around his knees. 'No. This room is . . . amazing. It's not perfect, but with practice you'll improve. You are incredibly gifted.'

Rachel blushed. 'Really?'

'Oh yes. Now, it's time to finish off your breakfast. I want to show you the gardens of the Palace, and later we'll pay Dragwena a visit.'

'The snake-woman I met yesterday?'

'Mm, but that's not a name she likes.'

'Sorry.' Rachel smiled hopefully. 'Can we play some more games first?'

'Later,' said Morpeth. 'First, I want to take my old bones

for a walk. Let's see how quickly you can finish your breakfast.' A plate of toast with several kinds of marmalade appeared next to Rachel. 'You do like marmalade, I hope.'

'Oh, I'm too excited to eat. I know – I'll imagine I'm full!'

Toast and marmalade filled her belly.

They both glanced at the empty plate and burst out laughing.

6

JOURNEY
IN THE SKY

Morpeth led Rachel down a flight of stone steps leading from the Breakfast Room. He stopped at a huge round door made from burnished steel. It possessed no markings whatsoever, not even a handle or a lock.

'Is that the door to the garden?' Rachel asked.

'Yes.' Morpeth held his palm towards the metal surface and it silently opened.

Rachel watched him closely. 'You used magic, didn't you?'

Morpeth nodded.

'Why do you need a big door with a magic lock to go into the garden?'

'Dangers lurk outside,' said Morpeth. 'Remember the black claws? There are massive wolves too, yellow-eyed with teeth bigger than your face.' He grinned. 'You wouldn't want them to get in and bite you in half while you slept, would you?'

Rachel stepped back, suddenly frightened. 'I don't want to go out.'

'There's no need to be scared,' he reassured her. 'The wolves only come into the garden at night.'

Rachel peered cautiously out of the door. A shining blanket of light grey snow buried the grass. In the distance, surrounded by triangular-leaved trees, a frozen lake sparkled. She saw no yellow-eyed wolves. Could they be hiding behind the trees? What, she suddenly wondered, if just by *thinking* about it she could bring a wolf to life?

'I'll show you it's safe,' said Morpeth. He ran outside, cartwheeled in a big circle and shouted at the top of his gruff voice, 'Wolves, wolves, wherever you be, I've a big fat belly if you want to eat me!'

Rachel timidly took a step into the garden and then dashed to Morpeth, gripping him tightly.

'Come on,' he said. 'I'll race you to the lake!'

Rachel ran fast, but Morpeth's short thick legs were a blur of speed.

'You'll never catch me!' he bawled. 'I'm faster than the wind, I'm quicker than a cat, I'm so fast you'd never know I'm fat!'

He zigzagged across the garden, arms spread wide.

Rachel couldn't catch Morpeth, but she knew she could beat him. Remembering her journey between the worlds, she simply imagined herself landing near the lake. After a momentary whoosh of air she alighted comfortably by the shore. Morpeth staggered and almost fell over her.

'H-how did you do that?' he gasped, collapsing by a mushroom-shaped tree stump.

'It was easy. I just thought about it, like you showed me.'

Morpeth shook his head vigorously. 'No! I haven't shown you how to do that. I never taught you how to move from *one place to another*. Even I cannot . . . only Dragwena can do it!'

'It wasn't hard. I did it before.'

'But that was between the worlds! Dragwena places a special magic there to help all children brought to Ithrea. You did this yourself!' He stared at Rachel with a look of wonder on his face. 'You *are* the child-hope.'

'I am the what? You said that before, Morpeth. What do you mean? What is this child-hope?'

'I mean—' He checked himself, recovering his composure. 'I mean . . . you are the sneakiest little girl I've ever met! Fancy pulling *that* trick on me! Come on, let's go for a skate on Lake Ker.'

He leapt onto the ice, gliding on a pair of bright red skates. 'Whoopee!' Morpeth sang, turning perfect circles on one leg. 'Come and join me, Rachel. This is fantastic!'

She quickly imagined sparkling pink skates under her feet and they danced a joyful duet across the surface, as if they had been practising together for years.

Eventually they returned to the bank of Lake Ker for a rest. The Palace towered above them. Inside its high wall hundreds of thin black columns and battlements, with tiny, odd-shaped windows, pushed against the sky. Every contour was harsh, angular and threatening – the stone absorbing the daylight as if it hated it. One enormous slender tower in the middle of the Palace stood higher than all the others, like a giant needle piercing the sky. At its top was a large window, green in colour, and formed – Rachel tried to make out the shape. It looked like an eye. Where had she seen that shape before?

'Who built the Palace?' she asked. 'It looks old and it's so dark.'

Morpeth shuddered. 'It was built many years ago. That's all I know.'

But he knew far, far more than this. He knew Dragwena had built it thousands of years before, when she first arrived on Ithrea. He did not know why the Witch had come. She trusted no one with that secret. But he knew that Dragwena hated this world, and also hated all the children she had drawn from the Earth and enslaved – though she drew them always, seeking something she would never explain.

One night, many years before, Dragwena had brought Morpeth to the eye-tower of the Palace. She had taken great delight in explaining how each rock, each layer of the wall, had been dragged from the mountains by hand – by the small blistered hands of generations of children. It took centuries of labour. Most of the children died from hunger or cold as they carried its stones through the snow – or fell from the towers. It was a story that lasted many days and nights. With her perfect and ageless memory Dragwena recalled everything, the exact form of death for each child. She forced Morpeth to suffer also, understanding what she had done, and yet compelled to carry out her merciless commands nonetheless.

Morpeth sighed, and considered Eric. He was with the Witch now, being probed and tested. There was an unusual quality about the boy. A strength, a skill, though different from that of Rachel. Dragwena had instantly sensed it. If Eric's abilities were not interesting enough, Morpeth knew, Dragwena would soon find out and kill him. The boy might already be dead. What should he do about Rachel? How could he conceal her remarkable gifts from the Witch? Even now, from the eye-tower, he realized Dragwena was probably observing every movement he and Rachel made.

Rachel had been looking over the snow-covered Palace gardens and beyond. The only other buildings were a few simple huts around the Palace walls. Small, hunched figures like Morpeth moved slowly in and out. In the far distance huge jagged peaks jutted out of the ground.

'Are those mountains far away?' she asked excitedly.

'Ah, the Ragged Mountains!' said Morpeth, rousing himself. 'Why don't we find out? Let's fly there and take a look.'

Rachel giggled. 'Can we? We haven't got wings.'

'Oh, haven't we? Then we'll have to *imagine* them!'

Rachel expected wings to sprout from his arms. Instead, Morpeth simply peered into the distance.

'Today,' he said, 'I think I'll fly on the back of a giant sea eagle. Look – here she comes!'

Rachel followed Morpeth's gaze into the creamy winter sky. From far away, low across the horizon, a tiny point sped towards them. As she watched it grew larger, until first she saw its wings, then a pointed white head, and finally curved talons, each dwarfing Morpeth himself, sunk into the snow nearby.

Morpeth jumped nimbly on its back. 'Come on Rachel, let's go!'

His great bird leapt into the pallid sky.

'Don't leave me!' Rachel cried.

'You know what to do! Hurry, or I will beat you to the mountains!'

Rachel concentrated. What was the most superb bird? Another eagle? A dove? In her mind she formed the image of a great white snowy owl, yellow-billed, growing out of the snow. Even before the owl had fully taken shape she vaulted onto its back, gripping the neck feathers. Within seconds Rachel had soared hundreds of feet above the Palace, the cold wind scudding through her hair.

'I'll catch you! I'll catch you!'

The snowy owl, following her command, swiftly caught Morpeth's eagle. Perched side by side on their giant magical birds of prey they grinned at each other, stretching their necks to see what lay ahead.

'Let's fly over the Palace,' Rachel said.

'No! Straight to the mountains! A race!' Morpeth's eagle blazed high and away.

'You can't fly faster than me!' Rachel called out.

'Try to catch me! Use your magic!'

Within minutes they swooped amongst the mountain peaks, diving into the valleys and shooting over the high tops.

Rachel wanted to lead. She told her owl it was faster than any eagle, the swiftest creature that had ever taken flight – uncatchable – and streaked into the vast sky. Morpeth caught her effortlessly. Time and again Rachel strove to get away, but he always matched her speed.

'Why can't I stay ahead?' she complained over the wind.

'Because I can always imagine catching you up!'

'Then I'll imagine you can *never* catch me up!' Rachel whispered softly in the owl's ear and it sped into the distance.

'I just imagined,' Morpeth laughed, catching up again, 'that no matter how fast you flew I would *always* be able to catch up.' He drew alongside her. 'Can you imagine something I could *never* imagine? Can you, Rachel?'

She pondered this until Morpeth held out his arm to indicate the arc of the land glistening below.

'Look at that!' he marvelled. 'Look at the world of Ithrea!'

Rachel felt her heart race and drank in her surroundings. To the west and north of the Ragged Mountains piled even more peaks, halted by cliffs overlooking an endless sea.

'The Endellion Ocean!' Morpeth cried. 'An ocean of ice!'

Eastwards everything was unending grey snow, a monotony only broken by the towers of the Palace itself. In the south, a few black smudges that might have been forests huddled under the snow. Where were the children Morpeth said lived everywhere, Rachel wondered? Could there be towns hiding under the snow filled with them? Could she fly to where they lived? Could she – suddenly Rachel gasped and forgot altogether about children.

She had seen the storm-whirls.

There were eight of them, immense hurricanes, twisting in pairs in the corners of the world. Rachel flew higher, into the thinnest air, to peer inside. Nothing she had seen before could prepare her for the sheer size of these twisting towers of grinding wind. Black clouds belched from their tops, spreading horizontally out over the whole world of Ithrea, pumping snow like wrathful breaths in all directions. And inside each storm-whirl there was lightning too, not one flash, but endless streaks of lightning, setting the sky above ablaze like a gigantic camera flashlight.

Rachel breathed deeply, trying to take everything in. What kind of world was Ithrea? She suddenly longed for colour – any colour. There was none. The sky was dull white, the snow grey. Even the sun glowed feebly; it gave off virtually no heat and Rachel could look directly at its disc without hurting her eyes. A monochrome world, Rachel thought. A winter world. Like a black-and-white photograph. She looked at Morpeth and his blue eyes blazed in the whiteness of the sky.

'Does it always snow here?' she called across to him, suddenly shivering.

'Of course,' he replied. It is the will of Dragwena, he thought bitterly, though Rachel was not ready to hear the reason yet. 'Time to return to Lake Ker,' he said. 'We can't fly around all day.'

'Another race?'

'Why not? You haven't beaten me yet!'

He tickled the nape of the sea eagle and it plummeted towards Lake Ker. Rachel did not try to fly faster. She simply pictured herself already landing by the lake.

Instead, she found herself hovering beside the green eye-window of the highest tower of the Palace.

Looking out of the window, a few feet away, was Dragwena.

The Witch gazed at Rachel, stroking her snake-necklace. Rachel stared back uncertainly, sensing something was wrong.

'Come away!' Rachel ordered her owl, tugging its neck.

47

The bird refused to obey. Instead it moved even closer to the window, a few inches from the glass. The Witch smiled, pressed her lips against the window and blew Rachel – a *kiss*.

Immediately, a blast of wind struck the owl.

Rachel gripped the neck feathers, trying to steady herself. 'Take me away!' she ordered it. The owl slowly turned its massive head and opened its beak. 'No, don't!' Rachel screamed, seeing what it was about to do. The owl bent closer. It bit her hands – and nudged her off its back.

Rachel shrieked, clutching hopelessly for its tail feathers. And fell.

An icy wind tore through her hair. Glancing down, she saw another large tower yawning below, its needle point ready to impale her.

Rachel shut her eyes tightly, remembering how she had slowed her fall between the worlds. But the darkness between the worlds was an endless fall; this time she had only a few seconds to decide what to do. She had almost given in to panic when an idea abruptly struck her. It was an image – the image of a feather, a small white feather, drifting gently downwards. Rachel furiously held it in her mind, picturing how small she would be, how light, how calmly she would fall, rocking slowly back and forth in the wind.

At last she dared to look around. Huge snowflakes surrounded her, tossed by the wind, and she was being tossed with them. The whole sky blossomed with their greyness, crystal edges pressing hard, pouring dark freezing water over her body.

Suddenly, Rachel realized why the snowflakes were so

large – it was because *she* was so small: she had become a tiny feather. She could feel her new body drifting amongst the snowflakes, a prisoner of the winds. A moment later she landed comfortably on a ledge. A breeze picked her up and she wandered on the wind, strange sensations tingling across her new near-weightless body. She continued to drift to and fro, descending gradually with the huge snowflakes.

Then, through the blur of snow, she saw a figure racing towards her.

'Morpeth! Morpeth!' she cried.

He plucked the feather from the air, his giant fingers gripping her inside a dark world. Rachel waited in the quiet warmth of his hand, feeling safe. Moments later Morpeth placed her in the snow by Lake Ker and she watched him say three words from a great height.

Slowly at first, she felt her hands reappear. Arms grew from her shoulders, her lips flew past them – and a frozen Rachel staggered and shivered in the snow.

'Oh Morpeth,' she cried. 'What happened? The snake-woman stood there. She blew that kiss and—'

'I know. I know.' He wiped wet hair from her cheeks. 'You are safe now. I promise.'

Morpeth led her back to the Palace through the large steel door. Once again he opened it using magic. Rachel felt too distracted to notice. How could any of this be happening to her? The strange woman, Morpeth, the Breakfast Room, the owl, changing into a feather. How could any of it be real?

'Am I in a dream?' she asked. 'Am I going to wake up in a minute and have to go to school?'

'I wish you were,' he said. 'Or that this was *my* dream.'

'Morpeth, I want to find Eric and leave this place. I want to go home!'

Morpeth did not reply. Instead, he escorted her back to the Breakfast Room, where dry clothes waited. As Rachel dressed she noticed that the room appeared exactly the same as when she first entered it. The slender fish with earrings had vanished.

Morpeth sat her down. 'Rachel,' he said, his voice shaking slightly, 'I know you are frightened, but I need you to be brave.'

She nodded, not understanding, but trusting him.

'What you did,' he said, 'is change your form. You became something *different.*'

'A feather.'

'Yes, but it should not be possible. On this world only one has that power.'

'Dragwena,' said Rachel. 'I bet she can do it.'

'Yes.' He leaned forward and gripped Rachel's hands. 'In a moment I must bring you to the eye-tower. Dragwena will force you to undergo a severe test. I cannot warn you what it is, for that would betray me. It will not *seem* to be a test. It will come as a surprise and I will not be able to assist you. Do your best. I will try to protect you if I can.'

'I don't understand,' Rachel said. 'You saved me. I know you'll help.'

Tears splashed over Morpeth's sunken cheeks. He knew he had already told Rachel too much about what would happen in the eye-tower. He must seem *ruthless* when he brought the child to the Witch – Dragwena would be watching him closely when he arrived, and others would be observing his every move on the way.

'Morpeth, what's the matter?' Rachel asked. 'Don't cry. I'm all right now. I feel much better. Why are you so worried? What kind of test is it?' She felt Morpeth suddenly withdraw his hands. 'I don't want to take any test. I'm frightened.'

Morpeth sat with his head buried in his gnarled old fingers. He breathed deeply, and for a few moments his body became almost unnaturally still. When he looked at Rachel again his eyes had lost their friendly sparkle. He spoke in a different voice, much harsher than before.

'Dragwena is calling. We must hurry.'

'I won't see that woman,' Rachel said. 'She made the owl bite me. Where's Eric? I want to know what—'

'Shut up!' Morpeth shouted.

Rachel stepped back in shock. 'Morpeth, what's wrong?'

'Come on,' he growled, grasping her arm. 'Fun and games are over, girl-child. It's time to see how good you really are!'

7

RACHEL'S TRIAL

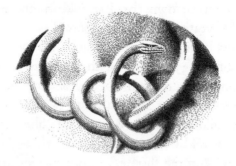

Morpeth trotted along several twisting dark passages, tightly holding Rachel's wrist, forcing her to run.

'Let go!' she protested, resisting him. 'I thought you were my friend.'

He laughed, dragging her up a vast flight of stone steps ascending the eye-tower. Rachel tried to understand what she had done wrong. Why was Morpeth behaving like this when he had promised to help her?

He eventually stopped outside a large arched door, flanked by two soldiers wearing short stabbing swords. In the middle of the door stood a snake-head handle, mouth open, as if ready to strike all visitors.

'I'm not going to see Dragwena,' Rachel told him. 'Not until I know Eric is safe.'

'Keep your mouth shut!'

'Don't tell me . . .' Rachel stepped back. 'I'm not doing anything else you say! Morpeth, why are you talking like this?'

He grinned. 'You'll soon find out.'

The door opened itself and Rachel peered inside the huge, dark chamber.

'You're on your own now,' said Morpeth. 'Keep your wits sharp or you won't come out alive.'

He shoved her inside and slammed the door.

Rachel, blinking in the semi-darkness, tried to get her bearings. She was drawn to the far end of the chamber, where a green window, shaped like an eye, gazed down on the Palace buildings. Dragwena stood beside the window, looking outward.

'Come in,' said the Witch, without turning round. Her voice was warm and inviting.

Rachel took a few steps towards Dragwena – and gasped. Eric's sleeping head poked from the blankets of a small bed.

'What have you done?' Rachel exploded, trying to shake Eric awake. He did not respond. 'If you've hurt him—'

Dragwena laughed softly.

'I want to go back home!' Rachel roared. 'Wake Eric up! Let us go!'

Dragwena turned, and Rachel saw a box in her hand. It was a plain black object, thin, that rattled. 'I have a present for you,' said the Witch.

'I don't want a present,' Rachel said stiffly. 'Tell me what you've done to Eric!'

Then she noticed a hissing sound coming from the box. Instantly, she had a sudden, almost painful desire to tear it open.

'What is it?' she asked, forgetting Eric. 'Oh, please let me have it!'

The Witch smiled and casually tossed the box in the air.

Rachel caught it, turning the box over and over, frantic to discover its contents.

'How do I get inside? I can't open it! I can't open it!'

'Isn't your magic powerful enough, child?'

Rachel held the box tightly, tearing at the lid, trying to picture a releasing clasp. There was something wonderful inside. She knew it would disappear if she didn't hurry. She gnawed the edges wildly.

Suddenly the lid ripped off. Rachel's grip had been so tight that the contents were spread over the floor. She looked down. In front of her was the board for a simple game she knew well: snakes and ladders.

What? she thought, intensely disappointed.

Then something happened that made Rachel change her mind – one of the snakes slithered to a new position. It twisted until it came to rest in the middle of the board. A second, much larger, snake uncurled until its head sat on the top row. All the other snakes, seven altogether, also jostled to find places. At last they were set, their tongues lazily tasting the air. Four ladders nestled between them. Three were tiny. One large ladder stretched from square three at the bottom diagonally right up to the top, two squares from the end.

'Do you like your present?' asked Dragwena.

Rachel smiled uncertainly.

The Witch knelt beside the board. 'Let's play a game. I like games.'

Two counters marched proudly from behind a chair, where they had come to rest after spilling from the box. A green counter span towards Dragwena. The blue counter jumped into Rachel's hand.

'You start,' Dragwena said.

Rachel nodded, fascinated, unable to take her eyes off the snakes. Her first throw of the game was a three. This placed her on the long ladder. She moved the counter up to sit on square ninety-eight.

'How fortunate,' said Dragwena. 'It will be hard to beat you if you play as well as that.' She took her own turn, threw a one and sighed. 'I'm rubbish at this,' she said, using the same words Rachel had spoken in the Breakfast Room, imitating her voice perfectly.

Rachel glanced warily at Dragwena. She knew this was no ordinary game. Could it be the test Morpeth had warned her about?

'What happens if I win?' she asked hesitantly.

'What would you like to happen?'

'To go home,' said Rachel. 'Both of us. That's all I want.'

'Throw a two or more,' said Dragwena. 'That is all you need. Then you can run back to Mummy and Daddy.'

'You *promise*.'

Dragwena imitated a different voice this time – Morpeth's. 'Of course! Don't you trust me, child?'

Rachel did not answer. Instead she picked up the dice, rubbing it against the soft part of her thumb. 'What happens if I lose?'

'That depends. It depends on how hungry the snakes are today. Continue to play. If you refuse I'll punish Eric.'

Rachel's heart leapt.

'Are you afraid?' Dragwena inquired gently, as if asking nothing at all.

'Of course I am! Why are you making me do this?'

'I have my own reasons,' said Dragwena. 'You are wasting time.' Her face transformed into Eric's. 'Don't let her hurt me,' Eric's voice pleaded.

Rachel considered trying to run for the door, then remembered the soldiers waiting outside.

'I won't need the soldiers if you have to be killed,' whispered Dragwena.

Rachel's hand trembled. She turned away from the Witch, no longer able to meet her gaze, pressing the dice hard against her palm.

I must throw a two! She concentrated furiously, as Morpeth had taught her, and released the dice. It clattered over the board.

Two neat dots faced up.

'I won! I won!' shouted Rachel.

'Nothing is as easy as that,' Dragwena said.

She touched Rachel's forehead. Instantly, she shrank to the size of a fingernail. Dragwena picked her up and placed her in the middle of the board.

'Now we'll see how strong you are,' said Dragwena. 'Watch out. The death-serpents are out to get you!'

One of the snakes immediately lurched towards Rachel, its head now twice the size of her body. Rachel ran across the board. Another snake turned towards her. She shrieked and jumped over its neck, dashing down the squares, towards the edge. Dragwena's own snake quickly uncoiled, spreading its thick body around the board like a wall, preventing any escape.

'What can I do?' screeched Rachel. 'It's not fair!'

'If you reach the final square you can still win the game. However, you might not like what's waiting for you.'

Rachel clearly saw what it was: the largest snake squatted on the final square. She would have to enter its mouth.

'Help me!' Rachel yelled, running up the board to escape a further snake zigzagging towards her.

'You have one chance,' said Dragwena. 'You need to use the ladders. Hurry, the snakes are restless!'

Rachel flew down the board to square three, hoping the ladder would take her up. It did nothing and the snakes continued to slide after her, chasing relentlessly. She stumbled and ran and jumped over their arched backs, but the snakes allowed her no respite. Finally, she no longer had the strength to evade them. The snakes closed in and trapped her in a corner. As they opened their jaws Dragwena, looking almost bored, sighed irritably.

Rachel stood facing the snakes. Terrified, she still tried to understand what Dragwena had meant about using the ladders. At last a sudden desperate idea struck her.

She gazed at the snakes and whispered 'Stop.'

They halted, their forked tongues pressing against her body.

Rachel addressed them together: 'Eat the snake sitting on the last square.'

Instantly they obeyed. After a fierce struggle the largest

snake was smothered and killed. Only two snakes now remained alive on the board.

Rachel spoke to one of them. 'Move the ladder to square one hundred.'

The snake wriggled down the board, placed the ladder between its fangs, and positioned it on the final square.

Rachel calmly walked up the rungs of the ladder to the last square, put her arms by her side, and looked defiantly at Dragwena.

And the Witch looked back at her. *How* she stared at Rachel! She breathed raggedly, glancing at Rachel and the dead snakes.

Rachel did not wait for Dragwena to regain her composure.

'Attack her!' she instructed the two snakes still alive.

They leapt off the board, heading for Dragwena's throat, but the Witch's own snake quickly darted forward and swallowed them.

'H-how did you do this?' the Witch asked, dumfounded. 'You should not be able to defeat the snakes! No child has ever done it!' She leapt in the air. 'You *are* the one!' she gasped. 'After all this time . . .' She reached down to Rachel and touched her head, bringing her back to normal height. 'Oh Rachel, Rachel,' she cried, hugging her. 'Forgive me. I had to test you. You have no idea how long I have waited for you to arrive.'

Rachel pushed her away. 'Go away! Don't come near me!'

Dragwena turned triumphantly. 'You hate me now. But soon you will learn to adore everything that I am. We will rule together on Ithrea, and on *your* world too.'

'You promised to let us go if I won. You *promised!*'

'I lied,' said Dragwena. 'I have never kept a promise to a child, and I never will.'

Rachel kicked the Witch hard.

Dragwena jumped back in surprise. Four sets of teeth momentarily appeared on her face, snapping at Rachel. As soon as Dragwena knew Rachel had seen the teeth she dropped the pretty-lady face entirely. The tattooed eyes which stared at Rachel were expressionless.

'You should not enrage me,' Dragwena warned her. 'I could destroy you in a second.'

Rachel backed away, appalled by the Witch's true appearance. 'What do you want with me and Eric? What *are* you?'

'A Witch,' Dragwena whispered. 'And soon you will also be one, Rachel. A very powerful Witch.'

'What? No, I won't,' Rachel said. 'You're . . . how dare you keep us here, playing these games? I don't care what it's all for. I *won't* help you.'

'Child,' replied Dragwena, 'do you think you have any choice in the matter? From now on you will always be at my side.'

Rachel felt sick with hatred. 'Let me leave!'

'In a moment,' said Dragwena. 'You are tired. First you should have a rest. After that – we'll see.'

Rachel inexplicably yawned. For some reason she did feel tired. She fought it, knowing the Witch was responsible.

'Your lids are drooping,' said the Witch. 'You can hardly keep them open.'

Rachel's eye-lids fluttered and closed. With a huge effort she managed to open them.

'I'm not tired at all,' she said, yawning again. 'I'm wide awake. I don't want to sleep. I *won't* sleep.'

'Get into the bed with Eric,' the Witch said. 'I know you want to.'

Rachel found herself crawling under the sheets, pulling the quilt around her. 'I'm not tired,' she said weakly. 'I won't do what you ask.'

'Have a long rest,' said the Witch. She tucked the quilt around Rachel's shoulders and kissed her on the cheek. 'I promise you will have lovely dreams.'

Rachel's face nestled into the pillow. 'I'm not tired . . . not . . . tired.'

In a few moments she was asleep.

While Rachel slept Dragwena reached into her mind and created a *dream-sleep*, the transforming spell needed to begin changing Rachel from child to Witch. Dragwena had never used such a powerful spell before on Ithrea. Would it work on Rachel? Countless children had come and gone, some gifted like Morpeth, but none had the magical intensity that Rachel displayed. Could she control Rachel? Already she felt Rachel's power swelling. If she acted quickly she could mould Rachel into anything she needed. Trembling with excitement, Dragwena planted the layers. Slowly, carefully, she chose memories from her past, hatreds and fears and longings, events and feelings that would overpower Rachel's mind, condition her, prepare her for a new destiny.

Once the dream-sleep was ready, Dragwena turned to Eric. She sensed a power within him she had never faced before, yet her testing earlier in the day had revealed no

magic in the boy – surprising given Rachel's extraordinary power. Still, he was young and did not have
Rachel's defiance. His personality should be easy to
break and reshape. She touched Eric's temple, probing
into the cortex, searching for the control roots of his
brain.

Instantly, the Witch was thrown across the chamber.

She screamed, every muscle in her hand clenching in
spasm.

An attack!

Dragwena lay on the floor, pondering, waiting to recover. What could it mean? After a few minutes she
activated her own mental defences, returned to the bedside
and delicately probed Eric's thoughts.

She sensed several layers of protection in Eric's mind and
was bewildered – no human had this gift. This was no
ordinary child. She should have realized that and been more
careful. Dragwena sat for over an hour, observing Eric
closely, knowing he was asleep, that the child had not
deliberately thrust out. When she felt ready she once again
delved tentatively within his mind, searching his memories
for a clue. Nothing – only a child's simple joys and
frustrations. Eric, she realized, was not even aware of his
abilities. Could they have been planted? By whom?
Dragwena sat back in frustration, wanting to study further.
Eric's tantalizing gift must wait, she thought. I will strip his
mind of the secret later. For now Rachel's power is all I
need.

Carefully, avoiding Eric's defences, Dragwena planted a
spell in the outer layer of his brain. It had been a long time
since she had used this particular spell – so weak that it was

almost undetectable, so simple that it would be hard to block even if detected.

The spell was perfect for what she needed.

8

the council of sarren

The Witch finished her work on Eric, left the eye-tower and met with Morpeth.

'You have instructed Rachel well,' she announced. 'Her abilities are great.'

Morpeth bowed. 'I did nothing. The child took control from the start.'

'That is obvious,' said the Witch. 'Her magic is beyond all except my reach. Take Rachel back to the east wing tonight and prepare a room with her wardrobe closer to my chamber. In the morning bring her to me. You will have no further part in her training.'

Morpeth nodded. 'Did you test her with the box?'

'Yes. And she conquered it! She defied it!'

'That has never been done!' marvelled Morpeth.

'Indeed. She will do many things no child has done before.' Dragwena glanced warily around the corridor. 'I have placed Rachel in a sleep that will start her transformation into a Witch. Tonight I want you to stay with her, Morpeth. Guard her personally. Do not allow her to be awakened until she is ready. Also, ensure Eric stays in her room tonight. He has no magic, but may prove valuable nonetheless.'

'As you wish. Will Rachel remember anything when she wakes?'

'Nothing important,' said Dragwena. 'Her past will vanish when the dream-sleep is over. She will remember nothing about her family, even Eric. Instead, her mind will be prepared for the final training she needs. I will undertake this myself.'

'What should we do with Eric?'

'Kill him,' said the Witch. 'Not yet, though. He may still be useful. I will tell you when.'

Morpeth bowed again and the Witch returned to the eye-tower. Morpeth arranged for two maids to carry the sleeping children back to the east wing and gave them Dragwena's orders.

Once he was alone again with Rachel and Eric, Morpeth buried his face between his knees. He sat for a long time, thinking about what should be done.

I must act tonight to save Rachel, he realized. Tomorrow will be too late.

Masking his face he left the Palace, treading cautiously across the snow towards the house of Trimak.

Muranta woke first. 'Wake up, Trimak, you old booby,' she

said, digging her arm into his ribs. 'There's someone banging on the door.'

'Well,' Trimak muttered sleepily, 'they can't be enemies making that racket.'

He put on a pair of old slippers and padded along the corridor.

Muranta lit a candle. 'Who can it be at this hour?'

Trimak listened to the heavy knocking, counting each rap. Four fast knocks, one slow, three more fast raps – Morpeth, and he was in danger!

'What's up?' Trimak asked, quickly shutting the door behind him.

'It's the girl, Rachel,' said Morpeth. 'She survived the box.'

'What! Did you see it happen?'

'Of course not! Dragwena does not allow me in the chamber at such times. But she could not contain her excitement. She intends to turn the child into another Witch.'

'Let's be careful before we act,' Trimak said, struggling to remain calm. 'This could be a trick. It would not be the first time the Witch has questioned your loyalty.'

'No, I'm sure this is not one of Dragwena's games,' said Morpeth. 'I tested Rachel earlier. She changed into a feather and shape-shifted from the Palace to the shore of Lake Ker. She did both effortlessly.'

'Then she *is* the child-hope,' Muranta whispered.

'Did Dragwena see everything you saw?' Trimak asked.

'She must have done,' groaned Morpeth. 'You know how closely the Witch observes during the trial period, especially gifted children. Once I realized Rachel's strength I tried to lead her to the mountains, but Dragwena drew her to the eye-tower.'

'You let her fly near the tower!' thundered Trimak. 'How could you let the Witch get so close?'

Morpeth lowered his face.

'Never mind,' sighed Trimak. 'I suppose if Rachel survived the box Dragwena knows everything anyway. Where is Rachel now?'

'In the east wing,' said Morpeth. 'Tomorrow morning Dragwena is moving her to the eye-tower.'

'Then we must act tonight, before it's too late.'

Morpeth nodded.

'I will call the Council of Sarren,' said Trimak. 'We will decide together what must be done.'

It was late in the kingdom of Ithrea. Steady snow fell across the whole night world, refreshing what little had melted during the day. Most of the slaves of the Witch – the *Neutrana* – were already asleep, enduring the troubled dreams of Dragwena, awaiting her commands. Amongst the Neutrana lived a few who had managed to free themselves from the Witch's control. They called themselves the *Sarren*, after a man now long dead who supposedly was the first to refuse to obey the Witch. Morpeth was one of the Sarren, as were Trimak and his wife Muranta, Fenagel, her father Leifrim and several others. They met rarely, communicating through special signs, obeying Dragwena's endless duties, while keeping watch – keeping watch on all the new children who arrived and, where they could, trying to help them.

Trimak sent the alert by personal messenger – extremely

dangerous, but the circumstances demanded it. Gradually over the next hours stealthy, coded taps on window and door awakened Sarren close to the Palace. They knew the danger call and slipped quietly from their beds. Each headed for Worraft, the guarded secret cave deep under the foundations of the Palace.

Within an hour over thirty of the Sarren had arrived.

Trimak glanced around, counting as shadowy presences hurried to find places on the stone seats along the walls of the great cave. He noticed Fenagel struggle in with Leifrim, pushing him along on a kind of wheelchair-stretcher.

'It's time to close the door,' said Trimak. 'We can wait no longer.'

Morpeth traced a circle on his forehead, and a wall of rock came down from the ceiling of the cave, blocking the entrance. No one could now enter the cave or leave it. The meeting could begin.

The gathered Sarren murmured nervously. They were concerned and with reason: no such conference had been called for many years. Trimak clapped his hands and silence descended.

'Why have you called us so recklessly, without warning, Trimak?' demanded a voice from the dark.

'In haste there is danger,' Trimak agreed. 'The reasons will soon be clear enough. Let Morpeth speak.'

Morpeth arose from his chair and addressed the assembly. 'I have important news,' he announced. 'I believe we have found the child-hope!'

Uproar broke out in the cave. Morpeth told them everything he had seen and Dragwena's plans for Rachel.

'Even if this is the child-hope,' someone called out, 'what can we do? Dragwena already has command of the girl. We are surely powerless to assist her.'

'We have a slim chance,' said Morpeth. 'Rachel has been left in a chamber I can reach. We can sneak back to the Palace and kidnap her.'

'Too dangerous,' snarled the same voice. 'Her spies will see us coming.'

'If many attempted the kidnap that would be true,' said Morpeth. 'But Dragwena trusts me. I can get safely back into the Palace without anyone noticing. If I'm seen I will say I am on the Witch's business. Everyone knows who I am. No one will dare to question me.'

Another voice said, 'What if this girl refuses to help us?'

Trimak stepped forward. 'I have considered this possibility.' He looked out boldly at the Sarren. 'If Rachel refuses to help us – then we will be forced to kill her *ourselves.*'

An awful silence fell on the cave.

'Trimak! Remember our pledge!' bellowed another Sarren. 'The shedding of child blood is the dark work of the Witch and her Neutrana slaves. I, for one, could not do this. How can you even suggest it?'

Several voices muttered their agreement.

Trimak sighed and held up his hand. 'I understand your fear,' he said. 'Do you think I have come to such a conclusion easily? Think: if Rachel will not assist us she is too dangerous to leave alive. We may hide the girl here for a while, but in time Dragwena will surely find and transform her. There will be no escape for us if this happens. With their strength combined they will quickly find and slaughter all Sarren.'

'And will you kill Rachel yourself, Trimak?' someone asked. 'Would *you* be prepared to do it?'

'I will do it if it must be done.'

'It should not come to that,' Morpeth said. 'If the child survived the box she has an innate strength Dragwena will not easily conquer; and remember, the Witch has had little time to work on Rachel's mind. If we act at once I am certain we can persuade her.'

Fenagel spoke up. 'Dragwena is so powerful. Is Rachel strong enough to fight the Witch? She seemed just like an ordinary, friendly girl when I was with her today. Even the simple magic of the Palace dresses came as a surprise. Imagine what Dragwena could throw at her! I think you're expecting too much, Trimak.'

'It's hard to argue against what you say,' said Trimak. 'But consider: for hundreds of years we have spoken about the legend of the child-hope, the girl who will defeat the Witch and free us all. I know at times we have all felt foolish, clinging onto this idea.'

Within the cave most heads nodded.

'But if we are to have any chance of defeating the Witch,' continued Trimak, 'then aid *must* come from the world outside. We all know this. Morpeth is our best weapon, but even combined with all our magic he's not strong enough to confront Dragwena. I can't promise any of you the child-hope is real. However, from what Morpeth tells us Rachel possesses magical powers far greater than any we have witnessed before. She *may* be the child-hope. No one among us has ever mastered skills she has developed in a single morning of play.'

He paused, to ensure that his next words were understood by everyone. 'Let me warn you all: if we do not try to use this girl's power to help us you can be sure Dragwena will not hesitate. She will take Rachel and turn her into an enemy whose ferociousness we can hardly imagine.'

He gazed at the faces in the darkness. 'Remember we speak now for all Sarren, many of whom cannot be here. To waver in our decision would deliver them all to Dragwena. I believe we have no choice. We must grasp the girl tonight, while we have a chance. If we wait even a few hours it will be too late.'

He peered around the cave. 'Are there any more questions? Does anyone have a different view?'

The cave was silent. Trimak waited several patient seconds before closing the discussion – the decision so grave everyone must have a chance to speak.

'In that case,' he said, 'I take it we are agreed. Morpeth will kidnap Rachel from the Palace tonight and bring her to Worraft. Now I ask you to return quickly and quietly to your homes. It will be noticed if you are away for too long.'

Morpeth again used his magic to open the door of the cave and the Sarren left rapidly, whispering to each other.

Once they were alone, Trimak noticed Morpeth deep in thought.

'What is it, my friend?' he asked. 'You have a trial ahead of you. Are you worried Dragwena may be lying in wait?'

Morpeth shook his head. 'I am not concerned for myself,' he said. 'Something you mentioned earlier has been gnawing at me. I wonder whether Dragwena does suspect I'm a rebel. She's certainly bored with me. It's obvious she wants a new, younger slave to replace her old guide.' He rubbed his chin. 'Perhaps, after all, this Rachel is not the girl she appears to be, merely one of the Witch's spies. Dragwena can make a creature look and behave as she wishes. Perhaps she transformed a Neutrana into the shape of a girl and gave her some extra powers just to tempt me.'

'Didn't you see Rachel arrive from Earth?'

'What I *saw* means nothing. Dragwena could have set me up. My heart tells me to trust Rachel, but Dragwena could easily have deceived me.'

Trimak bowed his head thoughtfully.

'There is more,' said Morpeth. 'Rachel has a brother who came with her through the Gateway. I must try to rescue Eric, too. Dragwena is bound to kill him if Rachel escapes.'

'Too dangerous,' replied Trimak. 'You must only worry about yourself and Rachel.'

Morpeth shook his head. 'We already ask so much of Rachel. Do you think she will forgive us if we do not try to save her brother?'

Trimak paced the cave, his expression anguished. 'Your safety and that of Rachel are too important to risk. I hate to be so merciless, Morpeth, but forget the boy. We have waited hundreds of years for this moment. We will lie to Rachel about Eric if we must.'

'That may not work,' said Morpeth. 'I have already sensed how quickly Rachel's magic is developing. If we lie, and she discovers this, she will never trust us. Never.'

Grudgingly, Trimak said, 'Oh . . . very well. But surely someone else can plan Eric's rescue?'

'No. Only I know the commands to lead them both safely from the Palace.'

'How will you bring them here?'

Morpeth grinned ruefully. 'A boy and girl over each of

71

my handsome shoulders, I should think. Dragged here on my tired old legs. I daren't use my magic so close to Dragwena. She knows my pattern too well.' He met Trimak's solemn gaze. 'Time to leave, I think. If Dragwena is preparing a welcome at the Palace, it would be rude to keep her waiting!'

He hugged Trimak and rapidly strode out of the cave.

Trimak now stood alone in the deep silence of Worraft. He thought about the work ahead for Morpeth and shuddered with fear. Have I sent my best friend to his death? he wondered. Could Rachel be a spy, or already under Dragwena's sway?

He knelt on the cold floor and, while he waited, felt the pressure of a small knife against his hip. He unsheathed it and deliberately held the blade towards the light, forcing himself to look at the sharp edge – to consider what might have to be done.

9

the child army

While the Council of Sarren debated Rachel slept. Her
body lay slumped in the east wing of the Palace where
Morpeth had left her, breathing slowly and peacefully at
first. Then her pulse quickened as the dream-sleep of the
Witch gradually took hold. The dream would spare her
nothing – only by feeling Dragwena's own desires and
hatreds could she be transformed into a Witch.

Within the dream-sleep Rachel experienced the past life
of the Witch.

Rachel saw things she would rather never have seen. She
saw lakes and streams; when Dragwena touched them they
turned to ice. She saw a snake, slithering from Dragwena's
neck in a silent attack. She saw a boy no older than Eric
being hunted by a pack of wolves. She witnessed children of

Ithrea long dead whom the Witch had killed. Dragwena forced Rachel to gaze into their faces and know their names. For a moment, Rachel even saw Morpeth as a young boy newly arrived on Ithrea – a boy with sandy-coloured hair and big blue eyes. 'Ready?' he asked. He opened his clenched hands and a tiny bright bird, no larger than a penny, flew into the air. 'I did it!' he gasped. Dragwena stood there, gazing fondly. 'You are my favourite child, Morpeth,' she said.

This memory, like all the others, lasted only a moment. Rachel could do nothing to stop them or shut them out. They streaked by as Dragwena selected all the memories of her past she needed Rachel to know, forcing her to watch, faster and faster, until each image became a blur of pain.

At last the memories stopped and Rachel, still in the dream-sleep, stood side by side with Dragwena herself in the eye-tower. The Witch's skin oozed its blood-red brightness, and Rachel watched spiders crawling beneath her teeth.

'Do I frighten you?' Dragwena asked softly.

'Yes,' said Rachel. 'You want me to be frightened. Why have you shown me all this? The things you have done . . . make me hate you even more than before. I'll fight you if I can.'

'You don't understand yet,' whispered Dragwena. 'I do not wish to fight. I already know that if I threaten Eric you will do anything I ask.'

'Yes,' said Rachel. 'I've seen what you do to children.'

'Children mean nothing. When you have as much power as I their lives are meaningless. You will soon have that power and feel the same.'

'I'll never feel that way. I don't want your power, Witch!'

'I would like to show you one more thing,' said Dragwena. 'It contains my most terrible memory, one that shames me. Do you want to see it? If you can resist my worst memory I will know that I can never use you. Then you will be free.'

'No. You'll kill me and Eric. I know you will.'

'This memory holds a secret I have shown no one else,' Dragwena said. 'It will also show me at my weakest. That could be useful if you need to fight me. Perhaps you can save yourself and Eric after all. Surely you want that chance?'

'Show me, then!' Rachel shouted.

Instantly, Rachel found herself thrust back in time. She gasped, realizing that she was no longer on Ithrea. She stood outside an enormous cave. The cave was surrounded by thousands of savage-looking children, each carrying swords and knives. Their faces were sweaty and ferocious.

'Where am I?' asked Rachel. 'Who . . . are these children? What have you done to them?'

'We are back on your Earth, in an age forgotten thousands of years before your birth,' Dragwena's distant voice answered. 'See how the children loved me then.'

Earth!

Rachel watched the Child Army standing with swords erect, chanting the Witch's name: 'Dragwena! Dragwena! *Dragwena*!' they cried with one great voice, adoring her. As the children called out Rachel saw Dragwena appear from a cloud. She swooped like a swallow over the army's raised swords, tenderly brushing the sharpened tips.

'What was this army for?' Rachel asked, trying to remain calm.

'I fought a battle against three Wizards on your planet,' Dragwena said. 'Always we have waged this war, Wizard and Witch, across many worlds and across all time. I had no interest in the children, but I knew the Wizards would come to protect the most fragile creatures on your world. They always do. But I had many years to prepare each child before they arrived, and when the Wizards came at last I surrounded myself at all times with my loyal Child Army. The Wizards did not dare attack me directly – they were afraid of injuring the children. That was their weakness, and I used it. I sent the children themselves to slaughter the Wizards. They hid underground. My children followed. I raised an army of a million, taught them my ways, and sent them deep inside the world with shields and swords of magic to seek out the Wizards and kill them.'

Rachel saw the shining look on each child's face as it held a sword aloft.

'They worshipped me,' said Dragwena. 'Each child would have killed with its bare hands if I ordered it. Their minds were full of hate. They hated the Wizards as I hated. They killed as I killed: without hesitation, without guilt.'

Rachel shivered, but also felt defiant. 'Do you think by showing me this I will do what you ask?' she scoffed. 'These children are twisted. Everything about you disgusts me!'

'Watch the final battle with the Wizards through my eyes,' said Dragwena. 'I have trapped them within the deepest cave in the world, and I go now to destroy them.'

Rachel felt herself inside Dragwena's body. She soared

into the cave mouth. Inside, all three Wizards squatted in tattered clothing. One Wizard stood up shakily when the Witch entered.

'Get on your knees, Larpskendya, leader of three,' Dragwena snarled. 'Kneel and beg. Or I will make the pain of your death last longer than this entire war.'

Larpskendya gazed calmly at her. 'You cannot harm us,' he said. 'Put down your weapons. You have already lost.'

'Lost?' Dragwena answered scornfully. 'How pathetic you are! This is where your great magic has left you – hiding in your rags! Will *you* stop me, Larpskendya? Will you take my sword and strike me down?'

'Not I, you fool,' he said.

Larpskendya turned to his companion Wizards and they all laughed at Dragwena.

Instantly, she uttered a spell of evil over her sword and thrust it into Larpskendya's heart. As it pierced his flesh a radiant blue light flashed from the wound. The light sprang from the cave and poured into the hearts of all the children waiting outside. Each child felt Dragwena's sword enter its own chest and howled in agony.

Dragwena stared in shock at the Wizards.

Lazily, Larpskendya plucked the sword out of his chest. The wound vanished. He met her disbelieving look, his eyes sparkling with many-coloured light. Then he touched his tattered robe.

Dragwena was brought to her knees, barely able to lift her face.

'You do not understand, do you?' Larpskendya said. 'Even *now* you do not understand.' He shook his head sadly. 'Your desire to kill us is so strong that you have forgotten the laws of magic.'

Dragwena stared. His words meant nothing to her.

'For every spell of evil there is a spell of goodness that will prevent it,' he explained. 'How could you have forgotten that simple law? You have been trapped, Dragwena. When you struck me with your sword we made every child in your army feel its pain and understand the evil enslaving them. They are coming now. They are coming for *your* blood, not ours. As you said yourself, they hate with your hate. They will show you no mercy.'

Dragwena listened, hearing the sound of thousands of children's feet running into the caves. As they came they scraped their knives against the stone walls, sharpening them. The sound was unbearable.

Dragwena tried to build a protective barrier at the mouth of the cave, but the spell merely burned uselessly in her mind. Her powers, she realized, were gone. The children continued to rush towards them, their cries deafening.

'Your magic has been stripped away,' said Larpskendya. 'You will never be allowed to rule over humankind again.' He stared coldly at her. 'What does it feel like to be as powerless as those you once enslaved?'

Dragwena said nothing.

'There are many forms of death we could have chosen for you,' Larpskendya said. 'Perhaps we should kill you, as I know you will never change your ways, Dragwena. But all life, even your life, has some meaning. Therefore, we offer another choice. I have created a young planet for you: Ithrea. There you will be banished for the remainder of your days. Many of your powers will be returned, those to help shape the new home to your needs. But there are no creatures such as these children to bend to your will, merely plants and a few simple animals.'

Dragwena considered the Ool World, the distant planet of Witches from which she came. Surely the Sisterhood would find her in time, wherever she was sent. They would always search for her, and if she was killed they would revenge her death.

'The Ool Witches will never find you,' said Larpskendya. 'The world of Ithrea is obscured from their leering view. You will be alone. Always.'

Dragwena spat at his feet. 'You had better kill me now, Wizard. I'll find a way back to this world.'

'Do you think I will leave this planet unprotected?' said Larpskendya. 'I will give the children of Earth new gifts to use against you if they should ever be needed.'

Dragwena laughed. 'Even you cannot create a child with the power to threaten me! I have worked on them for generations. They are weak. They can be made to obey, but have no flair for real magic. A million breedings could not make a human child with enough strength to concern a Witch.'

'We shall see,' said Larpskendya. 'In any case, know this, Dragwena: my song will always be on Ithrea. If I am called, I will return.'

The Witch cursed him. 'Get on with the banishment – before I tear out the hearts of the first children who reach us.'

The Wizards immediately held hands.

The next moment Dragwena stood alone on a new world. She looked about her. The skies were blue and the sun shone radiantly. Shimmering lakes sparkled in the sunshine and birds twittered amongst branches and leaves bursting with vitality.

Dragwena dragged her hands across her face. The loveliness of this world only enraged her. The destruction of the Wizards she had worked for, strived so long for, had been snatched away. Her hatred of them and the children who had turned against her returned, and she let out a scream of anguish.

I will return, Dragwena pledged. I will return and kill you all!

Rachel was lost inside the overwhelming hatred of the Witch. She fought to keep control, to remember who she was, but the Witch thrust further and further into Rachel's mind until she could no longer resist. At last, deep within the dream-sleep Rachel, too, swore to return and kill the Wizards and the children. As the Witch hated, so Rachel hated.

Lying in her soft bed in the Palace Rachel clenched her fists and dreamt of revenge.

10

awakening

Morpeth burst into Worraft, a sleeping Rachel and Eric under each arm.

'Far too simple,' he said, placing them on the cave floor. 'Something's wrong.'

'You rescued both!' marvelled Trimak.

'Yes, but it was too easy to escape the Palace. There were few Neutrana, and the east door stood unprotected. You know Dragwena always stations two guards there.'

'Were you followed?'

'I saw no one, but Dragwena has a thousand eyes.'

'Our scouts are close to the Palace and the cave,' said Trimak. 'They should be able to give us some warning if we're in any danger.' He looked with concern at Rachel. 'I see the child-hope still sleeps.'

'It's a dream-sleep planted by the Witch,' said Morpeth. 'She may not awaken for several hours.'

'What about Eric? Has the Witch been working on the boy, too?'

'Possibly,' said Morpeth. 'There is something strange about Eric.' He turned slowly towards Trimak. 'In fact, I know *exactly* what is unusual about him. I sense no magic, none. There is always a trace, even in the least gifted children.'

'Yes,' mused Trimak. 'Eric is different. Perhaps that is why Dragwena is interested in him.' He looked at Rachel. 'What kind of dreams would Dragwena give the girl?'

Morpeth grunted. 'Nightmares, without doubt.'

'Wake them up,' said Trimak.

'We can't! I've no idea what will happen if Rachel is woken too soon. We must let her wake when she's ready.'

'No,' Trimak said firmly. 'I understand your concern, but you said yourself that Dragwena's spell is intended to turn Rachel into a Witch. Even now the dream-sleep is probably conditioning the girl. We can't give the Witch any advantage.'

'It could kill Rachel,' said Morpeth. 'I've no idea how powerful this spell is. It is wrong to—'

'Do it!'

Reluctantly, Morpeth placed two bent fingers against Rachel's forehead. She moved, but remained asleep.

'Use *full* force,' Trimak demanded angrily.

'I daren't! If Rachel is the child-hope we can't risk her safety.'

'I can't risk the safety of the Sarren, either. Try Eric first. Perhaps the Witch also put him in a dream-sleep.'

This time Morpeth placed both hands against Eric's temple. He shot up, blinking in fright. Morpeth and Trimak studied his behaviour closely, watching as he tried to get a reaction from Rachel.

'The boy seems himself,' said Trimak warily.

It took far longer for Morpeth to wake Rachel. Eventually she stirred, and the moment her eyes opened she leapt on Eric, tearing at his arms, screaming with frenzy. Startled, Eric managed to stagger away. Morpeth jumped on Rachel, holding her down.

'I'll kill you! I'll kill you, child!' Rachel shrieked at Eric.

'Stop her!' said Trimak. 'What's happening?'

Morpeth pinned Rachel's arms to the floor. 'I told you, Trimak. I told you how dangerous it would be to wake her before she was ready!'

Eric approached Rachel.

'Stay back,' warned Morpeth.

Eric touched one of her kicking feet. Instantly, Rachel stopped struggling. For a moment she seemed lost, then gazed at her hands, feeling them come back under her control.

'What's happening?' she asked. 'Eric . . . I didn't hurt you, did I?'

Morpeth stared at Eric. 'You broke the Witch's control over Rachel. How?'

Eric shrugged. 'I didn't do anything. I just grabbed her foot, that's all.'

'But she changed the *moment* you touched her.'

Rachel jumped up. She clutched Eric and moved them both away from Morpeth. 'Don't answer any of his questions,' she told Eric. 'He's working for the Witch.'

'That's not true,' Morpeth protested. 'I know it seems—'

'Why did you leave me in the eye-tower with Drag-wena?' Rachel demanded. 'You knew what was going to happen inside, didn't you? You shut the door in my face.'

'I had no choice,' Morpeth said. 'Please try to understand. Dragwena watches all her servants so closely. If I had not dragged you all the way to the eye-tower, someone would have reported it. I had to appear merciless.'

'Why should I believe you?' Rachel said. 'How do I know you're not lying?'

Morpeth swept his arms around the cave. 'Look at this dark place,' he said. 'If I was a friend of the Witch do you think I'd bring you here? I'm risking my life doing this. So is Trimak.' He told her about the Sarren and their struggle against the Witch.

Rachel relaxed slightly. She explained about the snakes-and-ladders game and the dream of the Child Army and the Wizards. Both Morpeth and Trimak listened in fascination, never having heard this story before.

'Do you know what this means?' Morpeth whispered to Trimak.

Trimak nodded. 'It means the Witch has put her complete faith in Rachel. She will stop at nothing to recover the child.'

'Indeed, no place will be safe to hide her,' Morpeth said. 'We must protect Rachel in another way. We must work on her magic. She must learn how to defend *herself*.'

Rachel considered the meaning of her dream. 'At least I understand why Dragwena hates all children now,' she said. 'But I still don't know why she wants *me*.'

'The magic of children!' Morpeth exclaimed. 'Now it all makes sense! Dragwena has been bringing children to Ithrea for countless centuries, always testing, always hoping. From Rachel's dream we know the Wizards imprisoned the Witch here. All this time she must have been waiting for a single child with enough strength to help her get back. Rachel *is* that child!'

'But in the dream,' said Rachel, 'the Wizard Larpskendya told Dragwena she would always be alone, imprisoned forever on Ithrea. How did all the children get here?'

'If your dream is true,' said Morpeth, 'the Wizards made a mistake, or underestimated Dragwena. She long ago found a way to bring children from Earth.'

'The Wizard also mentioned he would develop magic in Earth's children, give them gifts to protect themselves if needed,' said Trimak. 'We have seen little evidence of that till you arrived, Rachel. Perhaps he meant you. You are to be our protection. You and Eric.'

'I can't do anything,' Eric said. 'Rachel's got all the magic.'

'But you smashed the Witch's control over your sister,' said Morpeth. 'Tell us how you did that.'

'I don't know,' Eric said. 'I just wanted Rachel back to normal. I didn't feel anything when it happened.'

'Mm,' Morpeth said, stroking his beard. 'What else do we know? The Wizard spoke about a song. What do you think he meant by it?'

'My song will always be on Ithrea,' Rachel whispered. 'That's what Larpskendya said. If I am called I will return.'

'Called how?' asked Morpeth. 'Called by whom?'

They sat for some time in the dark silence of the cave, pondering this.

'We're guessing at what the dream means,' Rachel said eventually. 'But I'm sure about one thing: Dragwena will search for me. Now she knows what I can do she'll never stop looking. You've betrayed her, Morpeth. She'll kill you and Trimak. Then she'll study Eric until she finds out how to use his gift.' She held her head erect, trembling slightly. 'I know what she'll do with me – turn me into her little Witch. It shouldn't be hard. I tried to stop her in the tower. I was useless.'

'Not useless,' Morpeth reassured her. 'You need training, to develop your spells and sharpen your magic. Then you'll be ready to face Dragwena.'

'I might never be strong enough,' said Rachel. 'I know what Dragwena's like. If she can't use me, she'll *kill* me. I'm too dangerous to live as her enemy.' She looked fiercely at Morpeth. 'I'm right, aren't I?'

'Perhaps,' Morpeth said. 'However, I believe that you are stronger than you realize; and I also believe that Dragwena can be defeated because she makes mistakes.'

'What mistakes?'

'She allowed you to slip from her grasp. That was foolish. She also trusted you with her deepest secrets too soon, when we – or Eric – could still reach into your mind and bring you back. And Dragwena does not realize I am a traitor. I've concealed my genuine thoughts for many years.'

'I wonder how well you know her,' Rachel said bluntly. 'I doubt you could hide your treachery for long. I don't think Dragwena makes mistakes. Perhaps she *let* me and Eric escape for some reason. Did you think of that?'

'Yes,' said Morpeth. 'We've considered it, but can think of no reason why the Witch would let you go so easily.'

Rachel made her fingernails glow bronze. 'Look at me,' she said. 'All this magic I've got. It's so strange. If I've got magic here why didn't I notice it at home? Why can't I use it there, too? It doesn't make sense.'

'All children have some magic on Ithrea,' said Morpeth.

'Dragwena is able to sense it when she draws children from Earth, so it must exist inside them there in some fashion. I've no idea why it can't be used.'

'Perhaps the Wizards don't allow it,' said Eric. 'They think it's too dangerous to use.'

Morpeth nodded thoughtfully. 'Have you ever seen the Wizards?'

'No,' Eric said. 'Have you?'

'No, nor anyone else on Ithrea,' said Morpeth. 'But I'd certainly like to meet the one called Larpskendya. I've got some good questions to ask him.'

Eric felt Trimak's beard. 'Hey, how old are you, any-way?'

'Pretty ancient,' sighed Trimak. 'Have a guess.'

'Eighty-six!'

Trimak laughed. 'Try again.'

'Younger or older?'

'Much older.'

'All right, a hundred and eighty-six!'

'Actually,' said Trimak, 'I am exactly five hundred and thirty-six years of age.'

Eric gasped. 'You can't be *that* old. You would be dead by now.'

'The Witch's power is responsible,' said Trimak. 'We have a saying here: she preserves those who serve. It helps keep her closest servants loyal. Morpeth is nearly as old as I am.'

'You were both stolen by the Witch from Earth, weren't you?' said Rachel. 'You are children who've grown up here.'

'Yes,' said Morpeth. 'Everyone on Ithrea was snatched away in a similar way to you and Eric. Dragwena does not let us grow gracefully into adults. I think she enjoys watching us get older and uglier in the same way together, until we have lost all our original features. The Witch also stunts our growth. It is as if she wishes to remind us we will always be children in her domain.'

'How many children live on Ithrea?' Rachel asked.

'Thousands have been abducted,' Morpeth answered. 'Some live around the Palace, those with the brightest magic, directly serving the Witch. Others are scattered around the planet.'

'But how can they live in this cold?' Rachel asked. 'How do they survive?'

'They live underground,' said Morpeth. 'They dig tunnels. They exist as best they can.'

Eric shook his head. 'But what do they eat? How do they grow anything?'

Morpeth grunted. 'Nothing much grows on Ithrea. They hunt for what meat they can find. Mostly burrowing worms. There aren't many. They cultivate a few herbs. They survive somehow on this, or die trying.' He glanced awkwardly at Trimak. 'Every year, from all over Ithrea, they make the trek across the storms and snows to the Palace. Dragwena insists they bring food for us.'

'For *you*?' said Eric.

Morpeth rubbed his round stomach. 'Yes. Dragwena could easily provide all we need, but she likes to watch the others struggle to bring the food here. She forces her Palace servants to eat, knowing it means all the others starve. Dragwena likes it that way.'

Rachel touched him gently on the shoulder. 'Does the Witch ever allow you . . . to die?'

'All the original children are now dead,' said Morpeth. 'Anyone who resists the Witch is killed immediately unless, like you, Rachel, they show promise. Sometimes Dragwena casts them out to the wolf packs, or she just leaves them to succumb to the cold. Perhaps those are the lucky children. Finally, the Witch kills us all, either because we grow too old to be useful or simply because she grows bored with us. No one dies naturally of old age on Ithrea. Dragwena is always there at the end of our lives, causing the final pain, enjoying the moment.'

Rachel and Eric fell silent.

'When I touched Dragwena's mind in the eye-tower,' Rachel said at last, 'I sensed there had been others like the Sarren in the past. Those who have tried to resist secretly. I think Dragwena actually wants you to rebel. I think she enjoys the challenge of letting you become a pest, then stamping you out. It's all just a game to her.'

'You may be right,' said Trimak hoarsely. 'But I'm certain the Witch has never faced a child such as you before, Rachel. She has never faced the child-hope.'

'*That* again,' said Rachel. 'What is this child-hope you and Morpeth keep talking about? Tell me.'

Morpeth glanced anxiously at Trimak, who nodded.

'The child-hope is a legend,' said Morpeth. 'That's all. No one knows where it came from, nor what it truly means, but it has been passed from generation to generation on Ithrea, even amongst the Neutrana. It tells of a dark girl-child who will come to free us all. The legend has grown over the centuries, but the original verse from which it springs is short enough:

'Dark girl she will be,
Enemies to set free,
Sing in harmony,
From sleep and dawn-bright sea,
I will arise—'

'And behold your childish glee,' Eric finished.

Everyone turned towards him.

'How do you know the end of the verse?' gasped Morpeth.

'I don't know,' said Eric, looking bewildered.

'Someone must have told you,' said Trimak.

Eric shrugged. 'I've never heard the words before. They just came into my head.'

Morpeth looked expectantly at Rachel.

'I don't recognize them at all,' she said. 'The words are so . . . strange. What do they mean?'

'Who knows?' Morpeth said bitterly. 'Perhaps nothing. Perhaps everything. Your hair is dark, your powers beyond anything we've seen before. We hoped *you* would know what they meant.'

'I know what some of it means,' Eric said.

'Tell us,' breathed Trimak.

Eric appeared almost bashful, as if the words held him in awe.

'*Enemies to set free*,' Rachel whispered. 'Are we the enemies?'

'No,' said Eric. 'Neutrana.'

Morpeth trembled. 'What about the last part of the verse? What or who will arise from sleep and dawn-bright sea? Do you know?'

Eric's face lit up. In a purely childlike way Rachel had not seen in him since he was a young boy he flapped his arms. '*Whoosh*!' he crooned, running in circles around the cave. 'Whoosh! Whoosh!'

Everyone watched Eric in fascination. Eventually he calmed down and came back, looking sheepish.

'What was all that about?' Rachel asked. 'Were you supposed to be flying?'

'No,' Eric said. 'I mean – yes, I might have been. Oh, I don't know!'

'What does *sing in harmony* mean?' Morpeth asked.

'Beats me,' Eric muttered, looking uncomfortable under their stares.

'*Beats me*?' Rachel said. 'Come on, Eric, you're not taking this seriously.'

'Yes, I am!'

'Be honest,' she said. 'Did someone tell you this verse before? Better let me know quick if you're faking it.'

'I'm not faking it!'

Rachel sat down until her eyes were on a level with his. 'All right,' she said. 'I believe you. Think a minute. In my dream the Wizard Larpskendya told Dragwena his song will always be on Ithrea. Do you know what that means?'

'No, I don't,' Eric said angrily. 'Stop getting at me.'

Rachel turned in frustration to Morpeth. 'I suppose you think I'm the one to free everyone. You think I'm your precious child-hope. Are all your hopes about me based on this little verse? A few lines about a dark child?'

'Yes,' said Morpeth. 'Exactly.'

'But the words of the verse . . . well, they could mean almost anything!'

Morpeth grinned. Wrinkles deep enough to snuggle inside appeared under his eyes and criss-crossed his sunken cheeks. 'Don't you understand?' he cried. 'Until now they could have meant anything. But *Eric* knows the words! Apart from myself, the only contact he's had on Ithrea is with Dragwena – and I'm sure the Witch would never have put these ideas into his head.'

'I'm scared,' Eric whispered.

'Of the verse?' Rachel asked.

'No. I'm scared of Dragwena.' He murmured this. Rachel knew how hard it was for him to admit it, especially in front of Morpeth and Trimak.

'So am I,' Rachel said. 'But I'm sick of being scared of her, aren't you?'

Eric nodded fervently.

Rachel turned to Morpeth and Trimak. 'I'm not sure if this verse means anything,' she said. 'But I bet Dragwena already knows we've been kidnapped. We can't have much time before she finds us. You told me that if I learned some new spells I might be able to fight her.'

'We'll begin your training at once,' said Morpeth. 'Eric can stay with Trimak.'

'No,' Rachel said. 'Eric and I stay together.'

'It's too dangerous,' warned Trimak. 'Dragwena will use him as a weapon against you.'

'I won't do anything unless you agree,' Rachel said flatly.

'It's too risky,' said Morpeth. 'We can protect Eric better if you are separated.'

'You have no idea how to protect him,' Rachel said. 'Stop

pretending you do. I can probably take care of Eric better than all the Sarren. You should know that by now.'

'Very well,' said Morpeth gloomily. 'Follow me.'

11

MAGIC

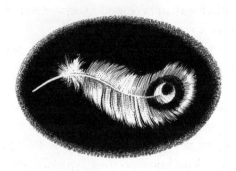

Morpeth led Rachel and Eric from Worraft. For some time they shuffled in silence under a low ceiling of cold corridors. As Morpeth padded along, red doors winked alight ahead of his footsteps, extinguishing the moment he passed. Occasionally he took them through one of the red doors. Each door always led to another almost identical corridor and more doors, in a seemingly endless series of upward sharp bends.

Rachel felt dizzy. 'How do you know the way?'

'Magic. This was built many years ago, the secret labour of a few Sarren. Dragwena knows nothing of it. You are the first children to come here.'

'Where are we going?' asked Eric, gazing round intently.

'To my study.' Morpeth stopped outside a door which looked like all the others. 'Now do you think you can remember how to find your way here from Worraft?'

Rachel looked at Eric and they both shook their heads.

'Good,' said Morpeth. 'Only a special kind of magic can guide you this way again.'

'Could the Witch find us?' Rachel said.

'In time she could. She would have to find Worraft first. There is no other way in here, and Dragwena does not even know about the cave. At least, I hope not.'

He blew on the door three times to open it and ushered the children inside.

Morpeth's 'study' was nothing more than a cramped oblong room, with a simple bed, a table and a single chair.

'What can you do to help me fight the Witch?' Rachel asked Morpeth. 'You know so many spells, and—'

'Me?' He laughed. 'I nearly collapsed just trying to keep up with you at breakfast!'

'What do you mean?'

'Do you remember those fish earrings? I had to use *all* of my power to alter their colour!'

Rachel gasped. 'I wondered why they kept changing!'

'You also played snakes and ladders against Dragwena and won. All children who have taken that test have failed: every one of them.' He put his hands on Rachel's shoulders. 'You *are* the child-hope. I'm sure of it.'

'But how can I defeat the Witch? What do I have to do?'

'You need to learn some new spells,' Morpeth said. 'You also need to practise. Dragwena has practised for centuries. When she commands, she is instantly obeyed. She can change shape in a moment.'

'But it's *hard* to change shape,' Rachel said dejectedly. 'I only did it because I was scared. What do I have to become to defeat Dragwena?'

'I don't know,' said Morpeth.

Rachel stared at him. 'I can't believe it. You expect *me* to know!'

'Well,' he said, 'let's not worry about confronting Dragwena for now. One step at a time. Will you play a magic game with me?'

Rachel sighed, recalling the sheer joy of making magic in the Breakfast Room, smashing melons into walls. Magic no longer seemed like a game.

Eric parked himself comfortably on Morpeth's bed and watched.

'I want you to try changing your shape again,' Morpeth said. 'What would be a clever disguise on Ithrea?'

'A snowflake,' Rachel answered at once. She quickly pictured herself as a snowflake drifting in the air. 'Well?'

'Same skinny legs as always,' said Eric.

'Don't be concerned,' Morpeth told her. 'It's much harder than you think. When we played in the Breakfast Room and rode over the mountains Dragwena put a special blanket of magic around us. But you soon began using your own magic. When you flew to the lake and changed into the feather, the Witch's magic didn't help you. You did those things yourself. You can do that here, now, but you must concentrate fully. Using real magic is extremely dangerous and requires all your attention.'

Rachel glanced around the room. 'Can I try to be something different? I don't really want to be a snowflake. I'd rather be a horse – or something that's *alive*.'

'A horse, however lovely, would hardly fit into this

study,' said Morpeth drily. 'I want you to fight against the desire to become just *anything*. You need to be more disciplined in your use of power.'

'I don't understand.'

'When you changed into a feather it saved your life,' he explained. 'You see, it is because you became what you needed to be, what you *had* to be at that instant. Dragwena will give you little chance to think when she attacks. You may be able to save us all if you can, at the moment of danger, change into the *right thing*, whatever that is. Now try to concentrate.'

Rachel forced herself to relax, to focus on the snowflake image. She ran fingers of ice over her body, colder, colder, until her brittle eyelids froze against the pupils. Shape next. Skin folding, bones condensing, until she shrunk to the size of a palm, then a finger, a thumbnail; then smaller still, so tiny she would hardly be noticed. She made her limbs and head disappear. She made her body fluffy and white, with sharp crystalline edges. It took an enormous effort, but for the first time Rachel was conscious that instead of instinctively reacting she could control the transformation herself. She blinked, opening her new snow eyes.

Morpeth and Eric had disappeared – at least Rachel thought so, before realizing she had been slowly drifting alongside Morpeth's trousers for several seconds. She landed gently on the floor. Hardness and dust pressed harshly against her. A few feet away Eric's giant shoe stepped back.

Before Rachel even had time to grow used to her snowflake-ness she noticed a pool of water surrounding her body. Am I bleeding? she wondered. Suddenly she understood: I'm not bleeding. I'm *melting*. I'm melting on the floor!

The next moment she had changed again: she was a drop of water.

Little currents of liquid lapped inside her new body from one side to the other.

Mm, she mused, no longer frightened, merely curious. A drop of water would be more interesting if she could . . . take off . . . like a plane!

Instantly she jerked from the floor, flying slowly at first, but speeding up as she learnt how to use her new wing-flaps. She hovered in mid air, gazing about. A few feet away Morpeth's nose loomed, as big as a bus. Rachel zoomed three fast circles over his head, then darted into Eric's ear, out again and over his cheeks, through his blond curls, onto his nose. A slide! She skied down the bridge of his nose and hung at the tip, swinging backwards and forwards. Looking up, she saw Eric's huge face gazing down from crossed eyes. Rachel flipped herself into a dive.

I'll allow myself to fall, she thought. I can't hurt myself. I'm just a splodge of water . . .

Her little body exploded as it hit the stone, splitting into hundreds of tiny water droplets that leapt away from the rest of her body. Panicking, Rachel tried to imagine herself as a girl again . . .

A deep voice – Morpeth's – blasted, '*No!* Stay as you are!'

Rachel waited anxiously. A moment later her tongue flew into the air. She watched her legs shoot upwards and wriggled her nose, a girl again.

'That was fantastic!' Rachel said. 'Can we do it again?'

Morpeth glared at her. '*You stupid girl,*' he roared. 'Do you know what would have happened if you had changed back when you were scattered all over the floor?'

'I—'

He gripped her arm. 'I'll tell you what would have happened: you would have come back as a girl in pieces! Your arms, legs and head would have been all over the room. *You would be dead!*'

'I'm – I'm sorry,' said Rachel. 'I didn't know. You didn't tell me.'

Morpeth sighed heavily. 'You see, when you change into another form you really *become* it.'

'I don't understand.'

'Think of a lizard. If you changed yourself into a lizard someone could chop off your tail and you could still crawl around, couldn't you?'

Rachel nodded.

'But if you changed back you might find one of your legs missing.' He grinned. 'I think I prefer girls with two legs, don't you?'

Rachel stared at the floor. 'I'll try to remember.'

'Good.' Morpeth flapped his arms. 'What a magnificent creature you became! I felt dizzy watching you shoot about.'

Rachel pointed at his face. 'What a big nose you have!'

Morpeth rubbed his thick nose playfully. 'I dread to think how big it must appear to a drop of water! Let's play some more.'

'First, why couldn't I change back to being me again?'

'It is much harder to change back to your real self,'

Morpeth explained. 'I don't know why. Only Dragwena is able to do it. However, when I saw you scattered all over the floor I sensed you might try.'

'*You* can change me back. You've done it twice now.'

'It's a gift from the Witch,' Morpeth said. 'Dragwena is always concerned there are enemies hiding inside everyday shapes like trees or birds or wolves. She gave me the power centuries ago to *unchange* things – to change them back to their true form. Until I reversed you back from the feather I did not know I could do it.'

'Why can't you change yourself into a feather or a snowflake?'

'That is a gift only you and Dragwena share,' Morpeth replied. 'You are the first child to have shape-shifted.' He gazed wistfully at her. 'You are the first to have done many things.'

'Maybe I'm a Witch,' Rachel said anxiously.

'I don't think so.' He smiled ruefully. 'Or, if you are a Witch, you are a very nice one.'

Eric lay down on Morpeth's bed and snuggled the pillow.

'Can I have a nap?' he asked, yawning. 'I'm really tired.'

'How can you be tired after what you've just seen?' said Morpeth. He looked puzzled, then relaxed again. 'I'm forgetting what a long night you had. Of course you can. I will wake—'

But Eric had already nodded off.

Once they were sure Eric was asleep, Rachel whispered to Morpeth: 'What will we do next?'

'Why not try being something more solid this time?' Morpeth said. He looked around the room. 'This place is a little bare, in my view. How about some more furniture?'

With a grin Rachel instantly transformed herself into a high-backed chair, with carved wooden legs.

'Can you hear me?' Morpeth asked.

'Yes,' she tried to reply, finding her mouth inside the wooden frame. She brought her lips onto the cushion, and placed her eyes above them. 'I can hear you perfectly!'

'Interesting,' he said. 'A chair that can talk. Whatever next?'

'A table!'

She lengthened her legs, made the cushion disappear, and transformed the seat into a big flat top.

'Hi,' she said breathlessly.

'Quite clever,' Morpeth said. 'Let's put you to a real test. Can you imagine you are *me?*'

'What? You mean make myself look like you?'

Morpeth nodded.

'I'll try,' said the little lips on the table.

Rachel observed Morpeth carefully, studying everything about him: his long arms, the flat bulbous line of his nose, the ancient sunken cheeks. She examined his leather clothes, trying to work out what the old garments must feel like to wear.

'Well?' she asked, rushing to finish.

'See for yourself,' said Morpeth, pointing to a small mirror on the wall.

Rachel dashed across expectantly. The creature staring back was a mess. The clothes were accurate, but Morpeth's beard was only half made and she had not even remembered to change his hair or square jaw. What looked back from the mirror was a crude Morpeth, with long dark hair and a pointed chin like her own.

She laughed – and realized Morpeth also had her small even teeth.

'Oh dear,' she said. 'I'm a sort of Rachel-Morpeth thing.'

The voice was also her high-pitched own. She had forgotten to change that as well.

'Mm,' Morpeth said. 'It's much harder to imagine being a person, isn't it? Tables and chairs don't have voices or teeth. You have to think carefully and remember everything about people, even the things you cannot see.'

'At least I got your nose right,' Rachel said, pressing it.

'That's not true,' said Morpeth. 'Your nose is much too big.'

Rachel checked in the mirror. 'No,' she said, twitching it. 'I think the nose is just like yours. It's exactly the right size.'

Morpeth frowned. 'Perhaps you're right.'

'Should I make the nose smaller? Would you like that?'

'Isn't it perfect already?' he asked. 'Oh, all right. Why not!'

Rachel made a snub nose. They looked in the mirror together.

'Not bad,' he said. 'But can you make me look *handsome*? There's a test for you!'

Rachel tried a few different combinations before she found what she wanted. The creature now standing next to Morpeth was a tall good-looking man with sandy hair and piercingly blue eyes.

Morpeth stared in astonishment. 'He is certainly more handsome. But does it look like me?'

'I don't know,' Rachel replied, uncertainly. 'I saw you as a boy in the dream Dragwena gave me. You look a bit like a grown-up version of him.'

'You may be right, Rachel,' he muttered, touching her face awkwardly. 'It has been so long since I was a boy. I had forgotten . . . what I used to be like.'

He stared sadly at the floor.

'I didn't mean to upset you,' she said. 'Perhaps . . . perhaps I can really make *you* look like this. Do you want me to?'

'I'm so old I don't care what I look like,' said Morpeth. 'Anyway, it is impossible—' He stopped and gazed sharply at Rachel. 'Go on then. Change me if you can!'

Rachel considered how to do it. How can I go *inside* him? she wondered. On impulse, she transformed into a speck of dust, so tiny that she could enter the pores of his skin. Small currents of air in the room moved her around. Rachel steadied herself, landed on his hair, felt the texture and dryness. She moved carefully among the strands sculpting them, made them lighter, silkier. Next she softened his cheeks, smoothed out the wrinkles and changed the colour of his eyes to a deeper blue. She made herself into a small pair of scissors to cut off his ragged beard. After several minutes of hard work she was finished – or almost. She reached into all his limbs, stretching out his body, making him taller. Feeling tired, she flew to the middle of the room and turned herself into a table again.

Morpeth sat in front of her, but not the wrinkled old dwarf Rachel knew. He was a tall young man, with curly thick hair and radiant blue eyes.

Morpeth gasped at his reflection in the mirror, pinching his face as if it were a mask. He blinked rapidly and his new blue eyes blinked back.

'You look very handsome now,' said the table.

'How did you do this?' he marvelled. 'You should not be able to change *someone else*. Only Dragwena has that power.'

'I don't know,' she said.

'Imagine you're Rachel again. Change yourself back,' Morpeth said firmly.

'You told me only Dragwena can do that.'

'That's what I used to believe. Now I am certain you can do it.'

Rachel knew what was needed at once. She saw herself as a girl again, wearing the soft leather of the Sarren. It was somehow easier than before. She did not even need to concentrate. Rachel walked confidently across the room to the mirror. A girl with large green eyes, a sharp nose and a small beauty spot on her left cheek peered back.

'I did it!'

Morpeth's jaw dropped open. Then he gazed at his own handsome face in the mirror, pulling faces to see his new expressions.

But Rachel had not finished. Suddenly ideas were occurring to her which even Morpeth could not have conceived. She pictured *another* Rachel in the room, placing it behind him. It stood there, as rigid as a plastic doll. She made it step forward. It moved stiffly, like a robot.

Rachel concentrated harder, gave it bones, ligaments and muscles that could move flexibly, like a real person. She made the second Rachel stretch out its arms and place small fingers around Morpeth's ears.

He gasped, jumping away.

'Which one is me?' asked both girls at the same time.

Rachel smiled and the fake girl smiled too.

Morpeth stared at both of them. At first they seemed identical. As he looked more closely he noticed that one of the girls had a slightly bland appearance. He grinned confidently at Rachel. '*You* are the real one.'

Rachel could also see the differences. She made the bland expression disappear.

'Which one is Rachel now?' asked both girls.

Morpeth studied each child closely. He touched their cheeks. He felt their hair. He picked them up. They were the same weight – Rachel had even considered that. Eventually, he shrugged.

'I don't know,' he said. 'I can't tell which is real. You *both* look real.'

Rachel giggled and wished the second Rachel to vanish. It disappeared at once.

Morpeth sat down heavily on a chair, and they stared in silence at each other.

'I – I don't know what to say,' he said. 'The things you are doing should not be possible. I have no idea how you've done them.'

'I can teach you,' Rachel said. 'It's not hard.'

Morpeth rubbed his handsome new chin. 'I am supposed to be teaching *you*,' he grunted. 'I see instead I have much to learn! I think—'

A noise from the bed distracted them both. It was Eric, talking in his sleep.

'He must be dreaming,' said Rachel.

'Shush! Listen to what he's saying.'

Eric twisted in the bed. 'Fifteen,' he said. 'Left. Eight. Right. Four. Left. Six. Left. Two.' He continued to say the strange numbers.

'What's he muttering?' Rachel asked. 'It sounds like a weird dream.'

'It's not a dream!' Morpeth jumped up. 'It is the way to this room through the corridors and doors. *Dragwena is coming.*'

'What do you mean?' Rachel cried. 'You said Dragwena wouldn't be able to find us?'

'Don't you see?' he said. 'The Witch has tricked us all. She was alone with your brother for several hours. She must have planted a finding spell within him!'

Rachel put her hand across Eric's mouth. Still asleep, possessing extraordinary strength, he ripped the hand away.

'Right. Four. Left. Six. Right. Two.'

Rachel burst into tears. 'Can't we stop him?'

'There's no time!'

Morpeth pressed a spot on the floor and a small exit appeared in one of the walls.

'Quick,' he said. 'We must leave at once!'

'But we can't leave Eric here,' Rachel insisted. 'We have to take him with us.'

'No!' Morpeth leapt towards the exit. 'He is under Dragwena's control. We can't help him now. Come with me.'

He jumped through the exit and held out his hand.

'I won't go without Eric,' Rachel shouted. 'I'm not leaving him!' As she tried to pick Eric up he kicked out savagely in his sleep. 'C'mon,' Rachel snarled. 'You're coming whether you want to or not!' She dragged Eric across to the exit into Morpeth's reluctant arms.

'We *can't* take him with us,' Morpeth said desperately. 'You must understand, Rachel. He's Dragwena's slave now! Leave, before it's too late!'

'Not without Eric!'

With no time to argue, Morpeth clutched Eric with one arm, reaching with the other for Rachel. 'I've got him! Now follow! Hurry!'

Rachel took a step forward, but a blast of wind startled her. The main door leading to the room had been smashed open.

In the doorway stood Dragwena.

The Witch glanced at Morpeth's escape exit, slamming it shut. Rachel heard him running away down the tunnel, calling 'See you at Hoy Point! *Hoy Point!*' as the sound of his footsteps disappeared.

Two Neutrana guards leapt into the room alongside the Witch.

'You must open the exit,' one said. 'Let us kill Morpeth.'

'No,' Dragwena answered. 'He can't escape. We'll deal with him later.'

Rachel wasted no time. She pictured herself as a sword, flying towards the Witch's head, but before she could complete the thought Dragwena knocked her to the ground.

'Tut, tut,' Dragwena scoffed. 'What nonsense has Morpeth been teaching you? My magic is stronger than anything he knows. Do you think you can challenge me, child? Did you believe I would ever allow you to escape?'

'I won't let you use me to harm anyone,' shouted Rachel. 'You'll have to kill me first, Witch. My magic's getting stronger. I can fight you now!'

With two fingers Dragwena wrenched Rachel from the floor, as if she weighed nothing.

'Soon you will want to be with me forever,' Dragwena said. 'You will not want to fight. You will forget everyone else. I will suck them all from your mind.'

'I *hate* you!' Rachel struggled to free herself. 'You brought us here, didn't you? The black claws in the cellar were yours!'

The Witch smiled appreciatively. 'I am indeed the claws and many other things unspoken on this world. None of this will matter soon. I will change you into my own creature.' She stroked Rachel's hair. 'You will kill lots of children and, I promise, you will *enjoy* it.'

Tucking Rachel under her arm the Witch flew rapidly from the room and along the corridor. All the doors opened before her. Rachel tried to imagine herself by the shore of Lake Ker again. Each time she did so a wave of pain smashed her mind, scattering her thoughts. The Witch would not let her concentrate for a second.

Within moments they were out of the corridors and into Worraft, through the entrance and heading upwards. Freezing wind struck Rachel's face and she realized she was outside. The stars shot past her head. She arched her back and looked up. Ahead, the luminous green window of the eye-tower raced towards them.

12

the kiss breath

After Dragwena shut the escape exit Morpeth ran for his life carrying Eric, still half-asleep, down the narrow tunnel. A few moments later he stopped to listen, holding his breath, expecting to be chased by Dragwena and an army of Neutrana. Hearing nothing, he collapsed on the floor, safe for a moment at least.

You fool, he raged at himself, thumping the wall. You were supposed to protect her. Now Dragwena has Rachel and you will never get her back!

Eric, now wide awake, watched him fearfully.

'What happened?' he asked. 'Where's Rachel?'

Morpeth pressed his thumbs against Eric's temple, but felt no trace of Dragwena's magic left inside. The spell Dragwena planted, he now understood, must have been shallow, snapping as soon as Eric awakened. Morpeth groaned. Why hadn't he thought to check the boy properly earlier? Eric was the perfect spy, a neat snare leading Dragwena to Rachel and the Sarren. All along, he thought, perhaps long before Rachel arrived, Dragwena must have recognized his treachery. The Witch had used Rachel and Eric to flush out the secret locations of the Sarren, trapping them together under the Palace – a place they could easily be slaughtered.

I was too confident, he realized. I believed I could conceal my thoughts from the Witch. Rachel knew I was wrong!

He forced himself to calm down, knowing he needed help quickly if there was to be any hope of recapturing her. Picking Eric up he headed swiftly down to the deep caves where Trimak was hiding. As he got closer he heard anguished sounds – the screams of men and the ring of metal.

A fight was taking place.

Morpeth padded towards the sounds and drew his own short narrow sword. He had never used it before in a real battle. He had not bothered to sharpen it for years. Beyond a final door he could hear voices clearly now. A deep voice, Trimak's, barked desperate orders.

'We must go inside,' Morpeth told Eric. 'I may not be able to protect you if I have to fight in hand-to-hand combat. Stay behind me, close. If I'm injured you must find other Sarren to look after you as best they can. Do you understand?'

Eric nodded his head, intensely frightened.

Morpeth thought bitterly: thanks to my stupidity there is no safe place for you now, boy.

He pulled Eric against his back and put his shoulder against the door.

He gripped the haft of his sword tightly.

And leapt into the battle.

Rachel was held in the black arm-claw of the Witch, flying towards the eye-tower. A sharp wind tugged at her hair as she flew upward, the other Palace buildings disappearing below. Dragwena's face glowed in ecstasy. She held Rachel with one bent arm; the other arm pointed in front like a gun-barrel, slicing through the night air.

Rachel knew time was running out. She tried using her magic to slide from the Witch's grasp. But every time she began forming a spell snake-hairs burst from the Witch's head, smothering her face, breaking her concentration.

'Do you think your child-magic can affect a true Witch?' said Dragwena. 'I command all the magic on this world. Nothing you do could ever harm me.'

Rachel kicked out, thrashing helplessly in the grip of the Witch's claw.

Dragwena soared upward, the green window of the eye-tower looming. They flew straight into the glass. Rachel expected to be cut to pieces. But the glass did not shatter. It simply liquefied for a second as they entered.

Once they were inside Dragwena threw Rachel down on the floor. She bled slightly where the Witch's nails had dug into her back. She ignored the pain, glancing towards the window, ready to leap out, but the thick green glass had re-formed.

There was a timid knock on the door.

'Enter,' growled Dragwena.

Three Neutrana soldiers hesitantly set foot in the room and bowed.

'What news of Morpeth?' asked Dragwena.

'There is no news of the scum yet,' said one of the men. 'He can't hide for long. Our men are fighting the remaining Sarren. We have ten times their number. Guards are placed on all the cave exits. We are hunting them down, one by one.'

Dragwena rubbed her hands, her expression gleeful.

'Kill them all,' she said. 'I want every single rebel found and destroyed. Burn their bodies. Round up their families, along with anyone suspected of helping them. There will be no more Sarren.' She spat at the Neutrana soldier. 'I will teach your people a lesson they will never forget!'

He nodded uneasily and turned to leave.

'Wait!' snapped Dragwena. 'Tell your men there will be a special reward if Morpeth's head is brought to me before the end of the day. I want the traitor found. If I read the child before me correctly, he will be taller than anyone you have seen before, handsome, with – ah! – bright blue eyes. Ensure they are torn out while he's still alive.'

The Witch relaxed slightly, put her arms by her side, and indicated Rachel. 'Listen closely,' she hissed. 'The girl and I are not to be distracted for the next hour. Inform your guards and my servants. *Under no circumstances* must we be disturbed.'

As soon as the Neutrana soldiers left the Witch leapt across the room and slapped Rachel hard across the face.

'Now, child,' she said. 'There have been enough games played with Morpeth and his friends. They will all soon be dead, if they are not already. I have delayed long enough. It's time to turn you into something more useful.'

Rachel dragged herself away across the chamber.

Dragwena followed her in a leisurely way. 'I think we should improve your appearance,' she said. 'Where should we start? Those small teeth of yours, perhaps.'

All four jaws of the Witch lunged at Rachel.

Morpeth dashed through the doorway. The cave was full of armed Neutrana, trained soldiers of the Witch. A few lay dead on the cave floor, but the number of dead or wounded Sarren were much greater – they had not expected a fight and most had no weapons. The Neutrana, knowing no mercy, were tearing them to pieces. Trimak stood in a defensive line with the small group of Sarren who did possess swords. Morpeth saw dozens of fresh Neutrana troops entering the cave from both ends.

'Over here!' he barked. 'There is an escape route!'

'What?' said Trimak, squinting in the dim cave light while trying to fight. 'Who are you?'

'Morpeth! Trust your instinct!'

Trimak looked at the man – not Morpeth, though it spoke with his harsh voice.

'It *is* me,' Morpeth shouted. 'Rachel changed my appearance!'

Trimak uncertainly ordered the Sarren to follow the stranger.

The few Sarren who were not already cut off followed the command at once, dashing across the cave. A great roar of alarm came from the Neutrana and they surged towards

Morpeth. Four heavily armed Sarren fought furiously to keep them back.

'You go!' one cried to Trimak. 'We'll hold them off for as long as we can.'

'No, Grimwold,' Trimak shouted. 'We must all leave! Now is not the time to sacrifice your life.'

'If *this* is not a good time, then what is?' Grimwold bellowed. A Neutrana blade cut deeply into his cheek. He ignored it, screaming at the Witch's soldiers. 'Come on then, try your best! I'll fight you all!'

'Follow your orders!' Trimak commanded.

The last Sarren slipped through the doorway opened by Morpeth. Once they had escaped Grimwold lifted his free arm, making a slashing movement above his head.

Instantly his own men leapt towards the door.

Trimak drew it shut. Inside the narrow tunnel were eight Sarren left with Morpeth, Eric and Trimak. All the other Sarren were dead or had escaped elsewhere. The survivors sat in exhaustion, breathing heavily, some noticing their injuries for the first time now the battle had ceased. From the cave the Neutrana hurled their bodies at the door.

'It will not take them long to break through,' murmured one of the Sarren.

Trimak turned to Morpeth. 'If you are really Morpeth,' he said, 'you will be able to seal the door.'

Morpeth opened his right palm towards the entrance, slowly melting the stonework until hardened rock smothered the doorway.

Even Grimwold, who was not easily impressed, looked in surprise at the sandy-haired man. 'The Morpeth I know is an ugly old devil,' he said. 'You must tell us who made you so handsome. I'd like to pay them a visit!'

'Where's Rachel?' asked Trimak.

'Dragwena found us,' said Morpeth. 'I couldn't stop her.'

'Then we must recapture the girl!' barked Grimwold. 'Does this tunnel lead anywhere?'

'It leads to many places,' said Morpeth. 'Most of the exits will be guarded. However, there is one route only I and Dragwena know about. It leads directly to the eye-tower. If we act quickly I think a small group could reach it.'

'The Witch's guards will be swarming about the eye-tower,' Trimak protested. 'Particularly at a time like this.'

'I doubt there will be many,' said Morpeth. 'The last thing Dragwena will suspect is an attack now. Especially an attack against her. Most of the Neutrana soldiers are still in the caves. There are probably few in the Palace itself.'

'What are we waiting for?' said Grimwold. 'I have wanted to kill that hag for so long.'

'Our aim must be to free Rachel,' Morpeth said. 'Dragwena would relish a direct fight. Somehow we must distract her.'

'Perhaps the Witch will be leading the battle in the caves,' suggested one of the Sarren.

Morpeth said quietly, 'No. Dragwena knows that battle is already won. She will work on Rachel immediately. The dream-sleep will already have half-prepared the child. Rachel did not have nearly enough time with me to develop her defences. It won't take the Witch long to break her.'

The Sarren picked up their weapons and solemnly made their way up the winding tunnel.

*

Inside the eye-tower Dragwena smiled at Rachel.

Then she took a narrow pointed blade from her dress and jabbed Rachel's palm.

Rachel jumped back, clenching her hand. 'What have you done?'

Dragwena's four sets of teeth grinned together. 'I have started the transforming spell. You will soon begin to look like me.'

The Witch glided across the room and lit a long tapered candle. Engraved on the candle was a circle, and inside it a five-pointed star. The flame flickered with a cold green light. The Witch retired to a chair, leaving Rachel standing alone in the middle of the chamber. For a few minutes they simply gazed at one another without speaking, the Witch kissing the head of her snake, while Rachel rubbed her hand, trying to decide what to do. She could hear a few people passing outside the corridor, whispering commands. Behind her the green window of the eye-tower stared down at the Palace buildings, but she knew there was no hope of escape in that direction.

Inexplicably, Rachel found herself relaxing. The wound in her hand no longer hurt. She breathed deeply. The candle gave off a delicious perfume. She sniffed the air, vaguely aware that most of the smoke was drifting towards her nose and mouth. She yawned – and flinched. Why was she tired? She blinked heavily, fighting to stay awake, recognizing the feeling from her last visit to the eye-tower yet unable to fight it, just as she had been unable to fight it before.

Dragwena's snake uncoiled slowly from her neck and lifted its head. Rachel tried in vain to turn her face away.

The snake moved lazily back and forth, tasting her eyelids with its tongue. Finally, Rachel could not prevent her lids from closing. With a huge effort she parted her lips, the sound taking an eternity to emerge.

'What – is – happening – to – me?'

'Happening?' replied Dragwena easily. 'Nothing is happening. We are simply sitting quietly, you and I together.'

Rachel fought to regain control of her mind. I have to stop breathing the smoke, she knew. I must put the candle out. She urged her frozen muscles to move.

At last she realized she did not *want* to move. Any thought of resisting the Witch had gone. A pleasant warmth spread up through her neck and shoulders. Her throat and lips tingled. She relaxed completely, forgetting Eric and the Sarren and the Witch. She lay on the floor and drifted into sleep. When she awoke the room was unchanged. Dragwena gazed kindly, the snake once again coiled around her neck.

'There we are,' said Dragwena. 'Do you feel better now?'

Rachel tried to nod her head.

'You see,' said Dragwena gently, 'I am not such a terrible creature after all.'

Terrible creature? Rachel wondered vaguely what she meant.

'We can talk if you like,' Dragwena said. 'We can speak with our minds.'

'Mm.'

Dragwena's lips were shut. 'Can you hear me?'

'Yes.'

'Do you remember your friends?'

The image of some children came into Rachel's mind. She did not recognize them.

'Do you remember the Sarren who kidnapped you?'

Sarren? The name meant nothing, though it hardly mattered to Rachel. All that mattered was to listen to the lilting voice of the woman.

'These Sarren told some lies about me,' the Witch said. 'They also tried to kill you. I rescued you when Morpeth tried to kill you. Do you remember? Do you remember when he tried to kill you?'

An image leapt into Rachel's mind of a dwarf holding a knife against her throat. She saw Dragwena rush over to knock the knife out of his hand.

Rachel smiled inwardly. 'Thank you.'

'You are welcome,' replied Dragwena, pausing, knowing Rachel was already within her power, needing only to be given a new purpose for her remarkable gifts.

'You are a special child,' Dragwena explained. 'I want you to be with me forever. We will rule together, you and I. My kingdom is so large. I will need your help. Look for yourself—'

Suddenly, Rachel saw herself flying through the silence of deep space. A vast sun blazed at her back and crowns of stars clustered around her neck and shoulders. She wore a black dress and when she lifted her neck a snake with ruby-red eyes caressed her chin. Rachel peered down. Below her, a small planet swirled with white clouds and sparkling blue oceans. She flew effortlessly towards it, sensing neither wind nor cold, skimming its seas and streams and soaring with outstretched arms across mountains and plains. And wherever she flew huge armies of children followed, fighting for places to watch her pass and shout her name.

'Rachel! Rachel!' they chanted, raising their keen-edged swords.

She felt a soft touch on her hand. Dragwena flew alongside her, fingertip to fingertip.

'Will you rule with me?' Dragwena asked.

Rachel realized blissfully there was nothing else she would rather do. She smiled as her own snake embraced Dragwena's in the formal greeting of Witches . . .

At that moment a scuffle outside the eye-tower distracted Dragwena. Neutrana guards, caught unawares, leapt to protect the chamber. There followed a short fierce struggle, immediately shattered by a cry of Sarren as they threw their bodies at the thick chamber door.

Rachel, still in the bliss-trance of the Witch, paid no attention.

The door reverberated as it was repeatedly hit. At last, even the great hinges of the chamber could no longer bear the onslaught and the frame came shattering down. As it did so a blast of cold air shot into the room, snuffing out the candle.

Rachel awoke gradually from her daze and glanced at the doorway.

Standing there, flanked on either side by his men, was Grimwold.

In one arm he held a huge sword; in the other a knife. Both were covered in blood. Dead Neutrana of the Witch lay outside.

'I've come to kill you, Dragwena,' he hissed.

Dragwena gazed at their swords in amusement. 'Do you intend to kill me with those?' she asked. 'If you are to kill a High Witch they must be magic swords, blessed by magicians themselves. Did you know that?'

'I don't care!' Grimwold roared. 'I will kill you or die trying.'

All three Sarren leapt at her. Dragwena casually lifted a finger and a transparent green wall appeared between them. Grimwold charged the wall. As soon as the tip of his sword struck the surface it leapt into the Witch's palm. He watched in astonishment as Dragwena calmly tossed the blade aside.

'I think I have seen enough weapons today,' she said. 'Let me welcome you brave men in my own way.'

She pursed the thin lips covering her four sets of teeth and blew a gentle kiss towards them. As if in slow motion the kiss-breath left Dragwena's mouths and moved lazily towards the men. When it hit the transparent wall it quickly spread inside, twisting. The Sarren glanced at each other uncertainly.

Rachel had been desperately trying to find her voice.

'G-get out,' she stammered. 'Get out of the chamber!'

Grimwold stared at Rachel, noticing her for the first time.

'The child-hope,' he said, gazing in wonder.

Inside the wall the kiss-breath swirled angrily, preparing its attack.

'Leave now!' Rachel screamed. 'Run!'

'Too late,' sighed the Witch, laughing at the Sarren.

Grimwold suddenly understood. He dragged his men towards the open doorway, but as they turned the kiss-breath ripped through the transparent wall, slamming them against the stone floor of the corridor.

The Sarren lay in a crumpled heap on the floor, their swords broken.

'No!' Rachel wailed.

Dragwena ignored her and went over to inspect the men's bodies.

Rachel held back her tears, knowing this might be her only chance to escape. She had to alter quickly, while Dragwena was distracted. What should she change into? Something too small to be seen. Her mind raced. A speck of dust! Yes, it could work . . .

As she transformed she quickly placed another Rachel in the room. Dragwena was still examining the Sarren, a smile on her face. Good. She had not noticed. Rachel became a speck of near nothingness, incredibly light, so light the merest breeze picked her up. She floated, allowing it to carry her towards the open doorway of the chamber.

The Witch lost interest in the Sarren. She stared suspiciously at the fake Rachel.

'Speak to me!' Dragwena commanded it.

Rachel tried to make the dummy Rachel talk, but it was too hard to do this and imagine herself as a speck of dust at the same time. She floated slowly out of the doorway. Dragwena's eyes widened in sudden understanding. She reached inside her dress, pulled out a curved blade, and stabbed the fake Rachel in the heart.

The real Rachel screamed – a human scream, loud and agonized, revealing her position.

Almost fainting from the pain, Rachel gave herself little

wings and flapped down the steep winding stairway, searching frantically for a window. There had to be a way out . . .

A whoosh of air sighed above – Dragwena flew towards her. A large tongue emerged from the Witch's mouth, tasting the air, seeking Rachel's presence. At the same time an impulse thrust into Rachel's mind, suggesting she change back into a girl. She felt her dusty body start to alter.

No! Rachel thought furiously, holding her shape.

A window – closed, but there was a crack in the frame through which she could squeeze. For a second she was in darkness, then a wider darkness tinged with stars.

A snowflake struck her like an avalanche. Rachel collapsed inside, shaking with the effort to stop herself transforming back into a girl.

She glanced back. The window was open. Dragwena stood there, extending an arm. Rachel tried to leap away, but a giant claw closed around her. In a moment, Rachel knew, everything Morpeth had done, everything the Sarren had struggled and died for, would be for nothing.

No! No! she thought. I will escape. I *will!*

She remembered her race with Morpeth to the lake. She saw herself looking into its frozen waters, far from the eye-tower.

Her stomach tugged and when she dared to look it was not the face of Dragwena but the gleam of frost on the shore of Lake Ker which met her gaze. Behind her, a shriek of rage came distantly from the Palace as Dragwena clutched vainly in the air.

Rachel shuddered, snowflakes crushing her head. She had no strength left to bring her body back. The snow continued to fall steadily, burying her in soft, bitterly cold clumps.

I'll just lie here for a while, she told herself. I'll think of what to do soon. I'll . . .

Exhaustion closed her speck-of-dust eyes.

13

JOURNEY IN
the snow

It was a bright, crisp morning in Ithrea and a light wind hardly stirred the feathers of the great white eagle, Ronnocoden. A mile above the eye-tower he soared, wheeling in great circles, closely watching events below.

The giant central gates of the Palace were open. Pouring from them was a vast army of Neutrana sniffer-troops, dressed for a long journey. They headed northwards towards the Ragged Mountains. Many had recently fought with fury against the Sarren in the tunnels of the Palace. The Witch allowed them no rest, nor herself. All night she had worked on the spell she needed: the Neutrana troops spilling from the gates now had the soft, odour-sensitive muzzles of dogs, which they pressed low to the ground. Only one smell had their attention: the scent of magic –

Rachel's magic. They fanned out evenly on a wide track. Every now and then one would eagerly sniff the snow at its feet, excited by some trail or other, before moving restlessly on.

The eagle lifted his head, following the sniffer-troops beyond the range of normal vision, to the far north. There, amongst the mountains and valleys of the Ragged Mountains, he saw even more transformed Neutrana, and also other creatures: wolves. Each was the size of a black bear, with bright yellow eyes. Like giant outlandish dogs they loped around, pushing their muzzles into the snow. And amongst the wolves stood Dragwena, stroking them, encouraging them, guiding them where to look.

Ronnocoden silently dropped lower. His keen stone-grey pupils watched as a figure white-on-white shuffled slowly towards the edge of Lake Ker. Below, the shape paused, adjusted its cowl, and lifted blue eyes in recognition.

Instantly, Ronnocoden tipped a wing to indicate the gardens were safe from prying eyes. Then he flew rapidly southwards, disappearing within seconds into the high clouds.

The creature on the ground reached the brink of the lake. It pressed its face against the snow near a tree stump shaped like a mushroom, muttered two words and stepped back.

A girl shot into the air.

The creature hurriedly wrapped another white cloak around her body.

'Morpeth!' Rachel gasped.

'You are alive!' He rubbed her freezing cheeks. 'I feared the worst. I thought – how happy I am to see you!'

'Oh Morpeth,' said Rachel, between chattering teeth. 'I'm freezing. I was in the snow for ages. I couldn't change back.' She gazed around anxiously. 'Where's Eric?'

Morpeth reached inside the deep pockets of his cloak. He pulled out a small fur jacket, thick gloves, padded trousers and a pair of snowshoes matching those on his own feet. He placed a small knife in one of her pockets.

'Eric is safe,' he said. 'He made his way with Trimak to a cave network several miles south, called Latnap Deep. I'm to bring you there.'

'I tried to help the Sarren,' Rachel explained. 'I just didn't know what Dragwena planned to do. Then she blew that kiss, and . . .' She glanced up imploringly. 'Dragwena used Eric to find me, didn't she? Morpeth, please don't blame Eric. It's not his fault that—'

'I know,' Morpeth reassured her. 'Eric's his usual self again now.' He glanced over the Palace gardens. 'Sooner or later one of Dragwena's sniffer-troops will pick up your scent. We must be a long way from here when it does.'

'Mm,' said Rachel, peering under her cloak. 'How do we get to these caves? By using magic?'

'I wish we could! But my magic's not strong enough to take us. Only you can zip about from place to place like Dragwena. I have to walk about on my stubby old legs.'

'I'll carry you with me,' Rachel said. 'I'm sure I can do it. We'll fly to Latnap Deep together.'

'Try imagining yourself just a few feet away,' said Morpeth. 'Keep the cloak around you. We mustn't be seen.'

'I've lost my magic!' Rachel whispered, after several tries.

'No, you're simply exhausted after using so much energy escaping from Dragwena. A rest will do the trick, but it might take several hours to fully recover. We'll have to go on foot.' He helped her put on the snowshoes. 'The Witch is frightened now. She can't believe you outwitted her!'

'She never looks frightened,' said Rachel, remembering the ease with which Dragwena had greeted Grimwold and his men in her chamber. 'She can't really be scared of me.'

'Oh, she is! The Witch has been searching madly since dawn. Fortunately, she thinks you are in the Ragged Mountains. I have never known her to become personally involved in a search.' He grinned. 'She must be extremely worried.'

'Why does she think I'd be there?'

'Remember when I left the room and said, "See you at Hoy Point"?'

Rachel nodded.

'It's a peak in the mountains. I never expected Dragwena to believe it. I only said it in the hope of misleading her in case you managed to escape.' Morpeth chuckled. 'It seems to have worked, at least long enough to delay her for a short while.'

'How did you know where I was? I thought no one except Dragwena could find me.'

'I guessed if you were in danger you would return to this spot. It's the place you flew to on our first morning together. Of course,' he said, 'you could have turned up in the Breakfast Room, or your bedroom in the Palace – but I gambled you would never go somewhere Dragwena could easily find you.'

'I never thought about it,' Rachel said honestly. 'I didn't have time.'

'Then we must be grateful to Dragwena at least for that!'

He carefully tucked Rachel's scarf about her neck and assessed her with a new purposefulness. 'Let's go. It is a long journey to Latnap Deep on foot. I had planned for the eagles to carry us there, but the sky is so clear that Dragwena's spies would certainly spot us. We can't take that risk.'

'How can you be sure Dragwena doesn't know about these caves?'

'I can't be certain,' Morpeth admitted. 'But Latnap Deep has never been used in my lifetime by the Sarren. We are relying on that.'

Morpeth pointed across Lake Ker to a distant wood shrouded in mist. 'We're going that way,' he said. 'Walk close to me. The ice is thin in places, and the wolves will not so easily spot our tracks.'

'Wolves?'

'I'll tell you about them as we go,' said Morpeth.

He gripped her hand, preparing to set off.

'*Ouch*!' Rachel cried. She looked down. In the middle of her palm a black puncture wound throbbed painfully.

'Dragwena did this to me in the eye-tower,' she said.

Morpeth examined her hand. 'It's nothing. Just a cut.'

'It's not just a cut,' Rachel said firmly. 'Dragwena said it would transform me into a Witch. She said I'd start to look like her.'

'How many mouths has Dragwena got?' asked Morpeth.

'Four.'

'And what about her skin? Are there any freckles on her nose?'

Rachel half-smiled. 'No, of course not.'

'In that case stop worrying. I see one mouth, and your

129

freckles are as bold as ever. Nothing about you is different. Let's go.'

He took her other hand and they set off on their snowshoes across the frozen waters of Lake Ker.

Rachel and Morpeth made their way steadily across the ice. As usual the sun shone weakly in the sky, barely piercing the high grey clouds.

'Tell me about the wolves,' Rachel said, as she struggled to keep up with him.

'They are Dragwena's special pets,' Morpeth explained. 'They were ordinary dogs once. Over the years the Witch fashioned them in her own way: made them larger, gave them snouts which can pick up the tiniest scent. Unlike most animals on this world wolves can *speak*. In the past I have been responsible for their training. They are intelligent and ruthless creatures, and every last one does the bidding of Dragwena.'

'Are there any near us?'

'Wolves are never far away.'

Rachel gazed nervously around, expecting huge paw tracks to be criss-crossing the snow. But there were no signs of wolves. The snows stretched out confidently, as if daring anything alive to disturb their featureless grey. Nothing moved or stirred. Even the pallid sky was empty. So quiet, Rachel thought. Was that good or bad? She cleared the snow of Lake Ker beneath her feet, wondering if bright fish might be shivering under the lake's surface, but there was just the impenetrable blackness of ice forever frozen.

'What's down there?' she asked.

'Nothing,' said Morpeth. 'Unless it can live without breathing. Unless it can live without moving or eating. Perhaps Dragwena has created such a creature, just to know that it suffers. Come on, we can't rest here.'

'But what other creatures live on Ithrea?' Rachel asked, staying close to him. 'I've seen so few.'

'Eagles live in the western mountains, helping the Sarren where they can,' he said. 'They only survive because Dragwena likes to keep a few alive, to hunt when she's bored. The wolves devour anything that lives on the surface. The only other animals live underground – if you can call them animals. Who knows what they might have been once, but most are now weak slug-like creatures, blind, slurping what scraps they can find from the deep earth. Even Dragwena can't be bothered to torment them.'

Rachel heard a tiny flutter. It was a pair of birds, streaking across the sky. They flew in perfect formation, their movements incredibly precise.

Morpeth pulled her down. 'Keep dead still,' he hissed.

'What are they?'

'Prapsies,' he said. 'Dragwena's spies. Half-bird, half-baby, and much faster than eagles.'

'Half baby?' Rachel whispered.

'They're weird, mixed-up things,' Morpeth said. 'Joke-creations of the Witch. Don't ask me to describe them. You wouldn't believe me.'

The prapsies zigzagged in several directions across the sky. They travelled in exact straight lines, occasionally stopping and hovering, without needing to slow down. At one point they passed over Rachel and Morpeth and she heard them chattering loudly – a babble of high-pitched voices.

Morpeth waited several minutes before continuing, and now they moved more cautiously. After walking for over an hour they crossed Lake Ker and headed towards the low hills. To Rachel the hills seemed miles away, and the murky wood even further. She noticed her hand throbbing painfully and glanced down.

'Morpeth!' she cried.

Where the puncture wound had stood a clear black circle now lay etched on her palm; inside the circle was a perfect five-pointed star. Rachel knew where she had seen that shape before – on the candle in the eye-tower.

'What's this?' she asked, looking squarely at Morpeth. 'It's some kind of Witch-mark, isn't it?'

'Yes,' he admitted.

'Does it mean I'm changing into a Witch?'

'You still don't look like Dragwena, if that is what you mean. Do you feel any different?'

'No, I don't . . . think so,' said Rachel. 'But this mark has grown in a few hours. If it's a Witch-mark Dragwena must have done something to me. I'm scared, Morpeth.'

'It's probably nothing,' he said, trying to draw her on.

'You don't know what it means, do you?' she said, standing her ground. 'What if it means I'll be a Witch by the time I reach Latnap Deep? Eric's there. I don't want to harm him, or anyone else.'

Morpeth regarded her gravely. 'I don't know what the mark signifies. No Sarren has ever had this mark. It could mean *anything*. Your first thought is for Eric's safety. That tells me you are still the Rachel I know. We must trust in that.'

They shuffled on, their snowshoes carving through the

snows. Morpeth kept up a fast pace and Rachel, thinking of Dragwena, did not complain. But after several hours of trudging through the everlasting cold she entered a state of exhaustion, her whole body numb with pain and weariness.

Morpeth chatted constantly, trying to keep her alert. Eventually they arrived at the low hills. Rachel was too weary to notice or care. Morpeth let her rest and made his way to the top of a small rise.

Due south lay the safety of Latnap Deep, so close now. Between them and it stood the trees of Dragwood. Which way to go? Dragwood was dangerous, full of Dragwena's magic, easily stirred. They could go around Dragwood, but that would take over an hour, and Morpeth sensed the detour was beyond Rachel. Not once had she mentioned her tiredness, or complained, but Morpeth saw her fatigue in every step – and he was too weary himself to carry her all the way to Latnap Deep.

He glanced at the sky. A bleak sunset had set in, casting deep shadows around the trees. Soon it would be dark and unendurably cold. Even with her furs, Morpeth knew, Rachel would not survive a night on the surface. Making up his mind, he trotted back and found her lying on her side, half-buried by snow.

'Wake up, sleepyhead,' he murmured, lifting her up. 'It's not time for bed yet. We're going to take a short cut through the wood. We'll be in Latnap Deep within the hour.'

The last rays of the sun vanished. Above them, a few lonely stars and the great moon Armath shone brightly. Morpeth prayed Armath would shine well – its cold radiance was their only hope to pass swiftly through the trees: there were no footpaths in Dragwood.

'Stay close,' Morpeth said, linking hands with Rachel, and stepping more boldly than he felt into the outer trees.

14

PRAPSIES

As soon as Rachel and Morpeth crept inside Dragwood towering trees enfolded them in near darkness. A few moonbeams sliced between the upper branches, stabbing the ground with a piercing brilliance. Rachel listened anxiously to the tremor of a light wind. It rippled through the treetops, causing the branches to creak like doors opening.

At first they made rapid progress. As they penetrated further into Dragwood the trees packed together, their high, gnarled roots making it harder to stay on a straight course. They stumbled along as best they could, Rachel always clutching tightly onto Morpeth.

Then Morpeth squeezed her hand.

'What's wrong?' she asked.

He winced as Rachel's voice rang in the air.

'Listen,' he whispered.

Rachel held her breath. 'I can't hear anything.'

'Exactly. There is a breeze but the leaves on the trees are no longer rustling. Nothing's moving. Look!'

He pointed at the canopy of the wood.

On every tree the leaves pointed stiffly, like outstretched fingers. The branches had also stopped swaying, as if stilled to listen. Morpeth and Rachel staggered warily on.

Then, without warning, a branch lashed at Rachel's head. Other trees also started to shake, thrashing their leaves, warning the trees ahead about the strangers.

'What's happening?' Rachel squealed.

'Dragwood has awakened!' replied Morpeth.

And they ran for their lives.

They ducked under the lowest branches, tearing through the leaves, tripping and falling, picking each other up and running on. Ahead, Rachel suddenly noticed a spot where the trunks thinned slightly – an opening to the edge of the wood. They dashed towards the gap.

As they neared it two huge branches reached over their heads, ripping off their white cloaks. Instantly, as if a million eyes had been opened, all the leaves in Dragwood lashed the air. Several nearby trunks swayed. They snapped their roots, pulling themselves out of the ground.

'They can't run after us, can they?' screamed Rachel.

'They don't need to,' said Morpeth.

Rachel watched as the uprooted trees were passed from branch to branch of other trunks, until six of them were slammed into the earth, encircling Morpeth and Rachel.

There was no way through the trees. Dragwood, now fully awakened, had no intention of letting them escape.

For a moment Rachel and Morpeth stood in silence amidst the trunks, while leaves showered them from above, and Dragwood decided what to do.

At last, two of the largest trees dragged their slashed roots forward and felt with their branches for Morpeth's throat.

'Wait!' snapped a voice behind him.

The trees froze instantly. Even Morpeth froze because he recognized the voice behind him at once: Dragwena.

He turned to see Rachel standing with her head proudly erect, hands on hips, addressing the trees.

'Do you not recognize me?' she purred, her voice so perfectly like the Witch that no one except Dragwena herself would have been able to tell the difference. Rachel reached into her pocket and thrust her knife against Morpeth's neck. 'Let me through with this creature,' she commanded.

She did not wait for the trees to react. She walked confidently forward, dragging Morpeth with her. Slowly, uncertainly, the trees parted and allowed them through, their branches whispering. She pointed imperiously at the last tree blocking her path and it scuttled aside.

Rachel and Morpeth walked quickly to the edge of Dragwood, Rachel holding the knife against his throat all the way.

'Keep walking – don't run,' warned Morpeth.

Twenty footsteps took them safely out of reach of the trees. Rachel released Morpeth and stuffed the knife back into her jacket. Immediately the trees realized they had been tricked. They crowded at the edge of the wood, whipping their branches.

Rachel eyed them anxiously, ready to run. 'Why don't they come after us?'

'It seems they cannot leave Dragwood,' said Morpeth. 'Their magic must be confined to its limits.' He grinned, then stiffened.

'What is it?' Rachel asked.

'Quiet!' Morpeth hissed. 'Stay still!'

Behind them, peering from the outer trees of Dragwood, were two flying creatures with human faces.

Each had the black body of a crow, but on its neck perched a small human head: a pink face, snub nose, tiny round ears and soft thin hair – the face of a *baby*. They were so bizarre that Rachel would have burst out laughing had Morpeth not looked so concerned.

'Mine,' said one of the creatures, its voice high-pitched and baby-like too.

'No, mine,' said the other. 'I saw it first.'

'I saw the trees moving.'

'I saw it first!'

'You would not have seen it if I had not seen the trees.'

Its companion stuck out a tongue and blew a raspberry. The other spat at it.

'Missed me.'

'Meant to miss you.'

Together they turned their heads towards Rachel and Morpeth.

'What are they?' one asked.

'A man and a girl.'

'They do not move. Men and girls move. These do not. Therefore, they are something else.'

'A puzzle. Let's have a closer look.'

'After you.'

'After *you*,' chirped the other, bowing – and they both glided down together. One perched itself on Rachel's head; the other landed on Morpeth's shoulder. Rachel tried not to blink. The one on her head bent down and pressed the tip of its tiny pink tongue against her cheek.

'Soft skin,' it said. 'Must be girl. Tastes nice.'

The other child-bird bit Morpeth on the ear. Rachel saw him tense, stifling a cry.

'Frozen man. Statue. Not real.'

'But I saw it move.'

'It does not move.'

'It moved! I saw it!'

'Rubbish!'

'You're rubbish!'

'You're rubbish!'

The child-birds argued like this for some time, while Morpeth and Rachel remained as still as they could.

'Let's go away and watch them,' suggested one of the child-birds, eventually.

The other scratched its ear with a claw. 'Agreed. After you.'

'After *you*,' said its companion, bowing – and they both flew off together. Each retook its original position in the trees and perched there, quietly twitching and staring at Rachel and Morpeth from a short distance.

'Prapsies?' whispered Rachel, trying to stay motion-less.

'Yes,' said Morpeth. 'Probably the same pair we saw earlier. They can't harm us, but nothing flies more swiftly. They could warn Dragwena of our presence. Don't move.

They are stupid creatures and quickly become bored. If we stay still they may just fly away.'

Several times the prapsies flew down and landed on or near them, then flitted back to the trees, continually arguing amongst themselves.

'Statues. Definitely statues.'

'Yes,' said the other. 'Warm statues.'

'Will we tell Dragwena?'

'No. Silly mistake. She will spank us if we tell her about statues.'

They giggled.

'Let's go then.'

'After you.'

'After *you*,' said the other, bowing – and together they sprang from the tree. But at that moment Rachel felt a cramp in her right leg and had to lift it from the ground. The prapsies immediately hovered, chattering wildly.

'Real child and man. Alive! Alive!'

'Pretend statues! Man and girl.'

'Rachel and Morpeth!'

'Morpeth and Rachel!'

'Tell Dragwena at once.'

'At once.' Somehow, while flying in circles, they managed to bow to each other. 'After you,' they said – and flew off together.

Morpeth hurled a stick, but they easily dodged aside.

'Tell Dragwena!' squeaked one child-bird.

'Tell Dragwena and the wolves!'

'Tell the wolves!'

'Tell the wolves!'

'Eat them up—'

'For supper!'

The prapsies sped off, heading northwards, muttering 'wolves, wolves, wolves!' in glee until they were out of sight.

15

wolves

Morpeth watched the flight path the child-birds had taken.

'They're heading for Dragwena in the Ragged Mountains,' he said. 'The journey is short for a prapsy. Now we have a race to beat the Witch to Latnap Deep.'

Rachel shivered. With the onset of night snow had started falling heavily, bringing with it a searing wind. Behind them the trees of Dragwood continued their urgent, relentless thrashing.

'Morpeth, I can't go much further,' she said. 'Can't we hide?'

'There is nowhere to hide on the surface from the Witch,' Morpeth said, gripping her tightly. 'We *can* get to Latnap Deep! It's not too far. Please – I know how tired you are. Make one last effort.'

Rachel nodded weakly, barely able to force a smile any longer.

Despite the danger they set off at an agonizingly slow pace. It was all Rachel could manage, and they had also lost their snowshoes in Dragwood, making every footfall heavy through the snow. They skirted Dragwood, heading westwards for a time through the slush of boggy land.

Eventually they turned south again. Ahead, a wide undulating moor rose gently before them, and normally Rachel would not even have noticed the effort of walking across. But her last reserves of strength had vanished in the slush, and she moved through a numbing exhaustion. Only fear of the Witch kept her dead feet moving. She planted one reluctant step in front of the other, too tired to think ahead.

Morpeth allowed Rachel to lean against his shoulder, protecting her face as best he could from the buffeting of the wind. They seemed to walk forever like this, freezing gusts piercing their clothes and Armath so bright that without their cloaks they were lit up for all to see in the snow.

At last Morpeth permitted Rachel another rest. He knew Dragwena would soon arrive – their clumsy footsteps would be like blazing beacons to her night vision and the wolves. Rachel slept, her face already half-buried by dark snow. Morpeth heaved her over his back. He lowered his face and walked steadily into the brunt of the wind, sheer desperation carrying his legs.

Then he noticed the wolf.

It was eight feet high from paw to shoulder. Thirty or more of the beasts had surrounded them without him noticing. Icy breath steamed around their muzzles, and their glistening yellow eyes gazed in an almost leisurely way at Morpeth and Rachel. The leader of the wolves casually trotted forward. It was Scorpa, a she-wolf:

ferocious, sleek and deadly. Morpeth knew her well, as he had trained her as a cub.

'Hello, old man,' Scorpa said. 'I see Rachel has made you handsome. It's a pity she forgot to change the way you *smell*. That was a mistake.'

The wolf pack grinned.

Morpeth roused Rachel. He had to shake her several times.

'Welcome, child,' said Scorpa, bowing courteously. 'To greet one who has escaped Dragwena herself is a rare honour.'

'Leave us!' Rachel tried weakly, using Dragwena's voice.

Most of the wolves stirred uneasily. Scorpa simply rocked back on her grizzled hindquarters and howled with derision. 'Not a bad try. But we are not so easily fooled as the trees of Dragwood.'

Morpeth held his knife against Rachel's throat.

'Leave us or I will kill her!' he growled.

A wolf darted in, plucking the blade from his hand.

'Not fast enough,' tutted Scorpa. 'Rachel has given you a lean young body, but it moves like a geriatric. Another mistake. Still, Dragwena will soon polish the child's rough edges.' She licked her lips, pawing the ground. 'I give you a choice, Morpeth: I can set the pack on you at once – or you can do me the honour of single combat. I promise the others will not interfere. At least you will have a chance to tickle my flesh before you die. What do you say?'

The other wolves moved back slightly, giving them space.

Morpeth abruptly raised his hands. A blue light shot from them, piercing the sky like a flare.

'Do you hope for rescue even now?' Scorpa scoffed. 'Come. I grow weary. Choose!'

Morpeth spat at her muzzle.

'I choose to fight!'

He moved into the combat circle. The wolf with the knife tossed the blade back and he gripped it in his right hand, close against his hip, warrior fashion. With his left hand he beckoned Scorpa towards him.

'Come on, then!' he roared. 'Or are you *afraid*, she-wolf?'

Scorpa bared her fangs and they slowly circled each other, probing for weaknesses. The wolf padded deftly and, when she pounced, there was no warning – her movement so swift that Rachel hardly saw it. Scorpa sunk her jaw into his thigh, then jumped aside. Morpeth stifled a scream but stayed on his feet – to fall would mean instant death. Scorpa pounced again. Feigning to attack the same leg, she changed direction at the last moment and caught Morpeth turning. Even as he realized his mistake her fangs ripped through his stomach, and when she raised her muzzle it dripped with blood and torn flesh. Scorpa leapt away at once, and Morpeth's weak slash at her underbelly missed.

'You have become feeble, old man,' gloated Scorpa, 'while I have grown strong. I am not the cub you bested long ago. I hoped for a better fight than this.'

Morpeth tottered in the circle, facing her again.

'An enemy is always at its most dangerous when it is desperate,' he growled. 'I taught you that, remember. Your strength never matched my cunning.'

But his words sounded hollow and Scorpa knew it.

'Time to finish you off,' she said, aiming for his throat.

She never reached him. As Scorpa leapt a huge white eagle, as large as the wolf itself, swooped out of the darkness, sinking its talons into her neck. At the same instant two other eagles dropped down, grasped Rachel and Morpeth and shot into the air. The wolves snapped at their tails, but the fangs fell short and the birds made their escape, carrying Morpeth and Rachel upwards into the cloud. Within seconds they left the wolves baying far behind and were heading south.

'Latnap Deep!' Morpeth urged, wincing with the pain of his injuries. 'Take us to the Deep, Ronnocoden!'

The great white eagle bent his head towards Morpeth to obtain the exact directions. With the onset of night he had circled with his companions within the safety of the low snow clouds, waiting for any signal. Now the great birds cut purposefully through the storm. Within swift, almost silent, wingbeats Morpeth and Rachel were carried through the sky, the eagles dropping out of the cloud at the last possible moment to avoid detection.

Morpeth fell from the back of Ronnocoden and pounded his fists into the featureless snow. Six times. Four times. Three times. A few feet away the snow collapsed over a secret door, and avid arms pulled them inside. The eagles instantly took flight southwards.

Rachel blinked in the bright light of the tunnel before them. Three Sarren stood there and, a little to one side, Trimak gasped at the blood pouring through Morpeth's jacket.

Trimak worked furiously to stem Morpeth's bleeding.

Scorpa had performed her task well: the stomach was torn open and Morpeth's life-blood pumped from the wound, spreading thickly.

Trimak knew how to repair broken bones, minor burns or light bleeding, but this – this was an injury beyond his abilities. Morpeth's grey face was already creased with the effort to remain conscious.

In a few minutes, Trimak knew, Morpeth would be dead.

Morpeth also knew. He looked at his ripped stomach and weakly lifted his head.

'Well,' he said, with a faint smile. 'I think this wound is beyond even your skilful hands, my old friend. I should have allowed Ronnocoden to carry us all the way here from the Palace, but feared the Witch would expect help from that direction. I made the wrong choice, travelling on foot. I have made so many mistakes . . . so many.'

'Heal yourself!' Trimak ordered. 'You have come too far to leave us now.'

Morpeth's face writhed in pain. 'Heal myself? I think even if my powers were at their full I could not repair this injury. And I have nothing left. Nothing.'

Trimak cast his face down to conceal his emotions. 'You brought back the child-hope!' he said. 'Against impossible odds you rescued her twice. There is still hope for us, thanks to you.'

'Guard her well,' Morpeth said. 'Rachel is so weary. Let her rest.'

'Always thinking of others,' said Trimak. He looked away, tears splashing down his cheeks.

'At least Dragwena will never touch me now,' murmured Morpeth. 'I have denied her that, at any rate.'

His body slumped against the tunnel wall and his bright blue eyes closed.

Trimak buried his face in Morpeth's shoulder, weeping with abandon, tears bursting from him.

Rachel staggered across to Morpeth. 'Don't give up!' she shouted at Trimak. 'What's wrong with you? Make him live! Do something!'

Trimak stared uselessly at the floor. Rachel put her hands on the blood pouring from Morpeth, trying to hold it in.

Morpeth was not dead, not quite. He managed to open his eyes. 'Rachel, nothing is wrong which you cannot right.' He looked sternly at her. 'It is up to you now.'

'Don't die!' Rachel pleaded. 'Don't die, Morpeth. I can't bear it!'

'You must,' he said.

His head sunk heavily into the hands of Trimak.

All the Sarren bent on one knee and raised their swords.

'No! No! No!' Rachel screamed. 'I won't let you die. I won't!'

She pushed Trimak off and gripped Morpeth's cheeks. He was still breathing slightly, shallowly. Rachel forced his eyes open and stared into them. What could she do? *There must be something!* She felt her mind tug – and looked down: where before there had only been a mess of bone and blood, Rachel suddenly saw the way to heal Morpeth laid out like a diagram. She did not wait to ponder how this could be. Precisely, like a scalpel, her mind sought the wound, the blood, each torn muscle, the veins, the epidermal layers. She acted immediately.

Beneath her Morpeth convulsed and lifted his head. His stomach moved beneath the muscles. Layers of new flesh grew from the tatters, sealing the wound. A new belly-button appeared with a *pop* where the old one had been torn off.

All the Sarren gazed in disbelief at Rachel.

'How did you do this?' Morpeth gasped.

'I – I don't know,' Rachel said honestly. She searched her mind for the source of her new powers, sensing a different layer of magic growing inside, more powerful, itching to be used. But as she explored for answers a wave of exhaustion swept her. Now Morpeth was safe she could barely keep her eyes open. 'I'm so tired . . .' she mumbled. 'Too . . . tired to think.'

'Then sleep,' Morpeth said. 'No one deserves it more than you.' He laughed, and his voice rang with life. 'Sleep, and when you wake up we'll have breakfast together again!'

'I want to see Eric,' Rachel said weakly.

'He is being well cared for.'

'I'm scared about the dreams I might have, Morpeth. Please. I don't want to go to sleep.'

'Have happy dreams,' he said. 'Dragwena is far away now. She cannot harm you. I won't allow her to get close. I promise.'

Rachel sat on Morpeth's lap, leant against his shoulder and fell asleep at once, too weary even to explore her new gifts and what they meant.

16

latnap deep

Rachel slept through the night and late into the afternoon of the next day. Ithrea's sun had begun its bleak sunset, spreading watery whites across the sky, when she finally awoke. She was in a soft bed which Morpeth had himself prepared. He lay slumped in a chair a few feet away, snoring gently.

Rachel crept quietly out of bed, careful not to wake Morpeth, and washed herself using a bowl left for her in the room. Fresh garments had been placed beside the bed: rough woollen pants and a thick brown linen shirt. They were not the magnificent clothes she could have chosen from her wardrobe in the Palace, but they fitted well enough and Rachel now preferred them.

She sat on the edge of the bed and coughed loudly.

Morpeth grunted and looked up with his bright blue eyes.

'Hello, handsome,' Rachel smiled. 'Am I too late for breakfast?'

Morpeth stretched and eyed her. 'Of course not! But we do not have as much choice here as the Breakfast Room at the Palace.'

'It doesn't matter. Anything will do.'

He patted his stomach. 'Lovely belly-button,' he said. 'An improvement on my old one. Much neater.'

'I don't know how I did it,' said Rachel, seriously. 'What does it mean? I know my magic's been developing quickly, but not that fast.'

'I've no idea,' he admitted. 'But I'm grateful. Look at me – handsome, supremely fit, a match for any Neutrana soldier!' He jumped four feet in the air, turned a perfect somersault and landed on his toes. 'I don't know what you did, Rachel, but I feel fantastic!'

'How is Eric?' asked Rachel.

'Ah! You may well ask. I think you'd better come and see the amazing Eric for yourself. You won't believe what he's up to. Come on.'

Morpeth linked their arms and escorted her to a room where Eric sat on a small chair. Rachel burst into tears, holding him tightly for several seconds, not wanting to let go.

'Hey, are you all right?' she asked at last, smoothing out his hair.

'I'm OK.' He laughed. 'Better look out! I can do things now. *Special* things. Tell her, Morpeth.'

Morpeth grinned. 'Remember our games in the Breakfast Room?'

'Of course,' she said.

'Pick something to imagine. Anything.'

Rachel shrugged. 'A flower?'

'Very well. Now watch.'

A moment later a daffodil floated in the air above Morpeth's head.

Eric poked his finger at the flower. It disappeared.

Morpeth created six different bunches of flowers and made them race around the ceiling.

Eric zapped them with his wand-like finger, one by one.

'He's got magic!' Rachel cried. 'He can do the things we can do!'

'No, you're wrong,' said Morpeth. He glanced at Eric. 'Make a bunch of flowers.'

'I can't,' Eric said. 'You know that.'

'Try again,' Morpeth urged him. 'Go on.'

Eric screwed up his face for several seconds, lips pressed hard together. Finally, with an irritated groan, he gave up. 'I can't do it. So what. Everyone's got magic here. That's nothing special.'

'I don't understand,' said Rachel. 'What power has Eric got?'

'I'm not sure,' said Morpeth. 'A very unusual power, certainly. I've never seen it before in any child brought to Ithrea. I think I would describe it as *anti-magic*. Eric makes magic disappear.'

Rachel frowned. 'I can do that, too. In the Breakfast Room we both made things disappear.'

'Not in the same way as Eric,' Morpeth said. 'See for yourself. Create something.'

Rachel made a single object, a replica of the perfectly built oak table her granddad had crafted shortly before he died last winter. It was an object she knew well, as he had shown her lovingly how he had made every detail – the joints, the secret drawer, the many layers of varnish, all patiently applied. Rachel took her time, forming the table carefully and then placed the image in the centre of the room.

Eric, without even looking at it, pointed. Instantly the table vanished. Rachel tried to rebuild it, but found that she could no longer remember clearly what it looked like. She concentrated furiously, but could only remake a table that looked slightly like the original.

Eventually, she stared in amazement at Eric.

'Try something else,' said Morpeth.

So Rachel made a lamp instead, focusing hard. That disappeared too, and again she could no longer recreate it.

'Now do you see!' Morpeth cried. 'Eric takes away magic *permanently!* Whatever you can create he can destroy, and it seems to be impossible to use that same spell again. It has gone *forever.*'

Rachel immediately thought of Dragwena. 'Can you destroy the Witch's magic, too?'

'Maybe. I'm not sure,' said Eric hesitantly. 'Some of it. Not her best magic. She can hide things. And I think Dragwena's got some magic that's lots of spells together, changing all the time. They could mix me up.'

'Why didn't you do any of this before?' Rachel asked.

'I didn't know I could,' he said. 'It did it by accident. Morpeth was practising his magic. He was annoying me. I wanted it to stop and – swish!'

Rachel pinched his nose, wondering what to say. 'You're . . . I can't do anything like this!'

Eric beamed happily. It was the first time Rachel had seen him look his old cocky self since arriving on Ithrea. I wonder, she thought. For a moment she pictured herself fighting Dragwena while Eric waved his anti-magic finger, undoing the Witch's spells one by one.

She sat down at a large stone table and made a fuss over Eric until Morpeth brought her a bowl of soup and a chunk of rough bread.

'No chocolate sandwiches, I'm afraid,' he apologized.

While she ate Eric edged closer to Rachel, looking closely at her hair.

'Ugh!' he said, pulling away. 'It's grey. Your hair's all grey.'

Rachel lifted her fringe. Her scalp felt dry and flaky. She dashed to a nearby mirror and parted her hair in several places. Everywhere, under the surface, it was white and thin. She yanked and a tuft filled her hand.

'What's the matter with me, Morpeth?' she asked in shock. 'Am I – am I growing *old* like you and Trimak because I've been using too much magic?'

Morpeth touched the strands. 'It's probably nothing,' he replied lightly. 'The stress of recent events. Using magic doesn't change you that quickly.'

Rachel continued to gaze in the mirror, trying to see if she had the typical wrinkles of the Sarren around her eyes. There were no wrinkles but there were *other* changes – her jaw felt tender and her eyes ached.

As she pondered this Trimak appeared in the doorway. He looked exhausted. 'Do you want to look around Latnap Deep, Rachel?' he asked. 'It's not . . . a pretty sight, I'm afraid.'

Rachel held Eric's hand, still rubbing her sore eyes, and entered the main caves.

They were full of injured Sarren. Small makeshift beds, little more than rags of clothing, covered the floor and dozens of men and women lay still or softly moaning. A few of the least wounded moved between them, administering simple medicines and offering comfort as best they could.

Rachel stared at the Sarren, appalled. 'What happened?'

'They fought the Neutrana under the Palace,' Trimak said. 'Most had only their hands as weapons. Only a hundred or so are left. The rest died in the tunnels, or on the journey to Latnap Deep.'

'You *walked*?' marvelled Rachel. 'You mean, you came all that way in the snow without Dragwena finding you?'

'It was a terrible journey,' said Trimak. 'Fear of the Witch drove us through the blizzards. I believe we only made it because Dragwena's spies were searching for a bigger prize – they were looking for *you.*'

Rachel gazed numbly at the injured Sarren, and suddenly everything she had endured, everything they had all suffered since she and Eric arrived on Ithrea, seemed too much to bear.

'It's all our fault!' she said. 'Dragwena *let* me escape just to trap the Sarren together under the Palace. Then she used Eric to keep track of me. Perhaps she's still using both of us. Dragwena might be able to find you all in Latnap Deep because *we're* here. Did you think of that?'

'Yes. Of course,' said Trimak. 'It's a risk we must take.'

'Is it?' asked Rachel. 'I know you believe I'm the child-hope. You want me to fight Dragwena. I know I must do that. But—' she held back her tears, clutching Eric. 'But—'

'You're frightened of the Witch,' said Trimak. 'I know. We all are.' His eyes moistened, and he hung his head. 'We are asking so much of you.'

Rachel held her long hair, no longer completely dark, in both hands. 'I don't mind that,' she said. 'But have you seen this? Look, I'm no longer your dark-haired child any more, am I?' She stared at Morpeth. 'I will do anything to keep you and Eric safe, but what have I managed so far? I couldn't even frighten a few wolves. Eric points his little finger and my spells are gone, just like that. How do you expect me to defeat the Witch? You have no idea how powerful she is. I think Dragwena might just be playing with us. She flies around and amuses herself by killing Sarren and stroking her disgusting snake. What can I really do to frighten her?'

For a moment there was a tense silence in the cave. Then Rachel noticed a man kneeling down a short distance away – a man Rachel recognized: Grimwold. 'I remember you,' she said. 'You gave me a chance to escape from the eye-tower.'

Grimwold's face was badly cut. One of his ears had been torn off.

'The child-hope,' he gasped. 'Then all those deaths . . . were not in vain.' He reached out, gripping Rachel's arm. 'Are you really the child-hope? Are you? How many more deaths must there be?'

Rachel read Grimwold's expression – his despair and

hope. 'Oh, that stupid verse,' she muttered. 'I don't know what it means. What use is it? I can't even *remember* it clearly.'

Grimwold kept his grip on her arm, and said:

> *'Dark girl she will be,*
> *Enemies to set free,*
> *Sing in harmony,*
> *From sleep and dawn-bright sea,*
> *I will arise,*
> *And behold your childish glee.'*

'It still doesn't mean anything to me,' said Rachel.

'I know another verse,' Eric whispered.

Everyone froze.

'A dark verse,' he said.

Rachel glanced at Trimak. 'Do you know what he means?'

All the Sarren shook their heads fearfully.

Eric cleared his throat, and said:

> *'Dark girl she will be,*
> *Fair hearts broken,*
> *Ancient wrath awoken,*
> *Children unborn,*
> *Wizards under lawn,*
> *Darkness without dawn.'*

As Eric finished all the Sarren covered their ears, howling with pain.

'What does it mean?' Rachel asked, bewildered.

'It means this,' Eric said under his breath. *'Fair hearts broken, children unborn, Wizards under lawn, darkness without dawn.* Dragwena's going to kill all the children and the Wizards, just like she told Rachel.'

'Why didn't you tell us this before?' said Rachel. 'Something this important—'

'I didn't know the words, until just now,' Eric protested feebly. 'Don't ask me why!'

'It's me, isn't it?' Rachel said. 'Dragwena needs *me* to fulfil the dark verse. She needs my power. And if she turns me into a Witch I'll help her do all these terrible things. I am the child-hope or . . . the *end* of all hope.'

Morpeth and Trimak looked at the floor, unable to meet Rachel's gaze.

'You don't know *anything*, do you?' she said, hardly able to contain her frustration. 'You expect me to know! Are we just going to wait for Dragwena to come and get us? I'm sick of it, hiding and running away. There must be something we can do. How long will it take Dragwena to find us?'

'Weeks perhaps,' Trimak said. 'Days more likely. The Witch may already know we are here.'

Rachel pulled Eric towards her. 'What are we going to do?'

Eric started to cry, big tears tumbling down his cheeks. 'Rachel, I don't know. You'll think of something. The Witch hasn't got you yet.'

And then Rachel heard someone laugh.

The voice was not human. Rachel recognized it instantly: Dragwena.

17

teeth

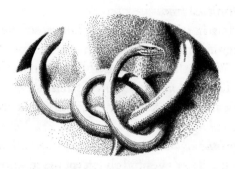

Rachel glanced wildly round the cave.

'*I am not in this dingy pit,*' Dragwena's voice scoffed.

Rachel thought, 'Then – where?'

'*Within you, child.*'

A thumping terror shuddered through Rachel. 'H-how can you be?'

'*Look at your hand.*'

Rachel opened her fingers. The five-pointed star of the Witch-mark, now thickly black, blazed on her palm.

'*I am finishing the task interrupted by the Sarren in the eye-tower,*' Dragwena explained. '*The wound I gave you then went deep. The transformation to Witch will be painless and swift now. Already your blood is thinning, altering in colour. Finally it will be vibrant emerald, too bright for your human eyes to bear. But by then your eyes will no longer be human, either . . .*'

Rachel tore at the Witch-mark with her nails. The blood

that poured out was yellow. Her mind shrieked: 'What have you done to me? This can't be happening?'

'*Your friends in the caves will certainly get a shock,*' Dragwena laughed. '*They think you are the child-hope to guide them home. What a surprise they will get when four Witch jaws thrust from your face, crawling with spiders.*'

Rachel felt her mouth. She noticed a solid hard mass burgeoning under the flesh of both cheeks.

'*In a few hours the change will be complete,*' Dragwena told her. '*You will no longer need sleep. Your eyelids will dissolve. Your nostrils will split and fold into sensitive flaps of skin, revealing extraordinary new scents. You will enjoy all this, I promise.*'

Rachel closed her eyes tightly, desperate to block out the voice.

'*That will not work,*' Dragwena said. '*I can now read your every thought, know your fears and hopes. There can be no escape. Do not struggle. Give yourself up to me willingly.*'

Rachel's entire body convulsed with fear. She gazed desperately around for help, stumbled and fell on the cave floor.

'Rachel, what is it?' said Morpeth, rushing to pick her up.

Eric walked across the room and did something he had not done since he had been little more than a baby – he put his arms around Rachel's neck. He squeezed her tightly, and Rachel sobbed into his embrace, wave on bursting wave of tears.

'I *know*,' he whispered. 'Dragwena's inside you, isn't she?'

Rachel buried herself in his shoulder, too despondent to answer.

Morpeth stared at Eric. 'How do you know what is happening? How can you possibly know?'

'I just know. Rachel needs to be alone.'

Morpeth lifted Rachel and carried her from the cave to a small chamber where there was some privacy. Eric held her hand tightly all the way, encouraging her with bright little smiles, not in the least embarrassed. Rachel knew Eric never normally behaved like this. Did it mean she could no longer survive without his help?

Morpeth placed her gently on the floor, wiping away her tears. 'There,' he murmured, lifting her chin. 'We are alone, you and I and Eric.'

'Not alone,' she said. 'Dragwena is in me. She knows *everything* I know.'

'What should we do?' Morpeth asked. He asked Rachel, but he also turned to Eric, and it was Eric who answered.

'I'm not sure,' said Eric, 'but I think that if the Witch can get inside her head, then Rachel might be able to get inside Dragwena too.' He gripped Rachel's shoulders. 'Try, Rachel. Go on. Find out things about the Witch.'

Rachel nodded bleakly. Clutching Eric's hand she made herself relax. She closed her eyes, clearing her mind. And then slowly, hesitantly, with the utmost care, she began to probe. She reached down until she touched another presence – a presence burning with its own ancient, ancient desires: Dragwena.

'*Look long and well,*' Dragwena whispered. '*I have yearned for this moment, child. I would have preferred to have caught you before you reached Latnap Deep, but that is no longer important. It is so long since I could openly read another's thoughts like this. Only Witches have this gift. We began to talk this way in the eye-tower. Now it is much easier. So you see we will soon be Witches together. I need have no secrets from you now. Look further.'*

Dragwena's mind spread wide in invitation, and Rachel streaked through the dark secrets of her memory. She experienced sensations that brought Dragwena comfort – the caress of her soul-snake; the joy of riding within a storm-whirl at the edge of the world, the spiders hiding within the safety of her throat. And wolves. Rachel felt what it was like for Dragwena to be amongst the pack: the smell of wolves together on the hunt, and the Witch belly-close beside them, running everywhere and nowhere, following the chase wherever it led.

'*Go deeper,*' Dragwena urged.

Rachel did. She witnessed the Witch on a long search. Amongst the Ragged Mountains of Ithrea Dragwena flew as a bird, and beyond to the high poles, where the ice froze on her gigantic wings.

'What are you looking for?' asked Rachel.

'*For Larpskendya. The Wizard told me he would leave his song on this tiny world. I sought out the scent of his magic to kill his presence, wherever it hid.*'

Rachel watched as Dragwena changed into dozens of creatures. As a shark under the vast Endellion Ocean the Witch sought, her body diving deep to the rocky bed, where her mouth became a limitless maw grinding through a million sea-creatures with fluorescent gills. For centuries she searched. The Witch scoured in every corner of the world, and beneath the world, and in the high skies, by day and night, until Rachel had seen the alien constellations flash by so often that she knew them intimately.

At last Dragwena's search ended.

'You never found him,' Rachel realized. 'You don't even know what Larpskendya's song is. But it's still here, somewhere, isn't it? Protecting Ithrea. Protecting *us*.' Her heart soared. 'I remember the dream-sleep,' she said defiantly. 'Larpskendya promised to protect the children on Earth by developing their magic. He said they would be able to use it against you if needed.'

'No child has ever come with enough magic to challenge me,' said Dragwena. *'But Larpskendya kept his word. For long ages I have drawn children to Ithrea, and their powers are always improving. You are the strongest of all, Rachel. But you are not strong enough to defy me.'*

'I wonder,' Rachel said. Could she really be the child-hope? And Eric? What about his gift? Was it a threat to the Witch? She sensed fear in Dragwena's mind then, quickly masked, but fear nonetheless, and felt grateful. 'So, you couldn't find Larpskendya. Good. What did you do next, Witch?'

'This was his planet, Larpskendya's world. I hated everything. I changed it!'

Rachel watched the Witch skimming over the original bright forest world of Ithrea. When she touched the trees they blackened and died. Dragwena dragged her nails into the rich soils and the lush flowers withered. She blazed across the vibrant blue skies, turning them to lifeless grey, and the snow a deeper grey, and filtered the yellow light from the sun until all colour and warmth was removed utterly. Even that was not enough for the Witch. She reached into the deepest edges of the world and created the storm-whirls, belching lightning and cloud. Then Dragwena turned on the simple animals, giving crows the faces of babies and changing dogs into wolves the size of bears, who could talk and comfort her in her loneliness. And one day, on a whim, Rachel saw the Witch take forever the singing voices Larpskendya had given the eagles.

'I'm not surprised by anything you do now,' Rachel murmured. 'I've seen how you enjoy killing and maiming for no reason. I'll never let you use me to do that!'

Dragwena's voice laughed. *'We shall see. Eagles, children, everything you know or feel now will be meaningless soon. Only the battle with the Wizards is important, the endless war. But all is not war, Rachel. There is the Sisterhood of the Witches to bring warmth too. Would you like to see it? Would you like to see my home world, the planet of Ool – the Witchworld?'*

Rachel knew that Dragwena was trying to entice her. But this time, unlike the dream-sleep or her experiences in the eye-tower, Rachel felt that she could withstand the Witch. Confidently, she said, 'Show me your home world, then. It must be ugly, if you came from there.'

Rachel found herself floating above a gigantic planet. The sky was deep grey, almost black, and the lifeless sun offered no warmth. As Rachel expected, she saw the storm-whirls – but unlike Ithrea, the whirls on Ool covered the whole planet. And inside, riding the whirl-tops, Rachel saw the Witches, millions of them. They flew on the raging blasts, practising their spells. As Rachel watched she felt a yearning to be there, riding with the Witches. Who were they? What were their names? All were female. Mothers? Sisters? They beckoned, lifting up their bare arms, imploring Rachel to join them.

Rachel wanted to fly amongst the Witches. She knew this feeling, dragging her inside Dragwena's desires, and resisted it. She dismissed the Ool World from her mind, and knew that Dragwena had not expected this.

'How did you bring the children from Earth?' Rachel demanded.

Rachel now saw Dragwena sitting alone in the unending snows of Ithrea. '*Larpskendya made sure I could not leave the planet. I was trapped, but I began a spell, a single finding spell. It required a dozen years, Rachel, to initiate, and a hundred more to perfect, and the making of it almost destroyed me.*' Rachel watched the years of the spell's creation flash by. During it the Witch hardly changed from her position in the snow, barely moved even her head. The effort to finish the spell made Dragwena ill: her blood-red cheeks swarmed with maggots and her teeth rotted as the cleaning spiders died.

'*Larpskendya made one mistake. He should never have told me he was developing magic on Earth. That gave me a faint hope. I put everything I had into creating this one spell. Finally it was complete.*' Rachel stared as Dragwena dragged her sagging body to the top of the highest mountain of Ithrea, breathing at the radiant stars. The spell leapt through the sky. It pierced the outer world and spread in several directions, hunting.

'*I waited a thousand years and longer,*' Dragwena said, '*until I was so weakened I wondered if the wolves themselves might finish me off. But at last the spell found your Earth. And then I was able to draw children from it, bring them here and make use of their magic to revive me.*'

Rachel recalled the Wizards and the Child Army. 'Why didn't you return? You pledged to kill the children who turned against you. I know how much you hated them, still hate them.'

'The magic of earlier children was not powerful enough. But I was patient and I waited. I knew one day a child would arrive strong enough to help me back – you, Rachel.'

'I can read your mind as well as you can read mine,' said Rachel. 'It is dangerous for you to let me inside you, Witch. I'll discover a way to hurt you.'

Dragwena whispered, *'No, child, you do not understand. I intend to keep you here, linked to my mind, until I am sure the transformation is complete. When you are fully a Witch I will return you to the caves and let you loose. First, I think you should kill the betrayers, Morpeth and Trimak. After that we must decide how to use little Eric. Your brother has strengths I cannot yet fully understand. If we are unable to master them for our own purposes, we will destroy him. Perhaps I'll let you kill your own brother, Rachel – if the army I have sent does not reach Latnap Deep first.'*

Dragwena opened her mind, and Rachel saw Neutrana soldiers marching. Five thousand of them, armed for close fighting and flanked by wolves, headed steadily towards the caves of Latnap Deep. The army would arrive soon and Dragwena planned to kill everyone inside.

Everyone except Rachel.

'I'll warn them!' Rachel raged.

'Try to get out. See if you can!'

Rachel tugged her thoughts away, expecting to find herself back in the cave with Morpeth and Eric. Instead, she remained inside Dragwena's thoughts. She searched for the exit. There was none. The original route was blocked, or she had forgotten it. Every path she tried took her down, deeper into the Witch's mind.

'Let me go!'

Dragwena laughed, the sound filling Rachel's ears. *'The transformation is quickening. Sense it! Can't you feel the change? You already have new powers beyond anything Morpeth can conceive. You are becoming a Witch. Join me. Don't fight. It is pointless. Soon—'*

Suddenly: a blast.

Rachel felt it slam into her, like the shock-wave of a bomb. Then a further boom, twice as hard, followed by high-pitched screams: *Dragwena's* screams.

'What?' the Witch gasped.

Another explosion, and this time Rachel heard something tear. She looked up, and saw light gashing through the tear, and above the light a corner of Latnap Deep. Eric stood there, his face burning with concentration.

'Get out!' she heard Morpeth shout. 'Head towards us!'

'No!' said Eric. 'Look for spells first. Quickly, Rachel, find them. I'm opening up Dragwena for you.'

The blasts continued, ripping into Dragwena's mind, slicing it wide. Rachel did not hesitate. She spread her thoughts, ignoring Dragwena's agony. Rachel searched in the most secret regions, until she found what she was looking for: *spells* – delicate and powerful spells, changing spells, fast spells and spells of such complexity that they required unfathomable knowledge to summon. And, nestled deepest of all, were the death spells – a rich variety of death. Rachel touched them all, filling her mind.

Dragwena's shrieking ceased abruptly. Rachel blinked,

finding herself lying in the caves of Latnap Deep beside Eric and Morpeth.

Eric kicked the walls in frustration. 'What did you find?'

Rachel felt confused. 'I . . . don't . . . where is the Witch?'

'Gone! I kicked Dragwena out of your head. I smashed her magic. She ran. She *had* to run, back to the eye-tower!'

'H-how did you do that?'

Eric shook his head. 'I don't know how. I just attacked her magic. That's what I do, remember. I knew Dragwena was keeping you in there with her spells. I felt you trying to find a way out, so I reached in and killed the ones holding you there.' He grinned. 'Dragwena couldn't make them come back. Like you, she didn't know how!'

Rachel spent a few minutes considering what she had discovered. All the spells, including the death spells, remained in her mind. Was there something she could use to attack the Witch?

Her left cheek ached. Absently, she touched it – and immediately withdrew her hand.

Teeth, new teeth, were boiling under her skin.

She stared at Morpeth. '*What do I look like?*'

His face twisted.

'Tell me!'

Morpeth left the chamber briefly, returning with a mirror. Gripping it tightly, Rachel saw several things: her skin was red, blood-red; her nose a formless spongy mass. She examined her eyes. The lids were missing. She forced her lips open and noticed, embedded in the gums, three new sets of teeth. They were almost fully formed, white and backward curving, pushing at the flesh of her cheeks, ready to burst out.

Rachel dropped the mirror. She stood still, too terrified to cry out.

Morpeth gripped her shoulders. 'Yes, you are changing, but you are still the Rachel I know! Do you want to kill us? Do you?'

Rachel numbly shook her head.

'Then – we still have hope.'

'Hope?' Rachel replied angrily. 'Look at me! I'm *still* turning into a Witch! Dragwena told me this would happen.' She turned to Eric. 'How long before I completely change?'

'I don't know,' said Eric. 'I can't tell.'

'Can you get rid of it?' Rachel pleaded. 'It's a spell. It must be. Can't you stop what it's doing to me?'

Eric frowned. 'No. It is a spell, but somehow it's part of you, too. I can't work out what's happening. I don't know how to stop it.'

Rachel clenched her teeth. The new jaws meshed together perfectly.

'Take me to Trimak and the others,' she ordered Morpeth.

Back inside the main caves everyone gasped when they saw her. Several Sarren instinctively drew their swords. She quickly told them everything, including Dragwena's army approaching Latnap Deep.

Rachel noticed a man, obviously afraid, barely able to look up. She clacked her new jaws menacingly. 'You *should* be frightened of me!' said Rachel. 'When I become a Witch Dragwena said I'd enjoy killing you.' The moment she thought this Rachel sensed death-spells rise up in her mind. The spells told her she could already kill them all if she wanted. To Trimak she said, 'Get everyone ready to leave.'

'Listen Rachel,' Morpeth said, 'I know you are trans-forming into . . . *something*, but that does not necessarily mean you must become like Dragwena. Your instinct is still to protect us.'

Rachel hesitated. 'You mean I could fight her? Good Witch against bad Witch?'

'Yes. Why not? Perhaps you are not turning into Dragwena's kind of Witch at all. You might be able to protect the caves if need be. We must be careful to make the right decision. Think! Everything Dragwena showed you could be a lie. There may be no army approaching Latnap Deep.'

Grimwold knelt nearby. 'No. I sent someone to check. The Witch's army is coming, just as Rachel described it.'

Rachel gazed around the cave at the anxious faces of the Sarren.

'There isn't much time,' she said. 'I don't believe I can defeat the Witch. None of the spells I have learned show me how to do this. But I think I can get you all to safety, and then . . . I'll go somewhere alone, a long way off. It doesn't matter where. I'll wait until the transformation is complete, and see what happens to me. I daren't remain close to you all now. I can't take that risk. I'm thinking . . . if I can draw Dragwena off, fight her, weaken her somehow, maybe there will be a chance.'

Morpeth said firmly, 'We will never abandon you to Dragwena. We should stay together, no matter what happens.'

Trimak pulled out a knife. 'Morpeth is right. I once pledged to use this against you, Rachel.' He threw the knife down. 'That was a shameful thought. I sense Dragwena is deliberately trying to separate us. Stay. We will do what we can to protect you.'

Grimwold nodded, and all the Sarren fit enough to stand raised their swords and knelt before her.

'No,' Rachel said, her lip trembling. 'Look after Eric. Just don't let me or the Witch hurt him! Don't . . .' She trailed off, knowing Morpeth or the rest of the Sarren would never be able to protect Eric from Dragwena. The thought that she herself might hurt Eric was unbearable. Would Eric be safer with the Sarren? Or with her? Or – for a moment Rachel had a terrible vision of Eric all alone on Ithrea's snows, hiding from both her and Dragwena.

Eric tapped her on the shoulder. 'Hey, you.'

Rachel turned, and felt her four new jaws turn with her.

'I trust you,' he said. 'Don't go without me, Rachel. Don't leave me here.'

Rachel pulled him close. 'Aren't you scared of me?'

He grinned awkwardly. 'Well, a bit. Your teeth look flipping terrible.'

Rachel laughed – all four jaws joining in.

'But I've got this,' Eric said, stabbing his finger at the cave walls. 'I won't let Dragwena scare me. I *won't!*'

Rachel tried to smile. Was bringing Eric with her the right thing to do? Or was that what Dragwena wanted her to do?

Grimwold paced the floor of the cave. 'I don't see how you can get us safely from the caves, Rachel. Are you expecting the Sarren to run from this advancing army? Look at us!' He swept his arms around. 'Most can barely walk. Where will we go? Where will we hide?'

'Describe the weather,' Rachel said.

'What?'

'Is it dark outside?'

'Well, night, yes,' he replied impatiently. 'The sun set over an hour ago. So what? That will not protect us. Armath is full and shining like a demon down on us all. Dragwena's spies will spot us instantly.' He turned to Trimak. 'Let Rachel and Eric go if they must, but I say the Sarren should remain in Latnap Deep, and fight as best we can. Once we go to the surface, we'll be virtually defenceless. At least in the caves we can match steel with the Neutrana.'

Several Sarren muttered agreement.

'You won't need to run or fight,' Rachel said, scanning them. 'I have new powers now.'

Those Sarren who had serious wounds immediately stood up and shook themselves, their injuries gone. Rachel found the new spells she needed pouring effortlessly into her mind. Dragwena's spells, she realized. What was the best spell? What kind of spell could surprise Dragwena and enable them to escape undetected?

'Move everyone to the high corridors of Latnap Deep,' Rachel said, making up her mind.

'Where will you take us?' asked Trimak.

'Nowhere is safe. I'll take you as far from here as I can.'

As Rachel spoke a tooth sliced through her cheek – followed by a huge jaw. All the teeth stretched forward hungrily, trying to reach the Sarren. She felt something crawl over her gums and knew it was a spider, born in the saliva of her mouth. She did not try to spit it out, knowing other spiders were also being born who would replace it.

'Better hurry,' she said bitterly.

18

mawkmound

Rachel sat for a few minutes alone, making the spell she needed to leave the caves.

When it was ready the world above the Sarren altered. High in the night sky of Ithrea seven clouds moved furtively towards Latnap Deep. From the west they came, moving swiftly with the light breeze, though not so swiftly that their movement seemed different from any other cloud in the sky. For several miles they crept along the horizon, hugging the low hills, before rising in one great mass to obscure the moon.

'Now,' Rachel said to a sentry.

He lifted the doorway a few inches and glanced cautiously around. Dragwena's army approached, visible in all directions. The Sarren huddled in the corridors beneath the door, uncertain what to expect. A cold mist poured into the crack, covering everyone in a milky wetness.

'Don't be afraid,' Rachel's voice announced. 'Let the air surround you. I have summoned the mist to protect us. We will fly as a cloud. It will lift you into the sky. You will not fall, and the journey will be short.'

The next moment everyone's body reared up from the ground, as if a soft pillow had been placed beneath them. They all hung in the corridor, their feet a few inches above the floor.

'I'm ready,' said Rachel.

Led by her the Sarren floated slowly upwards into the night air – singly, as the doorway was too small for more than one to pass. Gently, like steam drifting from the mouth of a kettle, they poured out of Latnap Deep. By the time the last had been sucked out of the corridor Rachel herself was a thousand feet in the sky.

The long, thin column of greyness rotated in the air until it lay parallel to the horizon and flat. There it hovered. From a distance the column now looked exactly like a narrow grey cloud. No one could be seen or heard within. It drifted briefly in the light winds, travelling westwards with the other clouds in the sky, hiding the light of Armath and stars.

'Prepare yourselves!' Rachel exulted, her voice travelling throughout the length of the mist. 'We're departing!'

The cloud came to a stop, while those about it continued to roll west. A moment later, and silently, it shot south-westwards, keeping low to the ground. Inside the cloud many panicked as their bodies felt the lurch. The cloud gathered pace, cutting through the night. Rachel sent a warming spell through it, protecting everyone from the freezing wind.

A lone prapsy, flitting high in the sky, saw the cloud pass underneath. It blinked several times. 'What's that?' it asked itself, but the cloud had gone, and the prapsy instantly forgot what it had seen. Instead, it kept watch on the Witch's army marching below – Neutrana and the wolves would arrive at Latnap Deep within the hour.

The cloud, only briefly airborne, came to a halt over some gentle hills close to the South Pole of Ithrea: Mawkmound. Rachel's journey through Dragwena's mind had taught her everything about the planet. Here there were no spies, she knew. Nothing lived on Mawkmound except for a few scrawny trees, somehow defying the winds.

The cloud gently fell to the ground and dispersed, spilling Sarren into the snow. Several men leapt to their feet at once, their swords high and ready. Grimwold and Morpeth stayed close to Rachel, their eyes alert.

Morpeth walked the short distance between them and held her hands. 'Are you sure leaving is the right thing to do?' he asked. 'We would feel safer if you stayed.'

Rachel clacked her new teeth. 'What about these?'

'I could get used to them,' said Morpeth, lowering his gaze. 'I'm not sure I could get used to being without *you*.'

Rachel stroked his lean chin. 'You know, I think I preferred your ragged beard. I liked the old Morpeth better.'

'I'll grow it again for you,' he said earnestly. 'When you return.'

'I could change you back now if you like.'

Morpeth grinned. 'Oh, I don't know. I can see over

Trimak's head for the first time in over five hundred years. It's nice not having to look *up* at everyone all the time!'

'I never noticed that,' Rachel said, trying to hold back her tears. 'Whenever I watched, everyone was always looking up to *you*, Morpeth.'

As she hugged him, Morpeth said, 'Where's Eric going?'

Rachel saw Eric wandering away across a distant snow mound. 'Come back,' she shouted. 'Eric!'

Eric ignored her. 'Dragwena is here, or was here,' he said. 'Magic has a smell.' He lay face down in the snow and spread his arms. Sniffing, he drew circular patterns with his hands. 'I'll find her!'

'No, Eric!' Rachel cried.

Without warning, the snow in front of Eric parted and a figure uncoiled from the ground.

It was Dragwena.

Before Eric could defend himself the Witch struck him hard across the face, knocking him several feet across the snow. He lay there bleeding and unconscious. 'Time for you later, boy,' the Witch said.

Grimwold was the first to react. He and several Sarren threw themselves at the Witch. Dragwena fixed each with a swift look, throwing them hundreds of feet into the dark sky. Before they fell Rachel glanced up, held them in the air, pinned like wingless butterflies against the stars.

'Very good,' said Dragwena, 'but not quite good enough.' She sent a piercing thrust into Rachel's mind. The pain made Rachel lose control for a second. That moment was all it took for the Grimwold and the other Sarren to tumble from the skies.

Tumble to their deaths.

'There, child-hope,' said Dragwena. 'I shall enjoy many such deaths tonight. Did you think you could escape? You fool. You stink. Don't you realize that? You stink of magic. I could recognize your smell anywhere now. The cloud was a clumsy device, easily followed. As for Eric, I knew he would not be able to resist using his unusual gift to search for me. It is all so easy. You are only children. I will always be able to outwit you.'

Filled with horror, Rachel gazed at the dead Sarren. She prepared herself, expecting the Witch to attack her immediately. Instead, Dragwena said, 'You must know you can't defeat me. Why fight at all? Come to me willingly and I will spare the remainder of your friends. Even little Eric. I promise.'

Rachel instantly read the Witch's mind. Dragwena was momentarily unguarded. She blocked the spell, but not before Rachel had seen the truth: Dragwena planned to kill the Sarren savagely.

'You are *afraid*,' said Rachel. 'Nothing else would have made you promise something like that. You are lying. You are afraid of Eric, and you are afraid of me!'

Dragwena's confident mask fell away.

'Why are you so scared, Witch?'

Dragwena did not answer.

Rachel paused, for the first time really sensing their differences. 'I know why,' she realized. 'I'm not turning into your kind of Witch, am I?' She touched the four jaws on her face. 'In fact, I'm not . . . turning into a Witch *at all.*'

'You cannot resist much longer,' said Dragwena. 'Stop trying.'

Rachel cast her mind over everything that had happened

– the stabbing wound in the eye-chamber, Dragwena's insistence that it meant one thing only. As soon as Rachel questioned herself she understood the truth.

She faced Dragwena. 'It was *you* who tried to convince me I was becoming a Witch,' Rachel whispered. 'Over and over you kept saying I would be like you, think like you, look like you. And I believed it.' Rachel felt her hair, her arms, her four lips, and smiled. 'My own magic was developing. But magic doesn't know what it wants. Morpeth taught me that in the Breakfast Room, when I had to choose the colour of the bread. I forgot that simple lesson. Magic wants to be used. But it needs control. My magic ached to do *something*. Without realizing it I used it. I was so sure that I was becoming a Witch that the magic worked to do exactly that. If I had gone on believing, I might have become your kind of Witch in the end. That was your plan, all along.'

Instantly, Rachel returned her body to normal. She faced Dragwena with one set of teeth, her hair dark. 'You dumb, stupid Witch,' she said. 'I know what you want – to return to Earth to kill the Wizards and children. But you need my help, don't you? You can't do it alone. And I won't give it! A soothing voice won't work on me now, or your other tricks.' She looked without fear at Dragwena. 'I've learnt a lot. I can destroy myself if I need to. Whatever happens, you won't be able to turn me into your Witch. I'll *never* allow the dark verse to come true.'

Dragwena probed her mind. Rachel captured the thought and threw it back.

Dragwena shrieked her rage over and over, her voice echoing across Mawkmound.

'Then I hope you are ready for a battle, Rachel,' Dragwena hissed. 'You are useless to me now. I can't allow you to live.' Her tattooed eyes were fierce. 'A *real* fight! I have not had that pleasure for many years.'

'A fight to the death,' Rachel whispered.

'Of course.'

Rachel tried to remain calm, unprepared for this. 'I know some interesting spells now,' she said weakly.

'True,' said Dragwena. 'You borrowed them from *me*. But I know all the defences against those spells. I hope you have a new weapon, or our contest will be brief indeed.'

'That would be telling,' Rachel said.

'Now you *do* sound like a Witch,' Dragwena laughed. 'Brave little girl, do you know how many ways I have to kill you?'

Rachel nodded. 'I know everything, all your spells.'

'No,' Dragwena said softly. 'You know only what I *allowed* you to see. When Eric helped you find the death-spells I escaped before you found the deadliest. There are spells even more powerful than those: *Doomspells*. You have no defence against them, child. Doesn't that make you afraid?'

'Everything about you frightens me,' Rachel answered. 'But you would not be wasting time now unless you were also afraid of me.'

Dragwena appraised Rachel carefully, even admiringly. 'What a pity it is to have to destroy you,' she said. 'Still, if you exist there will be others to follow, no doubt. Larpskendya has bred magic in the children of Earth well. I thank him for that. I will not make the same mistakes with new children I made with you.' She stepped back. Her soul-snake licked diagonally across her face, a gesture to start the battle. 'Since you are game enough to challenge me, do you want to start the first spell, Rachel? I think you deserve that honour.'

Rachel glanced at Eric, still lying face down in the snow. She had to get Dragwena away from him as soon as possible – away from Mawkmound. She transformed into a raven and flapped into the sky.

Dragwena did not follow her immediately. Instead she turned to the Sarren. 'Watch the final scene,' she exulted. 'It will be the last thing you ever see. When I return I'm going to burn you all to death.'

A moment later a second raven cawed and sped after Rachel.

Everyone on Mawkmound gazed nervously after the black birds as they winged into the brooding night.

19

doomspell

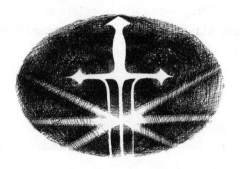

Rachel was not ready to fight. She flew in a panic, wondering where to go. Where would be a safe place to hide? She shifted her mind to the Ragged Mountains, far from Mawkmound. She flew effortlessly amongst the peaks and valleys, wondering how to use the new spells, knowing Dragwena had practised them for thousands of years.

Safety first, Rachel thought. Become difficult to find. She stilled the sound of her beating wings to utter silence. Thick flocks of snow burned her eyes, so she flew blind, yet still saw the world with perfect clarity. Armath was bright, so she changed the colours of her upper body to reflect the moonlight. In the distance the Palace jutted from the ground, impenetrable black against the near black of the sky.

Would Dragwena find her quickly? Yes. Should she attack or defend? The spells gave her different answers when she asked them. Was there anything she could do that

Dragwena could not? Something new, a weapon Dragwena had never seen before? The spells offered no answer to this. Then Rachel realized she had not guarded her thoughts. Furious with herself, she blanked them out.

Instantly Dragwena appeared alongside her, wingtip to wingtip.

'Too late,' said Dragwena. 'You must think of the obvious things first, child. I could hear your thoughts yammering from Mawkmound. And now I know you have no secret weapon, either. You should never have revealed that. Keep me interested, or I'll tear your heart out.'

Rachel shifted rapidly and at random: from the Ragged Mountains to Dragwood; from Lake Ker to the Palace, hurrying, never staying in one place more than a few seconds. While she moved she also changed her shape, trying to throw off the Witch. Eventually, Rachel merged with the black rock of the Palace wall, becoming a grain of the wall itself, and waited there anxiously.

Part of the wall nearby spoke to her. 'Is this the best you can do? I know the pattern of your magic too well now for shape-shifting to throw me off. You caught me by surprise with your speck-of-dust trick in the eye-tower, but that can never work again. Hurry, I'm getting impatient. Dazzle me with your magic!'

Rachel leapt into a wolf prowling the Palace gardens. She took on its scent. She leapt into a frog, felt its slime and mingled that with the scent of wolf and other smells, always moving. For the first time she recognised the distinctive smell of her own magic, and removed it. Shifting many miles, she masked all the smells, becoming a wisp of odourless air, drifting aimlessly.

This time Dragwena did not find her for several minutes, and Rachel only knew when a ragged black claw ripped her from the sky.

'Interesting,' said Dragwena. 'What next?'

Rachel imitated the Witch, and held her inside a larger claw. Dragwena followed until the giant black hands blotted out Armath, claw after claw building in the sky.

At last Dragwena herself pulled them both to the ground. 'Is copying all you can think to do?' she asked, looking bored. 'I hoped for a more interesting battle than—'

Rachel leapt into the Witch's soul-snake. She gripped its mind, held its fangs and made it bite Dragwena's neck.

Dragwena screamed, then regained control, but Rachel already knew what she wanted to do next – the snake had been only a distraction. She made her body bright and created *thousands* of other Rachels, equally bright, in the air. For a moment the whole sky was so fierce with their incandescence that even on Mawkmound the Sarren saw it and wondered. Quickly, she made each pretend Rachel soar in several directions – into the earth, trees, rocks, water, and air. All the fake forms she kept in her mind, concentrating to make them as real as herself, giving them one scent, one weight, one pattern of breathing, one pulse, scattering them all to the corners of Ithrea.

From high in the sky above the Palace several Rachels glanced down. Amongst them, her true form saw the Witch, just for a moment, confused.

Then Dragwena appeared alongside her face, laughing loudly. Rachel screamed and it was this, only this, which gave her away. She noticed too late that Dragwena's laughing form had appeared alongside all the other Rachels.

'Oh, very good,' said Dragwena. 'Excellent! If only you had thought to make all the other Rachels scream it might have worked. But I suppose that's too much to ask. It takes many years of training to become a real Witch, and you do not have that long, do you?' She smiled. 'Keep trying. I don't wish to kill you just yet.'

Rachel shape-shifted all over Ithrea, trying to give herself time to consider something new. What else could she try? Come on, she told herself. Think! Something *completely* different . . .

Dragwena casually followed Rachel's shape-shifting. She took her time, enjoying the game, hoping there would be a few more interesting surprises. Rachel had stopped, Dragwena realized, in of all places Dragwood. The Witch glided towards the earth, knowing exactly where Rachel had landed. But instead of the dark trees the Witch found a tropical forest waiting for her. Instead of dark earth between the trees she found sweet grasses bursting with life. And sitting cross-legged amongst the grass fronds was a Wizard with many-coloured eyes.

'Larpskendya!' gasped Dragwena.

'I told you I would always protect this world,' said Larpskendya. 'Did you think I would allow you to hunt Rachel down?'

Dragwena collapsed to her knees, burying her head in her hands. 'This can't be true!'

The instant the Witch averted her eyes, Larpskendya's body disappeared. Where it had been, a needle-sharp blade hovered in the air. Rachel controlled the blade, a combination of all the fast death spells she could muster. She launched it while Dragwena was confused, unprepared, and sliced into the Witch's body, tearing it to shreds.

The wind blew the tatters of Dragwena's remains across the snow, scattering them. Rachel transformed back into a girl. For some time she examined the shreds of bone and flesh and clothing, poking the remains gingerly with her feet, hardly daring to believe it had worked.

Then, behind her, Rachel heard a slow handclap.

Dragwena stood there, unharmed. 'Oh, well done,' she said. 'Brilliant! What a fantastic Witch you would have made. What daring! To seek out what I feared most and use it. I only just managed to shape-shift into a tree at the last moment.' She bowed elaborately. 'It is an honour to fight you. Shall we continue?'

Rachel watched the Witch's expression. There was no fear there, only pleasure and enjoyment of the battle. Rachel knew that Dragwena had not even started to fight seriously. At any moment Dragwena could launch an attack. Rachel ignored the spells clamouring in her mind and tried recalling Dragwena's memories. There had to be something else she could use! What was Dragwena's weakness? Where could the Witch never follow her? Of course!

Rachel transformed into a rocket, aiming for the edge of the sky. The clouds scudded over her face, the air growing thinner.

'What are you trying now?' asked Dragwena, taking the same form, following her upward.

Rachel focused on shutting out her thoughts, but Dragwena sensed she was doing exactly that and read her intention.

The Witch slammed them both into the ground below.

'Idiot,' Dragwena said. 'If you had not shut your mind, I would not have bothered to read it until too late. You might have escaped! A wasted chance. Since you knew I cannot leave Ithrea, why didn't you just imagine yourself already outside the planet? I could never have followed you. But you did the obvious thing: you made yourself just *fly fast*. You are still thinking like a child, Rachel.'

Rachel immediately tried to picture herself in space, outside the world. Her body hurtled upwards, then crumpled like paper – an invisible shield created by Dragwena held her in. Rachel recovered, flew across the sky, desperately hoping for a crack in the shield. There was none. The stars beckoned above, achingly close. Rachel clawed at their winking light, seeking a way through.

The Witch appeared alongside. 'I think our little battle is almost over,' she said. 'I was wrong about being able to use you, but perhaps I should have concentrated on your brother from the beginning.' She smiled, pulling Rachel's face close. '*Eric* has much I can use. With training, I sense he might be able to remove the bonds of magic Larpskendya has wrapped around this world. It may be *Eric*, after all, who helps me fulfil the dark ver—'

Rachel breathed a blinding spell at Dragwena. Their heads were so close that Dragwena did not have time to shut her eyes. For a moment blades of emerald attacked her face; then they vanished, leaving the Witch unharmed.

'I know defences against all your spells,' the Witch whispered. 'Eric will not fight like you. He is so young. He will be much easier to persuade.'

Rachel screamed and shifted again, but this time

Dragwena did not follow. She simply ripped Rachel from the sky and dragged them both back to Mawkmound.

Rachel saw Morpeth and Trimak and the rest of the Sarren turn towards them expectantly. Eric lay in Morpeth's arms, still unconscious.

'See their anxious little faces?' said Dragwena. 'I want them all to see you crushed, to see the end of their child-hope. Then I will kill Morpeth and Trimak slowly, over a hundred years perhaps. Eric can help me. The others are not important.' She laughed. 'Where is your precious Larpskendya now? Where is the Wizard who promised to protect you?'

Rachel had one last desperate idea. She craned her neck, pointing towards Armath. She drew a deep breath – and shouted out the verse of hope.

For a moment the air rippled delicately. Everyone on Mawkmound felt it, even the Witch. Rachel and the Sarren waited hopefully, but something was missing. The words faded in the night breeze, and Armath shone coldly above.

Rachel bowed her head, completely defeated. Defiance, bravery, all of her magic – none of it seemed any use now. Where was Larpskendya? *Where was he?* Rachel glanced at the Sarren huddled across Mawkmound and the small face of Eric cradled in Morpeth's arms, and could think of nothing left to try.

'Prepare to die, girl,' said Dragwena. 'I am summoning the Doomspell.'

The Witch walked slowly to the centre of Mawkmound and raised her arms. She incanted spells in the language of

Ool, her home world. Rachel knew a few of the words from the death spells in her mind, but most she did not recognize. Here, she realised, was one of the deadliest spells Dragwena had never revealed – a killing spell of incalculable power. Rachel searched for something – anything – to defend herself.

The Doomspell arrived slowly. Dragwena knew there was no need for haste now. From the frozen wastes of the north a gigantic storm-whirl tore itself from a corner of the world. Rachel saw it from many miles away, an inferno of blasting rage. As she watched, the storm-whirl spread out to cover the entire sky. Its immense shadow bulged over the land, obliterating snow and stars. Over the Ragged Mountains the storm-shadow poured and Armath, shining there, was consumed by it. Mountains and streams were devoured and a wind rose that began to blow fiercely over Mawkmound.

The Sarren were terrified, but they did not scatter. Instead Trimak and a procession of Sarren solemnly crossed the snows of Mawkmound towards Rachel, their bodies bent against the wind. Morpeth hesitated for a moment, glancing first at Eric, then Rachel. Eventually, he carried Eric some distance away across the snows. Rachel saw him place his jacket under Eric's head, lower him gently in the snow and mutter three words. Not a protection spell, Rachel realized – Morpeth knew his magic was too weak to protect Eric. It was simply an apology, one Eric would probably never hear. Morpeth kissed Eric on the forehead and quickly caught up with the others.

All the Sarren now surrounded Rachel. Those with swords pointed them at Dragwena.

The Witch laughed. 'Swords? How touching.'

The vast storm-whirl finally reached Mawkmound. It hovered over Dragwena's head, a mass of coiling black cloud as wide as the horizon. Dragwena traced a shape in the air. Instantly, the cloud changed shape, condensing into a single thin grinding tunnel of wind, the thickness of rope. Dragwena dislocated her jaw. It flopped onto her chin, and the tunnel leapt inside her mouth. She shuddered with ecstasy as it poured inside her throat.

The Witch closed her mouth and smiled at Rachel. 'Ready?'

'Yes!' the Sarren closest to Dragwena bellowed.

Dragwena pointed her mouth at him and released the Doomspell.

A thick pillar of black smoke streamed at extraordinary speed from her lips. Inside the smoke a thousand teeth rushed to the surface.

Rachel placed several rings of protection around the Sarren, but it made no difference. The first Sarren hit by the smoke was torn apart. Knowing all the others would be killed, Rachel transported the remaining Sarren to safety at the edge of Mawkmound – and met the full force of the smoke and teeth alone.

She shielded her body with several spells, but the teeth inside gnawed relentlessly. Rachel fought them with everything she knew: with defensive spells, with killing spells, with incantations of paralysis and, finally, as the teeth burst through, even with her nails.

But it was no use. Dragwena cackled with joy as the teeth began to eat Rachel's lips and eyes.

20

MANAG

Rachel felt the teeth tearing lumps from her face. They shredded her arms and legs. They attacked her neck and heart, seeing the quickest way to kill her, chewing hungrily at her flesh, whispering the words of the Doomspell, willing her to die.

Rachel endured everything. Her whole mind was focused on a single spell to deaden her body to the pain. She waited and waited until all the teeth clung to her body. At last, when she could hear the whisper of the last jaw of the Doomspell, its meaning was fully revealed.

Rachel made fists of both her hands and unhinged her jaw. Her chin dropped and her mouth gaped wide. Through a gargle of blood and air she choked out the words she needed. Immediately, the teeth stopped biting. The black column of smoke and teeth rushed inside her throat, filling her.

Rachel's torn and bloodied body gazed evenly at Dragwena. 'Get ready,' she muttered. 'Larpskendya taught me in the dream-sleep that there is a spell of goodness for every spell of evil, Witch. You'd better start running before it catches you!'

She coughed. Blue smoke emerged from her mouth, moving slowly towards Dragwena.

'What is this?' asked Dragwena, backing away nervously. 'You cannot use the Doomspell. It is mine alone.'

Rachel pressed her chest with both hands, continuing to cough, and the blue smoke advanced more thickly. She incanted words backwards in the Witch's tongue. The spell flooded from her lips and followed the smoke.

A look of understanding suddenly gleamed in Dragwena's eye. 'A reversal,' she whispered. 'You are reversing the Doomspell. Bad to good: no, it cannot work.'

Dragwena continued to retreat. The first wisp of smoke touched her leg. She screamed in pain – and ran.

The words streamed from Rachel. Dragwena raised her arms and flew upward. A tendril of smoke yanked her back and fisted her into the ground. The rest of the blue column rapidly encircled Dragwena, pouring into her nose and throat and eyes. There were no teeth inside, but the Witch wailed and writhed under the onslaught as if inhaling fire.

Then, as suddenly as they had started, the words ceased. The reversal spell was at an end. As it finished Rachel's wounds vanished. She closed her mouth and the last blue vapours disappeared.

Everyone looked at Dragwena.

She lay in torment on the ground, her whole body burning in a blue flame which still reached deep inside.

But the Witch was not dead. With a huge effort she lifted her head into the air, and rasped: 'Manag . . . Manag . . .' The smoke poured back out of Dragwena's throat like glue, flicked out by her tongue.

It rose into the air and formed into a clawed creature with green eyes and a mouth that spread across all Mawkmound.

The Sarren looked desperately to Rachel for an explanation, but she had no understanding or answer.

Dragwena sat up. A bright green light ran over her body, snuffing out the last of the blue flames. 'Did you think the Doomspell is only a few flashing teeth?' she scoffed. 'It is countless spells, whatever I need it to be. This time a reversal will not work.'

Dragwena kissed the air. Rachel's body stiffened, outlined by a ring of flickering green fire. Understanding, the Manag opened its great claws and dived to rip her apart . . .

Morpeth ran towards Eric, shaking him over and over.

'Get up! Wake up!' he pleaded.

At last Eric raised his head and got clumsily to his feet. He stumbled towards Rachel and stood in front of her, tiny against the Manag's hugeness. Pointing with both hands, he punched holes in the creature's frame, somehow holding it back. But the spell that formed the Manag kept changing, inching closer, defying him. At last its breath swotted Eric to the ground. He fell on top of Rachel, still wildly jabbing his fingers.

'I can't stop it!' he cried. 'I can't stop it! It's made up of millions of spells. There are too many. I can't stop them all!'

'Sing the verse of hope,' Rachel told him. 'Sing it! Sing it!'

Eric pressed both his hands into the face of the Manag. He twisted his head towards the Endellion Ocean and sang in a high voice:

> *'Dark girl she will be,*
> *Enemies to set free,*
> *Sing in harmony,*
> *From sleep and dawn-bright sea,*
> *I will arise,*
> *And behold you childish glee.'*

The Manag warily opened its eyes.

'Sing it again!' Rachel shouted.

'*Dark girl . . .*' Eric began, and this time Rachel joined him, two voices singing in harmony. Over and over they sang, not stopping, louder and louder, until they heard an ancient sound rumble from its sleep – an immense heart thudding across the night.

The Manag stopped. It hovered over Rachel, rearing back, and turned uncertainly towards Dragwena.

'Finish it!' the Witch shrieked. 'Kill her! Kill her!'

The Manag flexed its claws, still hesitating.

'Destroy her!' Dragwena commanded. 'I created you. I demand it! Do it!'

Lunging forward, the Manag opened its great jaws within inches of Rachel's head, but still withheld its attack.

The Witch raged wildly at the creature, and it groaned with the agony of her words, yet something else tugged at the Manag's will. It continued to hover, glancing first at Dragwena, then at Rachel. Finally it ignored them both and turned its apprehensive eyes westward. And now every-one's eyes followed it, for a remarkable transformation was taking place.

In the middle of the night, with Armath at its zenith high in the sky, a sunrise was beginning in the far reaches of the world.

At first there was only a dim orange glow over the western mountains. But soon the sun rose in all its glory and ascended at an impossible speed into the sky. It was not the meagre creamy sun that had shone for so long on Ithrea. This sun was wild and golden. Almost painfully bright, it heaved itself into the air, pouring through the clouds of Ithrea for the first time in thousands of years. The Sarren gaped in wonder as they followed it, incandescent beams flashing off their cheekbones. Dragwena staggered and uttered an agonised cry, unable to bear the touch of the sun's rays. She called the Manag and cowered beneath it, hiding her head between her knees.

The Sarren continued to watch events unfold. High in the sky, beyond the rising sun, the night air was still dark – then something equally impossible happened: Armath, the great moon, fell from its place low over the Ragged Mountains, splashing with a mighty explosion into the Endellion Ocean.

'What's happening?' cried Trimak.

'I don't know,' Morpeth said, watching the tremendous plume of sizzling water thrown up by the moon.

The green ring of fire surrounding Rachel vanished. As she rushed across to the others Morpeth saw points of light plummeting in her eyes.

'Look!' Trimak cried. 'Look at the stars!'

In the sky above Ithrea, one by one, and then in their hundreds, like points of light on wallpaper, the stars were falling from their appointed places, following Armath into the ocean. Meanwhile, the sun continued its galloping ascent until it stood high above their heads. Bright daylight now swept across Mawkmound.

Dragwena pulled her dress over her face, her eyes bleeding.

Morpeth was too astonished to care what had happened to the Witch. He pointed towards the waters into which the last of the stars had sunk. 'How can we see the ocean?' he whispered. 'It should be frozen.'

Their answer was not long in coming. The Endellion Ocean was *rising*, barely noticeable until now as it had such a long way to climb before toppling over the western mountains. As they watched its writhing waters spilled over the highest summits, flowing towards them at devastating speed, swallowing the land.

Morpeth pointed eastward. There, in a far corner of the world, where no Sarren had ever travelled, an even mightier ocean also swept towards Mawkmound.

'Why aren't I scared?' asked Trimak. 'This should be terrifying.'

All the Sarren realized they were filled with awe, not terror. But a despairing Dragwena called weakly to the Manag. She could barely raise her head. The Manag shrank and moved to surround the Witch, trying to use its bulk to shield her from the rays of the sun.

Rachel whispered to Eric.

He giggled and they both turned to face the advancing waters.

'*Come Larpskendya!*' they sang together. '*Come from sleep and dawn-bright sea!*'

And Larpskendya came at last: from the tumultuous foaming ocean a silver bird rose from the depths. He was of such size that the waters could hardly contain his beating wings. With slow, massive motion he swept from the waves and headed towards Mawkmound. He boomed out the words of the verse of hope, filling the air with a sound whose loveliness cannot be named. And his many-coloured eyes blazed with beauty.

Dragwena met his stare. As soon as she did so Larpskendya locked her in a gaze of fear – in his eyes she saw a million grim-faced children, sharpening their knives against a stone wall. She shrieked and pointed.

'Kill it!' she instructed the Manag. 'Kill the Wizard!'

Without hesitation, the great shadow left her shoulder. Larpskendya turned to meet the creature. As he drew closer the Manag dwindled until it was just a point of swift darkness against his dripping breast. A mile above the ocean they met and Larpskendya, hardly even needing to open his bill, ripped the Manag from the sky.

Dragwena lurched with pain as her spell-creature was devoured.

'I'll kill you yet!' she roared, racing towards the Sarren, her face contorted by fear and rage. 'Even in defeat I'll destroy you!'

'Form a guard!' cried Trimak, and the Sarren rushed to put themselves between the children and the Witch.

Dragwena lunged past the Sarren, unscathed by their swords. She ripped Eric from Rachel's hands and ran to a low mound. Rachel fired wounding spells, but Dragwena fought through them, heaving herself and Eric across the snow.

Larpskendya swooped across the ocean. He flew with immense speed straight towards the Witch, but Dragwena already held Eric close – she knew there was time to snap his neck.

'See this!' Dragwena howled at the silver bird. 'You cannot save him! One more child I *will* kill!'

As she tightened her grip Eric uttered one word.

Dragwena twitched with pain. She dropped Eric, staggering backwards. Blood poured from her ear. 'What is this?' she rasped. 'An *unmaking* spell? No. I . . . will not be denied . . . by a child!' Dragwena fumbled to retrieve him, but Eric danced easily aside and went to the safety of Rachel's embrace.

The Witch could not follow. She lay writhing on the ground and then, clenching her fists and fighting to regain control, she shrieked as she started to transform: her blood-red skin peeled and she was a snake; and then it peeled again and she was a mollusc, and a raven, and a wolf, and a black monster writhing with serpents; and a hideous creature between whose splintered teeth spiders rushed to escape. The Witch merged into all the forms she had ever taken, faster and faster, until the transformations were so rapid that they blurred together and her screaming voice became unrecognizable.

But Dragwena was not finished. Somehow, through an overwhelming hatred, she managed to leap from the confusion, black claws outstretched.

Rachel howled, and with the sound of it Larpskendya swept from the sky. His head raked the ground, plucking the Witch from the earth.

Everyone watched as Dragwena, a speck inside the enormous beak, somehow held it open. She gasped, trembling with the effort, her teeth slashing, trying to string together all her knowledge into a single venomous spike of death. But Larpskendya had no fear of Dragwena's magic. Gradually his beak closed until the Witch's arms buckled and her knees were squeezed against her bursting chest. At last, Dragwena could no longer endure and her spine snapped. She unhinged her jaw and uttered a final despairing cry.

'Sisters!' she shrieked. '*Revenge me!*'

Even as Larpskendya's beak shut, killing the Witch, a tiny green light rose into the air where Dragwena's body had been. Unnoticed by anyone, the light flew directly into the sky. It pierced the outer atmosphere and shot into space. Once there it snaked towards a distant star, towards a watchful, Witch-filled world . . .

21

the choice

Everyone on Mawkmound gazed in awe as Larpskendya hovered above them, his great wings thrashing the air. Eric ran across the mound and jumped up to nuzzle the huge bird's wing. But it was to Rachel alone that Larpskendya turned his many-coloured eyes.

And, in that brief moment, the Wizard imparted many things: an apology for the suffering he had allowed; a choice they all must make; and happiness, enormous tear-joyful happiness for what was to come. Finally, Larpskendya bent close to Rachel, touching her face. An extraordinary feeling shuddered through her.

'A gift,' he said. 'A gift no human has ever been trusted with.'

Rachel trembled, understanding it, and trying to find the words to thank him. But immediately Larpskendya wrapped around the gift a task and a warning.

At last the Wizard turned his head and soared upward and away into the western sky.

'Goodbye, Larpskendya,' Rachel said, casting her eyes down because she could not bear to look so closely at his magnificence.

Silence descended on Mawkmound as everyone else watched him disappear slowly into the distance, his tail dappled by golden sunbeams.

And then two immense shadows blocked out all the sunlight.

'Watch out!' cried Trimak.

Even as the children and Sarren gazed after Larpskendya, the oceans of Ithrea had continued to sweep towards them. Suddenly, like a flood to end the world, the mighty waves came crashing down on Mawkmound. There was no time for anyone to protect themselves, nowhere to run or hide. But instead of crushing everyone the oceans halted at the edge of the mound, and cast something towards them more gently than falling snow.

Morpeth gasped as, of all things, a Neutrana guard slid from the waters and landed by his feet. The man got up, grinning widely. 'I'm . . . free!' he cried, rubbing his head. Bowing in several directions, he announced his name to one and all.

'Free?' laughed a Sarren. 'You're a bit late for the fight, that's certain!' He pulled the newcomer away from the water. 'Where did you come from, anyway?'

But before he could answer, another passenger of the waves was unceremoniously dumped onto the mound.

'Muranta!' gasped Trimak, helping his wife up. 'How did you come to be here?'

'How do I know?' she replied irritably. 'One moment I'm at home, worrying about *you*; the next I'm picked up by that – that great wave' – she jerked her arm back – 'and now I'm . . . wherever this freezing place is!' She brushed water from her dress.

But there was hardly time to dwell on this either, as an awkward Leifrim toppled from the waves. A surge deposited him by Fenagel's feet, and his daughter bent to kiss him.

'This isn't possible!' said Morpeth. 'They couldn't. It's—'

'It's true!' Rachel shouted, her eyes filled with tears of joy. 'Watch!'

And now everything happened at once. All manner of creatures, animal and human, tumbled from the waves so quickly that no one pair of eyes could take it all in. Sarren came, adults and children from all over Ithrea; and bumping alongside were Neutrana, crowds of them, their expressions filled with surprise. On wave after wave they arrived, from everywhere Sarren or Neutrana lived, the waters delivering them up to Mawkmound.

Wolves came in their multitudes, Scorpa at their head, their great grey flanks covered in brine. Prapsies spilt on the surf, flitting about and speaking their usual nonsense.

They came and came, and still it never ended. Hundreds of thousands surged from the waves, until Mawkmound became a seething mass of all creatures who had once bent their backs to the will of Dragwena. Ronnocoden arrived with his proud eagle companions, beating their sodden wings and singing their hearts out, after a silence of centuries. And extraordinary creatures came that nobody knew – creatures that had lived and bred under the snows of Ithrea, forgotten in the darkness for untold years. They wriggled and slid and crawled over each other, teeth flashing, covering their sensitive eyes from a sun they had never seen.

Eventually it was at an end, and the waters retreated a little way, giving everyone a chance to spread out.

And how they spread out!

The wolves bayed and leapt onto the new wet grass that sprang from nowhere at their feet. Children petted the wolves, and raced after them in circles trying to stroke their fur, but hardly able to catch up. So instead the eagles let them climb on their backs and made short flights over the land, teasing the prapsies as they passed.

And the Sarren and Neutrana, for some reason over which they had no control, began to dance and sing and whirl together. Their voices clamoured with the birds in the air, who did not stop singing for a second, until the noise of shouting and laughter and baying and twittering became so great that the earth shook with it and boomed its happiness back.

Morpeth moved alongside Rachel and Eric and wistfully said the words:

> *'Dark girl she will be,*
> *Enemies to set free,*
> *Sing in harmony,*
> *From sleep and dawn-bright sea,*
> *I will arise,*

Rachel looked lovingly into his eyes:

> *'And behold your childish glee.'*

And she was right, for even as the Sarren and eagles and wolves and other creatures leapt and skittered and danced they slowly transformed, until they became children and puppies and eagle-young. Prapsies shook off their baby-faces and returned to being crow-chicks, their red mouths crying out for their mothers. Morpeth changed into a sandy-haired boy with bright blue eyes, and Trimak grinned from his dimpled chubby cheeks.

'Well,' said Eric, shaking his head and looking at no one in particular. 'Flipping heck!'

'Exactly!' laughed Trimak.

'But what happens now?' asked Morpeth. 'We're all children again. What are we going to do?'

With these words, as if he had initiated a spell, which indeed he had, though he did not know it, all the creatures of Ithrea fell silent and turned towards Rachel.

She traced a shape in the air. A doorway appeared, which led to the back of a cellar with thick stone walls.

'What home will it be?' she said. 'Ithrea or Earth? Larpskendya has given each of you a choice.'

A choice? The creatures of Ithrea stared blankly at each other. They had known the servitude of the Witch for so long that they hardly knew how to react. And how to choose? For nearly all of the children Earth was just a dim memory. The animals had never known Earth at all. To them Ithrea *was* home.

Puppies sat on their tails and yelped in confusion. Chicks huddled, cheeping uncertainly; and the strangest creatures of Ithrea slurped in their own tongues, wondering what to do. At last all the animals turned for advice to the children, but the former Sarren and Neutrana were bewildered. As Rachel and Eric watched, thousands of boys and girls started urgently questioning each other, trying to recall their lives on Earth, the families and friends who once shared their days.

And slowly, painfully, *all* began to remember.

'Oh Rachel,' said Eric. 'Look. They're . . . crying.'

It began as a few stifled sobs, but soon whole groups were weeping uncontrollably. They limped across Mawkmound, or fell to their knees, each child in its own world of grief as the images and words and feelings came hauntingly back: of long-dead parents, brothers and sisters, and priceless friends they would never see or touch again.

A young Leifrim, with spiky jet black hair, screwed up his face.

'My mother,' he said. 'I remember the way she held me, but—' He gazed about shamefully, hoping someone might help. 'What was her name? I can't—'

Fenagel put her arms around her father. She had been born on Ithrea. All her life she had known only its dark snows. But many had no children to comfort them, for the Witch had only allowed a few close servants this honour. Within minutes all the children on Mawkmound were bent in private tears, or clutching what loved ones they could find, gripped by an overwhelming sense of loss.

'No,' pleaded Eric. 'Rachel, please stop them. Use a spell. It wasn't meant to end like this. Surely Larpskendya didn't mean it to end like this.'

'Wait,' she said, her own eyes filled with tears. 'Larpskendya told me this would happen. It's not just dead families they're grieving for, Eric. It's what the Witch did to them, all those centuries of suffering.' She smiled through her tears. 'What happens next will be amazing.'

The anguish of the children went on for a long time. It

went on for longer than it had taken Ithrea's oceans to deliver them all to Mawkmound. It went on for as long as the last child still had the strength left to cry. Finally, the weeping ended and Mawkmound fell silent. The silence was so deep that even the Prapsy chicks seemed to realize they should not babble. They furled their stubby wings over their beaks and waited.

And a gentle wind stirred on Mawkmound.

Trimak was the first to notice it touch his cheek. It dried his tears, spreading warmth.

'Look!' he cried, pointing everywhere.

Until this moment no one had bothered to wonder what might be happening beyond Mawkmound. Now they saw the ocean waters had retreated into the far distance, melting all the snow. Black soil, scarred and lifeless, covered the whole world. Ithrea was naked. Even the grass had been torn from the ground. Not a single thing grew or stirred. A child sighed and her voice echoed across the barren emptiness.

'No,' whispered Trimak. 'Is this what we waited for all those centuries? Even the snows were more comfort than this.'

Rachel laughed. 'Then wish for something else!'

'Flowers?' he muttered. 'That would be something at least.'

Instantly, plant buds started shooting between his feet. He jumped aside and they quickly filled his footprints.

'What colour flowers?' asked Rachel. 'And what shape? What smell should they have? And how many?'

'How should I know?' said Trimak, trying not to tread on them. 'What do I know about flowers?'

Rachel grinned. 'Are you giving up already?'

'Nice ones,' he said, feebly. 'Pretty ones. What were their names? Oh . . . I don't know!'

The buds continued to spread out, but they stayed tight shut – waiting.

'White roses!' said Fenagel. 'Purple daffodils. Green daisies. Red – oh!'

The buds were opening into all the flowers named. They continued to spread across Mawkmound and beyond.

'Stop!' yelled Morpeth, and the flowers stopped.

'Roses that sing!' cried Trimak, and immediately the white roses began a tuneless whine, their petals flapping back and forth. 'Don't sing like me!' he told them. 'Sing beautifully, you stupid things!' And so the roses changed their tune. The sound was not beautiful, but it did sound stupid.

'Magic doesn't know what beautiful means,' said Rachel. 'Tell it, *you* stupid thing!'

Trimak fell about laughing, but others took up the challenge.

'Like happiness!'

'Like cockatoos!'

'Like gurgling babies!'

The flowers started singing like all these things.

'How can this be happening?' said Morpeth. Nearby, a girl pressed her ear against a humming buttercup.

Rachel winked. 'Magic. Larpskendya's given you everything you need.'

'To do what?' he said.

'To do what you like!' said Rachel. 'Don't be shy, Morpeth. Imagine something!'

Morpeth was lost for words. He nervously created a tiny sun in his palm and blew it into the sky.

'Oh, think *bigger* than that,' said Rachel. 'Look at what the others are doing already!'

Morpeth lifted his eyes and, wherever he gazed, he saw children everywhere testing their imaginations, making up the rest of Ithrea. Forests with legs marched up the slopes of the Ragged Mountains. Fenagel ran across the mound, jewels following behind her like obedient pets. Children wrote their names in the sky. Melon-shaped mountains began glistening in the distance, spitting out pips like volcanoes. A large stone rolled across to one boy and offered him a selection of sweets. As for the flowers, the first creations of the new Ithrea, they were soon forgotten, but they didn't care. They just carried on singing loudly. That is, until Muranta told them to hush. After this they just whispered.

In the distance, Eric saw a fire-breathing dragon rise up from Lake Ker. Amongst the other bizarre forms appearing everywhere he would hardly have noticed, but this dragon was heading for the little eaglets.

'Hey, cut it out,' he warned the giggling prapsy chicks, but the eagles had already turned the dragon into a beak. This chased the startled prapsies until they sent it pecking back after the eagles.

Eric said to Rachel, 'Isn't this all getting a bit . . . dangerous?'

'They can't hurt each other,' she told him. 'Larpskendya wouldn't allow it. Let them play. It's so long since they did.' Some toasted marmalade hovered in front of her mouth. 'You do like marmalade, I hope,' the toast said.

Rachel turned to see Morpeth smiling at her.

The craze of pure imagination went on and on, until some part of Ithrea belonged to everyone. Eventually Trimak called a brief halt to the magic and mischief.

'I know what I want!' he thundered. 'To stay! Ithrea is my home now. I have made my choice.'

'Brilliant choice!' boomed a voice. It came from Hoy Point in the Ragged Mountains. The ancient mountain lifted a cap and waved it enthusiastically. Behind Trimak a boy chuckled. 'Sorry,' he said, slightly embarrassed. 'Couldn't resist it.'

After this, with Ithrea beckoning with all its absurd wild loveliness, it was not long before most of Ithrea's creatures had also made their choice. Some asked for more informa-tion about Earth, but when they found out there was no magic on that world they soon lost interest.

To Rachel and Eric's surprise a handful of creatures did decide to return with them. A few deep-dwelling worms wrapped themselves around Eric's legs, and wouldn't let go. Scorpa peeled herself from a group of puppies and licked Rachel's knees so violently that she kept falling over. A pair of prapsies, for no particular reason, or at least no reason anyone could understand, crept onto her feet and mumbled something about flitting amongst new skies.

'I thought they'd just be normal crow chicks now,' said Eric. 'How come they can talk?'

'Larpskendya wouldn't take that gift from them,' Rachel said. 'The puppies can talk too. They just prefer barking.'

'That's right,' Scorpa said to Eric. 'Don't try petting me. I hate all that stuff.'

'I wouldn't think of it,' replied Eric, who had just been about to do so.

Ronnocoden suddenly flapped onto Rachel's shoulder. He stared imperiously over the heads of the prapsy chicks, as if they were beneath his attention.

Late in the first morning of the new Ithrea a simple ceremony took place. The bodies of Grimwold and the other warriors killed by Dragwena had been taken by the retreating waves, but they were not forgotten. Trimak marked the spot they had fallen with a cluster of swords: one for each of the warriors. He thrust the blades into the rich soil, and angled the hilts inwards, towards each other.

As the afternoon drew on, Eric said, 'I don't think any of the Sarren are coming back home with us, Rachel. I don't blame them.'

But he was wrong. One child decided to return to Earth.

Rachel watched for hours as he hugged and cried, and laughed and wept again, saying his farewells – farewells to countless other Sarren and Neutrana he had known. So many people, Rachel thought. Five hundred years worth of people. How do you say goodbye, a *final* goodbye, to those you have loved and shared all life and death with for that long?

At last, when he had embraced Trimak for what seemed like an hour, a leaving almost without words, as if they were not necessary, Morpeth was ready.

His face was so messed with tears that Rachel could barely meet his gaze.

'Are you sure you want to go?' she asked. 'All your friends are here.'

'Not all my friends,' said Morpeth, earnestly. He touched the lids of her many-coloured eyes and gave her a sly glance. 'You didn't just imagine these. I saw what happened when Larpskendya touched you,' he said. 'You have the Wizard's look now. Did you think I wouldn't notice? Larpskendya's given you a present, hasn't he?'

'Shush,' she said. 'I can't say what it is. A gift – and a task to perform.'

Morpeth clapped his hands in delight, then turned to see what wonders he had missed being created on Ithrea during the last few seconds.

'This is unbelievable!' he roared.

'And ridiculous!' laughed Eric. 'What's *that* supposed to be?' He pointed at a fat pig floating in the sky. It lay comfortably on a cloud, wearing sunshades, sipping lemonade. Below, on the ground, a little girl frowned up in concentration, obviously wondering what to make up next. 'That's just totally stupid,' said Eric.

'Oh, I quite like it,' smiled Morpeth. 'But look over there. Now that *really* does look stupid.'

And they stood pointing and peering at everything: burbling streams filled with frogs and skipping dragons and galloping rainbow-coloured horses, and things none of them could recognize, all growing and fading in the yellow-gleamy sky. Fish armed with rods hauled imitation Witches out of Lake Ker, and the comfortable fat pig now had a friend – the little girl, clutching its curly tail, was flying around Mawkmound. Instantly several other children joined in, or flew off in other directions, racing into the distance. Within seconds they were in every corner of the world, changing it, pouring out their imaginations, conquering the ancient winter world of the Witch.

Eventually, the sun began to set and one boy created a new moon. As he lifted his arms it rose slowly over the land, a crafty smile on its face. He pointed at the sky and a new constellation of stars gleamed warmly down.

Morpeth tried to take the whole fantastic world in with one last wide-ranging look, but it was not possible. Too much was happening.

'It's got, well, everything,' said Eric.

'No, it hasn't,' Rachel corrected him. 'Something's missing. Something dark and cold.'

Morpeth blasted, 'That's right! No *snow!*'

They all laughed, realizing that Ithrea's dark snows were gone forever.

'We don't really have to go straightaway, do we?' Morpeth almost begged. 'There's so much to see, so much to do!'

'I'm sorry,' said Rachel. 'Larpskendya told me it would be dangerous to leave the gateway open for too long. We must leave now.'

'Why?'

'I can't say.'

'Is it anything to do with Witches?'

Rachel nodded tightly. 'Don't ask anything else. I can't tell you until we get back.'

'If I go,' said Morpeth, 'can I ever come back?'

'I'm not sure,' said Rachel solemnly. 'Larpskendya didn't tell me. We might never be able to return to Ithrea.'

Morpeth nodded glumly and looked back at Trimak. Most of the other children had started heading off in different directions, but Trimak had not moved. He stood dead still at the centre of Mawkmound, his arm around his wife, Muranta. Rachel knew he would not take his eyes off Morpeth until his old friend left.

Morpeth walked reluctantly towards the cellar doorway, still glancing over his shoulder to see what the next child might conjure up. A worm took the opportunity to slip from Eric's leg and wrap itself around Morpeth's shin.

'Quick, then,' Morpeth said, clenching Rachel's hand. 'Before the worm and I change our minds.'

Rachel took one step inside the doorway. One of her eyes was in darkness; the other saw Morpeth still hesitating in the gleaming world of Ithrea.

'Are you sure?' she said. 'Morpeth, are you *sure?*

'Yes,' he said. 'No. Yes – I mean – oh—' He shoved her inside the doorway.

Rachel blinked. Dust hung thickly in the air, making it difficult to see. Her dad sat on the floor, his head in his hands, an axe at his feet. He glanced slowly upward and when his gaze met hers he broke into tears of relief.

'I thought you—' he stumbled, trying to find the words. 'You were in the wall. I thought—'

Rachel hugged him. When she looked at him again, her many-coloured eyes shone brightly.

'You're different,' he said. 'You've *changed.*'

Rachel kissed him. 'Everything has changed.'

'Where's Eric?'

'He's coming,' Rachel said. 'In fact, he's not the only one coming.'

'Rachel, what do you mean?'

'I mean—'

But there was no holding them back. Scorpa padded, prapsies hopped, Ronnocoden flapped . . . and Morpeth and Eric, dragging the worms as best they could, walked through the doorway.

the scent of magic

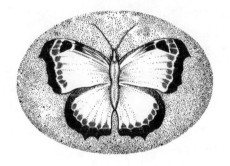

For Ciara, for everything

contents

1

eyes

'Rachel, wake up, get out of the dream!' Morpeth shook her gently, then more roughly when she did not move. 'Come on, wake up!'

'What?' Rachel's eyes half-opened.

Briefly Morpeth saw the remains of her nightmare. It dug into her cheek, as big as a dog: the gnarled black claw of a Witch. As Morpeth watched the thick green fingernails faded on Rachel's pale face.

'It's all right,' he said hastily, gripping her shoulders. 'Don't be afraid. You're safe, at home, in your room. There's no Witch.'

Rachel jerked awake and sat up, her breath coming in hurried gasps.

'Oh, Morpeth,' she murmured, '*never* wake me up like that. When I'm dreaming...I might...I could have hurt you.' She buried her face in a pillow, waiting until the cold jagged sensation of the fingernails had gone. 'You should know better,' she said at last. 'A spell might have slipped out.'

'Would you rather your mum faced those claws?' he answered. 'At least I can recognize them.'

Rachel nodded bleakly. 'But it's dangerous, even for you. Always let me wake up naturally, when I'm ready.'

Morpeth grunted, pointing at the sunlight filtering through the curtains. 'I waited as long as I could. Half the day's gone, and your mum was just about to get you up.' He picked a few strands of weed from her hair. 'Interesting smell these have.'

'Oh no,' groaned Rachel, noticing the staleness for the first time. 'I was in the pond again last night, wasn't I?'

'I'm afraid so.'

Rachel bit her lip. 'That's twice this week.'

'Three times.'

'I suppose I had the gills?'

'Yes, the usual scarlet ones, on your neck.'

'Ugh!' Rachel felt below her ears in disgust. 'How long was I under the water this time?'

'About an hour.'

'An *hour*!' Rachel shook her head grimly. 'Then it's getting worse. All right, I'm up.' She listened for a second. 'Will you check the corridor and bathroom are clear?'

Morpeth nipped out, returning moments later. 'Nobody about, and here's a couple of fresh towels. I'll stuff last night's sheets in the wash, shall I?'

Rachel smiled, taking the towels. 'Morpeth, you're my guardian angel.'

Slipping quietly into the bathroom, she used a long hot shower to remove the stink of the pond. Returning to her room, she sat beside the dressing-table mirror, half-heartedly brushing out her long straight dark hair.

Then she stopped. She put the brush down. She turned slowly to the mirror and examined her slim, lightly freckled face.

The eyes that gazed back were no longer quite human. Her old hazel-green eyes, matching her dad's, had gone. Replacing them were her new magical eyes. Spells clustered in the corners, behind the lids. They liked it there, where they could look out onto the world. Throughout the day they crowded forward, eager for her attention. Each spell had its own unique colour. Yesterday's spell-colours had started off scarlet and gold, surrounding her black pupil. This morning there was no pupil at all. There was only a deep wide blue in both eyes, the shade of a summer sky. Rachel had seen that colour many times recently. It was the colour of a flying spell, aching to be used.

Staring at her reflection in the mirror, Rachel said, 'No. I won't fly. I made a promise, I'm keeping it. I won't give in to you!'

'Give in to who?' asked a voice.

Rachel turned, startled. Her mum stood behind her, staring anxiously into the mirror.

'Mum, where did you come from?'

'I've been here awhile, just watching you. And *them*.' Mum studied Rachel's spell-drenched eyes. Their colour had now changed to a mournful grey. 'Those spells,' Mum said angrily. 'What are they expecting from you? Why won't they just leave you in peace for once?'

'It's all right, Mum,' Rachel mumbled vaguely. 'I'm … I'm still in charge of them.'

Mum wrapped her arms around Rachel's neck. Holding her tight, she said in the softest of voices, 'Then tell me why you're trembling? Do you think after twelve years I can't tell when my own daughter's hurting?'

A single tear rolled down Rachel's cheek. She tried to dash the wetness away.

'Let it out,' Mum said. 'You cry it out. Those terrible spells. How dare they do anything to harm you!'

For a few minutes Rachel leaned back into her mother's embrace. Finally she said, 'I'm all right, really I am. I'm fine. I am.'

Mum squeezed Rachel again and simply stood there, obviously reluctant to leave.

'You won't keep staring in that mirror?'

'No more staring today,' Rachel answered, forcing a smile. 'Promise.' As Mum walked slowly to the door, she said, 'You're missing Dad, aren't you?'

Mum halted at the door. 'Is it that obvious?'

'Only because I miss him too. I hate it when he's away.'

'His last foreign contract this year's nearly finished,' Mum told her. 'He'll be back in a month or so.'

'Thirty-eight days,' Rachel said.

Mum smiled conspiratorially. 'So we both count!' She turned to leave. 'Hurry down, will you? I've had just about enough of Eric and the prapsies today. I do love your brother, but he's nine going on six half the time, the things he teaches those child-birds.' She tramped back downstairs, muttering all the way.

Rachel finished dressing and made her way to the kitchen. As soon as she entered the prapsies covered their faces.

'Lock away your sparky eyes!' one shrieked, glimpsing her.

Oops, Rachel thought, quickly switching the glowing spell-colours off.

The other prapsy flapped irritably in front of her face. 'Eric could have been blinded!' it squeaked. 'His handsome face could have eye-holes burned in it!'

Rachel knew better than to react in any way. She put some bread on the grill and watched it brown, as if toasting bread fascinated her.

The prapsies hovered next to her nose, pulling faces. They were odd, mixed-up things, the joke creation of a Witch who had once used them as messengers. Bodily they were identical to crows, with the typical sleek, blue-black feathers. But instead of beaks they had noses; and instead of bird-faces, theirs were plump, dimpled and rosy-cheeked, with soft lips. Each prapsy had the head of a baby.

Mum swished by, waving the child-birds out of her way. They parted, then came back together, hovering perfectly over Rachel's head. One blew a raspberry; the other accidentally dribbled on her toast.

'How delightful,' Rachel said, throwing the slice in the bin. 'I wish I knew how they grew their baby-faces back again. I preferred it when they just squawked.'

Both prapsies showed her their toothless gums.

'Gaze at us, chimp face!' they cooed. 'We're so gorgeous. We're so beautiful! Ask Eric.'

Eric sat nearby at the kitchen table, casually turning the pages of a comic.

'You all right, sis?' he asked, glancing up. 'Enjoying the boys' company?'

'I'm fine,' she said dryly. 'But I'd prefer not to be within kissing distance. Do you think you might call the boys off long enough for me to butter my toast?'

'Sure thing.' He whistled.

Instantly both prapsies flew onto his shoulders. They perched there, scowling at Rachel.

'And shut them up for ten minutes,' Mum said in her deadliest voice. 'Or it's crow stew tonight.'

Eric pretended not to hear, but he did finger-zip his mouth. The prapsies sucked their lips in tight to prevent any more insults escaping.

Eric was a short stocky boy with a tough expression he often practised. His most striking feature was his hair – a blond mass of curls. Eric hated his hair. Mothers liked to touch the soft waviness of it. In a couple of years he was determined to get the locks hacked off. A skinhead. For now he had to be content with the prapsies messing it up as often as possible with their claws.

'I suppose the prapsies *slept* with you again last night?' Rachel said witheringly.

'Of course.' Eric grinned – and so did the prapsies – imitating him with eerie precision.

'I've watched them,' Rachel went on. 'They sit on your bed, with those big baby eyes. It's spooky. They copy everything you do. When you turn, they turn. They even imitate your snoring.'

'Ah, it's true,' Eric chuckled, 'They adore me.' He clicked his fingers. One prapsy immediately nudged the page of his comic over with its small upturned nose.

'Pathetic,' Rachel muttered. 'Three morons. Where's Morpeth?'

'I could tell you,' Eric replied. 'But what's in it for me?'

'He's in the garden,' Mum said, clipping Eric round the ear. She handed Rachel some freshly buttered toast. 'Eat a crust before you go out, won't you?'

After breakfast Rachel wandered into the back garden. It was a bakingly hot July day, with almost all of the summer holidays still left. Morpeth lay spread out by the pond. He was a thin boy, with startlingly blue eyes and thick sandy hair sticking out in all directions. An ice-cool drink lay within easy reach of his bronze arm.

Rachel smiled affectionately. 'I see you've settled in for the summer.'

'Thanks to Dragwena, I missed out on several hundred summers,' Morpeth said. 'I'm catching up as best I can.' He pulled a can of coke out of the pond and handed it to Rachel. 'I've been saving this. How are you feeling?'

'Pretty grim,' she said, easing into the garden hammock.

'You certainly smell better. I suppose you scrubbed with soap?'

'Yes, Morpeth, I did,' Rachel said, laughing. 'Why? Don't you?'

'Still can't stand the slimy feel,' he admitted. 'That funny sweet smell too, there's something wrong about it. Of course, we didn't have soap when I was a boy. Everyone smelt awful and no one cared a bit.'

Rachel couldn't quite get used to this new child-Morpeth. She had met him a year before on another world: Ithrea. Rachel shuddered even now to think of that desolate world of dark snow. A hated Witch, Dragwena, had ruled there. Morpeth had been her reluctant servant.

For centuries he had been forced to watch as Dragwena abducted children from our world. Rachel and Eric were the last to be kidnapped. When she arrived, Rachel discovered that all children possess magic they cannot use on Earth. That was why the Witch wanted them – to serve her own purposes. Morpeth had tutored Rachel, and she blossomed, discovering that she was more magically gifted than any child who had come before – the first strong enough to truly resist Dragwena. Eric, too, had a gift, and this time it was one no other child possessed. Uniquely, he could unmake spells. He could *destroy* them. In a final terrifying battle Rachel and Eric had fought the Witch's Doomspell and witnessed the death of Dragwena at the hands of the great Wizard, Larpskendya.

As Rachel gazed at Morpeth now, it was difficult for her to remember that for hundreds of years he had been a wrinkled old man kept alive only by the Witch's magic. Somehow he had defied the worst of Dragwena's influence, and when Rachel and Eric arrived he risked his life over and over for them. In gratitude, the Wizard Larpskendya gave Morpeth back all the lost years of childhood Dragwena had taken from him. He returned, as a boy, home – but not his own home. His original family were long dead, of course. So Rachel's parents had secretly adopted him – and here he was, a year later, a man-boy in a summer garden. A few other creatures had chosen to return from Ithrea with Rachel and Eric. Only the prapsies remained. The wolf-cub, Scorpa, Ronnocoden the eagle, and a few worms, had soon disappeared, deciding to make a new life amongst their own kind on Earth.

'What's wrong?' Rachel asked, noticing that Morpeth looked slightly uncomfortable.

'It's these shorts,' he pouted. 'Your mum forgets that I'm five-hundred-and-thirty-seven years old. I don't *like* stripy pants.'

'You couldn't wear your old leathers from Ithrea forever, Morpeth. You've outgrown them.'

'But they *felt* good,' he said. 'These shorts just look stupid. They don't fit properly, either. Your mum always assumes I'm the same size as Eric.'

'Are they too tight?'

'Too loose,' Morpeth said meaningfully.

'Mm. Dangerous.' Rachel smiled. 'Must tell Mum about that ... of course, you could go to the shops and buy your own.'

Morpeth gave her a grouchy shrug. Shopping meant setting foot out of the house and across the dreaded street. Traffic unnerved him. There had been no cars when he was a boy, or aeroplanes. The sheer *noisiness* of modern life made him constantly edgy, and he avoided roads whenever possible.

For a few minutes Rachel lay in the hammock next to the pond, simply enjoying the sunshine and the light breeze blowing over her legs.

'Morpeth,' she said at last, 'I was in bed for fifteen hours last night. I can't wake up. These things my spells are doing while I'm asleep... what's happening?'

'You know the answer to that,' he said bluntly.

Rachel shook her head. 'I know my spells want to be used,' she said. 'But they've behaved until now. What's changed? Why are they suddenly taking over like this?'

'They're defying you,' he answered. 'They're restless, impatient. Magic isn't something you can just tame like a pet, Rachel. Especially *your* magic.' He leant across and tapped her head. 'Your spells are far too intense, too ambitious, to leave you alone for long. And you stopped listening to their requests months ago, didn't you? You locked them out completely.'

'I had to,' Rachel protested. 'They were too tempting. Larpskendya made me promise not to use my spells—'

'I know,' Morpeth said. 'But your spells don't care about a promise made to a Wizard. They don't like being ignored. You won't listen while you're awake, so they come out to play at night – when they can take charge of your dreams.'

Rachel bent across to stir the surface of the pond. 'But why dump me under water?'

'Why not?' Morpeth said. 'Water must be an interesting place for bored spells to experiment. There's the challenge of how to enable you to breathe without lungs. And how to enable you to inhale water without damaging your body. Those things are difficult. They require many intricate spells, co-operating closely.'

Rachel thought of the gills. 'I can handle them,' she

insisted. 'Larpskendya warned me a party of Witches could detect my spells, even from space. That might lead the Witches to all children. I won't break my promise!'

'You already *have*,' snorted Morpeth. He stood up. 'You must take back control, Rachel. Give your spells something to do – room to breathe at least. And do it while you're awake, and you can restrain them.'

'Nothing terrible's happened yet ...'

Morpeth met her gaze. 'Are you going to wait until it does? I know you wouldn't strike out deliberately, Rachel, but what about your nightmares? What if your mum tried to wake you at the wrong time? This morning, for instance. Anything could have occurred. I saw the claw.' He stared earnestly at her. 'That's your worst nightmare, isn't it? And mine too: in my darkest dreams I'm facing Dragwena again. I'm hunted by a Witch.'

Rachel shivered. She tried never to think of Dragwena.

Bringing the drink of Coke to her lips, she noticed a wasp. It buzzed around the lid of the can, crawled under the tab and finally fell into the drink. Rachel sighed, absently tipping the wasp onto the grass.

'What spells just came into your head?' Morpeth asked sharply.

'Only the usual ones.'

'Such as?'

'Four spells: one to kill the wasp; a second to rescue it; a third to disinfect the can.' She watched the wasp, wings fizzing, stagger across the lawn, and smiled. 'And a warming spell to dry the insect's wings.'

'Which spell came first to mind?'

The killing spell, thought Rachel, and Morpeth read the answer in her face.

'I wouldn't have hurt the wasp,' she told him.

'I know,' said Morpeth. 'But it's interesting that the most dangerous spells offer themselves first. They always dominate the others.'

Rachel leaned over the pond and gazed at her reflection. Her eyes had turned a deep brown, like moistened sand. She looked for more vibrant colours, but her spells were unusually reticent – as if they did not want her spying on them. Why should that be?

For the first time in months Rachel turned her attention inward. What are you up to? she demanded. Several spells became silent, tucking themselves slyly away, not wishing her to recognize the mischief they planned.

They're waiting, Rachel realized – waiting until I fall asleep.

To Morpeth, she said, 'You'd better keep a close eye on me tonight.'

2

Ool

Heebra, mother of Dragwena, gazed out of the eye-shaped window of her tower.

Beneath her, in all its vast glory, lay Ool, home of the Witches. It was a freezing world. Dark grey snow plunged from the sky, filling the air, squeezing out virtually all light. Heebra had ruled for over two thousand years, and in all that time the snow had never ceased to fall. Valleys overflowed with it; animals quaked and bred under it; the tallest mountains of Ool had long ago been swallowed under its dismal bitter flakes.

Only the towers of the Witches rose above the snows.

As Heebra gazed out of the window her younger daughter, Calen, emerged from the shadows of the chamber.

'Will we watch the students fight?' Calen asked eagerly.

'So early? They were told to prepare for a night contest.'

'Let's surprise them, Mother. Make them fight now!'

Heebra smiled indulgently and signalled for the contestants to be made ready.

While she waited, Heebra surveyed the cold magnificence of Ool. The jutting towers of her Witches thronged the sky. Each tower was topped by an emerald eye-window, its height marking the status of the Witch who lived inside. There were millions of towers, but Heebra's outreached them all. It rose thick and black from the everlasting snows, decorated by the countless faces of the Witches she had defeated in battle. In Heebra's early rule many Witches had challenged her possession of the Great Tower. None dared any longer. A pity: it had been a long time since she had the pleasure of carving a new face into the stone.

Calen joined her by the window. 'Do you remember winning your first eye, Mother? A legendary battle!'

Heebra shrugged. 'It was nothing. A small tower. A lump of rock. Just a few hundred feet, and painfully thin.'

'Who cares about the size! You defeated twelve other students to win it.' Calen looked admiringly at her mother. 'No one had ever done that before. You were incredible, even then.'

Heebra studied Calen. It made her ache to see how much like her fabulous lost daughter Dragwena she had become. At less than four hundred years of age, Calen was a High Witch in her prime. Her skin was still blood-red, having lost none of its freshness. Her vision was also perfect, the tattooed eyes glowing under their bone-ridged brows. Even her sense of smell remained intact; sensitive nostrils, shaped like slashed tulip petals, could sniff out live meat hiding under the deepest snow. But perhaps Calen's best features were her jaws. All four were in spectacular condition. Despite numerous battles not one of the curved triangular black teeth had been lost or scratched. They glistened in her well-oiled silver gums, cleaned by armoured spiders that were supremely healthy, jumping alertly between the jaws in search of food scraps.

Heebra turned her attention to Nylo, Calen's soul-snake. He was restless, this one, like his mistress, a supple yellow body always on the move about her throat.

For all young Witches, Heebra knew their soul-snake was precious: as advisor, friend, shield and weapon – and a second set of watchful eyes. Most Witches needed their soul-snakes to be active throughout their lives. Heebra had long ago dispensed with Mak, her own snake. He was now golden and solid, hanging nearly lifeless against her breast. This, more than anything else, signified the magnitude of Heebra's power.

She drew her thoughts back to the eye-window.

'Well?' she asked. 'Do I know any of those in today's contest?'

'I doubt it,' said Calen. 'It's only a few students from the Advanced levels.'

Heebra smiled. 'Why do you always insist on observing such juvenile battles? Their spells are so uninteresting.'

'It's their passion I enjoy,' Calen answered. 'Don't you remember how thrilling it felt to win a blood-contest, mother?'

Heebra let her mind wander back. Once she had been

like today's students – aching for a chance to fight for her first eye. How she had relished that victory! Crushing her opponent, throwing out the dead Witch's servants, and living in *her* tower, still warm from her presence, with so many future contests and more elegant towers beckoning...

The three Advanced students were ready. Raising long bare arms, they flew to appointed starting positions in the sky, their sapphire battle dresses fluttering in the winds.

'Who do you think will win?' Calen asked, waiting for the contest to begin.

'It doesn't matter,' Heebra said. 'None are talented enough to get to the next level of magic.'

'How can you tell?'

As soon as Calen said this Heebra ripped Nylo from her neck. She stretched his jaw until it almost snapped. Calen waited fearfully, knowing that she had no spell powerful enough to threaten her mother.

With disdain, Heebra said, '*How can I tell?* I expect finer judgement than that from one who is to rule after me. You should be able to tell immediately! The mediocre quality of the students' flight alone shows that none will make a High Witch.'

Calen lowered her gaze. 'Of course. I should have recognized that.'

Heebra flung Nylo contemptuously across the chamber. Calen picked him up, though she didn't dare comfort him in front of her mother.

Together, in charged silence, they turned towards the battle.

Evening had settled in, so both switched to night-

232

vision. Slowly their tattooed eyes stretched across their cheekbones, meeting at the back of bald pitted skulls. Heebra and Calen could now follow the contest with ease. The students began, hiding in the dense storm-whirls of the upper atmosphere, launching their spells, breathlessly attacking and defending.

Heebra did not care. Annoyed with Calen, her mind turned as it so often did to her elder daughter, Dragwena. Where was she? Dragwena had ventured alone into the realms of remote space to conquer new worlds. For centuries Heebra had waited expectantly for her return. Later she sent out search parties, but they never found her. Standing here, watching the young students above struggling to survive in the charcoal grainy sky, Heebra's chest suddenly tightened. Was her superb, wild Dragwena still alive somewhere? Or did she lie dead on some hateful world, with no snow to anoint her grave?

'Do you want me to pause the contest?' Calen asked, sensing her mother's mood.

'No,' sighed Heebra. 'Let them finish.'

'It won't be long. All three students are starting to make mistakes.'

Heebra nodded, losing interest. What was the point of sharpening and practising their magic, she thought in sudden frustration, without any *Wizards* to fight? Her Witches had been slowly losing the endless war against the Wizards for millennia. In Heebra's own lifetime the Sisterhood had lost seven worlds they had previously conquered. Seven! Each time the Wizards retreated before her fleetest warriors could catch them. If only her Witches could find Orin Fen, the Wizard home world! But the location was unknown. Larpskendya, the Wizard leader, had moved the Wizards from their original planet, and obscured the way to their new one. Gradually, almost bloodlessly, he was winning the war – pushing her best Witches back, back, closer to Ool. The grip of the Witches had never been weaker.

'A defeat,' laughed Calen. 'At last!'

One of the students, her face flushed with excitement, drifted towards Heebra's tower. In her claws she carried the lifeless soul-snakes of the other students like trophies. But her moment of triumph was spoiled.

High in the sky a tiny green ball of light wandered through the clouds. Glowing intermittently, it staggered through the air as if in distress.

Heebra and Calen immediately forgot about the victorious student and flew from the eye-tower to meet the ball.

Calen gasped. 'It can't be!'

'It is!' marvelled Heebra.

All the Witches who had been following the student contest fell silent. None had ever seen this before: a dead Witch, her life-force returning. Only twice in the ancient history of Ool had such a long journey been made from space. What living Witch could have the strength to have travelled so far?

'Dragwena!' Heebra cried.

Her heart spasming with joy, she placed the green light lovingly on one of her tongues. Still breathing, Heebra realized. Still alive.

The injured life-force trembled inside, too frail to speak.

'Be well, my daughter,' Heebra comforted. 'You are home now.'

Inside the Great Tower Heebra unrolled her tongue carefully onto the hard floor.

At once the green ball started to stretch and grow at a fantastic rate. Dragwena's thighs bulged, forced their way out, the muscles soft, trying to harden.

'How she fights!' Calen marvelled. 'Look how she wants to live!'

Finally the transformation was finished – but Dragwena was incomplete.

'She has come too far to survive,' realized Heebra. 'She's too weak!'

The upper half of Dragwena's body was only half-formed. She had a single arm. The useless claw at the end of it flapped feebly in the air. Her eyes were covered in skin that would never open. Useless lungs lay collapsed inside her body. But her brain – the thing that had driven her all this way – was already fully developed. Dragwena could think. Somehow she heaved herself to a sitting position. She raised her malformed head, trying to draw breath. When Dragwena realized she could not do so she began to jerk pitifully.

Heebra ran across the chamber and supported Dragwena's head, while Calen fired renewal spells. But Dragwena was so weak that the spells merely injured her more.

She lay in her mother's arms, waiting to die.

'How could she be in this condition?' wailed Calen. 'She must have travelled further than any Witch before. Oh, sister!'

'Yes. There must be an extraordinary reason for her to have laboured so long.' Heebra gripped Dragwena's head and made a mind-connection. 'What happened?' she demanded. 'Who did this to you?'

Dragwena fought through her panic. She formed several images: Rachel, Eric, Larpskendya and the patterns of their magic. She formed a picture of the world of Ithrea and showed her mother the bitterness of her final moments there. The images shattered as Dragwena's oxygen-starved brain started to die.

'Not yet!' screamed Heebra. 'Not yet! Where is this world? Show us!'

Dragwena clutched her mother's soul-snake, her body shaking. A dim representation formed in Heebra's mind, marking the path between alien constellations – from Ool to Ithrea, and from Ithrea on to a larger blue planet with swirling clouds and filled with children – Earth.

Then Dragwena's four jaws flopped open. Heebra held her close, nearly crushing her daughter's body with love and anger. Dragwena's mind became dark, but she managed to flash a final image. It was a picture of the Dragwena of old, at the height of her powers, standing confidently next to her mother as they gazed down together over the vast skyline of the eye-towers. The wind swept through their shimmering black dresses, and their diamond and golden soul-snakes were playfully intertwined. They were invincible.

The image faded and Dragwena died.

Heebra sat entirely motionless for several minutes. She simply held her daughter. She said nothing. She barely breathed. When she did stand up Calen, almost blind with grief herself, stood well back in the chamber, knowing the power of the frenzy coming.

And how it came! Heebra burst out of the eye-tower window, carrying her rage. Streaking across Ool's black skies she headed everywhere and nowhere, out of control, lamenting through the blizzards. No other Witches dared fly that whole night, and for the first time in over a thousand years Mak stirred himself and held her in his scaly embrace.

Calen spent the night burying her dead sister's heart.

As tradition required she cupped it in one of her mouths, and used only her claws to dig down to the deepest ice under the snow. Here even the largest burrowing animals could never reach Dragwena's body. Then Calen flew back to the Great Tower, cultivating her anguish and hatred, and wondering what mood to expect from her mother.

Shortly after daybreak Heebra returned. Her face was now entirely calm, almost expressionless. She told Calen about everything Dragwena had shown her.

'Then we can find this Rachel and Eric and revenge her death!' exulted Calen. 'Let me go. The girl-child will be easy enough to find. Her reek was all over Dragwena's body.'

Heebra raked her claws thoughtfully against Mak. 'We will enjoy that pleasure soon enough. Dragwena travelled a remarkable distance to reach us. I doubt the desire for revenge alone carried her so far. I believe she wanted to tell us about this place called Earth. Only a Wizard has ever challenged a High Witch in personal combat, yet this Rachel child-creature found a way through Dragwena's defences. Think of that! We must find out more about these intriguing children.'

'If they are talented Larpskendya will protect them well.'

'No doubt.' Heebra laughed. 'Larpskendya will protect them anyway, even if they are useless. Feeble creatures always attract his sympathy.'

'Do you think Dragwena left Ithrea unnoticed?'

'She must have done. Larpskendya would never endanger its children by permitting Dragwena to escape.'

'In that case,' said Calen, 'the Wizards will not be expecting us.'

'They will,' mused Heebra. 'Larpskendya plans for everything.' She rolled a spider meditatively on her tongue. 'However, Ithrea is the closer world. Larpskendya would expect us to arrive there first. To surprise him we will bypass Ithrea, leave it in peace for now.'

'Even so, he is bound to leave some defences on Earth itself,' Calen said.

'True. How can we draw him away from there?' Heebra's eyes shone. 'What would terrify Larpskendya most?'

Calen stared blankly.

'The Griddas,' said Heebra.

At the mention of this name Nylo contracted, becoming a tight shivering curl around Calen's neck. Gridda Witches were considered almost demonic, even by the fiercest of Ool's other Witches. They were the largest and most savage of all the Sisterhood, their orange faces and hulking brown bodies unmistakable. Bred in small numbers, they were locked underground, only ever intended to be used as a last line of defence if Ool itself was besieged – or to lead the attack on Orin Fen, if the High Witches ever discovered the Wizard home world.

Calen stroked Nylo soothingly. 'We can't release the Griddas,' she protested. 'They're unpredictable. Even a few ... will create havoc.'

'Exactly,' said Heebra. 'That is the point. We will spread them wide, let them bring fear to as many worlds as they can quickly reach.'

'Mother, once their rage begins, the Griddas will be impossible to control. They may kill thousands.'

'I don't care how many they kill,' said Heebra. 'None of the other worlds have creatures like this Rachel. The point is that Larpskendya *will* care. He will be forced to use most of the Wizards to stop the Griddas. That will leave Earth vulnerable.' She stared at Nylo, then faced her daughter. 'What route should we take to Rachel's world? If you ruled, what would you advise?'

Calen looked uncertain. 'We should take our time,' she suggested. 'Move stealthily, avoiding our usual meeting places and rest sanctuaries in space. A scouting group would be best – just five or six Witches, difficult to detect. And when we arrive on this Earth world I would advise that we not kill Rachel and Eric immediately. They are too obviously targets for our revenge. Larpskendya may be watching them closely. We should start by observing the other children. Let's see what they have to offer. We can deal with Rachel and Eric, and the third, Morpeth, when we are ready.'

Heebra smiled. 'Good. Who should lead the scout group?'

Calen hesitated.

'One more surprise for Larpskendya,' said Heebra. '*I* will lead it. He will never expect that. I'll lead the way to Earth myself. Go. Instruct the Sisterhood of our plans.'

Heebra knew the journey would be a long one. She selected only the most durable and fiercely loyal High Witches to accompany her. Within days the preparations to leave were complete, and the chosen Witches, fed and ready, gathered together in the howling winds and lightning of a huge storm-whirl that touched the edge of space. Impatiently they awaited the signal to depart.

First Heebra launched the Gridda Witches. She sent them out in all directions simultaneously. Led by their pack-leader, Gultrathaca, the Griddas moved out in hunting teams, shrieking joyfully, their heavily muscled bodies coiled with power.

When they had gone Heebra gestured for the scouting party to move out into the darkness of space. Seeing her best Witches together like this reminded Heebra of the glorious wars of the past. Feeling young, she led from the front and, as the group moved in a graceful line away from Ool, Heebra considered what she had learned about the child, Rachel.

From Dragwena she knew the pattern of Rachel's magic. When they arrived on Earth the girl would be easy to find. And on the journey there would be endless time to decide the most fitting way to kill her.

3

MAGIC
WITHOUT RULES

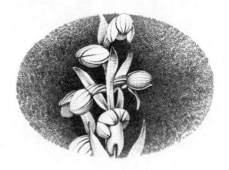

Morpeth lay fully clothed on his bed, alert and waiting. Even so he almost missed the faint sound. It was the rustle of hair moving against a ceiling.

He opened his door a crack and peered out.

Rachel floated in the corridor. The top of her scalp seemed to be anchored to the ceiling. Beneath it her body, wrapped in a pale yellow nightdress, swayed in a leisurely way. It was if her bones had become so weightless that the slightest motion of air could tilt and bend them. Her arms and legs drifted with the same relaxed rocking rhythm, like the motion of seaweed under waves.

Morpeth stepped into the corridor, careful to make no

sudden noises. Rachel's eyes were shut, but the skin of the lids jerked violently from side to side: a dream. Peering more closely, he saw her hair lift and move. Strands of it had bunched together and were rising from her head, feeling their way towards the corridor light bulb in the same slow purposeful way as sea anemones.

Then, apparently losing interest in the bulb, her hair dragged Rachel haltingly along the corridor. Occasionally she lingered long enough for a tuft to explore the complex whorls on the ceiling.

When she passed Eric's room, Morpeth tapped with the edges of his nails, not expecting an answer – but the door sprang wide at once. Eric stood there in his pyjamas, his hands covering the mouths of the prapsies. They fidgeted in his grasp, necks craned wildly, trying to get a good look at Rachel.

'Were you awake?' Morpeth whispered.

'Nope, until these two started bouncing off the walls.' Eric blinked, adjusting to the pre-dawn light. 'What's up?'

'Keep quiet and follow me,' said Morpeth. 'And leave the boys here.'

'Oh, Morpeth—'

'No. Come alone.'

Reluctantly Eric tucked the prapsies back under the quilt of his bed, resting their heads together on a pillow. Their eyes followed him mournfully.

'Please, Eric,' one pleaded. 'Let us come. We are so quiet. Watch.' It opened and closed its mouth silently.

The other prapsy giggled. 'You look like a guppy fish!'

'Shut up. Eric was believing me!'

'Sorry, boys,' Eric said, petting their neck feathers. 'Next time, maybe.'

He drew the bedroom door rapidly shut. Moments later the prapsies pressed their lips to the crack at the bottom. They began a low whine, like abandoned puppies.

Eric caught up with Morpeth at the bottom of the staircase.

'Blimey,' he said, spotting Rachel. 'What a sight! Is her hair alive or something? And where's she going?' He half-laughed as she passed the bathroom. 'The loo?'

'Shush. You'll see,' said Morpeth. 'Keep a close eye on her. I might need your help if things go wrong.'

Rachel entered the kitchen, making her way to the patio doors leading to the garden.

'It's locked,' said Eric. 'She'll never get out there.'

'She's more resourceful than you realize,' said Morpeth.

Eric heard a subtle click as the patio locks were disengaged without the use of a key.

'Impressive,' he said.

'Not really,' Morpeth answered. 'Locks are designed to be unlocked. For Rachel, this level of magic isn't even a challenge.'

The doors of the patio snapped forcefully open and Rachel glided into the garden. Her eyes remained closed as she came to a standing rest in the middle of the lawn. Then, twisting her head, she sniffed the late night air – and a sudden, distinctive aroma of many flowers struck Eric. The smell was rich and impossibly, overwhelmingly, strong.

'What's she doing?' Eric gasped.

Morpeth laughed. 'I don't know. There are no rules here, or only ones her spells make up. What happens next depends on whose turn it is.'

'You're joking,' said Eric. 'The spells take turns?'

'You'll see.'

Rachel, her eyes still shut tight, began to fly in rapid circles around the garden. With outstretched arms her hands touched everything: grass, leaves, the grain of the wooden fence, the silkiness of petals, the hardness of rose-thorns. She stopped, knelt, tasting the moisture on the grass and the damp acrid soil beneath. She sighed as she pressed her cheek against the toughest flints in the rock garden. She caught a moth and stroked it, deep and long across its fragile wings.

'I've seen this from her before,' said Morpeth, 'Her spells apparently enjoy the contrasts. Sharp and smooth, sour and sweet. She gets a pleasure from them I can't understand.'

'I wouldn't want to be that moth,' said Eric.

'She won't hurt it,' Morpeth assured him. 'If the moth struggles Rachel can somehow hold the delicate wings without damaging them.'

Rachel opened her hand, and the uninjured moth flapped confusedly away. She half-chased it, flapping her ears in imitation, but the insect was clearly too dull to interest her spells for long. She forgot it. She lifted her chin and raised her arms, soaring gracefully moonwards. Within seconds she was just a dwindling point of yellow nightdress against its scarred white disc.

'Flipping heck!' said Eric. 'Are you telling me she's still asleep?'

'Not just asleep,' Morpeth told him. 'It's much deeper than that – a slumber, compelled by her spells. Rachel herself has no control over any of this.'

'It sounds dangerous,' Eric said, staring up with concern. 'Should we wake her? I could destroy the spells keeping her asleep.'

Morpeth looked surprised. 'Can you actually trace the spells doing that?'

Eric nodded. 'Yeah. All spells have their own special smell. I learned that on Ithrea. The ones she's using a lot tonight, like the flying spells, are easy to recognize after a while. Rarer spells are trickier, but I can usually work them out eventually.' He licked his finger and grinned. 'Of course, once I destroy a spell that person can't use it again, so I have to be careful.' He squinted at Rachel's tiny speck body. 'I can't reach her from here, though. She's too far away.'

A dot of gleaming yellow casually sank from the sky. As Rachel alighted on the lawn her nightdress rose and settled smoothly over her knees.

'What next?' Eric wondered.

'Who knows,' said Morpeth, looking worried. 'It's always something unexpected, but her spells are especially lively tonight.'

Rachel altered her shape. It occurred instantly, not gradually. At first Eric thought she had vanished; then he noticed whiskers in the grass, quivering on a petite black nose: a field mouse.

'She's shape-changed!' marvelled Eric. 'I saw that on Ithrea, but I've never seen her do it here. Isn't it risky?'

'Rachel's spells wouldn't do anything to harm her,' said Morpeth. 'However, the cat might need to be careful.'

'The cat?'

Sophie, the family tabby, had uncurled herself from a comfy doze somewhere in the house. Drawn by a sudden tasty scent of rodent, she crouched low in the grass and deftly stalked her victim. When she was close enough to pounce, she waited for the mouse to run. It merely twitched its whiskers – and Sophie almost leapt out of the garden.

A *hundred* mice had appeared on the lawn, all squeaking Sophie's name.

As she sprang away the mice vanished with a giggle. Sophie, her fur on end, remained perfectly still for a while. Finally she returned languidly to the kitchen, settled herself on the floor and began primly cleaning her claws as if nothing had taken place.

'This is brilliant,' Eric said. 'Didn't realize Rach had a sense of humour. What next? A giant prapsy?'

Rachel had reverted to normal. She hovered for a few minutes above the ground. While her bare toes tickled the dewy grass, her head became unnaturally still, cocked slightly to one side – as if listening to the stars.

Then she disappeared altogether.

'She's *shifted*!' said Eric. 'Wow! One place to another.' Behind him, there was a rustle. He turned, expecting it to be Rachel. 'Oh no,' he muttered. 'We're for it now.'

Mum walked purposefully across the garden in her slippers and dressing gown.

'Well?' she asked, staring at Morpeth.

'Mostly the usual pattern,' he answered. 'But the mouse

trick is new, and Rachel's rarely gone so far from the house before. Her flying spells are really active.'

Mum nodded grimly. 'Two days ago just whizzing around the block seemed to keep them happy. Not any more, obviously. I've been viewing her from the window. Never seen such crazy stunts. I don't know how fast she's flying. I couldn't follow her.'

Eric gaped. 'You've been watching her, Mum?'

'Of course,' she replied matter-of-factly. 'Ever since this all started. Do you think either of you could leave the house without me noticing? I worked out the meaning of that pond smell long before Morpeth. Since then we've been taking it in turns to keep an eye on her.' She buttoned up Eric's pyjama top. 'It's chilly out here. Imagine how cold Rachel must be up – ' she flung her arms – 'wherever she is out there.'

'She won't feel it,' said Morpeth. 'Her spells will keep her warm.'

'She's back,' said Eric, 'with a weird thing in her hair.'

An exotic, long-stemmed plant, nestled in Rachel's fringe. In the lightening sky they could just make out its unusual green and red-brown flowers.

Mum's gaze narrowed. 'That's an orchid. I recognize it ... a Frog Orchid, it's called. They don't grow in this country. Spain, I think. Surely Rachel can't have gone that far?'

'If she shifted she could have gone anywhere,' Morpeth said.

Rachel plucked the orchid from her hair and longingly tasted its dainty petals.

Mum's voice became suddenly exasperated. 'I hate what that Wizard did to her,' she said. 'What kind of gift is it that allows Rachel to keep her magic, but not use it? Those spells of hers – playing games, fighting for control, using her. How can they be a gift? They're nothing but a curse, a worry for us all.'

'Docile little spells wouldn't be much use against Witches,' Morpeth told her. 'Larpskendya knew Rachel would need all her magic if she ever faced them.' He followed Rachel's tongue as it became a skinny tube that delicately probed the heart of the orchid flower. Her face was blissful. 'But I wonder if Larpskendya predicted Rachel's spells would behave quite like this,' Morpeth said earnestly. 'They're so suddenly, desperately alive, after being so quiet. Has there been a change? Something Larpskendya didn't anticipate?'

'Is there *anything* she can't do?' Mum asked Morpeth.

'I don't understand her limits,' he admitted. 'Neither does Rachel. On Ithrea she only had a few days to learn, and because of her promise to Larpskendya she hasn't experimented with her magic at all since she came back.' He watched wistfully as Rachel breathed on a clenched rosebud. It opened up its petals to her mouth as if she had offered a gift of sunlight. 'She's without doubt the most naturally gifted child I ever met,' Morpeth continued. 'On Ithrea Rachel learned to perform spells others took centuries to discover or never achieved. She did them without being taught, instinctively altering shape or shifting effortlessly between locations, or commanding the weather. No child had ever done such things; only the Witch, Dragwena.'

'You were pretty impressive yourself on Ithrea,' Eric pointed out,

'Not really,' Morpeth said. 'I could heal basic injuries. With difficulty I could change the shape of some materials, send signals. Of course, even that simple level of magic is beyond a lot of children.'

'Don't you miss it?' Eric asked hesitantly. 'I mean, you must hate Larpskendya for taking away your magic.'

'No, Eric, you're wrong,' Morpeth replied. 'I *asked* Larpskendya to remove it.'

'What?' Eric gasped. 'Why?'

'We daren't attract the attention of the Witches. I've used magic for so long that a spell is bound to slip out accidentally at some point. So I asked Larpskendya to take it from me shortly after returning to Earth – and he did.'

'I never knew that,' Mum said softly. 'You never told us.'

'It wasn't as big a sacrifice as you think,' Morpeth said, smiling crookedly. 'I'm an old man. Unlike Rachel's, my magic these last years was mostly content to snooze.'

That's not true, Mum realized, studying his face. You just didn't want Rachel worrying about you; that's why you didn't tell us.

Rachel sat cross-legged near the pond, her eyes still closed. As they watched, her cheeks swelled with cold morning air. When she exhaled the air in the garden immediately became tropical, and they breathed in the diverse, humid scents of a rainforest.

Then, without warning, Rachel dived into the pond.

'Shield your eyes!' Morpeth cried.

Eric half-heartedly lifted an arm. 'What's wrong? I don't—'

'Do it!'

Mum just had time to cover his face with a hand before extremely bright light flooded the garden. It was not the light of dawn. It came from Rachel. At last she had opened her night eyes. In sunshine the spell-colours varied, but in darkness they glittered one dazzling colour only – clear silver. For a moment opals of light swept across Mum, Eric and Morpeth, illuminating their clothes. Then Rachel settled back in the pond and set her gaze on the sky. Clouds, thousands of feet in the air, were lit up, pierced by the miniature searchbeams. The pond enlarged slightly to welcome her. She lay in the deepest part, and red gills appeared on her neck.

'That's new,' said Morpeth, peering cautiously between his fingers.

A third gill had materialized, this time on her throat.

Rachel lay in the pond, her mouth open under the water. As the others anxiously watched, her magic-skilful eyes scanned the skies for sights they could never have detected. Within minutes, their blazing silver light had attracted legions of moths and flies from the surrounding gardens and beyond.

Eventually Rachel emerged serenely from the pond. She floated back to her room, never once showing any recognition of her family. Eric was sent back to bed. For a while there were shrieks of excitement from his room as he told the prapsies what had happened. Downstairs there were only soft murmurings, as Morpeth sat with Mum and together they discussed what should be done.

Later that morning Morpeth had to shake Rachel repeatedly to wake her. Her eyes, when they finally opened, were bleary grey, like a summary of winter.

'I'm so tired,' she said, gazing in the mirror. Rubbing her face, she sensed the contentment of her spells. Most of them hung back from her eyes, seemingly satisfied, not pestering her to play.

'Last night's games took a heavy toll,' Morpeth said, explaining what had occurred.

Listening to the events, Rachel muttered angrily, 'You'd think my own spells hate me, the things they do…'

Morpeth gripped her shoulders. 'It's not that. They're just so fierce. There's a wildness about your magic I only ever saw in Dragwena. It yearns to be used.'

Rachel glanced uneasily at the saturated sheets. 'Mum can't have missed this. She knows, doesn't she?'

'Yes, your mum knows everything.'

'Oh, that's just *great*.'

'No, it's good news,' Morpeth said firmly. 'We need everyone's strength now.'

Rachel showered, dressed and made her way downstairs to a strangely silent kitchen. Even the prapsies were quiet. 'What's the matter with them?' she asked Eric suspiciously, pouring out a bowl of cereal. 'Are they sick or something?'

Eric raised his eyebrows. 'No. The boys have new respect for you, Rach. They saw you flying through the bedroom curtains. No more insults for a couple of days. They insist!'

The prapsies beamed at Rachel, flapping their wings and winking knowingly.

When they had finished breakfast and were all in the living room, Rachel said, 'I noticed something strange last night. It scared me, and I'm not sure what it means.' She sat on the edge of the couch, close to Mum. 'My information spells picked it up. You know the way they automatically record everything going on around me, whether I'm interested or not. It's usually just pointless junk, who's in the house, what's their heart-rate, the time the sun came up, pointless stuff like that. Last night, though, they went out a long way and picked up signs of magic. It wasn't mine. The magic belonged to other children. Thousands of them.'

The prapsies stopped prancing on the radiator.

'I thought Larpskendya wouldn't allow that,' said Eric. 'Didn't he say it was too dangerous to let the magic of children loose?'

'Yes, he did. He never normally interferes in the natural way magic wants to develop, but Earth is different. Larpskendya told me it's a special case, because of Dragwena. She was here for centuries before the Wizards discovered us, breeding her own kind of magic in children. Due to her, Larpskendya says, there's a streak of Witch in us all.'

'Ugh!' said Eric.

Rachel nodded. 'Larpskendya wanted to keep watch over us, not releasing our magic until he was sure it was safe.' She glanced at Morpeth. 'Larpskendya's not close,' she said, with certainty. 'He can't be; otherwise he would have warned us about something this important.'

'I agree,' said Morpeth. 'Try sending him a message.'

Rachel transmitted a distress call in all directions in the way Larpskendya had shown her.

'No answer,' she said, after a few minutes.

'What does that mean?' Eric asked. 'Larpskendya's not ... hurt is he?'

'Don't be stupid,' Rachel snapped, the idea unbearable. 'It just means ... he's not close, that's all.' She lodged the calling spell in her mind, ensuring that it would be sent accurately and far into deepest space whether she was awake or asleep. 'Larpskendya said he couldn't always be here,' she reminded Eric. 'We're not the only world he has to look out for.' But what, she wondered, could have been so urgent that Larpskendya didn't have time to warn us he was leaving?

'Well,' said Morpeth, 'for the time being we have to decide what to do ourselves. Tell me, Rachel, are any of the children your spells detected actively using their magic yet?'

'I don't think so,' she replied. 'But in the most gifted it's almost bursting to get out.'

'How far did you search?'

'Halfway across the world. It's the same pattern everywhere. And there was something really odd, Morpeth. A trace over Africa. So far away, but I've never felt anything that sharp.'

'What now, then?' Eric asked.

'We prepare ourselves as best we can,' said Morpeth, matter-of-factly. 'If levels of magic are so high, anything could be about to happen.' He turned to Rachel. 'This recent flowering of magic might explain why your spells have become so headstrong lately. I saw something similar occasionally on Ithrea: the magic of certain extremely gifted children reaching out, wanting to be together. Maybe that's why your spells have been so busy recently. They sense friends out there, almost ready to welcome. Spells enjoy companionship, too.' He held her gaze. 'We should start with a vigorous daily practice routine for your magic. That should satisfy those lively spells of yours. It might even put an end to their night-time adventures.'

Rachel nodded fervently – and the moment she did so, the moment she accepted that she must open herself fully to the entire richness of her magic – a wealth of fresh colours burst into her eyes. The colours came from dozens of spells new to her. These were small spells, minor spells, useful for particular occasions. They had quiet, almost shy, voices that rarely challenged the dominance of the major spells like the flyers and shifters. Now that she had at last noticed them, Rachel invited the spells forward. Respectfully, she asked each to identify itself for the first time, and they – in their mild, reserved way – tiptoed into her mind.

'Are you sure you know what you're doing, Rachel?' Mum asked anxiously, seeing the new soft pastel shades.

'No,' Rachel answered. 'I'm not sure about anything. But Morpeth's right: I've let some of my spells do what they want for too long.' She smiled. 'Safety first. We don't want any prying eyes, do we?'

She placed a blanketing spell around the house to prevent any magic seeping out.

Then she stared into the garden. She looked at the pond whose dank water she had swallowed over so many nights. She looked at the garden fence, shredded in places where her cheeks had rubbed against the surface. And she thought about Nigeria, in Africa, and the abundance of magic her information spells had sensed there.

'It's time to get my body back,' she said to Mum. 'No more dips in the pond. And from now on, if I fly some-place it's because I choose to go there. We'll start practising right now.'

4

the camberwell beauty

Dawn, and sleepy African birds were waking, as Fola trudged along the path from Fiditi to the river.

With one hand she reached over her head, expertly re-balancing the heavy weight of the washing basket. With the other she adjusted her *oja*. It made little difference: Yemi, her baby brother, was an awkward lump on her back no matter how she carried him – he would not stop moving and kicking!

'Be quiet! Stay still!' she said irritably. The tiniest things excited him: a bird doing nothing in a tree, a dog moping on the path, even the small plumes of dust thrown up by her feet.

Only a baby could enjoy such a tedious walk, Fola thought.

Absently she gazed ahead. In front, clear and boisterous, the Odooba river sliced through the forest. Fola knew from school how it cut a path between villages in southern Nigeria on its way down to the sea, but such details didn't interest her. She had seen its waters so often that she hardly noticed them. Reaching the bank she gratefully unloaded Yemi and the washing and stretched her aching neck muscles.

It was early, and still cool, but she was already tired. She had woken before dawn to prepare the yams and black-eye beans for the evening meal. There was still work to finish when she got back, and Yemi to mind all day. Fola did not complain. With Baba hunting in the rainforest, she was happy to help out. It was easier than Mama's day in the fields – long hours of hard work.

A few other girls from the village had already arrived at the river. Fola greeted them warmly as she wet the soda soap and doused the clothes.

While she worked Yemi sat in a sort of comfortable heap by her feet. He sifted dust. He blinked at midges circling his close-cropped hair. He saw a brown-black Asa hawk. It waved its big wings and he waved back.

Fola made sure that he was not too close to the river's edge, and engaged in the usual gossip with the other girls. A short while later she heard a sharp intake of breath. She turned to find Yemi sitting abnormally still.

'What is it?' she said. 'What incredible wonder have you discovered this time?'

It was a fly, and it had landed on Yemi's bare forearm.

He stared in awe, mouth wide, as the fly crawled towards his elbow.

Then, without even a friendly wave, the fly flew off.

Yemi started to cry. He covered his face and tears streamed out.

'Oh, don't be silly,' said Fola. She put down the skirt she was wringing out and picked him up. 'It's only a fly. You can't *make* them stay, you know!'

When Yemi continued to snuffle she rummaged for his special book. It was a pop-up book filled with pictures of butterflies. Yemi forgot the fly at once, stopped crying and reached out eagerly. Fola sat with him for a few minutes, helping him turn the pages. He stopped her, as always, at the page containing his favourite butterfly.

It was a Mourning Cloak, otherwise called a Camberwell Beauty. According to the book they came in many colours. The illustration showed a lovely bright yellow variety, with small patches of light brown dusting its wings.

'Want,' Yemi told her.

'Do you?' Fola said, amused.

He kissed the image of the Camberwell Beauty ardently.

'We don't have that kind in Africa,' she informed him. 'It comes from far away. We will never see one here.'

Yemi's face crumpled with sadness. He looked so unhappy that Fola spent longer than she should have done reading with him. When she returned to the washing Yemi flipped the pages back to his Camberwell Beauty. He studied it and frowned.

Fola took over an hour to complete the washing, beating the sheets and laying them out in the rising sun. When the last of the linen was nearly dry, she searched around for Yemi. He sat close by, still reading his book.

And he had a new companion – a yellow butterfly.

It was perched on Yemi's forearm precisely where the fly had been.

Fola blinked. There was no doubt it was a Camberwell Beauty.

Yemi grinned from ear to ear. He blew on his arm and the butterfly started fanning him. He wriggled his nose and it hopped on the tip. Then, slowly, like a ballerina, it rotated on spindly black legs until it faced Fola – and bowed.

She dropped the washing.

Sitting heavily down she noticed other flapping movements all around. Many more Camberwell Beauties were alighting from the northern sky onto the grass and soil surrounding Yemi. As Fola watched they all fluttered onto his right shoulder. Clambering on top of one another, they formed a neat pyramid. Yemi leafed through his picture book. Streaking light from the early sun reflected from the pages, making them difficult to read. Yemi squinted, then laughed. He glanced at his butterflies.

Instantly all their delicate wings opened, casting the pages in yellow shadow.

5

fish without
armour

Heebra's Witches were famished when they reached Earth. The journey had taken far longer than she had expected. Exhausted, their hungry soul-snakes shrivelled against their breasts, the scouting party only endured the final stretch because she drove them.

Yet here, at last, was the great prize: Rachel's home planet.

Despite their craving for food, Heebra held the Witches back – she needed to be certain there were no Wizards. Cautiously she circled the planet with two scouts. Larpskendya's unmistakable stink was everywhere – but his scent was old, and there were no other Wizards present.

Excellent. It meant the Gridda warriors were distracting well in far-flung places.

Shrieking with anticipation the Witches plunged towards the sunlit half of the world. A few defence satellites swivelled, registering their presence. Heebra easily damped the primitive electronic messages and, undetected, the Witches swept into the thermosphere. For a moment its hot layer held them up; then they adjusted their body shapes so that the searing heat merely sloughed off the useless dead layers of space-skin. Joyfully they emerged into the upper atmosphere, shuddering with rapture as coldness splashed across their new raw flesh.

'Feast! Feast!' Heebra ordered her starving Witches.

They dived through the swirling blue and white cloud. Into the deeps of the Pacific Ocean they sank, feeding on skipjack tuna and the great white sharks that hunt them.

However, this ocean was too warm for the Witches' liking, so they moved north. Swimming amongst the ice-floes of the Arctic they gorged on vast schools of herring.

'No weapons,' Calen marvelled, studying the fish. 'Unlike those on Ool, they simply gather in dumb shoals, apparently waiting to be eaten. Where is their armour and poison? I hope we find something more interesting to test us soon.'

But the largest creatures they could find were killer whales. These fled when the Witches tried to stimulate a fight. Heebra hastily drew the Witches towards land before they became too bored. She made base close to the North Pole. Here polar bear and oily seal flesh was rich and plentiful and concealment required only the simplest of spells. The temperature was too mild, but the occasional blizzards blew fresh and clear: a reminder of home. Within hours the Witches were already clawing at the frozen rock below the snows, energetically building the bases of new eye-towers.

Once they were settled, Heebra dispatched her five scouts. Across the globe the Witches probed, disguised in many forms, mastering the simple structure of the languages – and studying children everywhere. All the scout reports fascinated Heebra.

Calen was the last to return. Several hours after the others arrived Heebra saw her black dress rippling in the distance. Calen flew in typically flamboyant manner, bald head cutting through the wind, scudding low across the snow. She pressed her arms sleekly to the sides of her body, using only the tips of her claws to change direction.

'Well?' Heebra asked impatiently, as she alighted.

Calen transformed her face into a young boy she had recently met, indicating the tiny milk teeth.

'These children have nothing to scare us!'

'Obviously,' said Heebra. 'The other Witches are full of contempt. How do you judge them?'

'Where do I start? They're so weak. Frail liquid eyes, with no night vision or x-ray. They bleed at the slightest cut.' Calen laughed. 'Their skin *tears* – can you believe that! And soft internal organs, unshielded. That makes them vulnerable. They are also prone to endless disease and infections. And slow, Mother. Slow to react, think, move or sense danger. Nothing recommends them.' She tapped her skull. 'Above their brains is a fibrous hair-scalp growth. It ignites at the least touch – a ridiculous evolution!'

'Did you expect something more impressive?' Heebra asked.

'Didn't you?'

Heebra raked Mak's scales. 'Open your eyes. Their bodies may be flimsy, but this species are natural killers. Wars between them are happening everywhere on this planet. We have rarely known such a promising race. I see signs of Dragwena's healthy influence everywhere.'

'It's such a pity we can't use the adults,' sighed Calen. 'The magic they have as children decays early.'

'What do you think of their technology?'

'It's no danger to us,' scoffed Calen. 'A poor substitute for magic. They can't even detect our presence.'

'Agreed. We must concentrate on the children. Assess their magic.'

'Larpskendya is clearly interfering, holding them back,' said Calen. 'His influence has led to some peculiar features, such as child schooling. Instead of being free to practise their spells, the young ones sit behind desks, obeying the adults. How wasteful!'

'Larpskendya never usually influences the development path of magic on any world,' mused Heebra. 'Tell me why this planet is different.' She glared threateningly at Nylo who, remembering the last time Heebra had held him, hid his blunt head inside Calen's dress.

'These children have little discipline,' Calen replied warily. 'The youngest behave instinctively, seizing what they can – remarkably like our own kind. Larpskendya must fear that if he unleashes their magic the children could start along a destructive path.'

'Starting with the removal of the inferior adults,' agreed Heebra. 'Followed by a battle amongst the children themselves as the best learn to dominate.'

Calen smiled. 'How Larpskendya would hate that! It would be good to watch.'

'Can the children be used against the Wizards themselves?'

'Yes, they *will* fight for us,' Calen answered confidently. 'Their magic is brimming, and the simplest of spells is required to free it. We can train them as we would our own student-witches.' She laughed. 'We'll soon have them despising the adults. Larpskendya has the children so mixed up. Can you believe that when they injure an opponent they often feel guilt?'

'No matter how well we train them, no child could ever defeat a Wizard,' said Heebra.

'True, but these children like to be together, Mother. We could form them into large packs, give them a purpose. They would enjoy that. A hundred, perhaps, could distract a Wizard for long enough for us to finish him off. And there are so many of the little things. We could waste millions and not run out!'

'I wonder,' Heebra said thoughtfully. 'I have studied these children myself. They are contrary, often stubborn, and less predictable than you think. A few will resist us strongly; others will be difficult to master. The Rachel child is evidence enough. Dragwena obviously tried to train her, but somehow the girl held out. Remarkable: to resist a High Witch. No creature except a Wizard has ever done that.'

Calen shrugged. 'Rachel is probably unique. A single, extraordinary child.'

'Possibly,' said Heebra. 'I doubt it. On such a large world there may be many extraordinary children. And magic on this world is raw. Who knows how it will evolve?'

Calen said defiantly, 'In all our history of conquering, this is the first time we have discovered a species like these. What have we left to fight the Wizards? Larpskendya drives us back in humiliation closer to Ool every year. Is that what you want, Mother? An undignified death defending your own eye-tower from Larpskendya? Is his name to be whispered in awe amongst us forever?'

'*I* will decide what should be done,' growled Heebra.

Raising her muscular bare arms she glided into a bank of high clouds. For a while Heebra simply drifted amidst the polar winds, finding their touch pleasantly cool. A nest of spiders crept to the front of her jaws to feel the frost, and look out at the recently completed eye-towers of the Witches. The familiar sight elated the spiders, and Heebra licked them indulgently.

'Here are my instructions,' she said, flying back to Calen. 'Focus your training on the youngest. They are the most easily persuaded. Ignore all except the most gifted children or the most ruthless. Where you can set children against adults – parents, teachers, any others who regulate behaviour – do so. The most important thing is to work fast. Discover leaders, Calen. We can't train all the children ourselves. Find me those who will push and punish their own kind.'

Calen's tattoos sparkled with excitement. She started to leave, then turned back. 'You mention nothing of Rachel, or Eric. Surely you want revenge?'

'I haven't forgotten them,' said Heebra. 'Briefly I sought Rachel out myself. She was not difficult to find. Despite her efforts to hide her gifts, the quality of her magic blazes like a beacon on this small world.'

'What do you make of her?' Calen asked with interest.

'A startling member of her species. I can see why Larpskendya is so interested in her. And she has an unusual gift we can use.'

'A gift?'

'She has a direct connection with Larpskendya himself.'

Calen gasped, knowing how long the Witches had sought such a way to lead them to Larpskendya. 'Can we use this to locate him directly?' she asked.

'No, Larpskendya obscures the path back to him. But if we use the link carefully we might be able to use it to draw him to *us*.'

'Is Rachel calling for Larpskendya now?' asked Calen. 'We would not want him to arrive before we are prepared.'

'She calls him, of course she does!' laughed Heebra. 'Bewildered, confused Rachel – she is frantically sending out her signal. However, Larpskendya hears nothing. I've placed about her a damping spell the girl will never find.'

'When will you release it?'

'When we have trained enough children. When we are settled and I have decided how to set a trap for

Larpskendya. Until then he will get no warnings from Rachel. He will come when we are ready for *him*.'

Calen nodded. 'When the time is right do you intend to kill Rachel yourself?'

'She is hardly worth my attention,' answered Heebra. 'I have been thinking about a more interesting way to deal with her.' She poked a claw at Calen. 'You set much faith in the youngsters on this world, so I set you this task: find me another child capable of challenging Rachel. Find and train an executioner from her own species. Rachel's death will be so much more satisfying that way.'

'I may have already found such a child,' said Calen brightly. 'She is unusual in every way. I'll show her to you soon. A surprise!'

While Calen left to give the other Witches their orders, Heebra drifted for a few minutes longer in the polar winds, opening up her jaws. The spiders within rolled around, delighting in the direct touch of snowflakes.

Heebra dropped to the ground. A nearby polar bear raised its muzzle from the snow, wandered across and licked her feet. Heebra rolled with it playfully, tumbling over and over, careful not to injure the bear's thin hide with her claws.

Well, she thought; well now, Larpskendya. This world is your worst nightmare, isn't it? How these children must fill you with dread. I see why you have enslaved their magic, kept this world such a carefully guarded secret. You are afraid, aren't you? You are afraid because more than any other species these children are like *us*!

6

the hairy fly

Mum scooped porridge oats into Eric's breakfast bowl.

'More, please,' he said.

She crammed on one more dollop. 'Enough?'

'A bit more.'

Somehow she balanced two more spoonfuls on top of the porridge mountain.

'Surely that's enough …'

'Just a *little* bit more.'

Morpeth lounged nearby. 'It's already spilling over the plate,' he muttered. 'How are you going to eat all that?'

Eric picked up his spoon. 'I'm growing. I *need* this food, unlike some with the appetite' – he pulled a face at Rachel, sitting opposite – 'of an ant.'

'You want it for the prapsies,' Rachel said matter-of-factly. 'I've seen them slurping from your dish.' She laughed and sucked in her lips. 'They get it all over their faces.'

Mum sighed deeply. 'Eric, is that true?'

'Er...'

'No, don't tell me,' Mum said. 'I'd rather not know...' She picked up her handbag and a light coat. 'I'm popping out for about an hour – the mobile's on if you need me.' She stared at Eric. 'There had better not be any porridge in unusual places in my kitchen when I get back. Understood?' Eric nodded and she left the house.

A few minutes later Rachel noticed a commotion by the kitchen window.

'What's bothering the boys?' she asked.

Both prapsies were jabbering wildly, flying in tight spirals, too excited to speak. When everyone rushed over one finally found its voice.

'A big shaggy marvel!' it cried, peering through the lace curtains.

'A flying yowler!' the other said.

'Rubbish! A hairy fly!'

Eric blinked at the sun. 'Blimey.'

High in the pure blue sky, flying over the rooftops, a black shape turned smooth circles. 'Looks like a dog,' Eric said. 'That's ridiculous. It must be a kite.'

'No strings,' Morpeth said. 'And it's barking!'

'A Labrador,' whispered Rachel.

Eric nudged her. 'What's going on? Are *you* doing this?'

'Of course not.'

'Then who is?'

The Labrador was suspended in mid-air over the centre of a playing field. It lay on its back, big paws paddling the sky. Then it yelped, spun around, and shot straight upwards. Some boys, kicking a football around the field, didn't know whether to watch or run.

'Flipping heck,' Eric said. 'It's controlled by a spell. Magic, Rachel!'

She nodded, trembling slightly, trying to pinpoint the source, and calling to mind the defensive spells she had practised over the past couple of weeks.

The prapsies panted in Eric's ears.

'I could destroy the spell if you want,' he said.

'No,' Rachel answered. 'The dog's too high up. We'd injure it.'

'Why not use your own magic, Rach?'

'Not yet,' warned Morpeth. 'Don't reveal yourself until we understand what we're up against. Let's get to the field.'

They raced out of the house. The prapsies squeezed past Eric's shoulder before he could shut the door.

'Hey, come back, boys!' he called. 'You're not allowed out!'

The prapsies flew jubilantly over the houses and soon caught the dog. Chatting excitedly, they copied its stormy movements across the sky.

'Hey, come back!' one prapsy wailed into the Labrador's ear.

'Naughty dog!' the other cried. 'Quiet down, you shaggy wonder!'

Rachel led the way up the steeply rising streets towards

the field. As they approached, the dog's body started making new patterns in the air – long rhythmical shapes – a mixture of loops and straight lines.

Eric struggled to keep up with Rachel's long strides. 'It's flipping possessed!'

'No,' said Morpeth, tracing the dog's movements. 'It's a name.'

'What's a name?'

They arrived at the bottom of the field.

'That is.' Morpeth pointed at the sky. 'PAUL. Can't you see? The dog's writing the same name over and over again.'

They hurried to the top of the field, until they were directly under the frantic Labrador. The soccer boys had scarpered, leaving their ball behind.

'We're close enough,' Rachel said. 'Bring it down, Eric.'

Eric pointed his finger at the Labrador, putting an end to the flying spell, and the dog dropped from the sky. Just before it reached the ground Rachel spread a cushioning spell on the grass. The dog landed safely on all fours and fled down the hill, barking at the top of its voice. The prapsies pursued it gleefully, offering useless advice.

'Paul,' mused Eric. 'That doesn't sound like a dog's name.'

'No,' said Rachel. 'I think it belongs to *him*.'

She pointed to the bottom of the field. There, half-hidden in the thick grass, lay a plump spiky-haired boy about the same age as Eric. Propped on his elbows he was concentrating furiously on the dog, flicking his fingers, as if trying to send the Labrador back into the air.

Eric grinned. 'He can't do it. He doesn't understand that after I destroy a spell he can never get it to work again.'

'Stay back,' Morpeth said. 'Let him make the next move.'

Eric squinted. 'What's he doing now? He's looking at that ball.'

The leather football rose a few inches in the air, then slid low across the grass. It moved much faster than it could ever have been kicked.

'It's heading for us,' Morpeth remarked.

'Actually,' Rachel said, 'it's heading for me.'

The ball gathered pace, rising to the level of her head, a swift blur.

Eric jabbed his finger, destroying the spell, but the ball's momentum was so great that it continued to aim straight at Rachel. She made it swerve harmlessly around her shoulders.

'He did that deliberately,' Eric fumed. 'Let's get him!'

Rachel shook her head. 'No. Let's see what he does next.'

The spiky-haired boy frowned. The next moment Rachel felt a new spell, this time working on her.

'I can't believe it,' she said. 'He's trying to shove my face in the dirt.'

'Let me squash the spell,' Eric growled. Rachel gestured no, trying to understand something about the boy's magic.

'He seems inexperienced,' Morpeth said to her. 'Do you sense any real authority or subtlety about his spells?'

'No,' she replied, watching the boy anxiously repeat the same spell again. 'Just raw ability, freshly awakened – and powerful.'

'But why is he trying to hurt you, or that dog?' Eric asked.

Rachel was uncertain. Had this boy really tried to harm her and the Labrador? Or was he merely testing his own magic, and hers, curious about what they could both do?

They tentatively stepped towards Paul. When Morpeth was close enough to see his face, he noticed how frightened the boy looked. He gasped and juddered, his body jerking first towards Rachel, then away. Finally he sprinted off down the path.

'Come on,' Eric said. 'He can't escape that way. Hey, Rach, you could fly after him.'

'No,' she said. 'I don't want to show him what I can do yet.'

They followed the path to the bottom of the hill, where it curved sharply into a large flat meadow. The meadow was empty.

'Where is he?' gasped Eric. 'There's nowhere to hide. How could he have run away that fast?'

'He didn't outrun us,' said Morpeth. 'He must have waited until he got out of sight, then found a *different* way out of the meadow. Could he have flown?'

'No,' said Rachel, her face pale. 'It's not that. Someone or *something* else whisked Paul away. I felt a brief trace of magic, unlike the boy's. It was incredibly strong.' She sent information spells out for over a mile. All signs of Paul had gone. 'I can't detect anything. The trail ends here.' She dropped to her knees, where a single shoeprint of flattened grass marked the last place Paul had stood. Already the grass was springing back into place, as if he had never existed.

'Do you think Paul could have performed this vanishing act himself?' she asked Morpeth.

'I doubt it,' he said thoughtfully. 'Not so perfectly. It takes great skill to seal off tracks made by recent spells – and that boy was flustered. He must have had help – and from someone much more experienced.'

As they walked back home, Eric snarled, 'Whatever's going on I don't like this Paul. You saw what he did. Deliberately scaring that dog, and enjoying it.'

Morpeth rubbed his chin. 'Was he enjoying it? That's not what I noticed. I saw a boy at odds, either with himself or an invisible companion. Something was scaring him.'

As they arrived at the front gate the prapsies landed on Eric's shoulders. They noisily spat out dog hairs.

Rachel winced. 'They didn't bite the Labrador, did they?'

'Nah.' Eric pulled a face. 'Probably got that way trying to kiss it.'

He tucked the prapsies into his shirt before anyone on the street could see their flushed happy faces.

Morpeth guided them into the living room, relieved that Mum had not yet returned. For a few minutes they scanned the doors and windows, half expecting a rage-filled Paul to smash his way through.

'I thought you told us no kids could use their magic yet,' Eric said to Rachel. 'What's going on?'

Rachel trembled slightly, turning to Morpeth. 'Do you understand this?'

He shrugged. 'Something must have sparked off Paul's magic. Almost anything could have triggered it. An emotion, perhaps – anger or fear.' He thought of Ithrea: a favourite tactic of Dragwena, he remembered, was to panic children into releasing their spells.

'Do you think Paul's the only kid out there using magic?' Eric asked.

'Possibly. I doubt it,' Morpeth said. 'Or not for long. Whatever's caused this, we should assume that Paul is just the beginning. Hundreds of children may soon be spell-making.' He glanced at Rachel. 'Larpskendya never intended or wanted this, I'm sure. It confirms that he can't be close.'

We *are* on our own, Rachel realized. She fought against that idea, and noticed her spells withdrawing deep within her.

'I don't much fancy the idea of kids with magic,' Eric muttered. 'Imagine a bully who could use a blinding spell!'

'If enough children can use magic, we might have to prepare for worse than that,' Morpeth said gravely. 'On Ithrea, I saw all kinds of children arrive over the centuries. The strongest-minded resisted Dragwena's influence for a while, but some' – he paused – 'well, let's say some didn't try hard. They willingly directed their magic against other children. A few didn't even need Dragwena's encouragement. They enjoyed it.'

Rachel shuddered. 'Think of the damage a Witch could do here now.' At the mention of the word *Witch* Eric drew a sharp breath. 'It's what we've been thinking, isn't it?' she said bluntly. 'Whatever swiped that boy Paul away could have been a Witch. Let's stop pretending it hasn't crossed our minds. There was definitely something powerful with him.'

'Dragwena is dead,' said Morpeth. He came across and held her gaze. 'She can't harm you any more. And I see no evidence yet that there are other Witches here.'

Rachel nodded bleakly, wanting desperately to believe that.

'We need more information,' Morpeth said. 'Rachel, could you attune your information spells to find only those children actually *using* their magic?'

'Yes,' she said. 'I suppose that would tell us how many there are, and where. But we need to find out *how* they're using their magic as well. Are there other dog-tormentors like Paul out there? I want to get closer to them.'

'Good idea,' said Eric. 'And me and the boys'll come with you.' He shot the prapsies a special look. 'Extra protection.'

'No, I'm going to have to travel long distances,' Rachel told him. 'It's too difficult for me to do that with you hanging on.' She stared at Morpeth, seeing that he was about to object. 'I'll go on my own,' she insisted. 'It's safer that way.'

'Is it?' he asked, noticing her eyes glowing an almost painfully pure blue. 'Or is that the advice your flying spells are whispering?' Rachel hesitated, questioning herself. 'We need to be careful,' Morpeth said. 'Something attracted Paul here. What else could it be except your magic, Rachel? He probably knows where you live; and, willingly or not, he did attack you.' Morpeth glanced out of the window. 'Perhaps he's waiting for a second chance, when Eric and I aren't close enough to protect you.'

Rachel sighed heavily. 'I can't leave Mum here alone with *him* out there,' she said. 'I need you both to stay with her. Please, Morpeth. At any sign of danger I'll turn back. I promise.'

Morpeth wondered what to do. Was the boy Paul lurking patiently somewhere out there, preparing a better attack? And who was his invisible companion? A Witch, wanting Rachel dead? However, they did need to know more about this sudden use of magic – and sheer speed, unencumbered speed, was probably Rachel's best defence against an unknown opponent. Finally, he assented.

Eric shook his head. 'What do we say to Mum? She'll freak out.'

'Leave that to me,' Morpeth told him, knowing Mum would never accept his decision to let Rachel leave the house.

Rachel quickly kissed Eric, hugged Morpeth and squeezed past him. Unbolting the front door she hurried into the garden, trying not to think too much about what might be waiting for her. Outside the sky was clear and sunny.

A Witch could see me for miles, Rachel thought.

Feeling like a target standing in the porch, she quickly considered what shape to assume. Shape-changing was one of her special magical gifts. She had discovered it on Ithrea, improved it in her battles with Dragwena, and practised it repeatedly over the last couple of weeks. She didn't want to make a mistake now. What form to choose?

What would be the least conspicuous object in this wide-open sky?

A few swallows above swooped for insects. Carefully, making sure no one else was watching, Rachel transformed herself into one. Unfurling her sleek feathers, she flitted into the suddenly menacing skies.

7

the Blue-sky
Rainbow

Rachel soared into the warm summer morning air. For a moment she saw Morpeth, Eric and the prapsies glancing up through the lounge window. Then their anxious faces vanished as she used her tough swallow wings to beat a path upwards.

As familiar houses and streets dwindled the spiky-haired image of Paul swam back into her mind.

Practise your magic, she told herself, trying to shrug off the fear.

Tucking in miniature claws, Rachel deliberately threw her feathered body about the skies. Despite recent practice at home some parts of her spell-making, especially her flying spells, were still rusty. Come on, she thought, inviting her magic forward: surprise me!

Countless manoeuvring spells eagerly offered themselves. They promised wonders. Rachel selected two, tracing a wonderfully extended arc across the sky – a trick no swallow had ever attempted.

She felt nervous about remaining one shape for too long. How fast can I change if I really push hard? she wondered. She plucked out another bird-shape at random: a kestrel.

Lengthening her wings, Rachel hovered in the air, the terror of mice!

Something else, she thought. Don't stop to think.

In mid-flight, mid-flex-of-wing, she made herself alter again and again. A dove. A quick-darting hummingbird. A glorious swan, beating its ponderous wings. Rachel flew across the sky and up, up into its broad reaches, testing herself, transforming into every bird she knew.

And then a different spell suggested a *bat*.

Instantly her bird eyes shrivelled. Rachel sent out sonar clicks, and from a wrinkled, scrunched-up head she witnessed a place more beautiful than anything she had ever seen with her own or bird eyes. It was a fabulous new world, a bat world, without colour, but where each blade of grass, every tuck of air, had an exquisiteness of texture she had no words to describe.

You don't need these primitive wings to fly, her spells said. Just point your feet!

Giddy with excitement, Rachel transformed back into a girl and simply kicked her shoes through the air.

The turbulent wake of a supersonic jet caught her eye.

Catch it! Rachel commanded. A shifting spell willingly obeyed. The air lurched, flinging Rachel forward. There was no sensation of flight. Within a heartbeat, less than that, she stood on the nose-cone, peering in the cockpit. The pilot blinked in disbelief at the girl smiling at him through the window.

Rachel allowed the jet to fly on and focused on a remote cumulus cloud. How far away? she asked her information spells. 0.73 miles, they answered smoothly. Take me there! A shift took control, drawing her to the cloud – and then she shifted onto another cloud, and another, pushing herself to ever greater distances: a mile; five miles; ten; fifty. How about *eighty*!

Rachel chucked herself recklessly about the sky.

Eventually she stopped, skidding to a halt. Remember what you came out here for, she told herself angrily. Mum and the others are unsafe at home. Start searching for signs of magic …

How could she find the most gifted children? Magic has a distinctive smell, her spells reminded her – hunt out its scent. Her own nose was hopeless. Rachel allowed the spells to take charge. They grew her nostrils until each split into a soft, fleshy flap, like fragile petals that wavered in the breeze.

She sniffed – and immediately noticed the faint aromas of children's magic.

Some of the smells were sharp and pungent, others musky, fragrant, ripe or a mixture of these things, and all the traces were weak. To find those like Paul actively using magic she needed to search a wider area and shift faster.

Rachel made herself relax, permitting the magic to flood through her veins. The feeling thrilled: it was nervy and wild, like breathing immaculately clean air after a lifetime of mustiness. She had felt flashes of the same exhilaration when she fought Dragwena on Ithrea, but fear had spoiled any pleasure she might have enjoyed then. Now she turned confidently into the wind. Closing her eyes, she forgot about clouds. She sniffed for the tiniest vestiges of magic – and launched herself at them.

In great leaps she shifted, leaving home far behind. Cities blurred past. Seas surged up to meet her and receded like dreams of seas. Her body hugged a coastline, and she touched the wet rocks where a child had recently tried his first spell. But he had gone, and Rachel shifted again. Following a striking scent she entered a different country where the air was hot and the smells new.

Her shift had carried her to southern France.

Feeling exposed, she hid as a fly, settling on the needle-leaf of an Aleppo pine tree. She was in the mountains of Provence. At this time of the year, early summer, the air was already dry and hazy. Heat shimmered from the burning Gorges de la Nesque cut into the high mountains. And barely visible amongst the elegant pines on the steep slopes Rachel found a boy. He might have been four years old, probably less.

In a flawlessly blue sky he had created a *rainbow*.

It towered above the mountains, violet and red and yellow stripes dripping like paint onto the land below. '*Plus grand, plus haut!*' he shouted, laughing at the sun.

Rachel translated as best she could with her shaky

French – 'Bigger! Higher!' – and felt elated. There's no danger here, she thought – just a boy learning to use his newly awakened magic. Changing back into a girl she approached him with outstretched arms.

'Don't be scared,' she said, as he pulled back in surprise. '*Je suis Rachel. Qui es tu?*'

The boy stared intensely at her, then cursed when he realized he had forgotten about his rainbow. He squinted up to see all the colours vanish. Stamping his feet and scowling, he ran off down the mountains, his sandals slapping the hard soil.

Rachel considered following him – but a stronger scent had already attracted her attention. She hurriedly shifted again. This time, disguised as a wasp, she came down in Dortmund, Germany.

Where a girl, so young that she still required a bulky nappy, climbed an apple tree in a garden.

The child's mother stood nearby, too shocked to move. From the tree top the baby held out her arms, calling: '*Bär! Bär!*' At first Rachel thought the little girl must want her mother – then she saw the teddy bear lying in the grass. As Rachel watched, the bear's stitched button-eyes blinked. It sprang up. On felt pads it skipped across the lawn and clambered up the tree trunk, flinging its furry arms around the girl.

Both baby and bear turned together to gaze at the mother.

Rachel shook her head, trying to make sense of it. Perhaps this wasn't so strange. If young children experimented wouldn't they start with their toys? There's nothing actually sinister taking place here, she decided. Just a child at play.

While Rachel wondered how to console the distraught mother, a new scent hit her. It was different from the others. This smell was deeply rich and vast, as if a great shoal of gifted children had come together to make it. For the first time Rachel felt truly frightened. Could this be the magic of a *single* child?

Investigate, some of her spells advised. Flee, ordered the rest.

Rachel made herself shift towards the scent. She moved swiftly, back across France, skirting Spain, travelling southwards, until she reached a new continent: Africa.

The searing heat of the Sahara Desert blazed under her. She shifted at tremendous speed over the sand dunes, and became suddenly aware that her own gifts alone could never shift her at this pace. Something else had registered her presence. It knew she was out there, and drew her to it, a colossal, restless force heaving her into its own domain.

When she reached her destination Rachel felt herself almost yanked from the sky.

She staggered, a dazed girl, too shocked for a moment to think of concealing herself.

She stood in a Nigerian village, beside a round hut. The hut was made from mud bricks mixed with straw, and in the shade of one of its walls a baby boy sat on the baked soil. He was covered in beautiful yellow butterflies. Dozens of them rested contentedly on his fingers, his bare feet, his hair. They settled like jewels on his earlobes and his eyelids. The sight of so many insects should have been grotesque, but Rachel instinctively realized they were commanded by the baby. This little boy was the source of all the astounding magic that had drawn her here.

As soon as he saw Rachel the baby smiled. It was a simple, genuinely child-like smile of welcome.

'Yemi,' he said, pointing proudly at himself. 'Yemi.'

Rachel cried out with happiness as an astonishing feeling surged through her. It came from Yemi. He could only speak a few words, yet his spells already knew a full greeting. The magic welled freely out of him, so instinctive and yearning, so grateful to find it was not alone in the world.

Without thinking about it Rachel ran across, swept Yemi up in her arms and threw him into the air.

Momentarily he hung above her head, not falling. Kicking his bare feet, he struggled to keep himself aloft. When he did fall it was the helpless way any other baby would fall. Rachel caught and held him close, whispering her name into his butterfly-thronged ears. He blew the Camberwell Beauties onto her. They fanned out, adorning her hair with their yellow loveliness.

Then a gasp from the hut made Rachel turn.

Yemi chuckled. 'Fola,' he announced.

Rachel saw a girl half-inside the hut, clinging to the door frame. Her hair was braided and daubed with flour, and she glanced fixedly at Rachel, seemingly in awe.

'Hello,' Rachel said, withdrawing the spell-colours from her eyes to avoid frightening her. 'I'm sorry if I startled you. Did you see me arrive just now?'

The girl had trouble understanding Rachel's language.

THE BLUE-SKY RAINBOW

Finally, she nodded. 'Who are you?' she asked in heavily accented English. 'What you want with us?' She spoke mildly, and with great curiosity, glancing at Rachel's clothes and skin and hair.

Another voice, much harsher, coming from inside the house, shouted something – and Fola's collar was tugged. She resisted, clearly wanting to linger with Rachel.

'Is that your mum in there?' Rachel asked. 'Is she scared? She mustn't be. I won't harm Yemi. Please, if—'

The house voice rumbled menacingly.

'You make Mama afraid,' Fola said. 'Yes, the two of you. Have you come take Yemi away?'

'Of course not,' Rachel said. 'Are you his sister?'

'We hide him very safe,' Fola muttered. 'Yemi no suppose to be out. Mama keeps him in, then he escape.' She gazed at Rachel searchingly. 'He know you de coming, didn't he!' She was tugged again. 'Yemi, come!' Fola insisted.

She reached out an arm, but Yemi did not want to leave Rachel. He held her tightly and kicked out at his sister.

'No, do what she asks,' Rachel said. 'I'll come back. Soon.' Her magic sent waves of reassurance through to him.

After a short tantrum Yemi reluctantly slid into Fola's embrace.

'She no won you to come back,' Fola said sadly. 'Mama said that. Don't come back. Leave us alone.' But she gave Rachel a brief smile before drawing Yemi into the hut. The door was barred and a fierce argument started inside.

Rachel shifted away from the house, still tingling from the pleasure of just being with Yemi. For a while she drifted in the upper sky, thinking about him. His magic was so passionate, so joyful. Was he unique?

Before she could even begin to answer such questions another trace of magic demanded her attention. She wanted to rest, get back home and discuss what she had learned with Morpeth. However, she didn't want to ignore such a forceful scent – and this time it was familiar. She shifted.

And came down in Alexandria, Egypt.

Here, in the broad harbour where the river Nile meets the Mediterranean, there was chaos amongst the fishermen. These were tough, swarthy men used to the hazards of the sea, but nothing in their gritty lives had prepared them for this.

From the wet decks of their boats, the fish caught that day were slithering across to attack them.

8

the stone angel

Rachel saw the cause at once: on a jetty, close to the banks of the sea, stood a plump boy with spiky hair.

'Paul!' She shifted alongside him. 'What are you doing? Stop it!'

He turned despairingly towards her. 'I ca-can't! I daren't!'

Trembling, apparently fighting his own hands as they danced through the air, his fingers continued to orchestrate the biting fish.

'Get away from me!' he begged. 'I might – No! No!'

Suddenly he pulled in both arms hard. All the fish leapt from the boats – at Rachel.

She hastily created two counter-spells: one to deflect most of the fish into the water; another to rid them of the fury.

'What's happening?' Rachel demanded. 'Paul, who's making you do this?'

Before he could answer Rachel felt his body ripped away. One instant Paul was in front of her; the next he'd vanished, and as before the trail of magic was dead.

The fishermen crossed their hearts and watched Rachel from the empty boats.

A few of the fish had landed close to her. Their mouths opened and closed, and inside the soft jaws Rachel saw something she recognized: teeth; teeth that were curved, triangular and black – the teeth of a Witch.

She fell to her knees on the wooden boards of the jetty, gasping for breath.

Dragwena is dead, she told herself. You know that. She *is* dead.

But no fish on Earth had ever possessed a mouth filled with curved teeth like this. The triangularity and blackness could only mean one thing – another Witch was here.

The first three children, she realized, were using magic harmlessly enough. Paul's pattern was the same one she had seen with the Labrador – a deliberately cruel use of spells. But now she was certain Paul himself was not responsible.

Rachel could not wait to get away from the fish still flopping on the jetty. Shifting rapidly towards home, she was more than halfway back when a new scent struck her like a punch. It came from the opposite side of the world. She reeled in the sky, wanting so much to ignore it and get back, worried more than ever about leaving Morpeth, Eric and Mum without her protection. But something about this scent would not be dismissed.

Following the trail of magic Rachel streamed southwards. She passed over the equator, deep, deep into the southern hemisphere, leaving the sun's warmth far behind.

And alighted in a Chilean graveyard.

It was night in this part of the world – and winter. Snow had recently fallen. Rachel hurriedly transformed into the first bird she associated with cold weather – a robin – hoping that she blended in. Puffing out her chest feathers, she gazed about. The graveyard was enormous. Neglected tombstones lay flat on the ground; others poked up at odd angles, as if even the dead souls beneath had tried to push their way out into a cosier place. A fullish moon squatted near the horizon. All around Rachel the scent of magic was almost unbearably concentrated. Surely not another child, she thought. It must be a Witch. A trap?

She hopped cautiously among the mossy headstones. Nothing moved in the graveyard. There were no people tending or walking between the wilderness of graves, or obvious pathways guiding the way through. Rachel nervously flitted between a few scattered trees. Their branches were heavy with snow that crackled under her claws. Suddenly she wished for a sign of human life – any sign at all – a voice, or even a footprint to indicate that loved ones really did visit this place. There were no such reassuring signs. The snow hugged the ground as if it had always done so, and the moon watched Rachel in the spaces between the graves. It was entirely still and frozen and silent.

Eventually Rachel found herself drawn to one remarkably beautiful statue at the centre of the graveyard.

It was a stone angel.

There were further angels dotted at intervals, but this particular angel was different. It seemed new – freshly made – and the sculpture work was so fine that the smooth lines of the face appeared virtually human. Curious, Rachel flew warily towards it.

The statue was a female angel – a girl – and it knelt exactly as a living girl might kneel on the ground. But then Rachel noticed that it had no wings. And instead of the usual prayer-like pressing of hands together, this stone girl had folded arms.

The figure looked, Rachel thought, as if it was bored.

She glanced around. There were no children here, or Witches, nothing obvious to fear; there was only a great magic, centred on the unusual statue. Rachel shook off her robin shape, moved to within a few inches of the face and reached out her hand.

'Don't touch me,' whispered the angel.

Rachel froze – and saw the stone eyelids slowly open. The rest of the girl's face remained fixed. For a moment the two girls simply gazed at one another: stone at flesh. Then Rachel felt something probing her mind. A welcome greeting, similar to that from Yemi? No, she realized. It was infinitely more sinister than that – a measuring spell, trying to judge the strength of her magic.

Rachel prevented it – and saw the girl's eyes widen.

'How did you do that?' the girl asked, trying to hide her surprise. Her voice was flat – clipped and unfriendly – and it had no fear of Rachel's magical gifts. 'Tell me how you blocked my spell,' she insisted. 'Come on, spit it out.'

'What if I refuse?'

'I'll hurt you. I mean it.' The girl watched Rachel's reaction closely.

'Hurt me?' Rachel tried to sound unconcerned. 'Why should you want to do that?'

'You might attack *me*, that's why.'

'I don't even know who you are.'

'Target practice, maybe,' the girl said, shrugging. 'Can't be too careful. You're strong, like me, I can tell. Have you tried out your spells on other children yet? You know, experimented on them?'

'Experimented?' Rachel felt her heart race.

'Oh, don't go all weak-kneed,' sighed the girl. 'Don't tell me you're squeamish when it comes to other children. What a *good* girl you must be. How disappointing.'

She dissolved her stone body and stood up, twirling in the snow as if to display herself.

Rachel could now tell that they were about the same age and height. In all other ways they were different. Pale-complexioned and angular, the girl's thin fingers and wrists jutted from her grey pullover. Her fine hair was perfectly white – almost transparent – falling lankly over her narrow shoulders. Eyebrows that were bleached, nearly hairless, shone in the moonlight. But the girl's most astonishing features were her eyes. They were a washed-out blue, lighter in colour than any Rachel had ever seen.

'I'm Heiki,' the girl said. 'What do you make of me, Rachel?'

Rachel gasped. 'How do you know my name?'

'A secret. Are you afraid?'

'Do you expect me to be afraid?'

'Of course,' said Heiki. 'The other children were afraid.'

'Did you harm them?'

'A few.' She laughed. 'Not much. Most kids are pathetic, not worth the trouble. Are you like them, Rachel? Or can you fight?'

Rachel paused. What was she to make of this girl? Her accent was odd, not English, though she spoke fluently.

'Where are you from, Heiki?'

'It doesn't matter. Haven't you even learned that yet? We don't belong anywhere any more, Rachel. Special ones like us can go where we want. And we can do what we want. Have you used your magic against any adults yet?'

'Have you?' bristled Rachel.

'That's better! Get angry!' Heiki smirked. 'You sound more interesting when you snarl. Go on. Growl a bit. Grrr. I'd prefer you meaner.'

'Have you hurt any adults?' Rachel demanded.

Heiki did not answer, but her smile widened – and Rachel, suddenly, became aware that there was a third presence with them in the graveyard. It stood alongside Heiki, watching Rachel. Rachel could not see it, but she felt its casual observation on her, and recognized the pattern at once from her time with Dragwena: a Witch. Rachel took a step backwards and tried to control her trembling. Did Heiki realize, or was she being secretly followed?

'Who told you other children are pathetic? A Witch?'

Heiki's voice faltered. 'What ... do you mean?'

'I think you know very well,' Rachel said. 'A creature with four sets of black teeth and a snake.' She forced herself to look at the empty space to Heiki's right. 'They're ugly. Quite easy to spot.' She studied Heiki's guarded expression – and realized with horror that Heiki *did* recognize the description.

Heiki and the Witch were working together.

Flee! Flee! screamed Rachel's spells.

'How many Witches are there?' Rachel asked, unable to keep a quaver from her voice. She could no longer bear to look at the space next to Heiki. Jumping backwards, she shouted, 'Show yourself!'

Heiki smiled. 'What's the matter, Rachel? Scared of a few gravestones?'

'I think you'd better tell me what you know,' Rachel said, making herself step forward close enough to grasp Heiki's arm. 'Where are you from? Not this part of the world, anyway. You're a long way from home, aren't you? A long way from safety. Better tell me every-thing.'

'What if I won't?'

'I'll force it out of you.'

'Go on,' cried Heiki, her face excited. 'Just you try!'

Rachel launched a paralysing spell. Without harming Heiki it disabled her defences and immobilized her body, allowing only her lips and larynx to move. 'Tell me!' Rachel pressed, trying desperately to ignore the presence of the Witch.

'What are you doing?' squealed the girl, using her spells

to try to pull away. In that moment, Rachel sensed Heiki's great abilities. Fortunately, so far she could only partially control her magic.

'Tell me how many Witches there are,' Rachel said. 'And where they are.'

'You'll not force anything out of me!'

Rachel sent an information spell into the girl's ear, seeking access to her memories.

Heiki started to shake.

'What's wrong?' Rachel said, alarmed – the information spell should not have injured her.

'No! Please!' shrieked Heiki.

'I'm not—' Rachel began, then realized Heiki was not talking to her. She was communicating with the Witch.

'No, don't!' Heiki pleaded. 'Not yet! Let me fight her. I can take her on my own. I don't need your help. Let me—'

Suddenly Rachel gripped nothing. With a final groan of dismay Heiki's voice trailed off, leaving only the deserted graves. For a few minutes Rachel stood alone, feeling snow land and melt on her hot skin.

Then a new voice breathed in her ear.

'Hello,' it said. 'I am Calen.'

Rachel could see no face, but breath stirred the snowflakes above her head.

'I am the thing that frightens you most, child,' said the voice. 'Are you ready for what will happen next?'

Rachel could not move or breathe.

'Practise your magic, girl,' said the voice. 'The next time you meet Heiki she won't require my help.'

The voice faded on the breeze, but Calen left a sign – snow; not white snow but grey, falling with relish on Rachel and the tombstones of the dead.

9

games
without limits

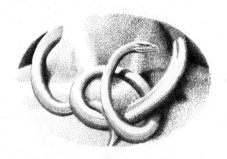

Rachel shifted frantically home from the graveyard. When she arrived in the garden Eric, Morpeth and Mum ran out to her.

'What's wrong?' cried Mum, seeing Rachel's haggard expression. 'What happened?' She clutched Rachel tightly, feeling her shiver. 'Oh, you're safe at least...'

Rachel blinked, trying to get her bearings. 'How long have I been gone?'

'Hours,' said Eric. 'What did you find? More dog-hating boys?'

'Worse than that,' she murmured.

Morpeth held her long black hair. A few grey flakes of

snow that had not melted on the journey oozed like oil against his fingers.

'Oh no,' he whispered. 'Please tell me I'm wrong.'

Rachel sagged against Mum's shoulder – and told them everything.

By the time Rachel finished Mum had long dragged them all inside the house and blacked out the windows. She sat next to Rachel in the living room, holding her in the near-darkness, and no one spoke for a while.

At last Eric said to Rachel, 'Do you think the Witch and this Heiki girl might be coming to get you, then?'

'Yes. I do.'

'Soon?'

'Probably.'

'Tonight?'

'Or earlier. I've no idea when.' Rachel gazed at the wall, her eye-colours a disenchanted grey flecked with black.

Morpeth immediately placed the prapsies on sentry duty. Seeing Eric's sombre mood, they took the task seriously, flitting between the corners of light peeping through the downstairs windows.

'Those two won't hold up a Witch,' Mum said, 'or this horrible Heiki.'

'They'll try, though,' Eric replied. 'They'll warn us fast, too, won't you, boys?'

Both prapsies waggled their heads while flying to inspect a crack in the ceiling. They stared at it with deep suspicion.

Morpeth scratched his chin. 'When Paul and Heiki were snatched away,' he asked Rachel, 'did you notice the same pattern of magic each time – Calen's?'

'Yes.' She glanced up hopefully. 'I suppose that's a good sign. Maybe Calen's the only Witch.'

'One would be enough,' said Morpeth, 'but we can't depend on there being a solitary Witch. The real question is why any Witch is here at all.' He leaned towards Rachel. 'Calen singled you out, told you her name, deliberately trying to frighten you. I'm wondering why she would do that, unless—'

'Unless she *knows* what happened to Dragwena on Ithrea,' Rachel said numbly. 'Unless Calen wants revenge.' She felt her throat tighten. 'And this strange new girl, Heiki...I bet she's being trained to fight me. Otherwise, why didn't Calen just kill me in the graveyard? It would have been easy enough.'

Mum held Rachel tightly, searching vainly for some words with which to reassure her.

'We will absolutely protect you in every way,' said Morpeth, joining Rachel on the couch. 'To help do that I'd like to know more about what Calen is attempting to do. Both Paul and Heiki appear to be under her personal instruction. Why? Are they being trained to attack you together? Or is Calen hand-picking talented children for another reason?'

'I bet this new Witch is just like Dragwena, or worse,' Eric said. With sudden passion he barked, 'Where's Larpskendya? He promised he'd be here for us. He promised!'

'I don't know,' said Rachel hollowly. 'I haven't stopped calling him. He doesn't answer.'

'Larpskendya wouldn't abandon us,' Morpeth said

firmly. 'But for now we have to find a way to survive without the Wizards. There has to be a way to fight back.' He paced the room, watched by the attentive prapsies. 'If we could eavesdrop on Calen when she interacts with children, we might understand this better. Paul is still trying to resist, we all saw that. Calen hasn't broken him, yet.'

'He might be tough,' said Eric.

'If Calen is anything like Dragwena, it doesn't matter how tough Paul is,' Morpeth replied. 'He won't be able to resist for long. We need to help him and children like him quickly.'

'Children like that aren't going to be easy to find,' said Rachel. 'The really gifted ones are scattered across the world.'

Eric laughed harshly. 'We'll find them all right. It's the end of the summer holidays tomorrow, remember. Any kids trained by Witches will hardly be able to wait!'

'For what?' asked Morpeth.

'To get inside their classrooms, of course,' Eric said. 'I bet any kids trained by Calen can't wait to use magic on their teachers!'

Before they went to bed that night Eric gave the prapsies strict instructions to stand vigil at all the windows and doors.

'They won't be able to be everywhere at the same time,' argued Rachel.

'Oh won't they?' said Eric. 'Have you forgotten how fast they were on Ithrea?' He clicked his fingers. Instantly the prapsies darted through the open doorways of the house. They moved at speed, so swiftly that Rachel knew they must be in another room a moment after leaving the last.

Eric slept uneasily on the couch. Rachel, Morpeth and Mum did not sleep. All night they huddled together on cushions in the shadows of the living room, planning and watching: watching the black windows, expecting an attack. No attack came. When dawn arrived the sun emerged cheerily as usual, as if nothing was wrong in the world.

Mum rustled up a breakfast of toast and eggs, which they ate in virtual silence. Mum was too distracted to notice the prapsies sucking tomato ketchup off Eric's plate.

'I've changed my mind,' she erupted suddenly. 'I don't care what I said last night. You're not leaving the house. None of you. I must have been mad, thinking to let you go.'

Rachel sat beside her. 'Mum, you agreed. I'll have Eric and Morpeth with me this time. We're just going to stay in the background and find out what we can. That's all.'

'But you have no idea what might be out there! I'm your mother,' she said simply, her tears flowing. 'How can I let you walk out of that door? How can I do that? I can't.'

Morpeth said to her gently, 'All the choices are difficult now, but we know a Witch is certainly out there. If we wait timidly inside these four walls Rachel and Eric are easy targets.' He saw Mum trying to formulate an objection, and said forcefully, 'Calen signalled her intentions clearly in the graveyard. On Ithrea fear prevented most children from taking any action against the Witch. Let me tell you: Dragwena took no more mercy on them for that. In fact, she despised their weakness and killed them sooner.'

Mum buried her face in Rachel's lap and Rachel silently motioned for the two of them to be left alone for a while. Morpeth and Eric went upstairs and made final preparations to depart.

'We can't take the prapsies,' Morpeth said. 'They're too noisy. We'll never shut them up.'

'Yeah, all right,' grumbled Eric. 'I know. If a cat yawns they freak out.'

He coaxed the prapsies back to his bedroom, whispering a few words of encouragement. As soon as they realized they had been locked inside, both child-birds clawed forlornly at the door.

Returning downstairs, Morpeth and Eric found Rachel still half-draped in Mum's arms. 'Let's go,' Rachel said, extricating herself with difficulty. 'Mum's agreed to let us leave if she can come with us.'

'No,' said Morpeth. 'That would be a mistake.' He faced Mum, and her stricken gaze. 'Rachel is going to have enough to concern her. If she has to protect you as well, that's an extra worry, another distraction. If Calen is anything like Dragwena, she'll probably try to hurt you just to get at Rachel.' He paused, turning to Rachel. 'That also goes for your dad. Now that we know something of Calen's purpose, he should be kept as far away as possible.'

'Too late,' Mum said. 'I called him yesterday. He's already on his way back.'

Morpeth sighed. 'I know how difficult this is,' he

implored her, 'but he mustn't come home. Tell him to go to a location not known by you, Rachel or Eric – a place never mentioned in this house.'

Mum stared furiously at Morpeth. 'If we're such a risk to Rachel, what about you? You're just an ordinary man now. Without magic, aren't you gambling with Rachel's life by accompanying her?'

Morpeth said nothing to this, and it was Rachel who spoke up.

'Mum, I need Morpeth with me. I need him.' She met her mum's intense stare. 'Morpeth took care of himself on Ithrea, and me and Eric. If you're with me, I'll just worry. All the time.'

Mum slowly nodded, and the four of them made their way through the hallway. For a while Mum stood partially barring the front door. At last her whole body seemed to cave in and she held each of them in turn and said a few words they could barely hear through her sobbing. Then she opened the door, her hands lingering on the heads of her children as they pressed past her.

'Close it, Mum,' Rachel said softly.

Mum did not close the door. She simply stayed where she was, clutching the frame as if by keeping the door open and by maintaining a gaze on her children she could keep them safe.

'I *will* protect them,' Morpeth promised, pulling it shut himself.

Rachel glanced anxiously about. Outside the house a milk float trundled up the street, followed by a stray dog. It was still too early for school children.

All three crept timidly along the path to the gate, scanning the pale cloudy sky.

'It seems safe,' said Morpeth. 'Can you detect any magic, Rachel?'

'No,' she said. 'But I don't want us standing out here like dummies. Get ready.'

Morpeth screwed his eyes painfully tight. Eric grinned.

As they had agreed the night before, Rachel turned all three into common sparrows. She had learned how to use such transforming spells on Ithrea, but it was complex and required all of her focus. She shifted them to a point high above the house. Morpeth looked uncomfortable and almost clattered straight into a tree. Eric, on the other hand, sped about with ease, as though he always went for a flight after breakfast.

'Come on,' said Rachel. 'I can't keep all three of us concealed like this for long. We need to hurry.'

She led them over the nearby streets. They skimmed close to the ground, faster than any bird, though not so fast that Rachel would miss any telltale smells of magic. Her scent flaps swayed delicately in the light winds either side of her beak.

'Phew, they're weird,' said Eric, watching the flaps quiver. He peered under his wing. 'Which school should we try first? Ours?'

'No, further out,' she said. 'There's nothing round here.'

They swooped across town, circling several infant and junior schools. The school day was now beginning, with children being called from playgrounds into assembly or first lessons. Rachel detected nothing unusual, so they searched in other towns.

Eric started trilling, a bizarre warble no sparrow had ever made.

'Stay close to me,' Rachel said. 'I've found something.'

Tracking a familiar magical signature over a hundred miles away, she shifted them towards it. Eric shut his beak as they passed over a large, four-storied junior school. Its red brick buildings appeared quiet and orderly. Dropping lower, Rachel hovered level with the third-floor windows.

Eric bumped against her wing. 'What is it?'

Within a classroom all the children sat attentively.

'I see nothing strange here,' said Morpeth.

'Check again,' Rachel told him.

Flying closer, Morpeth realized that he recognized one of the students.

'Paul!'

Morpeth narrowed his sharp bird-eyes. Paul and the rest of the class faced the teacher. The teacher herself stood stiffly, with her back to the students. On a whiteboard she had drawn a detailed head-to-foot picture of herself. In one hand she tensely held a pen; her fingers were white with the firmness of her grip. In her other hand she held an eraser, poised to use. Behind her, on the desk, the teacher had placed her shoes. Next to her shoes there were also her neatly folded pullover, several hair grips, a bracelet, earrings and a neckerchief.

Morpeth stared at the drawing the teacher had made of herself. The earrings and other items on the desk had been erased from the drawing, roughly removed.

'What's happening?' Eric breathed.

'Let's see.' Rachel used a cloaking spell to shift through the glass, and carried them to a position at the back of the classroom.

'Wrong answer again, miss,' they heard Paul saying. 'Call yourself a maths teacher? Surely you can do better than that.' He winked at a few of his friends. 'What shall we remove this time, eh?'

All the students were watching the teacher with a mixture of dread and fascination. Most were open-mouthed, uncertain what to think or do. A few of the braver ones edged away from Paul.

'Don't,' said one girl at the front of the class. 'That's enough, Paul.'

'Not yet, it isn't,' he muttered defensively. 'What's the matter with you lot, anyway? It's all just a bit of fun. I'm not going to hurt her.' He glanced at the teacher. 'Your glasses this time please, miss.'

Trembling slightly, the teacher rubbed out the glasses on the whiteboard. Then, with a flourish, she whisked off her real glasses and placed them on the desk beside the other items.

'Are you simply going to let him do this, Rach?' Eric growled. 'Don't just sit there! Do something, or I will!'

'Wait,' said Morpeth.

'Wait for what?' Eric asked angrily.

'For worse to come. Rachel, do you detect a Witch?'

She nodded grimly. 'It's Calen, keeping out of sight.'

'Stay calm, both of you,' Morpeth warned.

'Stay calm?' Eric protested. 'What's Paul doing to that teacher?'

'He's just denting her dignity a little,' said Morpeth. 'I doubt Calen will be satisfied. Keep watching.'

Paul settled back in his chair. 'Try this one, miss. Forty-seven times three hundred and fifty-five. That's not too hard.'

I'm not … sure,' she said, still facing the board. 'Paul, please don't make me do this. I—'

'Just answer the question,' Paul told her, his voice wavering slightly.

The remaining students had fallen silent. They stared nervously at the teacher.

'It's … it's … seventeen thousand six hundred and forty-two.' She winced, realizing the answer was wrong.

Paul looked awkward. He glanced at his classmates for support, but there was none. Through their silence the teacher could be heard softly sobbing.

'Hey, all right, I get the message,' Paul said self-consciously, shrugging off the accusing glances of his classmates. 'I'll stop, then.'

The teacher's arm, still gripping the eraser, dropped to her side.

Then, swiftly, it shot back up. In a frenzy she slammed the eraser into the whiteboard and effaced her whole body.

Paul, looking frightened himself for the first time, hesitantly looked around the classroom. 'No, Calen,' he said. 'This isn't funny at all.'

An icy voice boomed, blasting in all directions

through the room. 'Really? I think it is. Continue with the game.'

Paul shook his head. 'No. I've had enough, Calen. Really, I—'

'Had enough?' laughed the voice. The glasses, shoes and other objects on the desk were thrown at the walls. 'You think *this* is enough?'

Suddenly, a thick yellow snake curled about the teacher's waist. She tried to squirm away, but her body was not under her own control.

'What are you waiting for?' Eric fumed, and Rachel also glanced uncertainly at Morpeth.

'Don't lose your nerve,' Morpeth said. 'This is only meant to frighten. The Witch wants Paul to go further. Get ready to intervene only if we must.'

Paul stared in disbelief at the snake. 'Hey, what's going on, Calen? This wasn't part of the game we agreed.'

'You stopped playing,' said the voice. 'Therefore, I changed the rules.'

The snake wriggled up the teacher's back. It slid down her neck and across her chest and knees. Touching the floor it extended its body cobra-fashion, raising its sleek yellowness fully up – and stared directly at Paul.

'Finish the game,' the snake said silkily.

'No,' Paul objected. 'You said I could do what I wanted. This is just punishment. I want to stop.'

'But *I* don't want you to stop,' said the snake. 'And this is not punishment, Paul. Real punishment is fear, taken to the furthest degree. Take the teacher to that place.' The snake moved smoothly forward until its head was inches from Paul's nose. 'Did you hear me? Or am I wasting my time with you? Perhaps I should punish you instead!'

'No, please,' Paul implored it. 'Please don't. I'll do anything you want.'

'Will you?' The snake whispered a command.

'I won't do that,' he whimpered. 'No, I can't. Don't make me.'

'You want to do it,' said the snake seductively. 'You told me that you dislike this teacher. Now *show* me how much!'

Paul retreated from the snake. It followed him to the back of the classroom, close to where Rachel, Eric and Morpeth were hiding.

'Don't waste my time,' the snake urged him. 'Just do what I ask!' Its voice became impatient. 'Why can't you enjoy this? What holds you back? You have a worthless adult at your mercy. Don't waver, Paul. You've nearly finished. One more little step. It's so easy.'

'I ... can't,' Paul said, his expression agonized. He could barely raise his head. 'It's what ... I'm not ...' He began crying, not caring what his classmates thought.

'Stop that!' raged the snake.

Paul could not hide his tears. They choked out of him.

'You useless wretch!'

A shiver passed through the snake's coils. The next moment Calen, standing over seven feet tall, disdainfully surveyed the classroom. Nylo slithered in a close yellow spiral about her neck. The children were frozen in various postures, unable to move. Calen ignored them, striding angrily around the room, kicking over empty desks and chairs. She loomed over the teacher, releasing the spells that made her face the whiteboard. Shaking uncontrollably the teacher turned. When she saw Calen, her legs collapsed. Amused, Calen waited until the teacher had heaved herself back into her chair.

'I despise you,' Calen said. 'All you have taught these children is respect for weakness.'

Unsteadily the teacher sat up. For a few seconds she simply stared in terror at the creature above her. Then, with as much assurance as she could manage, she placed the tips of her fingers on the desk to limit their shaking and gazed directly into Calen's tattooed eyes.

'Leave. Nobody wants you here.'

Calen appraised her. She walked to the whiteboard and dragged her claws, tearing the surface to shreds. 'Do you know what I could do to you?'

'I've seen enough to guess,' said the teacher. Her blouse was ruffled, her eyes still red with tears, but her voice held steady. 'Paul doesn't want to follow you. Neither will the other children here, not willingly. Whatever you are, go back to the place you came from.'

Calen punched her claw in frustration through the wall. 'I would like nothing better!' She glared angrily at Paul. 'However, first this one must learn to do *what* he is told, *when* he is told, without argument.' She swivelled back to the teacher. 'Time to teach all your precious class a new kind of lesson.'

'What are you going to do?'

'Nothing complicated,' said Calen. 'Children only understand simple threats. Get up.'

The teacher had no magic with which to fight back. She rose at once.

'Walk to the window,' ordered the Witch.

Without hesitation the teacher pushed back her chair and strode towards the glass.

'Leave her alone, Calen!' warned Paul.

'Ah, defiance,' she cried. 'At last! Stop me, then, if you can.' To the teacher she said, 'Open the window and get on the ledge.'

The teacher obeyed. Releasing the locks, she pulled the window wide, staring down at the concrete playground over sixty feet below.

'What are you waiting for?' Calen asked the teacher. She waved a claw impatiently. 'I don't want you in this class any longer.'

'No, miss!' Paul leapt forward. 'Get away from the window!' Closing his eyes, he used a spell to slam it shut.

'Good,' said Calen. 'Resist me. Is this the way I have to teach you? Drag you every step of the way? Very well. Match my spells.'

The teacher, with a strangled cry, opened the window again. She stepped through onto the narrow ledge.

'Rachel!' Eric exploded. 'What are you doing? We must help her!'

'Get ready,' Morpeth said.

The teacher bent her knees and leaned forward on her toes, ready to dive.

'Jump,' said the Witch.

'No!' screamed Paul, lunging for the teacher's legs.

He reached her in time, but the teacher, with tears in her eyes, kicked him off.

And jumped.

As the teacher fell from sight the children closed their eyes, waiting for the sound of the impact. When there was none, a few of those furthest from Calen craned their necks to look out of the window.

And their teacher looked back up at them. She was unharmed. She stood in the playground, shakily feeling her arms and legs, unable to believe they were not pulverized.

Paul numbly blinked. 'I tried ... did ... did I do that?'

'No,' said Calen scornfully. 'That would be too much to hope for.' She shattered the spell concealing Rachel, Eric and Morpeth.

Eric did not think. He simply ran past the desks of gasping children and jumped on Calen's back, punching her face over and over. Calen did not bother to ward off the blows. Instead she allowed Eric to repeatedly strike her slashed nose and bony eye-ridges, interested in what the punches might feel like. Finally, as if he were a mildly irritating insect, she tossed Eric aside – but gently.

Paul was dumbfounded. 'Who saved the teacher? Him?'

'Partly. The girl did the rest.' Calen's gaze slowly took in the whole of Rachel. 'You helped destroy my sister,' she said. 'It is difficult to restrain myself from killing you.'

Calen's body shook – though not with fear. Everyone in the class could see that it shook with the effort *not* to fight – to hold back on Calen's deep instinct to crush Rachel at once. Her body instinctively readied itself for combat. Blood oozed into her skin, brightening her red face. Her claws lengthened. The ligaments of her arms and legs swelled and hardened. Her eyes, the only vulnerable part of Calen's head, became slit-like, retreating inside their bony covers. And her four mouths flew wide, the black teeth aching to taste Rachel's flesh.

But she held back.

'How many of you are there?' demanded Morpeth. 'How many Witches?'

'One is too many for you,' laughed Calen. She stared at Rachel. 'There is no Wizard this time to come to your rescue, child. And while you've dallied here, your baby friend has found a new home.' She eased her broad shoulders through the window frame and vanished, taking Paul with her.

'Yemi,' Rachel whispered.

Leaving Eric and Morpeth in the classroom she shifted in great leaps to his home. Arriving breathlessly, she looked through one of the open square windows of the hut. One half of the room was in total shade. Sobbing came from the darkness, from a figure on the floor. In the sunlit part of the house sat Fola, her arm reaching into the shade to comfort the figure.

'He gone,' Fola said to Rachel. 'Taken. By this.'

Fola bared her teeth, then searched for a way to make her meaning clear. Finally she placed both her wrists against her cheeks, pointed the fingers stiffly outwards and wriggled them.

Rachel immediately sent out her information spells,

searching for the distinctive scent of Yemi, Calen or any-thing that might represent a Witch. She found nothing. Shifting rashly, she had streamed across half the world before she realized something even more sinister: Yemi's was not the only missing scent. There were no keen traces of magic left anywhere.

All the children with the strongest magic had been abducted.

10

the finest
child

From paths and roads, from the doorways of their homes, from their beds, and from every place in the world children lived, the Witches stole them. Each continent yielded its number. The Witches carried some children away directly in their muscular arms; others, those who could quickly learn rudimentary flight, flew alongside their Witch, left to wonder where they were being taken. The smallest children, when they looked at the Witch on the journey, saw only another youngster, but more wild and free-spirited than any they knew – and more persuasive. Older children were rarely treated so delicately. The Witches did not bother to hide their true appearance, and these children either kept up or were dragged in terror to the north of the planet.

Arriving at the Witch-base, they were greeted by the eye-towers. There were five, arranged in a wide circle, thrusting assuredly into the upper clouds. Each child was appointed a Witch trainer, and deposited within her tower. Here their original clothing was removed, and they were rebadged within a unisex emerald body-suit. In the youngest children it became difficult to tell boy from girl. Training began immediately in the simplest fledgling spells: flight; entrapment; concealment; basic aggression and defence tactics. Mostly the children were taught in an atmosphere of fear, but Calen had studied something of the interactions between adults and children, and for the youngest a little time was set aside for play, and enough for rest, and there were even attempts at encouragement and soft spoken commands.

The Witches were learning.

Finally Heebra herself inspected the seventy-eight children selected and prepared by her Witches.

All the children stood in lines, completely motionless. They were at attention, undergoing an endurance test in the polar snows. In midsummer above the Arctic Circle the sun never quite sets. It shines day and night, and the children had been following its arcing journey up and half down the sky for a long time. Winds cold enough to freeze human blood battered them, but they were careful not to shiver or show the slightest trace of discomfort.

'Are these the superior ones?' Heebra asked.

'Yes,' answered Calen. 'The most gifted from each country. The finest children.'

Heebra flew between the tidily arranged lines, searching for weaknesses. 'How long have they been standing?'

'Over seventeen hours.'

'Without food or rest?'

'In most cases without even moving,' Calen assured her.

'What about this one?' Heebra pointed at a dark-skinned baby boy.

'Ah, that is Yemi. At least we think so. Yemi is the main word he uses, anyway. He's the youngest of all.'

Yemi sat happily packing snow around his feet. As Heebra observed him, several large yellow butterflies perched on his toes also observed her. Their wings were the size of his face.

'He brought the insects with him from Africa,' explained Calen. 'They're growing, changing. As Yemi learns to use his magic they also develop. Yesterday they were less than half that size.'

Yemi held out his arms to be picked up by Heebra.

'What does he want?' she asked.

'It is their peculiar way of seeking attention,' said Calen, She bent down and gingerly lifted Yemi with one claw, holding him at arm's length from her jaws. All four sets of teeth strained forward to reach him.

Heebra grinned. 'You make a poor human mother.'

'His softness is appetizing,' Calen admitted, retracting her teeth.

Heebra sniffed the air, closely studying Yemi. 'There is a magnificence about him. He could be dangerous.'

'He's too young to be a threat yet,' said Calen. She showered Yemi with spiders from her jaws, dropping them between his legs. He picked them up admiringly and showed the largest spiders to his own Camberwell

Beauties. 'Our real appearance does not appal him,' said Calen. 'In fact, unlike the older children, nothing seems to frighten him.'

Heebra examined Yemi's trusting face. 'It is the intensity of our magic that fascinates him. He is drawn to it. We must keep him close, train him separately from the other children, not allow them to influence the boy. Does he miss the mother?'

'Of course.'

'Keep him near you,' said Heebra. 'Learn how to become a convincing replacement.'

'You really think he's so special?'

'I have no doubt,' said Heebra emphatically.

Yemi tickled Calen's ankle.

'Later,' she hushed him.

Heebra looked amused. 'What does he expect?'

'He wants to play a game. It is how they learn.'

'Show me.'

Calen allowed Yemi to grip a gnarled foot-claw. Holding on firmly with both hands, he squeezed his eyes tight shut with expectation as Calen took flight. After a slow climb to a few hundred feet, she kicked him off. Yemi descended inexpertly, more like a paper aeroplane lost in the winds than real flight, but he landed softly enough. As soon as he touched the ground he held up his arms for another ride.

'Yesterday he could not fly at all,' said Calen. 'Remarkable progress.'

Heebra nodded, then returned her attention to the older children.

'I take it they have all passed first-stage training?'

'Some are advanced fliers already,' said Calen. 'And, as you see, the cold is no longer a problem.'

'Yes, they're disciplined enough,' noted Heebra. 'How can we obtain their loyalty?'

'They fear us anyway,' Calen answered. 'For now we can use that to control them. Some are surprisingly unwilling to injure the adults, even when pushed.' She glared at Paul. He stood in line with the rest, shoulders slumped, his spiky hair the only mark to distinguish him from the other taller children. 'Some can be charmed,' Calen said. 'A few have had particular experiences we can exploit.' She smiled, pointing out Heiki, who gazed haughtily back. 'That girl, for instance. I have lavished particular care on her. The rest need more work, but Heiki is dependable in every way. She could pass most intermediate student challenges on Ool.'

'So confident?' said Heebra. 'Then I'll test her. And if she fails it is *you* I'll punish.'

From her own place in the lines of children Heiki tried to follow the conversation between Calen and Heebra. They appeared to be discussing her. Good. Unlike the other children, she desired to be noticed. At first she had found all the Witches' appearance repulsive; but the longer she spent with Calen the more captivated she became. Calen exuded an effortlessness of power, imposing her authority in a brash, offhand, way. And yet, Heiki saw, at the same time her gestures were lithely keen and smooth – almost graceful. And no one else seemed to notice how tenderly Calen spoke to her soul-snake, Nylo. He idolized her, wandering freely about her torso, mirroring her many moods.

From the earliest days, Calen had paid Heiki special attention. Sometimes they stood together for hours, chatting like sisters, almost as if they were equals, discussing the merits of the other boys and girls. Heiki had already learned the names of the most impressive children – Siobhan, Paul, Veena, Xiao-hong, Marshall and, of course, that oddity Yemi. She didn't care about the rest, and was still trying to decide if any of them could be trusted.

Calen parted from Heebra and glided towards her.

'Justify my faith in you,' she said huskily. 'Prove yourself the best, and your reward will be as I promised.'

'I won't fail,' Heiki said. 'Am I going to be tested? What will—'

'You'll see. Prepare yourself.'

Without warning Heiki's body was suddenly wrenched from the ground.

She stood – alone – in a large field of virgin snow near the eye-towers. At the end of the field all the Witches gradually assembled, their black dresses swept back by the wind. Most stroked polar bears – the only pets hardy enough to take the scraping of a Witch's claw. The rest of the children were bunched at the feet of the Witches responsible for their training.

'The bears will come for you,' Heebra told her. 'The test is to get past them. If you make a mistake you will not be given a second chance. Do you understand?'

Heiki nodded vigorously, afraid that if she asked any questions Heebra would interpret that as weakness. One chance, she thought. I mustn't spoil it. She shivered, and realized: I'm meant to feel frightened. That's part of the test, too.

'Most of the spells taught you by Calen are worthless here,' Heebra said. 'You cannot fly, or shift, past the bears. Find another way to cross the snow.'

As soon as Heebra finished speaking the bears picked up their shaggy hindquarters and took up positions at mathematically equal distances across the field. There were no gaps. There was no space through which Heiki might dash to the Witches. In any case she knew she could never outrun an adult polar bear.

I can do it, Heiki told herself. I'm better than the other children.

The first line of bears loped steadily towards her. Prevented from flying or shifting, Heiki tried a wounding spell on the nearest. The bear merely came on faster. She cloaked herself in a fold of wind. The bears lunged forward, still seeing her. Heiki hurriedly sorted through her other new spells. She created a replica image of her body, placing it in hundreds of places on the field; the images simply faded. The nearest bears were almost upon her now, close enough for Heiki to smell half-digested fish on their pluming breaths.

She started to panic. There had to be *something* she was allowed to do!

Glancing desperately at Calen for advice, she found the Witch's eyes were expressionless.

Then Heiki noticed Yemi. Unseen even by the Witches he had drifted across the field.

Heebra and Calen consulted. They had not expected this, but made no attempt to remove him.

Yemi meandered vaguely in the air, like a lost balloon,

and landed amongst the bears. The nearest animal lumbered towards him. Teeth bared, it lowered its great head and … halted. Uncertainly, digging its paws hard into the snow to avoid crushing the boy, it sniffed him. Yemi raised his little hand and the bear tenderly nuzzled it.

The scent of a Witch is on him, Heiki realized – Calen's scent. Was that a coincidence? Or did he know that was the way to stay safe? Yemi pushed himself from the snow and floated serenely between the bears, heading for Calen. Sweeping all his butterflies onto his legs, he landed clumsily on her thick neck and smothered her bony red face in kisses.

Heebra's attention reverted to Heiki.

'You cannot copy Yemi's trick,' she said. 'Find a different way to us.'

The bears again turned smartly to face Heiki – but this time she was ready.

A Witch, standing near Heebra, flinched as her orange soul-snake suddenly uncoiled. It flew from her neck towards Heiki. The outraged Witch recovered immediately, but Heebra prevented her from retrieving the soul-snake.

'Wait,' Heebra ordered. 'Let's see if the child can control it.'

The snake landed in Heiki's sweating hands. Confused and angry, it wriggled in her grasp, not liking her unfamiliar touch or smell. Heiki tried wrapping the snake around her throat to calm it, in the typical style of a Witch. This only infuriated the snake more.

Intelligently, expertly, its coils began to choke her.

Heiki shrieked, trying to pull the snake from her neck – but its hold was too tenacious. If only she could use her spells!

The coils tightened a further precise notch.

Heiki was now shaking, close to losing consciousness. What to do?

What would *no* other child think of doing?

Abruptly, she relaxed. She ignored her sore throat and forced her rigid neck to untense. She flooded her mind with pleasant feelings about the touch of the snake. Baffled, the snake eased its hold slightly. Heiki continued to think the warm feelings, and gently stroked the underside of the snake's head. She fumbled in its reptile mind and understood its soul-name: Dacon. She called that name over and over. Dacon. Dacon. Eventually she had the soul-snake's amused respect and his peach-tinted eyes met hers.

'Walk across the field,' said Dacon. 'The bears suspect you are a Witch now. They will not attack – or, if they try, I will defend you.'

Heiki walked warily across the field. The grunting bears fell back, lowering their heads. Whispering soothingly to the soul-snake all the way, Heiki walked directly up to Heebra and stood defiantly before her. Calen, close by, glowed with pride.

The Witch from whom she had stolen Dacon wrenched him back, and Heiki felt a pang – as if something precious had been torn from her.

'Do you want to hold the snake again?' Heebra asked mildly.

Heiki yearned for exactly this. It was incredibly hard not to reach out for Dacon.

'You are indeed impressive,' Heebra admitted. 'Calen did not overestimate you. Time to receive your reward.'

Heiki gazed at Heebra's heavy golden soul-snake. It exuded a magical aura so extreme that she wanted to flee – but she was determined to receive her prize.

'I want—'

'I know what you want, child.'

Heebra reached inside her dress and pulled out a thin grey snake. It was tiny, with pale ginger eyes. She arranged it decoratively around Heiki's shoulders.

'A newborn,' Heebra explained. 'See if it likes you.'

The snake contracted against her skin, finding a comfortable place.

Heiki was too overwhelmed to speak. She stayed still, so much wanting the snake to feel at ease against her sharply breathing throat.

'It belongs to you now,' Heebra told her. 'Treat it well.'

'Does that mean …' Heiki gushed, 'does that mean I've become a Witch … like Calen promised?'

Heebra laughed. 'No. Not yet, child. It is a beginning. Touch your snake. It won't bite – not you anyway. How does it feel?'

The snake welcomed her touch. Heiki passed her fingers across its eyes and the snake did not move.

'Oh, is it blind?'

'Yes. All soul-snakes start life this way,' answered Heebra. 'Use your magic. As your talent improves so will that of your snake.'

'Can I give it a name?'

'Of course. But that is not the traditional way. As your magic develops so your snake will learn to speak. Then it will *tell* you its own name. And it will also give you a true Witch name. Our snakes name us all. No human child has ever been honoured in that fashion.'

Heiki gasped. 'Oh, I want to grow fast,' she said. 'What do I need to do?'

'You need to shed blood, without caring how much.'

'I'm ready.' Heiki's eyes shone.

'No, child. I doubt that. You are ready for a minor task, perhaps.'

'I'll do anything you want.'

'Good. I want you to kill one of your own kind.'

'One of my own kind?'

'A child.'

Without hesitation Heiki said, 'Yes, I will do it.'

'Don't you want to know why?'

'If you want it killed, I'll do it,' said Heiki. 'What's the child's name?'

'There are three. The main one is—'

'Rachel!'

Heebra nodded.

'I knew it would be!' cried Heiki, clapping and dancing in the snow. 'Oh, this is a perfect day, a perfect day.'

Heebra explained what had happened on Ithrea. She also told her about the endless war against the Wizards. Heiki listened avidly. The longer the story went on the closer she felt to the Witches. They were magnificent! In fascination she drank in the detailed description Heebra gave of Ool. Heiki wanted so much to fly inside a storm-whirl, battling for her own eye-tower. Heebra warned her about Eric's unmagicking gifts, but Heiki stopped her describing Rachel's powers.

'Please don't tell me. I'll find out for myself. I don't want any advantages.'

'Good,' said Heebra. 'That is the answer a true Witch would give. Tell me how you will defeat Rachel.'

Heiki thought about what she had learned. 'Finding her is easy. I know Rachel's pattern already. I won't attack straight away. I'll get to know her first, change my appearance and scent so she doesn't recognize me from the grave-yard. I'll make her feel safe, comfy; that way she'll reveal her spells.'

'Rachel has few weaknesses,' said Heebra.

'I'll discover them. Can she heal injuries? Other people's bad injuries?'

'Yes. What are you thinking of?'

'Oh, nothing, just an idea.' Heiki noticed that the tedious endurance test was over at last, and the rest of the children had been dispersed into the usual training groups. 'Can I take some of the others with me?' she asked. 'I need them to help me deal with Eric. I'm not sure how to handle him yet ... I'll think about it on the journey. It'll take us a few hours to get there, since I seem to be the only one who can shift.'

'Take anyone you like,' said Heebra. 'I am making you the leader of the children.'

Heiki smiled proudly and flew off to choose her team.

Heebra called Calen over. 'You selected Heiki well. An

independent, passionate child. It is as if she has been waiting her whole life for us to give her a purpose. Does she really believe your promise to transform her into a Witch?'

'She does,' said Calen, smiling. 'She wants to believe it so much.'

'I wish the other children were as amenable.'

'Do you trust Heiki to defeat Rachel?'

'I trust nothing,' Heebra answered dismissively. 'Rachel is too formidable to be treated lightly. Let Heiki decide her own tactics, but I want to approve them. And when Heiki leaves, you shadow her. Stay out of sight. Take Yemi with you, but keep him close – and be wary of him.'

'Wary? Of a baby?'

'He is not a typical human child.'

They both turned and watched Heiki making her selections for the team.

Heiki chose carefully, picking a mixture of those who were most talented and also those she believed would follow her orders without argument. When this had been done, she started formulating a plan, gesturing confidently, using others to translate for those children who spoke no English.

'I see there's no need for us to push them any longer,' Calen laughed. 'Young Heiki will be as exacting a taskmaster as any Witch!'

11

ambush

A small goldfish rippled the dark surface of the pond.

'Did you hear that!' screeched one prapsy, shivering with excitement.

'Shush,' the other cried. 'You'll wake Eric, boys.'

'But did you hear it?'

'I heard it!'

Like blurs, they sped together from the bathroom to the bedroom overlooking the night garden. Perched cheek-to-cheek they scrutinized the pond.

'There!' one cried wildly. 'An underwater devil!'

'A midget devil. Shall we tell Eric?'

'Don't be stupid, you mutant spanker!'

'You're stupid! Shush! Wait.'

'What?'

'Shadows.'

They both sensed the magic approaching the house.

'What is it? I'm scared.'

'Can't see it. Can't see *them*. Must be backside of house. Let's look.'

'After you,' said its companion, bowing gracefully.

'No. *After you*,' said the other – and they both flew off together.

From the living room they peered anxiously over the front street.

'See how they are creepily hiding?'

'They are scared of us!'

The prapsies' big eyes blinked violently. One licked the living-room window, wiping off the condensation; the other pressed a round face against the cleared glass. Together they twitched and gazed out over the empty street.

'What kind of things are they?'

'They are flying. Must be birds. Naughty birds, maybe. Should be in bed by now.'

'Big mad naughty birds!' A nervous giggle.

'Shall we chat to them?'

'Shut up and listen!'

'They are sneaking up, do you see?'

'I see them!'

The prapsies flapped their wings, trying to frighten off the dark shadows.

Outside nine large silhouettes emerged stealthily from the night sky. For a moment they gathered in front of the gibbous moon. Then they plunged towards the house.

'Eric! Eric!' shrieked the prapsies, fleeing upstairs. 'Rachel!'

Rachel's eyes flicked wide. Beneath her she heard glass being smashed – something invading the house. Two shattered windows, her information spells told her rapidly. One in the living room; another in the kitchen. What else? She heard frame wood hit the carpet – followed by the soft thud of shoes.

Eric blinked from a bed that had been placed close to hers.

'What's going on?'

'Stay quiet,' Rachel told him. She tried to decide who had broken in. Witches were large-bodied and heavy. These landings had been lighter.

'I think it's kids,' she said.

The prapsies were nutting the door of the bedroom. Eric let them in, pushing their quivering heads under the quilt.

'Morpeth and Mum are down there on guard!' he reminded Rachel. 'Come on!'

'Wait!' Rachel grabbed his arm.

'Get off! I'm going!'

She tugged him back. 'Listen, will you!'

Four more bodies had flown into the house. Rachel heard them squeeze through the gaping holes and land. Neat landings, Rachel thought. Both feet precisely together. Children using magic – and already experienced flyers.

'It's an ambush,' she said. 'Keep quiet. They might not know we're here.'

'What about Morpeth and Mum?' Eric fumed. 'I can't hear them!'

Downstairs glass tinkled underfoot. Even Eric's ears could now easily hear the sound of many pairs of feet tramping noisily around the living room. From his bed the prapsies kissed each other for comfort.

'Whoever they are, they're not trying to catch us by surprise,' said Eric. He lunged for the stairway. 'Morpeth! Where are you?'

Morpeth's gruff voice called up, 'I'm all right! So is your mum. Come to the kitchen.'

Eric tucked his quilt gently around the necks of the prapsies, calming them.

'Sleep, sleep, boys,' he said. 'Close your peepers.' The prapsies squeezed their eyes shut and pretended to nap because they knew that was what he wanted.

Eric and Rachel hurried downstairs.

They found Mum and Morpeth unharmed, standing by the dining table. Behind them a spiky-haired boy stood gazing out of the broken windows.

'Paul!' said a shocked Eric.

Eight more children were also crowded into the room. The curtains had been drawn back. All stared at the blazing broad moon, watching intently, as if unable to take their eyes from the sky.

Paul turned to Rachel and his eyes brimmed with tears.

'Oh, it is you, it *is*,' he murmured. 'I never thought we'd find you. You've no idea what we've been through to make it here.'

Eric glared at him. 'Where's your ugly Witch, Calen?'

'She's ...' – Paul choked on the words – 'given up on me. Oh, I don't mind, don't think *I* mind,' he said, but his face sagged awkwardly. 'Not good enough, you see. Wasn't *ruthless* enough.' He spread his arms, indicating those around him. 'None of us were.'

Rachel saw how distressed all the children looked. Heiki was not with them.

'How many Witches are there?' she asked. One, she thought, please just one.

'Five,' Paul answered.

Rachel tried to stay calm. Morpeth seemed unfazed by the news, and she gripped his hand.

'Why do you keep checking the windows?' he asked.

'We're being chased.'

'By Witches?'

Paul laughed bitterly. 'You think Witches can be bothered with the likes of us? We're the *rejects*.'

'Then who's chasing after you?'

'Kids, of course. Better kids. The *favourites*.'

Mum gasped. 'Why?'

'You've no idea what's going on, have you?' said Paul. 'The Witches make us fight, to see who's the best. They weed out those not up to scratch.' He glanced at his companions. A few dropped their heads. 'We lost too many battles. They've made us target practice.'

Eric asked, 'Target practice for whom?'

'For the favourites. They've caught us once. Banged us about a bit, then gave us a head start. Next time they'll finish us off. We can't outrun them. Most are quicker fliers than us. Hey, we haven't got much time, They're—'

'They're here,' a girl whispered. She staggered back from the window.

Outside a new group of children hung in a line against the rooftops. They made no attempt to conceal themselves. Kneeling or sitting at ease in the air, they all stared boldly at Rachel.

Morpeth studied Paul closely. 'How did you find us?'

'All the kids know this address,' Paul said. 'And the scent of Rachel's magic is hardly difficult to find.' He glanced at her. 'You've left trails everywhere.' From the darkness outside a child called his name, and he shrank away from the window. 'Look, are you going to help us, or not!'

Morpeth noticed that Paul and the other children's injuries were not serious – a few bruises and superficial cuts. 'I see no evidence you've been involved in a real fight,' he said.

'That's because Ciara drew them off!' bellowed Paul.

'I'm listening,' said Morpeth evenly.

'Ciara's a girl who's good enough to fight with the best kids, but she won't. She helped us get a good head start. The Witches went after her for that. They've probably killed her already.'

'We should get everyone away from these windows,' Mum said.

'No,' Morpeth replied firmly. 'We can defend ourselves better if we keep them all in sight. Those inside and outside the house.'

Mum looked curiously at Morpeth. 'Don't you believe this boy's story? Isn't Paul the one who's been resisting Calen?'

'I'm not sure what to believe yet,' Morpeth said. He turned to Rachel. 'Send out your information spells. If

334

Witches are attacking or have recently attacked anyone there should be some clear evidence.'

Rachel did so, and distantly sensed powerful spells being used. Some were from a child, a child raising all its defensive spells against massive forces.

'Two Witches,' Rachel breathed. 'Two Witches against one child. They're fighting now. She won't stand a chance.'

'How far away?' Eric asked.

'Hundreds of miles.'

Eric thumped the table. 'If I could get close, I could destroy the spells.' He gazed at Rachel. 'Can *you* get there in time to help her?'

'I'm needed here. I can't leave you!'

'Please,' pleaded one of the girls. 'You mustn't leave Ciara to fight on her own!'

Far off Rachel could sense Ciara's pain. She was torn: leave a poor, unknown girl to fight alone, or leave Mum with only Eric and Morpeth to defend her against the magic of the *favourites*.

'Morpeth,' she said bluntly. 'Tell me: what should I do?'

'Go,' he told her. 'Ciara can't survive long. We *can* defend this house for a while, I'm certain. Trust me: if there are five Witches out there who want us dead, even with you here we won't be able to stop them. Get to that girl, before it's too late.'

Rachel glanced at Mum who half-nodded, half-shook her terrified face.

'Wait!' Morpeth whispered in Rachel's ear. 'Can you put a scent-tag on me? A trace you could follow?'

'Yes,' she said.

'Do it.'

Rachel quickly completed the spell, and made the scent-tag difficult to detect.

Then, a long way off, she felt a child's defences suddenly shatter.

With a final agonized glance at everyone, she shifted.

As soon as Rachel left Paul buried his face in his hands.

'I'm so sorry,' he said. 'So sorry.'

'Pretty nicely done,' said another, older, pale-skinned boy, slapping Paul's back. So far this boy had been silent throughout. 'Heiki reckoned you would be the best to convince them,' he said. 'She was right. I thought you'd mess it up, actually.'

Paul half-raised his head. 'Marshall, no one here gets hurt. That's what we agreed.'

'Whatever,' said Marshall, dismissively.

He waved to the children outside. At this signal they swarmed towards the house, some calling out the names of friends inside.

'How could you do that?' Eric raged at Paul. 'How could you!'

Tears poured down Paul's face. 'I couldn't … I—'

'Oh, shut up,' said Marshall, brushing him aside.

Morpeth drew Eric and Mum close, furiously trying to decide how he could protect them.

'I suppose that Witch Calen is with you,' Eric snarled at Marshall. 'You don't have the guts to be doing this on your own.'

'We don't need her help with Rachel out of the way,' Marshall said.

Eric raised his hands. 'Do you think I'm just going to let you do what you want? I'll snuff out all your spells.'

'Will you, now.' Two children, strength boosted by their magic, grasped Mum's arms and legs. 'We've been taught all about your weird gift,' Marshall said to Eric. 'So this is what's going to happen. You and Morpeth come with us. Mum stays here. If you interfere with any of our spells we have orders to kill Morpeth on the journey. And just in case either of you try anything funny we're leaving some kids behind to take care of Mumsy.'

'Don't you dare harm her!' raged Eric.

'We'll do what we want.'

'Your performance isn't very polished,' Morpeth said, gazing levelly at Marshall. 'You're under orders, aren't you? Whose orders? What have you been told to do with Eric's mother?'

'What do you care?' Marshall said. 'Heiki doesn't mind much what happens to her, or you for that matter. It's Eric she's got special plans for.'

Paul glanced up. 'Their mum wasn't part of the deal. And what are these plans for Eric? I don't remember anything about them.'

'Heiki didn't trust you with everything,' Marshall said.

'Marshall,' Mum tried, her eyes pleading with him. 'Look, I know... you're not impressed by me... adults generally. I suppose without magic we just seem—'

'A hindrance,' finished Marshall. 'That's right. Parents are worthless now.'

'Says who?' asked Eric angrily.

'Heiki.'

'Who's that? A Witch?'

'A girl. You'll find out.'

'It sounds like she scares *you*!' Eric said scornfully.

'Maybe she does,' Marshall muttered.

Behind them, came two panted breaths.

A girl stooped to look. 'Hey, what are these?'

The prapsies shivered in the doorway. They had crept from Eric's bed and had been fearfully watching, ready to fly at anyone who tried to touch him.

'We are biters!' one cried, opening its gummy, toothless mouth.

'Oh, they talk,' the girl gasped. 'I want one!'

There was a flurry as many of the children reached out, but the prapsies were too fast – and dodged away.

'Leave them alone!' Eric blasted at Marshall. 'Fight *me*, you coward. Or are you scared?'

'I'm not scared of you,' growled Marshall.

'You *are*,' Morpeth said, in a voice he made sure all the children would hear. 'All this brave talk. There's nothing behind it except fear of the Witches and what they'll do. Are you on trial yourself, Marshall?' He saw Marshall's eyes widen slightly. 'This task is a test you've been set, isn't it?' Morpeth said. 'Your behaviour … is being *watched*.'

Marshall glanced nervously out of one of the windows, then regained his composure. He sniffed the air surrounding Morpeth.

'No magic,' he said sarcastically. 'And I hear you're an old man in a boy's body. That's a curious thing.'

'Perhaps,' replied Morpeth. 'But I am what I am. What are you, Marshall?'

Marshall shrugged. At a signal from him the two children holding Mum gripped her tightly, while the remainder started to pull Eric and Morpeth towards the broken windows.

Eric peered at the street chimneys. 'Where are you taking us?'

'On a nice trip,' Marshall said, as if he was announcing the start of a picnic.

'Where?'

'You don't want to hear. A long, cold journey.'

'Then you'd better clothe us better than this,' Morpeth said, indicating Eric's pyjamas and his own lightweight clothes. Without waiting for an answer from Marshall, he strode into the spare room. Mum joined him, her hands shaking as she helped to look for trousers and shoes. She found a coat that fitted Morpeth, and pushed past a few children to go upstairs to get one thick enough for Eric.

'You've had enough time,' Marshall said to her, when she returned empty-handed.

'But I can't find anything!' she shouted. 'How dare… no, look, let me check under the stairs, please… I think…'

'Just get on with it,' Marshall hissed.

Morpeth took his time getting dressed, all the while looking steadily at Marshall. 'You weren't told what to do if you got any opposition, were you? What was the instruction from your Witch or Heiki? – just do away with me or Mum if we got difficult? Well, go on, then. Are you going to kill us for putting on a few clothes?'

Marshall said nothing, and Mum, discovering Dad's duffel coat at last, flung it around Eric's shoulders. She fumblingly pulled some of her own gloves – the only ones she could find – over his fingers, trying to find a reassuring smile.

'Let's go!' Marshall blasted finally. 'Come on!'

'Not yet,' Morpeth said. 'These clothes won't be enough if we're flying far. We'll need magic to keep us warm as well.'

'You'll get no special protection from me,' sneered Marshall. 'I've listened to you for long enough.' He gazed at the other children. 'You know what Heiki and the Witches will do to us if we fail,' he said. 'Get them to the windows!' The galvanized children dragged Eric and Morpeth across the room, while the two with Mum struggled to hold her back.

Morpeth caught her terrified gaze. This time he felt that he could make no promises. 'I won't let them harm Eric,' he said anyway. 'Trust that.'

The children finished hauling Eric and Morpeth to the window. At Marshall's signal they flew up the walls of the house and over the peaked roof, into the chilly night air. The prapsies followed a short way behind. They wanted to stay near Eric, but the children swiped at them whenever they hovered too close, so they stayed as near as they dared, shouting insults at the children holding his arms and legs.

While Eric could still be heard by Mum he craned his neck, calling hoarsely, 'Wait for Rachel! She'll be back soon.'

Marshall swept alongside him. 'I don't think so,' he said. 'Heiki has her now.'

Rachel arrived breathlessly over a dense oak wood.

Sensing the two departing Witches, she swooped down, searching in the undergrowth. Was she too late?

A girl lay on her face, draped across the roots of a tree. Her hair was ginger, curly, and smeared with blood – yet somehow she was alive. Rachel knelt beside her. Drawing on her healing spells she knitted the skin on the girl's back where it had been slashed by the Witches. She set the femur of her broken leg. She lowered the swelling where a claw had fastened about the girl's throat. Any doubts Rachel had about being lured into a trap were removed by the piteous state of her injuries.

Eventually the girl sat up. She swayed, seemingly dazed.

'You're safe,' Rachel said softly. 'Don't be afraid, Ciara.'

'Where have the Witches gone?'

'I'm not sure, but they're not close. I can't sense their presence.' She smiled. 'I'm Rachel.'

'We've heard all about you. The child who defeated a Witch! Wow!'

'I had help,' Rachel said distractedly. Her information spells scanned for any approaching danger. 'Why didn't the Witches finish you off? They had time.'

'Who knows?' the girl said. Her eyes glinted. 'Did you know the Witches are training a bad girl to get you? I've met her. Scary thing. Bite your head off.'

Rachel nodded. 'Where have the Witches been keeping the children all this time?'

'Mostly at the equator. That's where they train them.'

The equator? An odd choice, Rachel thought. And she wondered about this strange girl. She had not asked about Paul or the reject kids once. Was she in shock from the Witches' attack? Possibly, though she also appeared so composed. That was it, Rachel realized. This girl looked *poised*, as if ready for anything.

'We must get back to my house,' Rachel said urgently, explaining what had happened. 'Can you fly?'

'Of course.' The girl rose stiffly. 'I'm your greatest admirer, by the way. You'll murder that Heiki girl!'

Rachel sent her information spells after the scent-tag she had left on Morpeth. For some reason he had moved away from the house. 'Something's wrong,' she said. 'Let's hurry.'

'On the way I will teach you all my spells,' the girl said eagerly. 'And you?'

'We'll see.'

The girl clapped her hands in delight. 'Two friends! That's what we are!'

Rachel flew rapidly towards home. The girl matched her speed.

'You're very good,' Rachel complimented.

'I'm hopeless. Can't do shape-shifting like you, or anything.' As Rachel prepared to shift, the girl screamed. 'Sorry, that hurts so much. Please don't.'

'But we have to get back. It'll take over an hour if we can only fly!'

'No please,' begged the girl, sagging into her arms. 'Hold me! I'm still feeling so weak.'

Rachel embraced her tightly and flew as fast as she could, waiting for the girl to recover.

Heiki smiled to herself. Perhaps this was going to be *too* simple. Rachel was impressive, but easily fooled, like all the others. Far too trusting. Of course, she had gone to great lengths to be absolutely sure to convince her. Relying on Rachel's ability to heal injuries, she had allowed the Witches to really damage her badly before they left.

That's the difference between me and you, Rachel, thought Heiki. I'll go through any amount of pain to get what I want. How much pain can you endure?

'Please go more slowly,' she implored Rachel in a feeble voice, as they sliced through scattered, wispy cloud. 'I'm so very frightened.'

12

ocean

Morpeth counted a troupe of twenty-seven children.

Ten carried him and Eric by the arms and legs, keeping them separated. The rest formed a guarding ring. Marshall was up front, the obvious leader. Paul flew alongside him, occasionally glancing apprehensively back to Eric. There was no sign of a Witch – and no sign of Rachel.

For a while they travelled eastwards, soaring over crop-laden fields, lit by stars and the waning moon. Then Marshall turned the troupe towards the Arctic. Leaving land behind, they headed off over the churning waves of the North Sea. Intensely cold, blustery air now carved into the children. The troupe had magic to ward off the severe winds, but Eric's and Morpeth's only protection were jumpers, gloves and coats. Morpeth knew from Ithrea how to keep his limbs moving constantly to ward off frostbite, but Eric had no such knowledge. Against the raw wind Dad's big heavy coat wasn't enough. Within minutes Morpeth sensed Eric starting to fade. Was this the fate Heiki had planned for Eric, he wondered – to kill him slowly during the flight?

Not while I live, thought Morpeth.

'Eric needs more protection!' he roared over the winds.

Marshall heard him, but said nothing.

'I expect Heiki wants her cargo delivered alive,' Morpeth called out. 'If you botch it, Marshall, if we die of exposure on the journey, she won't be happy.'

'I'll insulate them,' he heard Paul say to Marshall. 'Leave it to me.'

Marshall wavered, then said angrily, 'The minimum of warmth for Eric. Just enough to make sure he doesn't freeze. As for Morpeth, he gets nothing. Do you hear? Nothing.'

Paul extended a thin warm blanket of air around Eric's face and neck. His gaze lingered on Morpeth, but he was clearly too nervous to ignore Marshall's warning.

Left utterly exposed, Morpeth gritted his teeth and bore the pain as best he could. He flexed and unflexed his fingers, trying to hold the image of Rachel in his mind while he turned his attention to the children carrying him. They were uneasy. It was obvious to him that Heiki and the Witches must have presented this task as some sort of brazen game or adventure. Most were not fooled. Morpeth spoke to them. As they flew higher into ever colder air he asked the children questions about families and friends, to remind them what they had left behind. They did not answer, clearly under orders, but their grip loosened, and their bodies moved slightly closer to guard him from the howling winds. Soon they were bending low to hear his rough voice.

Paul's layer of warmth kept Eric alive, but his body was still pierced by the cutting gusts. As time went by he fell in and out of consciousness. The prapsies stayed close, trying to convince themselves that Eric was well, tears freezing against their cheeks.

'Wake up, you precious wonder!'

'Oh wake, will you!'

'I'm scared, boys. Eric is ill.'

'No, he is sleeping.'

'Is he? Is he just sleeping?'

They kept trying to wrap their wings around Eric's exposed cheeks, but the children transporting Eric always attempted to grab them. The prapsies could never get close enough to touch him.

At one point Eric briefly awakened.

'Go away, boys!' he rasped. 'You can fly faster than these kids. Hide. They won't find you.'

The prapsies shook stubborn heads, and continued to wilfully follow, blinking and twitching and flying into the wind, trying to use their own bodies to buffer Eric from the worst of it.

Most of the time Morpeth and Eric were kept too far apart to speak. Once the groups holding them drifted close enough to exchange a few brief words.

'Where are they taking us?' Eric managed to whisper.

'I don't know.'

'Where's Rachel?'

'Not far behind, I'm sure. She will come. Stay alert, and keep moving your hands.'

Eric looked up fiercely. 'Morpeth, don't let them hurt the prapsies! Promise me!'

'I…' Morpeth couldn't find any words. He knew that if these children wanted to harm the prapsies, he couldn't prevent them.

At a growled order from Marshall the groups split apart again. For another hour they flew purposefully northwards. Morpeth began to feel desperately tired, wanting so much to sleep. He understood what that meant – on Ithrea he had seen thousands of children succumb to a last blissful drowsiness shortly before they froze to death in the snow.

He sensed the pity of those children carrying him. They obviously wanted to help, but were afraid. Afraid of who? Not Marshall. Morpeth had seen him looking increasingly troubled at the head of the troupe. Someone else. Morpeth glanced at the roof of the sky, but saw nothing.

At some point he heard Paul wail, 'Let's at least take them lower, into calmer air!' The children holding him all raised their voices in agreement, but there was only a stony silence from Marshall.

Gradually Morpeth's strength faded. His face sank lower and lower, until his eyes were fixed only on the silver and black waves. Without bringing warmth, dawn broke at last, tingeing the surf pink. For a while, Morpeth had no idea how long, the children descended. Then he smelt the tang of salt, and heard the bleak, persistent call of gulls. A blinding whiteness cut across his eyes.

They had crossed land.

Ahead, a gigantic continent of snow stretched as far as he could see.

Where were they? Greenland? The Arctic? Morpeth urged his stiff neck muscles to move. Glancing across, he saw the group of children carrying Eric drop him onto the thick snow. Eric lay on his face, without moving. The prapsies, themselves shivering with cold, landed on his head, nipping his ears with their gums, trying to wake him. Moments later Morpeth himself was softly deposited nearby. He dragged his legs across the snow and felt for Eric's pulse. There was a heartbeat – just. Severe frostbite had set about Eric's lips and hands – Mum's gloves had not been enough. Morpeth held Eric's face away from the snow and peeled off the gloves, rubbing the finger joints and tendons.

'Wake up!' he bellowed, striking Eric hard. 'You must wake up!'

The prapsies winged about Eric's head, entreating Morpeth to hurry.

'Eric has slept long enough!'

'He is colder than bones!'

All the children who had been transporting Eric and Morpeth ascended to a point high in the sky. They hung there, solemnly observing, while the relentless Arctic winds thrashed their faces. Finally an argument broke out between Marshall, Paul and the children who had carried Morpeth.

'Come down and see us!' Morpeth shouted up, still struggling to wake Eric. 'Come and see what you've done! Or are you afraid, Marshall?'

'I'm not afraid.'

Hesitantly, Marshall descended with Paul to land. When Marshall saw Eric's blistered skin, split lips and swollen, misshapen fingers, he turned away.

'It's not so easy to allow someone to die, is it?' said Morpeth. 'It takes a long time for a Witch to convince a child it enjoys that.'

Paul could not bear the sight of Eric. He stepped forward to help him.

'Don't touch, you idiot!' cried Marshall. 'You'll get us all in trouble.'

'We can't just leave him this way. Look at his fingers!'

'We're not allowed to help him.'

'You control the troupe,' Morpeth said to Marshall. 'What's stopping you?'

Marshall glanced nervously upward. 'Are you blind? I'm not in charge here.'

Morpeth followed his gaze and sensed what must be hidden in the sky: a Witch, too far away to see, but nevertheless there, watching the behaviour of each child. Fear, Morpeth thought, knowing from long experience what the mere presence of a Witch could make children do. Suddenly he thought of his old friends, and wondered if the Witches had also discovered Ithrea. No: he could not bear to consider that...

'Only the strongest will survive,' Paul said remotely. 'That's what Calen said.'

'What have you been told to do?' Morpeth asked Marshall. 'Leave us here to die?'

'No. Bring you both to the pole, if you can survive the

journey. That's what Heiki wants. She didn't particularly care if you made it or not.'

Morpeth leant close to him, and whispered, 'Is that what *you* want, Marshall? I expect you're hoping the Witch who trained you will be satisfied with just our two little deaths. Let me tell you: she won't be. This is just the beginning. She will make you kill again and again. She won't leave you in peace. There will *never* be enough deaths to satisfy her.'

Above them a girl shouted down, 'Hey, what's going on?'

'I've got to go,' Marshall said. 'I can't be seen talking to you.'

'Give me time to revive Eric!' demanded Morpeth.

'Too dangerous.' Marshall's eyes flitted upward. 'He'll have to travel as he is.'

'Eric is just like you,' Morpeth beseeched him. 'Scared, trying to survive. Are you just going to let him die on the wind?'

Without answering Marshall kicked his feet from the snow, pulling Paul with him towards the other children.

'You *can* fight back,' Morpeth cried up to them. 'Look at each other! Can't you sense your own strength?'

If they heard neither boy replied, and Morpeth turned his attention back to Eric. He tried carving a hole to get them out of the wind, but after a few inches the snow was too compacted to dig through. So instead he took off his own coat, wrapped it around Eric and brought their bodies together for warmth.

Finally Eric half-opened his eyes. The prapsies squealed

with joy, cooing like doves in his ears. Morpeth wiped the frost off his lips.

'Only the strongest survive,' Eric mumbled. 'Isn't that what Paul said?'

'We're the strongest,' Morpeth told him.

Eric had lost all sensation in his toes. For some reason this frightened him more than anything else that had happened. 'T-talk to me, old man.'

'I'm here,' Morpeth said. 'I won't leave you.'

'Where are the prapsies?'

'Breathing on your hands.'

Managing to sit up, Eric gazed affectionately at the child-birds. 'I c-couldn't feel you, boys.' He coughed. 'Hey, I don't feel so good.'

'It's all right,' Morpeth reassured him. 'Rachel will be here soon.'

Eric nodded, trying to believe it, and peered at the glistening green uniforms of the children. 'What are they w-waiting up there for? Why don't they just finish us off?'

'Because they don't want to,' Morpeth said earnestly. 'They want to stop.'

The quarrel above had gradually spread to the entire troupe, with Paul and the children who had listened to Morpeth arguing most passionately. When it ended all the children gazed down and Eric and Morpeth discerned a spell at work.

All the winds about them ceased, a warming breeze replaced the slicing wind.

'No!' screamed an enraged voice – and from her hidden location Calen streaked across the sky. She aimed straight for the troupe, her claws extended, and initially Morpeth thought she intended to tear them to pieces. But she restrained herself, and instead flew over each child, flinging out her scorn, promising punishments – and giving new orders.

Yet again the icy winds tore at Eric and Morpeth.

'We're not done yet, old man,' Eric rasped. 'I'm not waiting for Rachel.' He held out his puffed-up fingers. 'I've still got these. If the kids back home have done anything to Mum, they've done it already. I'm not just going to lie here till they decide to finish us off. Help me up.'

Morpeth hauled Eric into a seated position. Eric raised his numb hands.

'Come on,' he coaxed, blowing on the tips. 'Don't let me down now.'

Above, Calen hissed instructions to four children. Separating from the troupe, they sank fast down the sky.

Eric pointed his fingers – and the four fell helplessly. Lying in the snow, they called for the others, their flying skills gone.

'Ignore them!' Calen said. At another of her commands, half the troupe swooped down. This time they came from several directions at once, front and behind, zigzagging evasively.

Eric knocked two more from the air.

'Quick!' he barked. 'Turn me round!'

But before Morpeth could swivel him, the rest of the attackers were on them. Morpeth sank his knuckles into the nose of the first, but the rest hit hard, sending Eric and Morpeth sprawling across the snow. Breaking off, the troupe members flew to higher regions where Eric's powers could not reach.

Eric and Morpeth regrouped, sitting back to back, while the prapsies recklessly flung themselves between Eric and the troupe, hurling abuse.

'What now?' asked Eric, squinting up.

Stung by another order from Calen the troupe had drawn together. They were massed against the sun, and Eric could hear a few of the children weeping.

'They're going to come after us in one go,' Eric realized. 'All together. Wait. What's that?'

It was Yemi.

From the cloud that had concealed Calen, he floated serenely towards the children. He was surrounded by his devoted butterflies. They were now enormous, the size of cats.

'Go back!' Calen shouted. 'Go back!'

Yemi faltered, then came on, drawn by the frightened noises within the troupe. His Camberwell Beauties surged forwards like a flock of immense slow yellow birds. They mingled with the children, touching those with tear-stained faces as if trying in some instinctive way to offer comfort. Unnerving and baffling, the butterflies milled in the sky, so big and so many that the troupe was virtually lost under their beating wings.

Finally Calen fought a path through to Yemi and yanked him away. The butterflies followed him reluctantly, their antennae bowed.

'That must be the baby Rachel mentioned,' marvelled Eric. 'Did you sense his power?'

Morpeth nodded, watching in awe as Yemi twisted uncomfortably in Calen's claws, unhappy about being carried away.

Once Calen had Yemi under control, she turned back to shriek at the children. This time they were too terrified to argue. The entire troupe clustered into the tightly knit shape of a fist. Together they dropped down, heading directly for Eric and Morpeth.

Eric closed his eyes. 'What do we do now?'

'Survive,' said Morpeth, preparing to take the first blows.

The children descended on them like hail.

13

BATTLE

Rachel returned home with Heiki sagging in her arms.

On the way back Heiki deliberately slowed her down. Whenever Rachel tried to shift, she faked pain. Every time Rachel tried to fly fast she wept deliriously, pretending that the shock of the Witches' attack had unhinged her mind. Rachel responded by holding her close, and flying gently, gently on the night winds.

During the journey Heiki shared some spells – nothing useful, just enough to gain Rachel's trust. Rachel warily joined in, but Heiki could tell she was not revealing her most subtle weapons or defences. Fine, she thought, not wanting too easy a contest. She made certain the voyage back lasted long enough for the troupe with Morpeth and Eric to get safely away. The last few miles were difficult –

Heiki could barely wait to see Rachel's reaction to the surprise she had prepared.

A cool dawn wind blew through the broken windows of the house.

Mum was inside, talking with the boy and girl who had been left behind.

'What are you doing?' Heiki shouted at them. 'What about the punishments? You were supposed to perform them as soon as Eric and Morpeth left!'

'They changed their minds,' said Mum thickly. Drawing the children close, she hurried across to Rachel, always keeping her gaze firmly on Heiki. The boy and girl shivered, trying to hide behind Mum's back.

'This is obviously Heiki,' Mum said hastily. 'I've been hearing all about her nastiness. Be careful, Rachel.'

Heiki grinned – and the curly ginger hair, freckles and endless weeping vanished, replaced by the washed-out blue eyes.

'The girl from the graveyard,' gasped Rachel. She turned to Mum. 'Where are—'

'Don't take your eyes off her!' Mum warned. 'Morpeth and Eric were taken. These poor kids' – she clenched the boy and girl – 'don't know where, but *that one* does.' She glared at Heiki. 'She planned it all.'

Rachel thundered at Heiki, 'If you've harmed them …'

'I *have* harmed them!'

Rachel sniffed the air. The scent-tag she had planted on Morpeth led from the kitchen, ending abruptly just above the house. 'Tell me where they've been taken!'

'Do you think I'm just going to *give* you that

information?' Heiki said scornfully. 'You'll have to fight me for it. Come on: a battle. Only us two girls. The finest children. No Witches, I promise.'

Rachel scanned the area. There were no Witches; Heiki was telling the truth about that. It showed how certain she was of success. She studied Heiki's fierce, Witch-trained eyes and felt afraid.

'Stop playing games,' Rachel said. 'I can't believe you want any of this. The Witches are making you behave this way.'

'That's not true,' Heiki replied. 'The Witches want you dead, but I couldn't wait to fight you anyway.'

'Why?' Rachel stared in disbelief. 'What have I ever done to you?'

'Nothing. I've just got to know which of us is the best.'

When Rachel looked confused, Heiki shook her head and said, 'You'd better catch up, girl. The future's a magic world. Forget grown-ups. Mums and teachers and grannies don't matter any more. Calen told me the Witches are going to make all the kids battle each other anyway – only the best will be allowed to fight the Wizards.'

For a moment, staring at that excited angular face, Rachel had a picture of the future: adults probably killed outright, the weakest children pushed aside, the gifted honed into a Wizard-hating elite – led by a handful of the most ruthless children, like Heiki.

No, Rachel thought, thinking of Dad. That mustn't happen.

'Better get on with it,' Heiki said. 'Morpeth and Eric may still be alive, but they can't last much longer.'

'Tell me where they are!'

'No.'

'You will!'

'Make me!'

Attack spells instantly offered themselves. Rachel ignored them. She had to get Heiki away from Mum and find Morpeth's signal! Maybe his scent-tag could be picked up close to the house ...

She glanced briefly, agonizingly, at Mum – and shifted.

Nothing happened, and seeing Rachel's bewilderment Heiki laughed. Rachel tried again, suddenly becoming aware of a spell she had never experienced before. It was a *counter-shifting* spell. Heiki was holding her back.

Rachel switched to simpler flight spells and escaped through the kitchen window. She flew into the early dawn sky, swiftly, though not too swiftly until she was certain Heiki followed. Once they were safely past the streets of the town and over open countryside, Rachel decided to really test Heiki's speed. Her fleetest spells took control, yet no matter how rapidly she travelled Heiki kept up effortlessly.

'You don't get away that easily,' Heiki said, smiling. 'I've got a particularly nasty spell I want to try out. It would be a pity not to use it, Rachel, because Calen and I created the spell especially for you. We call it a *multi-signal-hunter-slug*. See what you think.'

'No. Don't ...'

Heiki parted her thin lips and blew the hunter at Rachel.

The hunter was alive. Slug-shaped, mottled and black, it wriggled in a methodical manner away from Heiki's mouth. Rachel did not need to ask her spells for protection. They came forward immediately, a complex layering of defences. Frenetically, they sought combinations that might hold off the hunter's threat.

'You can't stop it,' said Heiki. 'Not in time. What are you going to do, Rachel?'

Rachel's information spells investigated the hunter. As it swam towards her head she realized she couldn't evade this weapon, or retreat from it, or ever shift fast enough to avoid its bite. Only one choice, her spells told her: become nothing. A hunter needs a victim.

Become nothing? Rachel wondered. What did that mean? She was flesh and muscle; she breathed, sweated. How could she become nothing?

Flicking its tail the hunter came for her. It was close now.

Rachel – still with Heiki flying alongside – came to a dead-halt in the sky. Heiki and her weapon also stopped. All three were anchored against the mottled clouds, unmoving. For a moment the hunter was perplexed. Then it lunged at Rachel's heart.

Hide! shrieked her spells.

Trying not to panic, Rachel masked the obvious signals. She scattered her magical scent. She disguised her panting frost-white breath. She bleached all colour from her body and even her clothing, until she was virtually transparent, the pale blue sky visible through her face.

Still the hunter came for her.

How can it detect me now? Rachel wondered – then realized how many alternative signs it had to choose from.

Like her heart, her poor hammering heart. Rachel could not prevent the thudding, but she could suppress the tiny vibrations each beat made. She did that. The breeze ruffled her clothes and stirred her hair. Rachel held all the strands stiff, even the finest hair on her wrists. Her eyes were open, dry, needing to blink. She did not blink. Broken light patterns reflected on her eyes from passing clouds. Rachel froze the patterns.

Gradually the hunter slowed. It opened a hot mouth next to her left eye – and waited.

Utter stillness without movement or sound.

The hunter angled left and right, baffled. Where were its signals? Sensing warmth it turned. Here, behind it, was pigmented skin and moist breath and movement.

'No!' wailed Heiki, suddenly understanding.

The hunter was designed to strike without mercy, and Heiki's cry only brought it on more speedily. Before she could fend it off the hunter sank through her legs. It ate deeply, burning through the flesh and bone until her thin ankles were fused together. By the time Heiki had called off its attack the entire lower half of her body was charred and smoking in the cold sky.

Rachel watched, appalled. Then she saw that incredibly Heiki already had the worst burning under control – soon she would be fit enough to continue her spell-making. Rachel quickly shifted, scurrying above the Arctic seas. Putting space between herself and Heiki, she extended her scent flaps, sniffing for any trace of Morpeth's tag.

At last, she found it: a feeble signal – but enough to follow.

Rachel tracked it northwards, shifting over the deep waters of the ocean. If she could smell the trace, did that mean Morpeth was still alive? The signal would probably linger for a while, she realized, whether he was breathing or not. She thought of Eric – and an image of his face, pallid and dead, jumped into her mind. No!

She tore across the ocean.

Heiki was not far behind. While Rachel followed a weak scent, Heiki knew exactly where Morpeth and Eric had been taken. She outflanked her, cutting in giant precise shifts over the Norwegian Sea, and simply waited. She did not bother to hide.

Rachel almost flew into Heiki. Seeing her – just in time – she held a position above the waves and viewed her opponent. Heiki's burnt legs still sizzled and cracked as they contracted in the cold air, but the injuries were mending rapidly. Heiki seemed at ease, strands of her thin white hair blown in all directions by the wind. She opened her palms and Rachel saw new weapons cradled there. Death-spells.

Heiki held them like treasured pets. 'Are you ready for these?'

Rachel beheld Heiki. Her face was contorted with excitement. It was a brutal face – terrifying, almost inhuman. But she *is* human, Rachel reminded herself. To have any chance of finding Eric alive, she knew she had to avoid the death-spells. Even if she could defeat them all, it would take too long. She thought: before a Witch got hold of you, Heiki, you must have behaved differently. There has to be a way to get through to you . . .

361

Cautiously, Rachel drifted towards Heiki, opening her hands and mouth to prove she hid no obvious weapons.

'Giving up already?' enquired Heiki.

'No, I've come for a chat.'

Heiki laughed. 'Go on, then.'

'What prize have the Witches offered you for defeating me?'

'Something special.'

'I doubt it,' Rachel said. 'I bet I can guess. They promised to change you, didn't they? They promised to turn plain ordinary Heiki into a Witch.'

Heiki's mouth gaped. 'H-how do you know that?'

'I was offered the same thing, on another world.'

'And you didn't want it?' Heiki was amazed. 'You refused?'

'I didn't like the killing I was expected to do in return.'

Heiki shrugged. 'Only the best survive. No point getting squeamish.'

Rachel studied her closely. 'Why did you order those kids to punish my Mum? She's no contest. Where's the challenge in that?'

'Parents are rubbish,' Heiki said vehemently.

'You don't like them, do you?' Rachel edged closer. 'Why not? What makes you dislike parents so much?'

'No magic. The Witches—'

Rachel cut her off. 'No. It's not that. It's something else, isn't it? What are you holding back?' Heiki appeared suddenly uncomfortable. 'This hatred of adults,' Rachel said, 'it's … got nothing to do with the Witches, has it?' She leapt in the dark. 'You hated parents *before* the Witches came!'

Heiki said nothing.

'What happened?' Rachel pressed. 'What did yours do that was so awful?'

'I won't tell you anything.'

'Did they hurt you?' Rachel drifted nearer, until they were almost touching. 'No, it isn't that, either. What happened? Can't you tell me? Is it too painful?'

'Shut up!'

'You were *abandoned*, weren't you?'

Heiki flinched, as if she had been struck.

'Shut up!' she screamed.

'Is that what the Witches promised you?' Rachel asked. 'Revenge on adults. Is that what all this is about?' Heiki's face darkened, her lips trembling with emotion. It was then, for the first time, that Rachel saw Heiki for what she truly was: an unwanted teenage girl, encouraged by Calen to hit out at everyone.

'You don't like anybody, do you?' Rachel whispered to her. 'Because no one likes you.'

'How dare—!' began Heiki, then tears burst from her bitter, angry face. The tears came so suddenly and with such energy that Rachel instinctively reached out a hand to console her.

Heiki shrugged it off, keeping her face covered to hide her feelings.

'The Witches like me,' she murmured at last. 'Calen likes me.'

'No,' said Rachel. 'She doesn't. Calen's just playing with you.'

Heiki clenched her eyes, holding back the rest of the

tears. 'I don't want your pity!' she muttered. 'I *am* special. Better than other children. Calen told me so!'

Rachel searched for hope in Heiki's resentful expression – but the brief moment of frailty had gone.

'They'll never make you into a real Witch,' Rachel told her. 'Calen's lying.'

'You're wrong. I'm *already* a Witch!' Heiki caressed her throat and gazed proudly down. A lean grey snake lay against her neck. 'See!'

Rachel studied the infant snake and saw at once that it was a fake. It could barely breathe or hold its ginger eyes open – as if what little life it possessed was already fading. She lifted its limp head, and the snake did not even try to stop her.

'Look at it carefully,' Rachel said. 'Do you really think Calen's soul-snake was ever like this? They've given you a scrawny toy, to keep you happy. A Witch's joke.'

'That's not true,' cried Heiki, her cheeks flushing. 'It's just young and weak because … because it's a baby and my magic's not very powerful yet.'

'There's no link between your magic and this mechanical thing. I'll prove it.'

Rachel cuffed the snake. Its jaw flopped open, and all its snake-colour faded immediately. White and semi-rigid, it lay unmoving in Heiki's hand.

Heiki leapt back, stifling a scream. With great tenderness she examined her snake, delicately rubbing its scales. She breathed on the nostrils, hoping that might bring it back to life. When the snake did not respond she glared at Rachel.

'You've killed it!'

'I didn't,' said Rachel earnestly. 'You saw I hardly touched it. A real soul-snake can defend itself. No living thing dies like this. Why can't you understand?'

'You'll say anything, won't you?' snarled Heiki. 'I was confused. I see what this is all about now. You're just scared to fight!'

'No, believe me,' Rachel implored her. 'That's not—'

'It was just a baby! It needed to learn like me, that's all!' Heiki stroked the snake's flaccid neck longingly. 'I...I might never be given a new one...' She became silent; then her face darkened with controlled anger. 'You had better run, Rachel. Try to find Eric. Go on! It won't make any difference. Even if you reach him before me the troupe will get you anyway. They know your appearance, and your magic scent. I've instructed them to kill on sight.' She smiled ferociously. 'And they do exactly what I tell them.'

'Did—'

'No! I'm not listening! I'll give you a few seconds head start...'

Rachel said, 'Are you sure you want to fight, Heiki? If so, better make sure you don't lose. No mistakes. Calen wouldn't accept that.'

Heiki bent the hardening snake into a curve. Pressing it forcefully against her neck, she uttered a few soothing words to its blank face. Seeing this, Rachel knew that any chance of influencing Heiki had gone. If she enjoys stroking its lifeless body, Rachel thought, perhaps she can never be convinced.

'Two seconds,' said Heiki.

Rachel pulled Heiki towards her – and widened her eyes. Dazzling silver light flashed out. For a moment only, Heiki was caught off guard. Snatching the snake from her neck, Rachel tossed it towards the sea. While Heiki dived after it, Rachel shifted.

A few precious seconds …

She sensed Morpeth was achingly close now. *Where was he!*

Suddenly, a lonely sound – the caw of a gull – followed by the crash of waves against shore.

Land.

Rachel swept across the last of the ocean. A narrow pebble beach lay ahead. Walruses crowded in the surf, and beyond them rose sheer ice cliffs. Rachel flew above their massive height and discovered snow, the beginnings of a vast continent extending north. At first she could see nothing except a remorseless whiteness. Then she noticed green dots. As Rachel closed in the dots widened, gained limbs, became children, dozens of them, plummeting from the sky, attacking two others on the ground.

'Morpeth! Eric!' she screamed.

Flinging herself at them, Rachel dropped beneath the thin cloud. Heiki was behind, closing rapidly, matching Rachel's movements. They swooped down together, so fast that no ordinary human eye could follow their speed.

Rachel made straight for the cluster of children.

But it was Heiki who landed first.

14

victim

A familiar girl with long black hair strode confidently up to Morpeth.

'Rachel!' Filled with joy, he staggered towards her as best he could.

Another girl landed some distance behind. This one was thin and white-haired, identical to Marshall's eerie description of Heiki. Morpeth shouted:

'Rachel! Can't you see she's behind you!'

Ignoring him, the black-haired girl addressed the troupe. 'Attack her! I showed you how!'

The children wavered, staring uncertainly at each other. Then they leapt straight onto the black-haired girl herself. 'What?' she gasped, trying to get away. Marshall was one of the first to reach her. He swiped her legs, pulling her down. As soon as she hit the snow the whole troupe sprang from all angles, pinning her arms.

'No!' screamed Morpeth. 'Leave her alone!'

Barely able to walk any longer he tottered over, trying to pull them off.

'Eric!' he pleaded. 'Help me!'

Eric raised himself from the snow. Getting to his feet he managed to take a few steps – *away* from the fight.

'What are you doing?' roared Morpeth. 'Get over here!'

Eric ignored him. Gingerly prodding the snow by his feet he found the prapsies. They lay together, a mess of feathers in a snowdrift, stunned and bewildered – though not badly hurt.

'Never mind the prapsies!' Morpeth cried. 'Do something! That's your *sister*!'

Eric continued his thoughtful inspection of the child-birds. He tucked in a few misplaced feathers, tested wing muscles for damage, pinched their rosy cheeks.

'Eric! What are—'

'It's not Rachel,' Eric shushed him. 'Be quiet, will you.'

To Morpeth the girl looked exactly like Rachel, even possessed her distinctive magical scent. 'Surely…'

'Trust me,' Eric murmured.

Cross-legged, the white-haired girl sat in the snow, staying out of the fight.

For the first time Morpeth gazed closely at her. She gazed back, forcing out a meagre half-smile. The face was wrong, but Morpeth knew that smile. He turned back in astonishment to the dark-haired girl. Not Rachel, he realized – Heiki.

A *switch* of appearances.

The troupe had been completely fooled. They engulfed Heiki. As Morpeth watched, for one extraordinary moment she held them off. Dragging herself upright, kicking at the grasping hands, Heiki hauled herself across the snow and tried to get away. But before her dazed mind could make a shifting spell – or even begin to understand what Rachel had done – the troupe leapt on her again, and slammed her into the ground. They did not stop to think about what damage they were doing. Terror drove them. Somewhere close, in the sky above, Calen observed. She would punish any hesitation. And Heiki also looked on.

They could see her not far away, calmly expecting her orders to be followed. Hadn't she demanded they be ruthless? The children followed her orders well, using fists and feet and spells. Amidst the snow turning to grey slush, they continued on and on with an incessant mechanical battering, waiting to be told by Heiki or Calen to stop.

Morpeth pleaded with the white-haired girl, 'Rachel, surely that's enough!'

Tears streamed down her pale blue eyes, and it was odd to see those soft wet tears against that hard brittle face.

'Nearly. I can't take any chances,' she whispered. 'You've no idea how strong Heiki is.'

When several seconds passed containing no sounds at all except the crunch of fists, Rachel undid the reversal spells, and shouted: 'Stop!'

The real Rachel, her hair dark and flowing in the wind, sat in the snow. At first the troupe could not understand what they were seeing. Their minds fought against believing it. Finally the truth sank in and their arms no longer came up and down on the girl beneath. Stumbling, crawling, desperate to get away, they peeled off Heiki.

Rachel lowered her face – not wanting to see what they had done.

The children formed a wide circle, surrounding Heiki. She did not need all the room they offered. A small heap against the reddening snow, she lay spread out in all her injury.

'Is she … alive?' Paul asked.

'Yes!' rasped Heiki, her voice strangled. Somehow she found the strength to dig an elbow in the slush and prop herself partially up. All the children retreated further away – despite Heiki's appalling wounds they were still frightened of her.

'Get me up,' she demanded.

The children wavered uncertainly, many looking at Rachel for guidance.

'If you … don't …' Heiki said between short gasping breaths, 'I will make sure … the Witches … kill … you all … I …' Her face slipped to the ground. 'Help me,' she begged, sounding suddenly pitiful.

A few children, led by Paul, started walking towards Rachel.

As soon as she saw this Calen burst from the sky. With a single claw she plucked Marshall and two other children by their necks and hoisted them into the air.

'You timid maggots!' she cried, addressing all the children. 'Follow me!' She pointed at Heiki. 'Except her. Leave her here.'

The older members of the troupe, many glancing despairingly at Rachel, raised their arms and flew into the air. Slowly they fell in behind Calen, following her northwards.

'Can't we do anything to keep them here?' Eric called across to Rachel.

'Let them go,' she answered dejectedly. 'I'm too weak to do anything now. So are you.'

'I'm not too weak.'

'You can hardly stand up, Eric.'

He tried – and collapsed when his frozen knees refused to lift him. The prapsies covered his hands, trying to warm them with their downy feathers.

In small groups, the remaining children rose from the snows. They picked up the four children whose flying spells Eric had destroyed and formed a sad, bedraggled line across the sky. The youngest were the most reluctant to leave. Bunching together, they clung tightly to Rachel's side and squeezed between her legs. Finally even these toddlers lost their nerve. Holding hands they glided off together, pointing their mournful eyes towards the Pole.

'Why won't they stay?' Eric muttered in frustration. 'Surely they realize nothing good's waiting for them out there!'

'Of course they do,' said Rachel. 'But they know I'm not strong enough to directly challenge all the Witches. What else can they do except follow Calen and hope they don't get punished too much?'

None of the children had stayed behind to assist Heiki. Fitfully, like a bird trying to make it home on a single ruined wing, she managed to flap awkwardly on her left arm. The right arm was dislocated, hanging limply by her side.

An easy victim, Rachel thought. A single spell would be enough to finish her off now.

'Well?' Eric asked. 'Are you going to let Heiki escape, after what she's done?'

Rachel's voice shook with emotion. 'There'll *always* be another Heiki somewhere,' she whispered. 'Should I kill everyone who comes after me? What about all those kids who've been in contact with Witches already. They're a danger, aren't they? Isn't that what Heiki would do – hunt them down just in case they're a threat?'

Eric did not reply.

Morpeth shuffled up to Rachel and held her tightly. Together they watched Heiki pass overhead like a broken shadow.

'I'll help you,' Rachel called up to her. 'Let me.'

'No,' rasped Heiki. 'I don't want your help. I'll make it back on my own.'

'Even if you do, what kind of welcome do you think Calen will offer?'

Heiki said nothing, trying to heave her body further up the sky. The troupe were a long way ahead, leaving her ever further behind as they gradually dwindled, fading against the brightness of the Arctic morning.

'I can't believe Heiki's trying to make it back to the troupe,' Eric said. 'Not after Calen did nothing to help her.'

'She's never faced a Witch's punishments,' Morpeth said quietly. 'She has no idea what Calen will do to her.'

And then, overhead, he heard the flutter of wings.

'A whirling baby!' marvelled a prapsy.

It was Yemi, clinging to his butterflies. All this time he had been waiting patiently for Calen. Where was she going with the children who made the shouting noises? They frightened him, and he was worried they might hurt Calen. As Calen flew away, he stayed quiet and still, as he had promised, but he felt scared. Then he noticed a familiar magic on the ground below. It filled him with the happiest of feelings. He floated down to greet it.

Rachel stood in the snow, surrounded by Yemi's Camberwell Beauties. They circled her, landing on her head, making the prapsies nervous. Two of the largest, their wings revolving like helicopter blades, carried Yemi himself gently down.

Rachel held out her arms.

But before Yemi reached her a warning shriek made the escorting butterflies cover his eyes. It was Calen. Leaving the other children she raced across the sky, calling Yemi's name over and over. Some of his butterflies waved their antennae excitedly at Calen; most hovered closer to Rachel.

'Come, Yemi!' Calen yelled. 'Don't make me angry.'

He hung uneasily just out of reach of Rachel's hands. Some of his Beauties pulled his toes towards her; others tugged him towards Calen. Yemi looked longingly at them both.

'Don't struggle over him,' Morpeth warned Rachel. 'You're too weary to fight Calen.'

'I know,' Rachel whispered – yet she could not stop herself. She opened her arms even wider, inviting Yemi inside. He sank lower, more certain, giggling at his butterflies.

As he touched Rachel's outstretched fingers a smell came over the wind, from the direction of Calen. It was a female smell – sweet, faintly musky – and palpably human: the smell of his mother.

Deeply confused, Yemi glanced at Rachel, then Calen, his butterflies flapping uneasily about the sky.

'Yemi, come.' It was his mother's gruff voice, emerging from Calen's four mouths.

'That's not your mother,' Rachel said.

Calen shifted. She reappeared as a faraway speck at the front of the troupe, leaving the powerful scent of mother lingering behind. 'Follow me!' she called.

'Mama!' Yemi wailed. 'Mama!'

'No!' Rachel cried. She projected a new smell – the scent of Fola, mingled with cornflower and other smells of his home she recalled. 'Go to your sister,' she insisted. 'Remember, Yemi! Go to your real home! Go home!'

For a few seconds Yemi's soft brown eyes blinked at Rachel. Then, without a glance at Calen this time, he shifted. It was a single immense shift that instantly placed him thousands of miles south. Rachel clapped her hands in joy, knowing where he had gone – and looked defiantly across the sky at Calen.

'A small victory!' Calen conceded. 'How long do you think Yemi's dull family can keep him occupied? He'll return to me soon enough.' She turned her back on Rachel and continued to lead the ragged troupe north.

Eric was still reeling from the sheer magnitude of Yemi's shifting spell. He had never felt such awesome power or control, even from Dragwena.

'That was no ordinary shift,' he said. 'Yemi didn't just use his own magic. He used the magic of the troupe kids to help him.'

Rachel shook her head. 'No, that's not possible. Even a Witch can't do that.'

'Well, he did,' insisted Eric. 'He took what he wanted. A bit from every child, not too much. Not greedy. Just what he needed.'

'Yemi's peculiarly gifted, isn't he?' Morpeth said. 'His magic seems completely distinctive, unlike that of other children.'

'In every way,' Eric said. 'His spells are weird. They're not like yours or Rachel's, or Witches', either.'

For one magnificent second Rachel thought of Larpskendya. She trembled, the possibility too wonderful to bear.

'More like a Wizard?' she said, hardly daring to ask. 'Is his magic like Larpskendya's?'

'No,' Eric sighed. 'It's not Larpskendya, Rachel. That baby's magic is not like *anything* we've seen before.'

As the last of the children ebbed over the horizon with Calen, Eric rummaged in his bulging, lively coat.

'Hiya, boys!'

The prapsies beamed merrily out of the pockets.

Eric's hands were too numb to feel the touch of their feathers. One prapsy rubbed the side of its delicate head against his fingers.

'Flipping heck!' it said, licking them distastefully.

The other prapsy rolled its eyes. 'Oh, don't be fussy. It's still Eric.'

'I know, but he's ice pops. You're so moody!'

'Shut up, you dinky warbler!'

'Ugly, cutted lips!'

'Are my lips cutted?' A sorrowful eye turned to Eric for reassurance.

He rubbed both prapsies' cheeks with his coat sleeve, not wanting to touch them with his cold fingers. 'They are cutted,' he said, 'but they look good, boys. In fact, you both look great. You *are* great: like eagles.'

The prapsies crooned delightedly.

'Time to sort out your frostbite, goldilocks,' Rachel said.

Eric smiled. 'Do the old man first. Age before beauty.'

'Don't these hurt?' She examined his swollen fingers.

He grinned. 'Can't feel a thing.'

'I suppose that's because you're tough?'

'Dead right.'

Rachel repaired the worst of Eric's frostbite. The spells needed were basic enough, but she was tired, so it took some time to finish. Then she attended to Morpeth.

'Save your strength,' he objected.

'For what?' she said huskily. 'What's more important than this?'

Morpeth's back was deeply bruised where he had taken

on most of the blows aimed at Eric. Rachel anaesthetized the stinging and carefully mended the worst of the broken blood vessels. Finally she wrapped everyone inside an insulating warmth even the stabbing Arctic winds could not pierce.

For a while they simply gazed northwards, feeling hungry and weary and anxious.

'What a miserable place this is,' Eric said. He shaded his eyes, trying to find any details in the whiteness stretching eternally ahead. 'I bet the Witches love it.'

Rachel explained what had occurred at the house. 'If you want, I can take you back home,' she said seriously. 'It will be safer there.'

Eric shook his head. 'No way. I don't want to give the Witches or anyone else a reason to go after Mum again.' He kicked the snows in frustration. 'Damn! Where's Larpskendya?'

'He'll come,' Rachel said tightly. 'He will come.'

'If we want to find the Witch-base we need to follow the children quickly,' Morpeth told them. 'Before their scent fades or is masked.'

'Brilliant,' Eric muttered resignedly. 'I can't wait to meet all five Witches!'

Morpeth gazed at both of them. 'There is an alternative. We could try to find a quiet place to hide and survive, until Larpskendya arrives.'

'No,' Rachel said. 'That will leave all children at the Witches' mercy.' She thought of Paul, and wondered how long it would take Calen to finally crush his spirit. 'I'm not just letting the Witches do what they want any more,' she said. 'We must at least try to find out where their base is.'

All three stared northwards, steeling themselves to go on. The wind had picked up, and with it came a light snowfall, squalling into their faces.

'I can still detect Heiki's scent,' Eric remarked. 'She's wounded, leaving a big trail of magic. It's, well, *leaking* out of her.'

Rachel sent out her information spells. When they returned, she found unexpected tears welling in her eyes. 'Heiki's falling further and further behind,' she said. 'She's attempting so hard to keep up, but she can't. Her injuries are too bad to repair this time.'

'Does she think we're coming after her?' Eric asked.

'It's nothing to do with us,' murmured Rachel. 'She's still trying to impress the Witches. Heiki's doing everything she can to hide her weakness, especially from Calen.'

Eric frowned. 'Why bother? Hasn't that Witch already given up on her?'

Rachel shared a look of understanding with Morpeth. On Ithrea it had taken all of her willpower to resist the allure of Dragwena. And she had only needed to resist for a few days. Heiki had spent far longer with the Witches, being made to feel utterly special.

Poor Heiki had fallen half in love with Calen's glamour.

15

ARRIVALS

Heiki hauled her frail body towards the Pole.

She was too weak to shift. While she still had the strength she flew. When that left her she limped on ankles that had never fully recovered from the hunter. Finally she crawled. It took her over an hour to make the last few windswept yards to the perimeter of the Witch-base.

Calen met her. She stared contemptuously.

'Why have you returned? There is only more punishment for you here.'

Heiki knelt shamefully in the snow. 'Please help me. Please. I am in pain...'

'You failed,' said Calen. 'There are no second chances for a failed Witch.'

'I'll do anything,' Heiki promised. 'I'm still willing. Don't give up on me.'

'I asked you to make me proud. You could not even do that.'

'Please. Give me another chance.'

'No. There is no chance for you now.'

Calen clenched Heiki's scalp and carried her like an unwanted bag between the towers.

'What's going to happen to me?'

Calen did not reply. Seeing Heiki fiddling with the baby snake, she snatched it from her neck and tossed its hardened body to the ground. Heiki started to cry. She tried not to, but she couldn't stop the flow, and was too weary to wipe the wetness away.

She gazed up at Calen. 'Am I ... to be killed?'

'Do you even need to ask?'

Calen flew to her own eye-tower and dumped Heiki inside.

Later Calen was summoned by her mother.

Nervously, she made her way to Heebra's vast tower, expecting to be severely punished for Heiki's failure. Nylo squirmed against her throat.

Heebra stood gazing out of the eye-window. For several minutes she ignored Calen. Eventually she said, 'Heiki, your favourite, the child you personally trained, was defeated.'

Calen bowed her head in humiliation.

'You were also mistaken about the other children on this world,' said Heebra. 'They can be instructed, but many are defiant or unpredictable.'

'If I have more time ...'

'More time!' screamed Heebra. She turned to face her daughter. 'It will take an *age* to forge the children into an army loyal enough to threaten the Wizards!'

'Then—' faltered Calen, holding Nylo close, 'do you recommend ... we leave?'

Heebra's four jaws twisted from anger to amusement. 'Leave this marvellous world to the Wizards? I think not. No. A new plan: we will drag Larpskendya here as fast as we can!'

'I don't understand.'

'Larpskendya has always been the great prize,' Heebra said. 'I've always known that if we could kill him we could quickly crush the Order of Wizards. For the first time I have an advantage. When the two girls battled I reopened the channel between Rachel and Larpskendya. He cannot communicate, but he sees everything that frightens his preferred child, sees with her eyes.' Heebra smiled. 'Heiki served her purpose. I always knew Rachel would defeat her. However, even their little skirmish will have horrified the gentle Larpskendya.'

'Surely he will be too cautious to come.'

'No,' Heebra said. 'He will come for his Rachel, count on it. A scout report has already reached me that he is rushing here to protect his cherished Witch-slayer.'

Calen's mouths widened. 'Are we ready? Larpskendya will not be alone.'

'He *is* alone!' exulted Heebra. 'The Griddas have accomplished far more than I ever expected, Calen. We sent them over a wide area. The Wizards needed to scatter to confront them. Larpskendya is presently isolated, with no companions to hold his hand.' She drew Mak against the skin of her nostrils and sniffed his ripe fragrance. 'Best of all, Calen, Larpskendya is injured. A Gridda slashed him at the Leppos world! I've made sure others in the area have orders to harry and harm him all the journey to Earth. Our Griddas won't allow him to recover. When Larpskendya arrives he will be exhausted.'

'Will he?' Calen said uncertainly. 'His power is immense. Even with your capability amongst us, are we enough with only four other Witches...'

'Only four?' Heebra laughed. 'Good. Then you did not detect the coming of the rest. In that case I'm sure Larpskendya will not have done so, either.'

'The rest?' Calen glanced round.

'I summoned them as soon as I realized how to set the trap.'

At a gesture from Heebra hundreds of High Witches suddenly appeared. They packed the sky with their magnificence, their black dresses streaming in the breeze. Seeing Calen's surprise, most were amused.

'How many?' Calen gasped.

'Seven hundred and fifty-six of our best. They just arrived, fresh and itching to fight. Take control of them, Calen. Let those who wish it start building their own eye-towers, but make sure all the new sisters remain hidden. Rachel expects to find only five Witches. She should continue to believe that. We must have no mistakes now.'

'Larpskendya is bound to suspect a trap,' Calen said. 'He will be cautious, survey the position, and not show himself until he is ready.'

'Agreed. So we must make him desperate. When Rachel sees the fun I have planned for the other children here, Larpskendya will dash the final distance. That will draw the last reserves from him.'

'What fun?' asked Calen, intrigued.

'I want you to create a single prison, isolate the children there and panic them, while Rachel watches.'

'Panic them? How?'

'Start by executing Heiki,' said Heebra. 'I want to make a special example of her. If her death does not bring Larpskendya move onto another child – any child, I don't care who.'

Calen nodded. 'How do you want me to execute Heiki?'

'As you wish,' said Heebra. 'Wait. A better idea. Choose something – a device – all children will recognize, no matter where they are from.'

'One of their own kind of murder machines?'

'Or something even simpler, perhaps. Talk to the youngest children. Find out what kind of games they share or like to play, and use something from those to frighten them. It's fear we want now, Calen. Build it up. Terrify all these children, and let Rachel witness it. Make Larpskendya hurry the final stretch.'

'And later? How will we dispose of Rachel?'

'After I've used her to capture Larpskendya we'll both deal with her, each in our own way.'

Calen left the eye-tower to carry out her orders.

Heebra glided across the chamber and seated herself. From the height of her meticulously shrouded eye-tower she could observe everything for dozens of miles. Rachel, Eric and Morpeth approached within a primitive spell. Heebra knew exactly where they were. She had deliberately drawn the Witches and all the polar bears away from their perimeter guard to ensure that the children came all the way into the base. The trap was almost complete.

For the first time since arriving on Earth Heebra permitted herself to relax completely. The view outside pleased her more and more. Snow rarely fell in this part of the world, but it did not melt. Her Witches could make a home here with little difficulty. The first stage would be to replace the disgusting sunlight with Ool's sensuous darkness. Next they would make the snows pour eternally.

But such matters could wait. With enormous anticipation Heebra imagined Larpskendya tearing through space, consumed with tiredness and injury, seeing through Rachel's eyes, trying to arrive in time to stop the bloodshed.

But he would not stop it. Not this time. This time she and hundreds of her most superb High Witches were ready for him.

16

IMPRISONMENT

Within a cloaking spell Rachel, Morpeth, Eric and the prapsies followed Heiki. They observed her meeting with Calen. Without realizing it, they entered the Witch perimeter watched by hundreds of pairs of tattooed eyes.

'This could be Ithrea,' said Eric. His voice was barely audible.

'You don't need to whisper,' Rachel told him. 'Our voices can't be heard.'

'I'll whisper anyway.'

The prapsies would not settle. Constantly twitching, they rolled their eyes and tasted the falling snow with suspicious pink tongues.

'Why are they fidgeting so much?' Rachel asked Eric.

'They're jumpy, that's all.'

THE SCENT OF MAGIC

One prapsy sniffed the air. 'A Witch, maybe.'

The other puckered its lips. 'Spine-gutters!'

'Shush, boys, I'll look after you,' Eric promised, petting their feathers.

'No, listen to them,' Morpeth said. 'Remember they spent hundreds of years on Ithrea as Dragwena's pets.' He stroked their neck feathers. 'How many Witches? Can you tell?'

'We see them stinkers!'

Morpeth nodded impatiently. 'But how many?'

'Many!'

'Too many to count?'

Both prapsies peered shrewdly upwards. 'See there!' They covered their faces.

Ahead, the Witch towers had appeared. There were five of them, each over four hundred feet tall, arranged in a faultless circle. Harsh emerald light radiated from the eye-windows, easily penetrating the meagre snowfall.

'There's no cover for us out here,' Morpeth said. 'We daren't get any closer.'

'To see what's happening we must,' Rachel insisted.

Cautiously she drew them towards the nearest tower. Her spells begged her not to. They wanted her to survive. They told her to shift. They pleaded with her to disguise herself, abandon Eric and Morpeth, and just get away. Rachel pressed on, ignoring their increasingly frantic warnings.

In an area of flat undisturbed snow between the towers, they stopped.

'Gutters!' squealed both prapsies.

For the first time the Witches showed themselves. Clothed in their skin-tight black dresses, three soared between the eye-windows, entering and leaving so swiftly that their bodies appeared to be inescapably everywhere at once. One Witch, Calen, passed directly over Rachel. She did not look down.

'They can't see us,' Rachel said, trying to reassure herself.

'Or they're pretending not to,' suggested Morpeth.

Eric spotted a new structure. 'What's that? It wasn't there earlier.'

A rough building made from ice was beginning to form inside the ring of the eye-towers. It was three stories high – and growing. Two Witches made short flights around the structure, relaying orders. As floor after floor took shape, Morpeth could not understand how the building was being constructed. Then he saw the meaning of the blurs scrabbling across the slabs of ice.

'The children are making it!'

Dozens were at work. Supervised by the Witches, the children used their hands and magic to compact the snow into blocks of ice. They moved at speed, shaping the walls and ceilings, taunted by the Witches, who allowed them no rest. Morpeth, Eric and Rachel watched in awe as the entire building was completed in less than an hour.

'What's it for?' Eric asked.

Morpeth said, 'It's obviously purpose-built, not made to live inside. Some kind of … prison. See how cramped it is? Each room is just big enough for a child to stand up in, with a single window. And notice: all the windows point in one direction only – towards *us*.'

Rachel shuddered. Was that a coincidence? It had to be…

'They've finished,' Eric said. 'What now?'

'Wait,' Rachel answered.

The Witches drove the children to their appointed rooms. They stood at the empty frames of their ice windows, gazing mournfully down.

At first Rachel thought the children were looking directly at her. Then she realized they were peering down the walls. At the base of the ice prison two Witches waited either side of a small doorway. One was Calen. She opened the door – and a figure shuffled out.

It was a girl, still badly injured: Heiki.

She stumbled forward, hauling numerous pieces of wood and a length of rope across the snow.

'What is it?' Eric tried to make out the shapes.

'I don't know.' Rachel strained to determine a purpose. 'The parts are so heavy. She can hardly carry them, even using her magic.'

Morpeth gazed around at the pinched, nervous faces of the children. 'They've been told what's going to happen,' he said, suddenly understanding. 'Each child has a perfect view.'

Eric frowned. 'A perfect view for what?'

'To witness whatever's planned for Heiki. To watch the spectacle.'

Once or twice Heiki dropped her load or tried to rest. Each time Calen flew over and struck her ankles, forcing her to move on. Eventually she hoisted herself far enough away from the foot of the prison for all the children to have a clear view. Calen hissed instructions in her ear.

Nodding, Heiki, piece by piece, erected a device.

'Oh no,' said Eric, recognizing it. 'No, please.'

It was a Hangman.

Rachel shuddered, almost fell. She had prepared herself for many things, but not this. Pity for Heiki poured through her – and dread. At the same time her shifting spells automatically leapt forward – awaiting a command to leave.

Heiki finished making the angular base and frame. Pausing a moment, she raised the length of rope from the snow and attached it to the Hangman. Calen tested the rope's resistance by making Heiki jerk it several times. Then Calen folded the rope into the shape of a noose, picked Heiki up and used her head to measure the size needed. Rachel numbly tried devising a defence, but against five High Witches her spells offered nothing that would work.

Get away! Get away! they screamed.

The Hangman was complete. Heiki leaned heavily against the base, and as she stared up at the knotted rope any resolve she had left faded. She covered her face and wept. All this time she had still been trying to impress Calen. Knowing the Witches never respond to pity, she kept her chin up, hoping the defiant attitude Calen had once so liked might make a difference. But Calen gave her no encouragement, and, now that the Hangman was waiting for her, Heiki fell to her knees. She pressed her lips to the black hem of Calen's dress and pleaded.

'Please. Please don't—'

'No second chances,' Calen reminded her. She lifted

Heiki by the scalp, displaying her to the children in the ice building. When Heiki squirmed to pull away, Calen simply tightened her grip.

Morpeth glanced at the rest of the children. From the windows all their haunted eyes were on Heiki, including the youngest. They were obviously being forced to watch. Paul and Marshall stood in adjacent rooms, their expressions petrified.

'Stop this,' Morpeth muttered. 'Rachel, somehow... we must...'

Rachel nodded wildly. She had no idea how.

Calen raised Heiki's thin neck towards the noose.

'Listen to me,' Eric whispered. 'Calen is using two spells to control the rope. I've worked them out. I think I can destroy both. Rachel, if you try—'

Morpeth tapped him on the shoulder.

'Rachel,' Eric went on, 'if you attack Calen at the same time, I'll—'

Morpeth tapped him again.

'What!'

Eric felt the hairs on his neck tingle.

Above them, winking from the sky, the Wizards had arrived.

17

the trap

They came in a great stately procession: twenty Wizards.

Singly they came, unfolding from the clouds in majestic robes of crimson and turquoise and burnished gold. And as they came they announced their names in jubilation:

'Areglion! Tournallat! Hensult! Serpantha! ...'

The names meant nothing to the children, but the Witches shrank back. A stupefied Calen stepped away from the Hangman.

'Mother!' she screamed at the sky. 'You promised only Larpskendya!'

Hensult and Serpantha took up positions at the epicentre of the sky. They were shaped like men but taller, as tall as the Witches. Impassively they waited, until the air sang in a manner that tortured the recessed ears of the Witches.

A final cream-robed Wizard had arrived. His many-coloured eyes were untamed.

'Larpskendya!' Rachel cried joyfully, her heart lurching as she took in the sight of him.

For a moment the Great Wizard acknowledged her gravely. Then he and the other Wizards shifted, unfurling in the snow beside Heiki.

Larpskendya picked her shaking body from the Hangman. He wiped away her tears.

Heiki had expected punishment. When Larpskendya simply took her in his strong arms she found herself unable to think clearly. He held her, without words, until she stopped trembling. He touched her injured arm, mending it. At last Heiki gazed up, but she could not meet his eyes. She could barely speak.

'Why ... are you helping me?'

Larpskendya seemed surprised. 'Why wouldn't I?'

'After what I've done ...'

'Haven't you been punished enough? Do you want more punishment?'

'No,' she murmured. 'Oh ... but I've done some terrible things.'

'And you might have done worse,' he answered firmly. 'There is a harder trial ahead, because of you. Will you help me, Heiki?'

Before she could say anything Calen's voice rang out. She had recovered from the entrance of the Wizards, though Nylo still cowered against her throat.

'Twenty Wizards,' she shouted. 'Twenty is not enough.

What is the largest number of Witches you can defeat in personal combat, Larpskendya? Five? Fifty?'

She raised a claw – and one hundred recently built eye-towers shimmered against the sky. Witches soared from them, drawing short curved daggers from their black dresses.

If Larpskendya's Wizards were afraid they did not show it. 'Not impressed?' said Calen. 'A few more, then.'

Exactly six hundred and fifty-six further towers appeared.

Witches swarmed from the eye-windows, so many that their weaving bodies cast half the snow in shadow. Morpeth strained his neck. He could not see beyond the Witches. They crowded all around him, and above him, bathed in luminous green light.

Eric gaped in despair at the sky. 'I don't think even Larpskendya can beat this many,' he whispered, poking the prapsies deep inside his coat. 'We're going to have to fight, too.'

'Wait for a sign,' Rachel said, squeezing his hand. 'Larpskendya will show us what to do.'

The Witches took up rehearsed battle positions in the sky, coming together in packs that surrounded the Wizards. Each pack contained only blood-related sisters – the most ferocious fighting combination. When they were set, each Witch's soul-snake licked diagonally across her face – the traditional signal of battle readiness.

But they did not attack.

Larpskendya was still calm. 'Do your worst, Witch,' he said to Calen, 'as your kind always will. We are prepared.'

He linked hands with the other Wizards, placing Heiki inside the circle they made.

393

'Perhaps Rachel and her friends would like to join in,' said Calen brightly.

The cloaking spell was laid bare, exposing Rachel, Eric and Morpeth. The children in the building stared in amazement. The Witches merely seemed amused.

'Stay where you are,' Larpskendya warned Rachel.

He consulted with his companion Wizards and said a few urgent words to Heiki. Briefly she argued with him. Then she sneaked a distraught glance at Rachel and started walking across the snow towards her.

'I can't believe it!' Eric blasted. 'Flipping heck, Larpskendya's sent Heiki here. To us!'

'Let her come,' said Rachel, meeting Larpskendya's steady gaze. 'He obviously can't protect her if he has to fight so many.'

'Are *we* going to protect her?' Eric asked defiantly. 'After what she did!'

Heiki shuffled across the snow. Her head was lowered. Unable to bring herself to stand alongside Rachel, she took a position instead awkwardly next to Morpeth. Rachel nodded curtly, showing that she tolerated Heiki's presence, nothing more. Conflicting feelings flooded her. Larpskendya wanted this, but could she trust Heiki?

The Wizards drew closer, standing back to back.

'Are you sure you want this fight?' Larpskendya thundered at Calen. 'Most of your High Witches are here. Even if you defeat us, how many of you will be left to defend Ool against the Griddas? I cannot believe Heebra was foolish enough to let them loose.'

Calen laughed. 'Tell her that yourself. A final surprise!'

All the Witches joined in her mirth, dispersing to leave a gap in the air.

Inside Eric's coat pockets the prapsies began whimpering. It was a sound they had never made before.

'What is it?' said Rachel, trying to decide how to aid the Wizards.

Eric caught his breath. 'Can't you … can't you feel it?'

The whimpers of the prapsies rose in pitch, became screeches.

Rachel could sense the reason clearly now – a huge outbulging of magic.

'Here it comes,' said Eric, clenching his teeth.

In one movement everyone – Witches, Wizards and children – looked up.

Across half the sky a new tower had appeared. It was so immense that all the children had to turn their heads to take in its scope. Rachel found her gaze drawn to the eye-window. A bulky shadow moved behind the glass. For a moment the shadow turned towards her. It moved – then stopped – then looked directly at Rachel. Under its detailed inspection Rachel could not breathe. She had faced Dragwena's death-spells with more equanimity than she now faced this shadow. It could kill her effortlessly, she realized. And it wished to. How it wanted to harm her!

She managed to turn her head.

Slightly, almost imperceptibly, she saw Larpskendya's whole body shiver. Rachel knew then that whatever owned this shadow, he had not anticipated it.

Heebra, leader of the Sisterhood of Ool, burst from the

tower. In a single leap she covered the distance to the Wizards. For a few seconds she merely stood by Larpskendya's side, enjoying his discomfiture. Then she bowed and said, courteously:

'Greetings, Larpskendya. Flesh to flesh at last. I have waited for this.' She examined his shining robe and the other Wizards. 'Shall we dispense with these illusions?'

As she touched his shoulder all the other Wizards vanished. Larpskendya was alone in the snow, his robe shredded. Heebra sniffed. 'Is this tattered mess, this rag, really the celebrated Larpskendya? I expected better. Did you hope to dazzle my Witches into submission with your trick? Or simply divert their attacks?'

Larpskendya was silent. His shoulders slumped, and for the first time Rachel noticed the appalling nature of his real injuries. Three deep slashes crossed his throat. They had clearly been made by a Witch's claws, though much bigger claws than any Rachel had seen before. The wounds were recent, still bleeding.

'I see my Griddas occupied you well,' Heebra said. 'But I knew you would survive. You were always a worthy opponent, Larpskendya.'

'I am not your enemy,' he answered.

'You have killed Witches,' said Heebra. 'Do you deny it?'

'Only when they gave me no choice. I took no pleasure in it.'

'A pity,' said Heebra, laughing. 'You should have done. I will certainly take pleasure in *your* death.' She prodded his neck injury. 'You took the life of my daughter. How long should I make you suffer for that?'

Larpskendya said nothing, knowing no words would make a difference.

'You will not retreat inside your silence,' Heebra told him. 'I have dawdled long enough on this world. I've a desire to commit some violence, and for you to witness it.'

'It is my death you want,' Larpskendya replied evenly. 'Leave the children.'

'It will take more than your death to satisfy me. I think I will kill all the children here. Their lives mean nothing to me.'

'Spare them,' Larpskendya said. 'If you do, I will submit.'

'You would surrender? Without a fight?' She sounded amazed.

'*If* you promise not to harm the children.'

Eric screamed, 'Don't believe her! Larpskendya, what are you doing? She'll kill us anyway!'

'Trust him,' Rachel whispered, never taking her gaze off Larpskendya.

Heebra hesitated. Obviously Larpskendya was protecting the children, as she knew he would, but she had not expected such a simple surrender. She gazed curiously at him. Even in his weakened condition, she knew, Larpskendya could probably destroy hundreds of her best Witches before they overpowered him. The Witch-packs could not wait to fight, but it suited Heebra to avoid conflict. Test his resolve, she thought. If this is another trick like his fake Wizards, expose it.

'Very well,' she said. 'I agree to your terms. Dragwena's blood-honour must be satisfied first, of course. So, I will spare all the children except two. Give me Eric and Rachel. That is *my* condition.'

There was silence. Larpskendya's expression was unreadable.

'Yes,' he murmured at last. 'Do as you wish with Rachel and Eric.'

Most children could not believe this answer. They gazed at him in shock. Several of those imprisoned in the ice prison wept. Eric began shouting insults at Larpskendya at the top of his voice, and the prapsies joined in. Morpeth was stunned, unable to accept what he had heard. Even Heiki shook her head, her emotions in turmoil. At least, if Heebra kept her promise, she might now live through this…

Only Rachel kept her gaze on Larpskendya. She stared at him, her faith unwavering, and he stared back, his gaze filled with determination and asking for her courage.

'Do you promise to obey my Witches?' Heebra asked, a green nail under Larpskendya's chin. 'You will not resist?'

'I will not resist.'

Heebra gestured for the Witches guarding the imprisoned children to empty the ice-structure, and Larpskendya permitted himself to be led inside. Heebra warily surveyed the skies, prepared for a trap. Could she have missed something?

'Take him to the top,' she ordered. 'Hurry. And bind him hard.'

Over a third of the Witches escorted Larpskendya into the prison. At first, most were too nervous to touch him. When he continued to offer no resistance the Witches grew bolder. They bound his wrists and ankles. They fastened his mouth with spell-thread, preventing any utterance of spells. As soon as this was done the ecstatic Witches lost any fear they still had. Snarling with joy, they hauled Larpskendya up the stairway, dragging him against the ice steps to the summit. Faster and faster up the floors they rushed, and as they moved they tightened the spellbindings until Larpskendya bled.

Rachel was unable to watch.

'Oh, Larpskendya,' Eric said, his anger spent, replaced by a feeling of utter desolation and emptiness. 'What have you done?'

Calen flew up to the Great Wizard's window and placed the edge of her curved dagger against his throat. She trembled with excitement.

'Let me!' she cried.

'No,' said Heebra. 'Let him see his favourites die, first. Start with the girl.'

Morpeth searched for anything with which to defend Eric and Rachel. He glanced at the assembled children. A ragged bunch, they huddled disconsolately in the snow. Morpeth appealed silently to Paul and Marshall. They saw him and averted their eyes. Ashamed, Morpeth realized, too afraid to risk the punishment of the Witches.

'We have a Witch-slayer amongst us,' said Heebra. 'Who wants to fight Rachel?'

Hundreds of Witches clamoured to be noticed. Heebra picked the first ten at random. Those chosen assembled in a semicircle, awaiting Heebra's signal to begin.

Morpeth immediately moved in front of Rachel. Eric took up a position behind, guarding her back. He tried to shoo the prapsies away, but they remained in his pockets, thrusting their soft mouths at Heebra.

'Come on then, you ugly hags!' Eric bellowed. 'As many as you like!'

'Wait,' said a voice.

It was Heiki. Her ashen, thin face shook with fear as she walked the short distance across to Rachel. When she was by Rachel's side, she turned to face Heebra – not calmly, but she faced her. She fumbled for a wrist, and Rachel clutched it.

Morpeth brought their hands together, and drew all four close: a fragile shield.

Heebra lifted a claw to start the attack, but a faint noise on the breeze distracted her. It was such an odd sound in that dread-filled atmosphere that everyone noticed it.

The sound of giggling.

Yemi had arrived. Floating between the Witch towers he swished back and forth as if nothing could be more entrancing. As he closed on the children guarded by the Witches he showed them a new dance he had learned: upright, jigging on his toes, waving his arms. His Camberwell Beauties jigged with him.

'What's he doing here?' Heebra growled at her daughter.

'I…don't understand,' Calen apologized. 'I didn't summon the boy. He should be with his family. I left countless spells to hold him there.'

'Remove him!' said Heebra, gazing suspiciously at Larpskendya.

Calen flew from the prison to intercept Yemi, but she

could not catch him. Each time she reached out her claws he squeezed away, teasing her.

'No games,' she insisted. 'Come here.'

Yemi continued to elude Calen. Over and over he slipped from her grasp.

Heebra nodded appreciatively. 'His flight has achieved a deftness and precision even you cannot master, Calen.'

Rachel clung to Morpeth. She could barely control her feelings. Ever since Yemi arrived she had been deliberately ignoring him. While his greeting magic bathed her like a warm stream she sent it back with cold, definite rejections. How she yearned just to hold him, but when the Witches launched their assault on her he must not be near...

'Leave him,' Heebra told Calen, when it was obvious her daughter could never again catch Yemi unless he wished it. 'Just don't antagonize the boy.' She stretched up to her full height, looking down on Rachel. 'Are you ready to defend yourself?'

Rachel did not reply, She stared at Larpskendya. And the Great Wizard stared back. He was burning for her to notice him.

'No use expecting assistance there,' gloated Heebra. 'Bound with spell-thread, he is as powerless as one of your own adults.'

Rachel looked into Larpskendya's many-coloured eyes. Inside them she saw a picture: Yemi. A movement showed Rachel what Larpskendya wanted her to do. She blinked. No. That couldn't be correct. She must have misunderstood. She narrowed her eyes, peering more closely.

'No!' Rachel yelled. 'I won't do it!'

Larpskendya's eyes overflowed with tears. But they were also hard, insistent, willing Rachel to trust him.

On Heebra's signal the Witches designated to kill Rachel opened their jaws. Death-spells streamed from their connected mouths.

Eric had time to destroy the first two, but the shock wave of the third threw him and Heiki into the air. They landed several feet away and lay in the snow, still. Moments later the stunned prapsies tumbled like stones from Eric's pockets.

Morpeth pushed Rachel down and spread his body across hers, trying to take the impact of as many blows as he could. But the death-spells merely knocked him savagely aside – and sank into Rachel.

The instant the first spell struck her Rachel wept, but not from the pain. She felt no pain. As soon as the spell touched her body she deflected its aim.

Without taking her eyes from Larpskendya she turned all the attacks of the Witches – every lethal one of them – on Yemi.

18

the Butterfly child

At the first touch of the death-spells Yemi's butterflies transformed.

The same dainty yellow wings that a moment earlier had been idly flapping became a hardened shield. Across his entire body they spread: he felt nothing.

Most of the Witches immediately stopped their attacks. Two did not stop. They had waited a long time for a fight, any fight, and hardly cared whether it was Yemi or Rachel they dispatched. Then one was thrown backwards. Howling, she pressed her smoking eyes into the snow. The second Witch fell to her knees, one of her lungs punctured.

'Leave him, you fools!' ordered Heebra. 'Can't you see what the boy's doing?'

Calen stared in amazement. 'He's throwing their *own spells* back at them!'

The attacks ended and everyone gazed at the space containing Yemi.

For a while he could not be seen. Steam from the snow boiled by the death-spells rose all about him. When the haze lifted everyone saw that he had no wounds. The attacks had not even dented Yemi's mood. With simple curiosity he grasped at the rising tendrils of warm air. His yellow shield had vanished, separated once again into the many and delicate butterflies. A few of these had scorched wings, nothing worse.

Most of the Witches, seeing their two injured sisters, expected Heebra to approve a renewed assault.

'Wait!' she said. 'Don't touch the baby!' No Witch was dead, she realized with relief. Only a blind Witch, humiliated, but too badly injured to launch any more attacks. 'There has been no sister killed,' Heebra called out. 'Contain yourselves. I will destroy anyone who attempts a spell against Yemi or Rachel!'

Her Witches obeyed restively, whispering in murderous tones.

'What kind of organism is he, Mother?' asked Calen, flying across. She kept her distance from Yemi. 'Is he something of Larpskendya's making? Not human, surely.'

'Human, yes.' Heebra answered. 'An exceptional evolution of magic. He must be unique – a rogue – even in this species.' She glanced warily up at Larpskendya. Even spellbound, she knew he had somehow managed to summon the boy. What else was he planning? She saw a look pass between him and Rachel.

'Cover the Wizard's eyes!' she raged at the nearest Witches. 'Bind him completely and press his face to the floor!'

Larpskendya's head was pushed below the window. Rachel shivered, not knowing what to do next – he had not had time to show her. Hearing her own laboured breathing, she realized how quiet it had become. Yemi's baby voice could be heard grumbling at Calen – an eerie noise in this place filled with so much despair. The only other sound was the rustle of dresses. It came from hundreds of Witches circling almost silently overhead, watching her.

Eric and Heiki lay stunned and scattered across the snow. The prapsies, half-senseless themselves, twitched beside Eric's neck, trying to console him with their babble. Morpeth was closer. Instinctively, Rachel made her way towards him.

Heebra saw this, but was more interested in Yemi. Calen's attempts to charm him into her arms had failed. At one point she did manage to pluck a butterfly from his nose – but Yemi snatched it back, scowling at her.

'He no longer appears to like me,' Calen said.

'He never liked you,' Heebra replied. 'It was your magic that interested him. It seems that he is no longer impressed.'

Calen peered uncertainly at the Camberwell Beauties. 'What are these strange insects, Mother?'

'Merely butterflies, nothing more,' said Heebra. 'Yemi's magic changes them into what he likes or needs.'

'But he's only a baby. How can he do this?'

'His magic is far more advanced than his human understanding,' said Heebra. 'The baby mind of Yemi senses no threat, but his magic recognizes it. I want you to take him away from here, Calen. There is a bond between Yemi and Rachel that could be dangerous, and some sisters still want to harm him. Let's remove that temptation.'

Calen nodded and reached out for Yemi. Expertly, he shifted a short distance away.

'Stop grasping at him,' Heebra told her. 'You know he craves human-type gestures. Offer him the simple affections he wants. Behave more like a mother. Caress him. Put your lips on his cheek.'

'A kiss?'

'Yes, as nearly as you can.'

It was a painful spectacle. Calen's mouths were not made for such tender gestures. As she pressed them closer to Yemi's face, the jaws reached out alarmingly – his warm smell and touch, mixed with their own juices, driving them wild.

'Get on with it,' Heebra said. 'I want to finish Rachel off.'

Yemi pushed the teeth away in disgust. Thrusting back from Calen, he started to drift hesitantly towards Rachel. He gave her his best smile, but she ignored him. Why? Confused, he continued to send out hopeful magical inquiries for her company, entreating her to be his friend.

Only by steadfastly not looking at Yemi could Rachel manage to keep up her spiky rejections. All she wanted to do was take him far, far from this dreadful place, but that was not possible.

Reaching Morpeth, she felt for his injuries. Gently, with the utmost care, she probed his back. His spinal column was severed in several places, her spells told her. I could repair the damage, she thought bitterly, but the Witches will never allow me to complete the task. Realizing this, her tears fell on Morpeth's face. As they did so he opened his bright eyes.

'We're not finished yet,' he rasped. 'I'm not finished, and neither are you. Pull me up.'

'I can't,' Rachel murmured. 'Your spine is broken.' Keeping still, trying not to attract the attention of the Witches, she used her magic to make him feel slightly more comfortable.

'Don't do that,' Morpeth said. 'I need to remain conscious. The pain helps. Tell me what happened.' She explained the way Yemi's butterflies had responded to the death-spells.

'Of course,' he said, a spasm rocking him. Furiously he fought to stay conscious, his body shaking with the effort. 'Keep up the Witch attacks on Yemi,' he urged. 'Make them continue. It's a chance.'

'I can't,' Rachel protested. 'Morpeth, don't you understand? Heebra's called her Witches off. They won't touch him now.'

Morpeth stared at the sky. The main force of the Witches stared back at him, wheeling above his head like flocks of colossal birds. Most simply kept watch over him, but a few swooped lower, shouting insults and slashing their claws above his face.

'They're impatient to continue the fight,' Morpeth said,

his voice barely audible now. 'Good. That is what we want. Come closer to me.' Rachel put her ear to his lips. Moments later, when she lifted her hair from his cheeks, he was unconscious.

Rachel did not try to wake him. She rose immediately and headed towards Eric. On the way she paused briefly by Heiki and did her best to ease her breathing – that would have to do.

Eric's body had fallen into a small hollow. He should have been covered with falling snow, but the recovering prapsies had kept the flakes off him. As Rachel approached they were busy licking his face and butting him with their plump chins, trying to nuzzle him into wakefulness.

Rachel gently nudged them aside – and used a fast-healing spell to rouse Eric.

'What's going on?' he asked, reaching straight for the prapsies to reassure himself they were safe.

'It's all right,' Rachel whispered. 'Listen, we haven't got much time …'

While Eric levered himself sorely up, Rachel tried to harden her heart to Yemi. It was the only way …

'Are you ready?' she asked.

Eric nodded.

Nearby, Heebra watched her daughter still trying to interest Yemi. He would no longer let Calen close. The boy's magic has already outgrown her, Heebra realized. From now onward, she would need to train Yemi herself, using—

Suddenly, behind, she sensed a death-spell being prepared.

She turned. It was the blinded Witch. Tottering in the snow, she sniffed for Yemi, trying to identify his smell over the stench of her own burnt skin. With every moment her strength improved.

Rachel's doing, Heebra sensed at once. Rachel is healing her.

The blinded Witch opened her four mouths in a single penetrating attack.

'Stop!' Heebra cried, forming a spell to kill her own Witch.

'Now!' Rachel called.

Eric lifted his finger – and Heebra's spell evaporated. She tried to remake it – and could not. Never having faced this situation before Heebra, just for a moment, was confused.

The blinded Witch launched her spell.

It never reached Yemi. This time his butterflies were ready. One swallowed the spell. Another sent it back to the blinded Witch. She fell dead instantly.

Six blood-related sisters of the dead Witch came after him at once. None of the other Witches interfered. This was now a clear retribution kill, and they had every right to revenge the death. The sisters unsheathed their teeth and drew together, flying vertically down the sky.

Heebra hastily placed a shield around Yemi that no spells could penetrate.

Again, Eric destroyed it.

The sisters descended on Yemi. As they approached they altered formation. Splitting the pack, they came after him in twos – a classical triangular attack. The eldest sister led them, an experienced fighter, patiently withholding the decision about what death-spell to use until the last possible moment. Finally, her soul-snake named it – and the mouths of all the sisters simultaneously filled with flame.

Instantly those flames tore down their own throats. All the other Witches stared in disbelief as the entire family of sisters fell soundlessly from the air, their black dresses burning like rags in the wind.

There was silence, absolute silence. And then, from the remaining Witch packs, there came an outraged pouring forth of wrath. Heebra saw all her Witches preparing to join the fight against Yemi. With so many dead sisters now strewn across the snow, nothing could hold them back.

'Step aside,' she said to Calen, striding across. 'Yemi is too dangerous to leave alive. I will dispose of him myself.' She exuded all her magical power to attract Yemi. 'Come boy,' Heebra said, smiling. 'I know you want to.'

'No!' screamed a voice.

It was Paul. With a great cry he flew across the snow. He did not come alone. He came with Marshall and all the other children in one tremendous line of fast flight. The guarding Witches restrained a few, but most bridged the short gap to Heebra.

Paul arrived first. He threw himself at her face. Heebra swatted him aside, but she could not stop all of them. The children surged into her, driving her back from Yemi. For a few moments Heebra lay under their small hands, feeling the irritation of clawless fingers and simplistic spells.

Then, in one easy move, she threw everyone off, made a final lunge for Yemi – and breathed into his mouth.

The words went into his body.

'Oh no,' said Eric.

Yemi wailed. It was a high-pitched cry, followed by dozens more: his Camberwell Beauties. Yemi clutched at them in despair. He coughed, sagged, held his throat. Something hurt inside. He reached for Heebra's dress, not understanding that she was the cause. Heebra kicked him off and walked away.

'Why didn't you stop the spell?' Rachel railed at Eric. 'Yemi's no match for Heebra! Why didn't you stop it? Why, Eric?'

'I didn't see it,' he murmured. 'She…she…disguised her spell from me.'

Yemi crawled a few yards after Heebra. Then he fell on his face. At the same time his butterflies shrank back to their normal size – in his pain Yemi had forgotten them. The Camberwell Beauties had lost their magical properties. A cloud of yellow, they rose.

Abandoning him.

'No!' wailed Rachel.

Racing across the snow, she swept Yemi up, placed him in her lap and cradled his head. Gently opening his mouth, she sent her information spells into his body to discover the kind of weapon Heebra had used. And then she felt it – deep inside Yemi – an extraordinary spell of his own trying to form. She bent her face towards his, and his mouth opened wider.

Heebra saw the danger. 'Kill Rachel!' she ordered her Witches. 'The boy can do nothing without her now.'

Yemi's breath was only a murmur. Rachel pressed her

lips to his. The new spell struggled up his throat, trying to reach her, to live. She drew it out, holding it in her mouth.

'Stop her!' shrieked Heebra.

As Rachel blew the spell outwards, Heebra flew across the snow, trying to capture it. But the spell slipped through her claws. In a rippling circle, on a thrilling breeze, it flowed in all directions away from the Pole.

Rachel stared wildly at Eric. 'What kind of spell is it?'

'Some kind of awakening,' he cried. 'And I think I know what it's looking for.'

'What?'

Eric's eyes shone. 'Children, Rachel. It's looking for children!'

19

awakening

Yemi's spell left the Pole, expanding rapidly across the ice and snow.

The first children it reached lived in the Norwegian fishing town of Hammerfest, in the far north of the world. It was late here, after midnight, but the summer sun shone as it always did at this latitude on the warm sleeping children. Like a sigh the awakening spell entered the open windows. Where windows were closed it swept down a chimney. Where there was no chimney it squeezed between the smallest cracks in timber or brickwork. Nothing could stop it.

It passed across beds; a light touch – only a breath – but children awoke at once. Youngsters in dozens of homes clenched their toys. Babies rattled their cots together to the same rhythm. Older children leapt from their mattresses and ran to windows as the magic they had always possessed was released.

The spell gathered pace. There was no time to waste. Spreading in a great ring over the Arctic seas, it pushed out: across Baffin Bay into Canada, over the Kara Sea into the West Siberian Plain, down northern Finland, following the smell of children to Ivalo and beyond. And, from their rooms, in countries hundreds of miles apart, children who had never met suddenly sensed each other.

The spell moved on. It flowed with the Mackenzie river down to Fort Good Hope, Alaska. It slashed by the Canadian-American great lakes: Michigan, Ontario, Erie. But Yemi needed more. So he sent the spell into the dark portion of the northern hemisphere. In Naples, Italy, it found two boys stealing car tyres; they changed their minds. It blew across children dreaming in Tashkent and Toulouse. When their eyes opened, they glimmered silver.

The spell crossed the equator. It delved in attics, school yards, shanty huts. It followed kids playing truant in Peru and caught them. It found girls skipping in Australia and made them trip. It sought underground, into filthy sweat shops and inhuman places where child-slaves perpetually dwell. Here children dropped their tools and held hands, knowing nothing would ever be the same again.

Into deep Africa the spell travelled, to a special destination: Fiditi. There it discovered Fola, and woke her. From her mat she wept when she recognized the voice of her brother.

The spell gushed across the entire globe. It did not stop

and it did not pause or slow down until every child in the whole wide day-and-night world felt its radiant touch.

But – at the pole – Rachel knelt in the snows, with Yemi trembling in her arms.

He was barely alive now. Heebra's death-spell gripped and gripped him in its savage joy, and Rachel's own magic could only slow down its biting attack. Yemi's warm brown eyes were vacant, almost shut.

But he still commanded his awakening spell. He changed it. No more gentleness. Yemi had never intended just to awaken the magic in children. He needed their magic. It was the only way he knew to fight Heebra's death-spell.

His awakening spell became a *feeding* spell.

Only the children at the Pole were spared. Without warning, Yemi felt for the new magic of all other children – and took it. There was no time to be kind. Yemi knew only his pain, his terrible need. So he ripped away the magic of each child on Earth – left them nothing – and pulled it like a great tide towards his aching body.

A sound came then that emptied all tranquillity from the world.

It was a scream. It was the sound of all the world's children, billions of them, screaming at the same time. They could not bear this loss. For a few moments every child had known how empty their lives had been without magic; now that emptiness returned, and they would not accept it. They reacted angrily. Following their stolen magic the rage of all children streamed to the Pole.

Rachel cradled Yemi's head as the early traces of children's magic entered him. At first the magic was a trickle creeping under his lids. Then he opened his eyes wide and it poured inside, until his little body seemed about to burst with an unbearable brightness. He sighed, relaxed, breathed again. Rachel felt the magic rolling down his throat, into his lungs, his poisoned veins and near-dead heart, attacking Heebra's malice.

Healing him.

But close behind the magic came the rage. It had almost reached the Pole.

Rachel had no idea what it meant. The disarrayed Witches felt it, and looked to Heebra in bewilderment. How they looked for her leadership now!

Heebra recognized what was coming. She knew that nothing could withstand the anger Yemi had unknowingly unleashed. It was too vast. It was a pulverizing fist of anguish. No living thing at the Pole would survive this anger: not her, not Larpskendya, none of her Witches; none of the children; even Yemi would be smashed. It would obliterate everything.

There was barely time to decide what to do. Heebra stared at Yemi. How she detested this rogue child, unable even to take pleasure from the Witches he had killed. Rachel she had underestimated. I see now, she thought, how you could have fought so magnificently against Dragwena. For Larpskendya she felt only the ancient hatred. There was no time to enjoy killing him now. Somehow, even thread-bound, she had allowed him to outwit her. That hurt most of all.

Heebra wanted to observe the death agonies of her enemies, but she knew she could not even have that pleasure. She must save her High Witches. All the finest were here. If they died the majesty of Ool would die with them.

Tenderly she whispered a few words to Mak. He raised his heavy golden head, ready to protect her for the last time.

'What is it?' asked Calen, flying over. 'What's happening?'

'I have no time to explain,' said Heebra. 'Lead the sisters away, every one. Fly close in one direction, and I will keep a safe path open for as long as I can.'

Calen trembled. 'Mother, no, surely. I will not go without you. We will stand and fight together!'

'This is not a contest I can win, with or without your help,' said Heebra. 'Take my Witches from this miserable world. You are their leader now!'

'I am ... not ready to rule,' Calen beseeched her. 'I can't—'

'Get away!' wailed Heebra, sounding an alarm across the sky.

Uncertainly, in small nervous bunches, her Witches rose from the snows. Calen drew them south and Heebra spread her four jaws wide. A narrow cone of green light emerged from her lips. Understanding, the Witches came together inside it. Upwards into the thick clouds they flew, continually glancing back at Heebra.

'Hurry!' roared Heebra – and then she roared again.

The rage of the children had struck the pole.

Heebra prepared herself. She had faced High Witches of the greatest intellect and imagination. She had defeated countless Doomspells. This was worse: like a thousand barbarous Doomspells. She raised Mak high, attracting the rage to her.

And the rage eagerly followed. Mak swallowed what he could. When he could take no more Heebra opened her own jaws. The rage flowed in. She held her arms wide, buckling and shuddering as the fury filled her.

The children at the Pole did not watch, or watched, if they could bear it.

Heebra contained the rage for as long as she could. Finally, with only a few of her Witches still on the Pole, she relented. The anger burst as fire from her nostrils, and then from her mouths and eyes – not little tongues of fire, but huge swollen torrents, blasting in all directions. Heebra threw her smouldering head from side to side, spewing the cleaning spiders from her jaws. Mak flopped against her neck, still desperately trying to shield her.

Heebra had time for a final bitter realization: the Griddas; she should never have released them. Only she had been able to contain their ferociousness. With her gone they would take control of Ool, and their first act would be to slay Calen, the new Witch leader. Calen would try to rally a defence, but Heebra knew her daughter was too young and inexperienced to lead the High Witches. When Calen most needed the Sisterhood they would desert her.

In her darkening mind, as her mouths closed for the last time, Heebra pictured what would happen. Calen would not hide. She would wait defiantly at the Great Tower while the Griddas gleefully climbed the walls. Calen would meet her end alone: motherless, sisterless, with only a brazen Nylo to defend her.

Heebra lay her burning head down upon the snow, and died.

20

flight

All the children gazed numbly at the smoking remains of Heebra.

The rage ended with the last vapours rising from her body, but a few scattered Witches still lay burning in the snow. No one spoke. The scene was difficult to bear, and for a long time the children simply stayed close to each other and tried to make sense of what they had witnessed.

Rachel left Yemi in Eric's care and tiptoed around the dead Witches until she found Morpeth. He lay on his back in exactly the same position she had left him, his eyes shut. Afraid that her touch might injure him further, she knelt close, asking her spells to determine the safest places to work on. With a subtlety and carefulness Rachel did not know they possessed, the major and minor spells combined to knit the bones and cauterize the internal bleeding.

Eventually Morpeth's eyes parted. 'It seems I'm not dead after all,' he murmured, managing a semi-smile.

Rachel kissed him and moved across to Heiki. Her wounds were less serious, and there was nothing wrong with her throat, but throughout the healing process Heiki said nothing. Her washed-out blue eyes were tense, not quite able to meet Rachel's.

At last, in a voice that cracked, she asked, 'Can you …' She stopped, but Rachel could read the words Heiki tried to say: forgive me.

As answer Rachel simply lifted her hand and felt Heiki's pale cheek. It was only a touch, the slightest of pressures, but Heiki reacted as if struck by a spell. She started to weep, and, seeing that, Rachel found herself also weeping. For more reasons than either could name they held each other and wept over and over, their hot tears melting tiny holes in the snow. Finally, Rachel tilted her head at the ice prison still containing Larpskendya.

'Shall we go to him together?'

'Yes!' Heiki took Rachel's hand; arm-in-arm, they flew to the Wizard. Halfway up the glistening white walls of the prison, Heiki faltered. Wincing with pain she started to slip down. Rachel caught her and carried her the remaining floors to the top.

Larpskendya lay on his side against the harsh ice. The fleeing Witches had left his arms, legs and head grotesquely tied with spell-thread. The thread was impervious to magic, so Rachel and Heiki worked with their fingers and nails only. Slowly, taking great care, they gradually loosened and removed the thick, cutting cords.

The freed Larpskendya turned at once to Rachel and Heiki. He stood shakily, towering above both girls, and drew them into his wide embrace. As they lay inside that warm space, they had never known such peace.

'Well,' Larpskendya said at last, 'we are only beginning.'

They glided to the snows below, and Rachel once again took Yemi from Eric.

Larpskendya went straight to Morpeth. He finished repairing his injuries, and then, as Morpeth struggled to his feet, Larpskendya knelt. He knelt before Morpeth, and gripped Morpeth's arm, and for a moment, when their eyes met, Morpeth saw Trimak, Fenagel and the Sarren he had left on Ithrea. All of his old friends were there, playing with magic in the glades.

'Safe and well,' Larpskendya told him quietly. 'They owe you so much, but I wonder if I owe you even more. Two worlds you have guarded now for me. How can I repay that debt?'

Morpeth shrugged self-consciously. 'There is something I miss. I—'

Larpskendya knew what he wanted. Morpeth gasped as he felt his magic seeping back. Familiar old spells trod noisily into his mind, searching for the usual places they liked to stay. Morpeth tried to thank Larpskendya, but he was too overcome to speak.

Larpskendya left him and attended to the rest of the children. They were gathered in various states of mind: disturbed, relieved, frightened, and weary, so weary from their long appalling ordeal. Most looked at the sky as if they did not really believe the Witches had departed. Larpskendya moved amongst them, reassuring each child, especially the youngest, giving them all the time they needed or wanted. He took a spiky-haired boy aside and spoke at length. Paul could not take his eyes off the Wizard.

Eric wanted to approach as well, but the prapsies kept shoving their heads out of his coat and poking tongues at Larpskendya.

'Stop it, boys,' Eric warned them. 'Don't you recognize who that is?'

They turned around and wiggled their feathery backsides at the Wizard. He looked up, catching them at it.

The prapsies gulped, hiding behind their wings as Larpskendya strode across.

'That won't do any good,' Eric said. 'You're both for it now. Me too, probably. Start bowing fast.'

Both prapsies bowed at Eric.

'Not at *me*,' he sighed. 'Flipping heck ...'

He tried to twist them to face the approaching Larpskendya, but the Wizard had already bridged the gap. He picked both prapsies up and swung them close to his face. One stuck out a tongue, tasting his ear. 'Ugh!' it said. Larpskendya laughed and placed both prapsies on Eric's shoulders. And then Larpskendya bent towards Eric, and they shared words Eric would never forget or tell.

Finally Larpskendya brought Yemi, Rachel, Heiki, Eric and Morpeth together. Rachel spread Yemi on her lap. He was a thing of astonishing beauty. Unendurably vibrant colours teemed in his eyes, spilling from the edges, too much for him to bear. Yet he still tried to cover them with his small hands, as if not wishing to let them go.

'All the magic of the world's children is inside him,' Larpskendya said. 'Our little thief does not want to give it back. We must help him.'

'Let me,' said Rachel.

She knelt alongside Yemi, prising the fingers from his eyelids. She kissed him.

With a tiny cry he suddenly wept.

He threw his arms around Rachel's neck – and his eyes opened. Spells instantly burst out, not one spell but dozens, then thousands, all wanting to be first. They emerged in every imaginable colour and left the pole, heading determinedly back to their original owners. In a few minutes the transformation was complete. Morpeth listened closely – and heard a sound.

It was a sound of surprise – a blissful intake of breath from all children.

With the release of the magic Yemi became himself again, and his Camberwell Beauties returned. They covered Rachel's body, their skinny black legs trying to draw her closer to him. Paul and Marshall came warily over, along with the other children, and the butterflies fluttered on them all, one or two landing on each child.

'Home,' Rachel beseeched Larpskendya. 'Can we take him home? Can we?'

Immediately Larpskendya shifted them, so smoothly that none of the children felt a thing.

It was dark; night-time in Fiditi. They stood outside Yemi's house, and normally at this hour it would have been quiet. But the entire village bustled with life. All the children were awake – and busy. One young girl skimmed like a dragonfly over the river Odooba. Her silver eyes lit the surface, attracting mosquitoes. From the dense rainforest nearby came the noise of a group of screeching Colobus monkeys. Two boys had woken them. Perched alongside in the frailest upper branches of a tree, they laughed and screeched back. Eric saw a toddler trying to fly over a leafy bush. He didn't quite make it, and ruefully rubbed his scraped legs. Two teenage girls kneeled face to face outside a hut, changing the shape of each other's hair. A scruffy-looking boy sat at a window, idly blowing clouds back and forth across the sky.

Morpeth gazed at Rachel wistfully. 'Can you believe all this? And things like it must be happening everywhere tonight across the world. Everywhere!'

'I know.' She thought about the little French boy, so recently crying for his lovely melting rainbow. Was he running back up to his mountains now? Or perhaps he had already learned how to fly ...

A bird shot past Morpeth, landing like the tamest of falcons on a thin boy's wrist. A girl lay dreamily on her back, watching a tuft of grass rise from the ground and tickle her brother's neck.

'I wish,' Eric said to Paul, 'that I could be everywhere at once tonight. To see it all.'

'Don't you feel jealous?' Paul asked. 'I mean, you're the only kid in the world left without magic.'

'No one else can do what I can,' Eric said simply.

Both prapsies nodded so hard their heads nearly snapped off.

The front door of Yemi's house opened – just a crack. Inside there were whispers. Finally Fola came out. Her eyes gleamed silver, like the others, and when she saw Larpskendya she curtsied over and over, not quite sure how to behave.

'It's all right,' Rachel reassured her. 'Join us. What's wrong?'

Fola lingered at the door, obviously waiting for something. Then, almost creeping forth, Yemi's mother emerged. She looked horrified by what had happened, afraid even to look at any of the village children – as if their eyes might burn. Yemi threw himself on her. She shrank back. When Yemi insisted, following her, his mother reluctantly let him settle against her chest. At his touch she relaxed slightly, but still stroked his head as though it was a breakable and slightly strange object.

Fola shrugged at Rachel. 'Mama not ready yet. We must be gentle to her, and them all.' She indicated a few adults nearby.

Until now Rachel had not noticed the rest of the adults. Compared with the animated, eyes-glowing children they were like shadows, mainly staying in the background. All appeared hopelessly bemused, some uncertain about approaching their own children. One father crouched under his hovering daughter, obviously expecting her to simply fall from the sky. A few parents stayed indoors, too afraid even to come out.

Rachel thought of Mum, and suddenly wanted her close. And then she thought of Dad, and felt anxious. She spoke to Larpskendya – and they shifted again to Rachel's home.

Mum and Dad were standing in the front porch, looking outward. Seeing Rachel and Eric, their faces broke with relief. Rachel looked happily at her dad. He was well, and tearful, and almost crushed her with one arm, while doing the same to Eric with the other. Then, seeing Larpskendya, Dad broke off for a moment and, almost formally, shook his hand.

Finally everyone turned to look at the world beyond the porch. There was so much to see. Overhead, girls danced on a slanting roof. Higher up a group of kids Eric recognized spiralled like midges around a block of council flats, their laughter carrying for miles in the mild summer air. Boys played cricket in the clouds. Other children were off alone, accompanying planes, following birds, or a hundred other things they had woken in the night. A boy in a wheelchair chased down a greyhound. One small girl simply read a book by the light of her own incandescent eyes. And all around, wherever the children stood or ran or flew, they left their telltale individual trails: smells new to the Earth – the scents of magic.

'I knew you would be safe,' Mum whispered to her children, watching it all. 'As soon as I saw all this happening—' she flapped her arms around – 'I *knew*.' She turned to Larpskendya. 'There's no changing things back the way they were, is there?'

Larpskendya shook his head.

Morpeth marvelled at the activity all around. 'Look at the magic they're performing!' he cried. 'On Ithrea we saw some amazing things, at the end, but those people had practised for centuries. How has it taken these children such a short time to learn similar skills?'

'No world has ever been held back as long as yours,' Larpskendya explained. 'Or had its magic released so quickly.' His voice became filled with humility. 'I have no idea what else might happen tonight. There has never been such a flowering! This' – he indicated the sky, grass, moon, and children who moved so gracefully between them – 'is your future, the beginning of an indescribable adventure for all children. Soon making magic will come as easily to you as breathing.' He smiled. 'And then, of course, it will no longer seem like magic at all.'

Everyone looked down the street, where a scared dad hollered at the sky. His young son was diving recklessly through narrow alleyways, far too excited to notice.

Rachel sidled up to Morpeth. 'This new world's going to be dangerous for the adults, isn't it? Everything will be different for them as well.'

Morpeth nodded. 'Most will be envious of their children. And kids won't automatically do what they're told any longer, either. If parents try to make them … well …'

'Anything might happen,' whispered Rachel, shuffling closer to Mum and Dad. A chilling image jumped at her: of kids taking control, and parents, not safe to go out alone, having to be escorted and cared for by their own children.

Heiki stood next to Larpskendya, watching a girl copying a leaf falling through the air.

'When this all settles down,' she inquired, 'won't the kids form into packs? Magic gangs, selected by skill, with the toughest in charge? That's what the Witches planned.'

'Yes,' said Larpskendya. 'That will happen in some places.' He stared at her. 'Everything you can imagine may happen now.'

'Can't you tell how our magic is going to develop?' Rachel asked him. 'Don't *you* know?'

'Magic evolves differently on all worlds,' he told her. 'But Earth is uniquely bountiful. There has never been a race as gifted as yours, so early in its history.'

'Is that why the Witches are interested in us?' Heiki wondered.

'Yes. They want you so much. And you are not a secret from them any longer.'

Morpeth shivered. 'For how long are we safe?'

'I cannot answer that,' Larpskendya said. 'But the Witches will never leave you in peace now. They will regroup and return in larger numbers. The endless war against us is all they know, and they have seen how useful you can be. Yemi, especially, will tantalize them. Who knows what he will be capable of soon?'

Rachel gently touched the deep claw marks still on Larpskendya's neck, but they did not heal.

'Leave them,' Larpskendya said. 'As a reminder of what I have unleashed.' He turned sadly to address Morpeth, Eric and Rachel, Mum and Dad. 'There is a new enemy now: the Griddas are loose. I knew Heebra was becoming desperate, but I never thought she would release their fury.' He hung his head. 'I pushed her too far, too quickly, these last years. That was a terrible mistake.'

Over Rachel's house two shining goal posts had appeared. Moonlit figures passed the football perfectly.

'They don't fear the arrival of the Griddas yet,' Morpeth said gratefully. Whatever the future held, tonight his heart felt light, and he could barely follow all the children teeming amongst the night clouds. He wanted to join them.

'That is true,' Larpskendya said solemnly. 'Why should they fear?' And then, suddenly, in a deliberate, measured way he assessed all those children pressed so closely to him. Finally he gazed at Rachel, as if he saw in her a summary of all their worth. Her eyes, staring into his, were the colour of gladness.

Larpskendya's expression became almost desperately, achingly hopeful.

'I want to show you something,' he said. 'You need to understand the great challenge ahead.'

'Show us what?' asked Dad suspiciously.

'Another world. A precious world. For many lifetimes the Witches have wanted to crush its loveliness.'

Eric blinked uncertainly. 'Is it far?'

'Far and near. Nowhere is too remote for you now. We can fly there.'

'What? Tonight?'

Larpskendya smiled. 'Why not?'

'What about the prapsies? I'm not going without them…'

Larpskendya swept his arms, taking in the scope of the sky. 'We'll take everyone.'

The prapsies chuckled haltingly, not sure what he meant.

'What do you mean, everyone?' Dad asked. 'You mean all the youngsters here?' He indicated the nearest children. 'All *these*?'

Larpskendya's eyes shone. 'No, you don't understand. I mean *everyone*. I mean every child and adult on your world. All of them.'

'Yes!' Rachel cried. 'Yes!'

Larpskendya breathed in and suddenly Rachel felt a tightening inside her, as if millions of minds were being drawn together. When she looked up she saw children all around lifting their chins to the same constellation of stars in the western sky.

Eric glanced at Mum and Dad, thinking they wouldn't enjoy this one bit. But he was wrong.

'Like this?' Mum stretched her arms out timidly. 'Well, am I doing it right?'

Larpskendya laughed, a long and booming laugh that shook off any final fears he may have had. 'Yes, that will do well enough,' he said. He paused and gazed at Rachel, Morpeth and Eric. 'Are you ready?'

They nodded tightly.

'Blimey, boys,' muttered one of the prapsies. 'What's going on?'

But there was no time for its companion to answer. From homes, from ships, from jets at thirty thousand feet and mines deeper still, and from the child-filled skies, everyone in the world raised their eyes.

And, a moment later, only animals and plants breathed on this Earth.

the
WIZARD'S
promise

contents

1

schools without children

As Rachel awoke, her information spells automatically swept the house for threats. They probed into each room, an extra set of senses watching out for her.

Nothing out of the ordinary, they reported. Mum lay in her usual morning bath. Dad was in the study, trying to touch his toes. The information spells delved further out. In the garden, two froglets were wondering whether to make a break for it across the dangerous lawn. Next door's dog hid behind a shed, thinking no one else knew about his juicy bone.

Rachel smiled, peering out of her bedroom window. A flock of geese passed by, and, just for a moment, as she gazed up at those birds, and listened to the familiar sounds of home and garden, it was as if nothing had changed in the world.

Then a group of under-fives cut across the sky.

The youngsters flew in tight formation, led by a boy. Rachel guessed he might be three years old, probably less. The group travelled with arms pinned neatly to their sides, little heads thrust proudly ahead. Their eyes all shone some tint of blue, the distinctive colour of flying spells.

The slower geese scattered nervously when the children crossed their path.

Getting up, Rachel brushed out her long dark hair and strolled downstairs to the kitchen. Her younger brother, Eric, sat at the dining table. A bowl of cornflakes crackled satisfyingly in front of him.

'You know, if I had magic,' he said, tucking in, 'I wouldn't bother with flying or the other stuff. I'd just use a spell to keep the taste of cornflakes in my mouth forever.'

'You'd soon get sick of it,' Rachel answered.

'No,' Eric said earnestly. 'I wouldn't.' He waved his spoon at the departing toddlers. 'Those little 'uns are probably long-distance racers. Must be, practising like that. They're so *serious*. At their age I was still happy just chucking things at you.'

'Mm.' Rachel glanced round, expecting to see the prapsies. The prapsies were a mischievous pair of creatures – feathered body of a crow, topped with a baby's face – that had once served a Witch on another world. Usually Eric put them up to some prank when Rachel first came down in the morning.

'Where are the boys then?' she asked warily.

'I let them out early for a change,' Eric said. 'Told them to find me a gift, something interesting.'

'Did you send them far?'

'China.'

'Good.'

Rachel stared up at the rooftops of the town. It was a typical morning, with children all over the sky. A few were up high and alone, practising dead-stops in the tricky April winds. Most children had simply gathered in their usual groups in the clouds, friends laughing and joking together. A few houses down Rachel saw a boy cooing. As he did so a pair of doves, tempted from some thicket, rose to his hand. Further away a girl drifted casually across the sky, plucking cats from gardens. The cats trailed in a long line behind her, complaining mightily.

'Hey look!' Eric cried. 'Lightning-finders!'

Six teenagers were heading purposefully south, their arms raised like spikes.

'It's a brand new game started up by the thrill-seekers,' Eric said. 'You search for heavy weather, find the storms and dodge the lightning forks. Most competitions are held in the Tropics, where the really big storms are. I bet that's where those kids are off to.' He gazed wistfully after the teenagers, who had already disappeared over the horizon.

'What happens if they get hit by the lightning?'

'Bad things, I suppose,' Eric said. 'It's risky, but that's the whole point. Wouldn't be exciting otherwise, would it?'

Rachel shrugged. The new magical games didn't interest her much. She was more interested in those children stationed in the air, watching the skies for Witches.

Nearly a year had passed since the baby boy, Yemi, had released the magic of all the children on Earth. In that first glorious Awakening, there had been a superabundance of magic – enough for the Wizard leader, Larpskendya, to transport every child and adult on Earth to Trin.

When Rachel thought of that purple-skied, plant-filled world, it still hurt. The plants of Trin had a language of leaves so rich that even the Wizards could only guess the meaning of their graceful movements. But the plants were dying. The Witches had poisoned them. On a whim, they had contaminated Trin's soils. And slowly, as their magic drained away, the Trin plants were losing their minds. Each year the great leaves waved ever more frantically in the breezes as they struggled to hear each other.

It was not possible to stay on Trin for long. The special blossoming of magic following the Awakening soon faded, and the adults and children had to return home. But everyone understood: if the Witches could do this amount of damage to Trin, a world that meant nothing to them, what would happen if they returned to Earth? So everyone had prepared. For months children practised their defensive spells. Night and day they patrolled the skies, anticipating a massed attack of Witches that never came.

Meanwhile, Ool – the Witch home world – wrapped itself in hush. A battle, the Wizards knew, was taking place: a battle for control, between the High Witches Rachel and other children had fought before, and the more ferocious warrior-breed, the terrifying Griddas. For a long time Ool had been silent.

Larpskendya had no doubt the Griddas had won. It worried him because the Wizards knew so little about them. The Griddas had been bred by the High Witches, bred to be savage warriors, and kept underground. But the former High Witch leader, Heebra, had made the mistake of releasing them.

And, having tasted freedom, the Griddas had turned on their makers.

As Rachel gazed up at the sky, her slim freckled face perched on her hands, she wondered how ready the people of Earth were to face the Griddas. She also missed a friend. 'I wonder,' she said, half to herself, 'how Morpeth's doing? I miss him.'

'He's only been gone a few days,' Eric protested.

'I *still* miss him.'

'Actually, so do I, but it's his only visit back to Ithrea in ages. Larpskendya's picking him up in a few weeks.'

While Rachel thought fondly about Morpeth, three girls landed beside the garden pond. They walked across the lawn, waving hopefully through the glass doors of the patio.

'Oh no, part of your fan club,' groaned Eric. 'Do they never leave off?'

A few children always loitered near the house, curious to get a glimpse of Rachel. Her reputation drew them, and the sheer quality of her magic. Every child on Earth wanted to be closer to it.

'I've seen those three before,' Eric muttered. 'Two nights ago. It was raining, pouring down, but did they care? Barmy nutters.' He pulled a face, attempting to scare the girls away. 'Clear off!' he yelled. The girls smiled sweetly back. 'They never flipping listen to me,' Eric said. 'Why don't you give them a shock, Rach? You know, send them to the Arctic or something. It'll take them at least an hour to fly back.'

Two of the girls nudged each other forward, trying to get Rachel's attention. The other one looked steadily at Eric.

A little ruffled, he self-consciously smoothed out his baggy pyjamas.

Rachel laughed. 'I'm not the only one with admirers.'

'Can't you get rid of them?'

'Oh, I think we should let that pretty-looking girl in,' Rachel said. 'I can tell she wants to talk to you.'

'Don't you dare!'

The girls stood outside, hoping for a conversation. Rachel, however, had entertained too many admirers lately. She turned away from their stares, feeling a desire to get out of the house.

'Come on,' she said. 'We'll go for a walk.'

'You're joking, aren't you?' Eric said. 'There's no chance of slipping out quietly. The sky's thick with kids.'

'I'll shift us, then.'

'Where to?'

'Let's find the prapsies. Creep up on them, give 'em a scare.'

'Hey, nice idea. Just let me get dressed.'

'*I* could dress you.'

'No way,' Eric snorted. 'I'm not having your spells fiddling with my pyjamas.'

He thumped up the stairs, colliding with Mum.

'Careful,' Mum groaned. Pinning back her wet hair, she smiled at Rachel. 'Going out, love?'

'Yep.'

'You'll need a disguise from the fans, then.' She inspected her daughter critically. 'How about an older look? Add three years on and lose the freckles. Blonde and fifteen?'

Rachel smirked. 'Blonde's out, Mum. Hair fashion's changing.'

'What's in vogue these days?'

'Silver for boys, long and slicked back. With the girls, anything crazy.'

Mum shrugged. Children regularly used magic to alter their appearance now. Nothing surprised her any more.

'You want to come along with us, Mum? I'll take you wherever you like.'

'No, you go off and enjoy yourselves. I'll potter about here.'

Eric reappeared, wearing jeans and his woolly parka coat.

'Ready?' Rachel asked.

'I was born ready.' Hoiking up his collar, Eric noticed her new round-cheeked face. 'Good disguise,' he said. 'You look dumb. That's realistic. Better hide your magic scent, too.'

Rachel did so, kissed Mum lightly on the cheek – and *shifted*.

Immediately, without any sensation of flight, she and Eric had travelled a few miles from the house. Rachel was one of the few children in the world who possessed this skill – the ability to move instantaneously from one place to another.

They stood on the outskirts of town. Above them a boy flew by on some errand or other, his dad perched on his back. Rachel heard their laughter. Magic did not survive the passage to adulthood, but adults who wanted to fly could still enjoy that special thrill through children.

Rachel and Eric tramped up a long path. It brought them to Rachel's old nursery school.

'Oh, it's closed,' Eric said. 'I hadn't heard.'

A thick chain on the school gate barred the way inside. No notice of explanation was provided, or needed.

'Same everywhere,' Rachel said. 'This was the last one. Closed last week. You know what little kids are like – just want to be out playing.'

At first it had seemed an ominous development when children stopped turning up for school. But if you could fly, why sit in a classroom? The best teachers soon realized that traditional schooling offered nothing that could rival the fascination of magic. Why bother with textbook geography, with the world at your disposal? Children now went all over the world for their education, and teachers not afraid of flying in the arms of their students went with them.

'It's funny,' Eric noted, as they walked away. 'A couple of kids from my old school took the Head of Maths out flying yesterday. Did I tell you? Wanted to know about vectors and something called thrust quotations. Reckoned it might help them manoeuvre better in high winds.'

'Was he able to help them?'

'Yeah. They were practising with him last night,' Eric said.

'What? They took him out in the dark?'

'Sure. Why not. He was game for it, apparently. A true test for his theories, and all that. They say he enjoyed it, but it was a while before he could talk normally afterwards.'

A couple of sprinters swerved around Rachel. They flew close to the ground, the wind from their passage messing her hair. Eric laughed – knowing they were deliberately trying to goad Rachel into following them.

Flying games were the most popular new sports – fiercely competitive, fast and visible, with rules that were usually easy to master. Rachel could have won them all, and local teams were always trying to get her attention, but such displays didn't interest her. She led Eric from the nursery lane into an adjoining field. There were some rusty swings here and a dilapidated rocking horse. It was the sort of desultory old-style playground only a few children still used.

'Feebles,' Eric said, seeing two children there.

'Don't call them that,' Rachel snapped angrily. 'I *hate* that word.'

'It's what they're being called, Rach, whether you like it or not.'

A young boy and girl, seven or eight years old, sat on the wooden horse. The boy wore shorts and a wind-cheater, and looked cold. The girl had a long white skirt. She had hitched it up over her knees to help her clamber onto the frame. They sat astride the horse, rocking each other back and forth as best they could.

Eric sighed, glancing at Rachel. 'You're going to play with them, aren't you?'

'Just for a bit.'

'That's what you always say. Then it becomes hours.'

Rachel grinned. 'I like being with them. Anyway, these are new. I'm going to introduce myself. And don't call them feebles.'

The children on the rocking horse were the least talent-ed children. Spell-gifts were not evenly distributed. After the initial rush of magic following the Awakening, it was discovered that a few children in each country had little magic – so little that it went virtually unnoticed. In a world where many children could fly effortlessly, others could still only dream of flying. None of these children could take part in the spell-games sprouting up all around, so Rachel had instead set up a programme where the most magical children spent time with them.

In the clouds above a boy the same age as the little girl

sped by, way out of her reach. She longingly followed him until he passed over some hills.

'Hey, who are you two?' Rachel asked, rushing over and putting the brother and sister at ease. The girl lifted her arms, wanting to be picked up. The boy hung back shyly.

'Get on,' Rachel said to them both, lowering her back so they could climb aboard. Then, gently, she rose skyward.

'I'm not scared,' the boy said fiercely.

Rachel laughed. 'I can see that!'

'Up! Up!' the little girl told her. 'Go faster!' As Rachel increased velocity, the girl cried out, 'I'm falling. I'm falling off!'

'No, you're not,' Rachel whispered into her ear. 'I'll never let you fall off!'

The girl gripped her neck, so happy to be paid attention by a child with magic.

For a while Rachel took directions from the brother and sister about what to do. They wanted to transform, so Rachel shifted halfway across the world. Soon the little girl and her brother were disguised in Asia, creeping in tangled forests, sneaking up on tiger cubs.

Finally, after Rachel had exhausted them with many kinds of magic, she took them back home. 'I'll come here tomorrow, if you like,' she said.

The girl sucked her thumb. 'Will you?'

'Promise.' Rachel fixed a time.

She left them with a wave and shifted back to the nursery, where she found Eric scowling. 'Hey, what's going on?' he said. 'I'm stuck out here, left like a twit by the kiddy swings. You said we were going to find the prapsies!'

'We are, we are. Stop moaning and climb on.' As Eric scrambled onto her back some of Rachel's favourite spells, her shifters, eased forward into her mind. She felt her whole body supercharging with exhilaration as they loosened up all their tremendous power.

Eric saw her eyes light up: a thousand glistening shades of blue.

'Get ready,' she told him, balancing on her toes.

'Oh-oh,' Eric said. 'A big trip, then. Where are you dragging us off to?'

'Wouldn't be a surprise if I gave it away.'

'How far? Come on. Just tell me.'

'Everest!'

'Oh no, not the flipping Himalayas again!' He seized her collar.

'Are you ready or not?'

'Yeah, yeah, I suppose.' Eric took a deep breath and half-shut his eyes. 'But you'd better keep me warm. I'm warning you, Rach. Last time we went there you nearly froze off my –'

Rachel launched into the chilly sky.

2

GRIDDAS

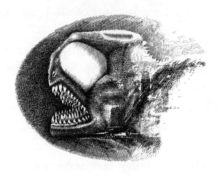

Gultrathaca, pack-leader of the Griddas, entered the eye-chamber.

She was accompanied, as always, by her watchers. The watchers were spiders that lived inside pits criss-crossing her face. As Gultrathaca walked across the chamber floor, they flowed down her body, searching for traps. Some skittered over to the emerald green eye-window. Others lurked in Gultrathaca's footfall, or waited at the doorway.

At fourteen feet tall, Gultrathaca was twice the size of a High Witch. Her imposing orange head was rectangular and all bone, bone impenetrable where it protected the brain. Like all Griddas she had no exposed nose or lips, no yielding part for an enemy to exploit. Nothing protruded from her face except five jaws. Four of these pointed forward. The fifth jaw was clamped to the back of her skull. Her eyes were vast, covering over half her face, and entirely solid – like shaped stone.

As Gultrathaca squeezed her body into the chamber, she said, 'What are you waiting for? Join me.' Seeing there was no danger, her watcher spiders swarmed happily onto her face.

Gultrathaca opened the eye-window – and gazed out in triumph.

Beneath her Thûn, greatest city of the Highs, lay in ruins. For thousands of centuries the High Witches had imprisoned the Griddas underground, while they built their eye-towers in the freedom of the skies. The first action the Griddas had taken after defeating the High Witches was to smash all those eye-towers. Knowing how much the High Witches loved them, the Griddas took each of the stones into their massive claws and crushed them.

Only one object remained intact to mark the reign of the Highs: this place, Heebra's old home, the Great Tower itself.

The last of the fighting Highs lay at its base. In the end, when all the other towers had been taken, the surviving Witches had come here to make a final stand. For several days, incredibly, they had held Heebra's tower against all the power and frenzy of the Griddas. Their bravery was soon forgotten. The eternally-falling grey snow of Ool covered up the High Witches. It settled over their intricate black dresses; it smothered their lifeless red faces and beloved soul-snakes. As Gultrathaca looked down now, only one High Witch remained, poking above her sisters. Piled atop them, she stared up as if in defiance of everything. Then her dead eyes too filled with snow, hiding the tattoos forever.

Gultrathaca intended to destroy the last of the towers. First, though, she wanted to walk amongst Heebra's old possessions, her personal items, clawing them. And – there was another reason.

'Come closer,' she said. 'Are you afraid?'

Jarius, a junior member of Gultrathaca's pack, hung back from the eye-window. Having spent most of her life in tunnels, she had never been so far up. 'How can you bear it?' she asked, trembling.

'We need to reach higher still to leave this world,' Gultrathaca told her. 'You can be trained to bear it, as I was.'

Jarius edged hesitantly forward. Like Gultrathaca, her body was all raw heaviness. Bony extensions erupted from her chest and shoulders. Her thick brown fur was untearable. Under it bunched layer upon layer of muscle. Each muscle was constantly gorged with blood – continually battle-ready, even in sleep. Such excess of power was of little benefit to mere survival in the tunnels under the cities, but there was a reason for it: the High Witches had deliberately bred the Griddas this way. In the event of an invasion of Ool, the Highs had always planned to retreat underground, where the Griddas would keep them safe. From birth that was all the Griddas were ever intended for. They could not recall a time when they had not lived, bred and died in the tunnels, waiting for the call to protect.

Jarius forced herself to step nearer the window. Outside it was dark, virtually black, but for her it was still too bright. Lowering her eye-shields, she looked across the sky. She did not look down; not even her own watcher spiders could bear to look down.

'This is an unnatural place,' she gasped, clutching Gultrathaca. 'I – I am frightened.'

'I know. Step closer.'

'Do not make me do this.'

'I must,' said Gultrathaca. 'We cannot stay in the home-tunnels if we wish to confront Larpskendya.'

Jarius shuffled up to the eye-window. For several minutes she stared outward. She could endure it, but only because she knew Gultrathaca would not allow her to step away.

'Now put your head out,' ordered Gultrathaca.

'No!' Jarius attempted to draw back, but Gultrathaca caught her face and bent it towards the ground. When Jarius tried to clamp her eye-shields shut, Gultrathaca held them open. In Jarius's panic, new spiders gushed from her mouths: soldiers. The soldiers ran onto Gultrathaca's claw, trying to loosen the grip. To oppose them, Gultrathaca unleashed her own soldiers; soldier against soldier, the same number – a stalemate.

Gultrathaca made her stare down the tower walls for a long time. When she was finally released, Jarius threw herself to the back of the eye-chamber. She squeezed into an unlit corner, needing to feel safe. The soldiers disengaged. Both groups of spiders studied each other warily, professionally. Then they returned to their owner's jaws.

'It was necessary,' said Gultrathaca.

'Why!'

'To show you what can be achieved. Look below. It is possible, now.'

Calming herself, Jarius approached the window again. She gazed at the faraway ground – only briefly, but she could do it. 'Is this the treatment we can all expect?' she demanded.

'There will be worse to endure than this,' Gultrathaca

told her. 'Knowing how dangerous we are, do you think the Wizards will allow us to live quietly in our tunnels? No. We are loose now, they know that. They will endeavour to destroy us immediately, while we are all still on Ool, contained in one place. That is why we must leave as soon as possible.'

'And go where?'

'Anywhere. Everywhere. I have seen the sun-fed creatures of other worlds, Jarius. You have no idea what strength we have compared to them.'

Jarius remained beside the eye-window. She knew it was important for her to impress Gultrathaca. She had already disgraced herself by being the last of the pack to leave the home tunnels. Worse, it had taken her countless attempts before she dared go onto the surface during daylight hours. Snow terrified her. When it first struck their bodies, the other pack-members had not screamed – but Jarius had.

I've been brought here as a test, she realized. If I perform badly this time the pack will desert me altogether.

Encouraged by her soldiers, Jarius thrust her face boldly out of the window. She made herself peer down.

'There,' said Gultrathaca. 'It is not impossible, after all.'

'No, I am used to it now.'

'Are you?'

'Yes,' Jarius said firmly. To show how steady her nerve had become, she put her head further out. All her spiders deliberately took up relaxed postures, trying to show Gultrathaca that they were completely unconcerned.

Gultrathaca was not fooled by the spiders. She understood exactly how Jarius felt. Only a year earlier, a High Witch had come to drag her out of her own tunnel. How she had implored for mercy! Like the meekest of infants she had begged, rather than face that horror of light!

Yet Gultrathaca adapted – swiftly. Within a day she was helping the other pack-leaders adjust to the snow. And within a week she could fly, not well, not with the elegance of a High Witch, but even so. And finally the moment arrived when punishments were no longer required to make her leave the ground. The time came when Gultrathaca could open her eyes and actually enjoy it. That special morning Heebra herself had travelled alongside her. Like pack-sisters on a jaunt, they had circled the city.

Jarius, however, understood none of this. She pressed her face into the air, wincing at the touch of snowflakes.

Gultrathaca did nothing to put her at ease. All the other pack-sisters had been made to prove themselves. If Jarius could not cope with the eye-tower, she did not belong in the pack. There could be no compassion for those Griddas too frightened to leave the safety of the tunnels – not even for blood-relatives.

Jarius tried not to shiver. Her soldiers finally persuaded her to open her eye-shields a little more. While staring out, she said, 'What was it really like? What was it like to be amongst the first Griddas to leave Ool and fight the Wizards?'

'It was exhilarating.' Gultrathaca laughed. 'And terrifying.'

She recalled the moment. At the brink of the clouds, she and the other hand-picked Griddas had waited for Heebra's command to move out into the emptiness of space. It was to have been a last decisive offensive against the Wizards. To support it the Griddas, for the first time, had been released from the tunnels of Ool to spread as much havoc as possible.

'We weren't meant for such places,' Jarius said, waving in disgust at the sky. 'We were intended for stone floors and ceilings, not this.'

'That is what you think now,' said Gultrathaca. 'That is what the High Witches wanted you to believe. But you are more impressive than they ever knew.'

'I will never fly. Not willingly.'

'No,' Gultrathaca said. 'That is obvious.'

A few healer spiders fussed over Jarius's eye-shields. They were checking for any damage Gultrathaca might have caused earlier. Finding none, they polished the hard eye surfaces.

'I hear Calen, the new High Witch leader, hasn't been found yet,' Jarius said.

'Leave Calen to me,' Gultrathaca replied. 'She is not the threat her mother Heebra once represented.'

'But surely while Calen is still alive the imprisoned Highs will always be a threat. I don't understand why you haven't just killed all those left in the cells.'

'That would be too easy,' Gultrathaca said.

'Too easy?'

'You have no idea what the Highs denied us.'

Jarius regarded her blankly.

'Tell me,' Gultrathaca said, 'what is the most repulsive aspect of a High Witch?'

'Her soul-snake,' Jarius replied at once.

'You think so? At one time we possessed our own soul-snakes. We knew their friendship. Our ancestors were High Witches.'

Jarius stared at her in disbelief.

'When I left the tunnels I learned a great deal,'

Gultrathaca said. 'The Griddas were an experiment. The High Witches wanted something better adapted to the tunnels. So they took a few of their own Witches and put them into the dark to see what would happen. Our soul-snakes joined us underground. But after hundreds of generations we became so altered that the snakes could no longer bear the taste of our skin. They left us. Nor was this musculature' – Gultrathaca raised her hugely swollen arms – 'and the constant desire to use it, to fight, originally part of us. The Highs designed us this way.'

Jarius shook her head, not quite able to believe this. The senior pack members did not bother to share such information with her, given her low status.

'We also mature far more quickly,' said Gultrathaca. 'The Highs wanted that, too; fast-breeders, capable like them of fertilizing our own eggs. That way they could produce a Gridda army whenever they needed it. Of course, we could never be allowed to grow in numbers that might threaten the High Witches. Imagine if we had wanted to share their food or their precious skies! But they found a solution for that. They culled us.'

'Culled?'

'Killed us off,' Gultrathaca said. 'We didn't question why our pack-members never returned from the wars. Why should we have done? Weren't they dying in glorious battles? The truth was that the Highs didn't want us in their wars. They simply killed a certain amount of us from time to time. That kept our numbers in check. For the Highs it was the easiest solution.'

Jarius stepped away from the window. To die in such a manner filled her with such shame that she was unable to speak.

'Now you see why I keep some High Witches in the worst of the tunnels,' said Gultrathaca. 'Let them fester. I'll never release them.'

Jarius lowered her head, preoccupied with what she had learned.

'The High Witches always despised our kind,' Gultrathaca said, 'but their reign is over. There will be no more culling. From now on the Griddas will breed in numbers even the Highs could not imagine.'

'Won't we fill the tunnels?' Jarius asked. 'They are already crowded.'

'That doesn't matter. You will soon learn to think beyond tunnel boundaries. You must, if we are to leave this world.'

'How far can we get,' Jarius said, 'if the Wizards stand in our way?'

'Not far, perhaps. We need to find Orin Fen, the Wizard home world, and kill them there. Until we do, Larpskendya and his kind will always be safe – and we will not.'

'The Highs never managed to find their home world.'

'Perhaps they searched in the wrong way,' Gultrathaca said. 'Perhaps they needed the help of an infant.'

'An infant?'

'Heebra did not die at the hands of a Wizard, Jarius. A human child was responsible. The returning Highs spoke of talents they had never seen before in the Yemi boy. I believe he may have the skills we need to find Orin Fen. Or perhaps he has other gifts we can use.' Gultrathaca joined Jarius by the eye-window. 'You have been gazing down for many minutes, without needing to look away,' she said. 'Had you noticed?'

'No,' Jarius admitted. 'Is that so?' She realized many of her watchers had genuinely forgotten their earlier fears. They now stared with simple curiosity at the snow pulsing against the stone and glass. Springing back and forth from the window, Jarius found that she was able to look out without flinching. There was still fear, but she could master it.

Jarius is ready, Gultrathaca thought. Or as ready as she could ever be.

'Our youngsters will adapt better than us,' she said. 'They will barely know the tunnels at all, Jarius. It will be so much easier for them.' She sniffed, picking out the distinctive aroma of Gridda infants. As she had requested, one pack had been driven to the surface. 'I wanted you to be here for this,' she told Jarius. 'For the first time Griddas are due to be brought directly from the birthing chambers to see the world. Let's observe how they behave.'

A pack of recently hatched Griddas showed at a tunnel entrance near the base of the eye-tower. The first one to emerge howled when the daylight touched her eyes. She would not have come further except that her sisters shoved her from beneath. Finally all twenty-four blood-related sisters were on the surface. They huddled together, beating at the falling snow as if it was trying to strike them. A searing wind blew into their faces. The sensation of that wind was so unusual and so appalling to the young Griddas that all their spiders acted as though they were being attacked. They formed hopeless little shields around their owners' faces, trying to use their bodies to fend off the winds.

As Jarius watched the youngsters, it seemed that they might have stayed in their crouched position forever if they had been allowed. But an adult Gridda prodded them forward. Awkwardly, trying to fend off the adult, the infants were hurried towards the entrance of Heebra's tower. Their spiders hurried after them, not wanting to be left behind. Bounding in long leaps, the infants bent their backs low, tunnel-fashion. It never occurred to them to check how high the eye-tower was. In the tunnels there was rarely any reason to look up.

The last of the infants were pushed inside the tower entrance. The pounding of their bodies reverberated through the stone as they made their way up the enormous stairway.

'What are you going to do with them?' Jarius asked.

'I am going to test them, of course,' answered Gultrathaca.

Jarius glanced across. 'Test them how?'

'I want to see how quickly newborns can be made to adjust. I intend to bring them to the eye-window and throw them out.'

'What? But they can't fly. They don't know how yet!'

The infants were closer. Jarius could hear their fearful, confused chatter. The first watcher spiders, baby-sized like the infants they belonged to, preceded their arrival. They called back, warning their owners about the strange green light of the window.

'It is unfair to ask them so soon,' Jarius protested.

Gultrathaca shattered the eye-window. Shards of glass and ice showered the chamber, blown back by the wind. 'I agree,' she said. 'That is why I have prepared you, Jarius. I want you to show them how it can be done. I want you to jump first.'

3

COUNTRIES
WITHOUT BORDERS

'Rachel, skip the tourist run and do some proper flying,' Eric complained.

'Why don't you just relax? Take it easy. Enjoy the sights.'

'I've *seen* the sights.'

'Speed,' she groaned. 'Is that all you get excited about?'

'What else is there?'

With Eric loosely hitched on her back, Rachel cruised over the Himalayas. Below them some of Earth's tallest mountains offered alluring views of their frozen tips: K2, Nanga Parbat, the majestic precipices of the Annapurna range. Rachel breathed in the coldness, cherishing the winds gusting through her hair.

Above Makalu, the Earth's fifth highest summit, she found children plunging feet first. As their bodies impacted the north face, a great sheet of snow broke away. Gleefully they rode the avalanche, racing each other down the slopes.

'I think we can match that,' Rachel said. 'Ready for a dare?'

'Yeah. Why not!'

Rachel immediately dived towards the nearest ridge. As her trajectory spells took charge Eric attempted to keep his cool. 'OK, tell me when,' Rachel said. 'Don't mess up, now.'

Eric tried to calculate how long before they hit the ridge – but they were travelling too swiftly.

'I can't...slow down...*now*!' he bawled, screwing up his eyes.

Rachel deliberately waited. At the last possible second her manoeuvring spells kicked in. She dragged her shoes against the slope, showering Eric with ice particles.

'Very funny,' he muttered.

'Too fast for you, eh?'

'I wasn't scared a bit,' Eric said stiffly, wiping the ice and snow from the hood of his parka. 'Do it again if you like. See if I care.'

'Later, maybe. Let's check out what's going on at the other peaks first.'

Rachel returned eastwards, swooping over the Everest region. The fittest of adults had failed to climb a handful of these mountains, but children had conquered them all. As Rachel flew by Everest itself, there were hundreds circling the summit. Some carried adult relatives or helped friends whose magic was not strong enough to reach this altitude on their own. Many of the world's best flyers were here on this day of near-perfect visibility. One was a teenage girl. She plunged and rose at will in the thin air, and then returned to a crèche of toddlers to show them, more slowly, how she had done so.

'What about the prapsies?' asked Eric, seeing no one he recognized. 'I thought you were taking us to see the boys.'

'Let's stop off for a tan first.'

Eric shrugged. 'Where? The Caribbean?'

'Maybe.'

Rachel changed direction and gave control to her shifting spells, heading west.

'Florida Bay,' she announced, as they arrived.

They were a long way from shore, perhaps four miles. A few adults were dotted about, churning the surface in their pleasure boats, but they were outnumbered. In these warm latitudes the waters abounded with children. They did not require boats. Their magic allowed them to swim directly with the life of the sea. As Rachel looked on, she saw boys following dolphins, half in and half out of the surf. Two girls were arching their backs, shadowing a group of hunting barracuda.

'Hey, what's *he* doing?' Eric called out.

A slim boy was out alone amongst the waves. With smooth underwater kicks he followed a broken fishing line. The line led to a marlin, twisting on a barb. The boy caught the thrashing head of the marlin, held it steady and wrenched out the hook. Eric gave him a salute. Seeing this, the boy saluted back, then broke from the waters and headed further out to sea.

Rachel followed him for a while. There were fewer children this far from shore, but an exclusive few specialized in underwater spells. They were able to dive down to the pits and trenches at the bottom of the world.

'Deepers!' Rachel called out, craning her neck. 'Way down! Right under us!'

Over a mile below, the deepers were holding onto the

flukes of sperm whales, hoping to witness an encounter with giant squid. Rachel's information spells reported that among the diving children was a magical signature she knew. It belonged to a little French boy whose rainbow she had once spoiled on a hot summer's day.

She smiled, shifting back over land.

Amongst the steaming sawgrasses of the Florida Everglades, they passed over a baby petting the crusty hide of an alligator. Nearby some brothers were chasing raccoons up a tree, giving the animals a head start.

Typical sights.

There were youngsters here from all parts of the world. The national borderlines between countries had never meant much to children, and now they meant nothing at all.

Eric laughed, seeing a small girl. 'How would you like to try that, Rach?'

The girl was hunkered down in the dry dirt next to a diamondback rattlesnake. The snake had been minding its own business, but the girl wanted to play. Planting her elbows on the ground, she nudged the snake's slatted mouth with her nose – daring it to strike.

'Too easy,' Rachel replied.

'You're joking!'

'Only one snake, and not especially poisonous.' She glanced around for a new direction to take.

'Let's move on,' Eric said, and, as he guided her around Florida, Rachel soon knew why.

A thin boy in shorts and a dirty long-sleeved shirt stood in the shallows of the Okeechobee river.

'A spectrum.' Eric whispered the name in awe.

Rachel alighted in the muddy waters and walked over to the boy. As they approached the boy took no notice of them. He kept so still, so perfectly still, that his ankles made no ripples whatsoever.

'They're so rare,' Rachel said. 'I've never been this close to a spectrum before.'

'It's their leader,' Eric remarked. 'It's Albertus Robertson himself.'

'Is it? Are you sure?'

'I know them all.'

'How? They all look similar to me.'

Eric shook his head. 'No, Rachel, they don't.'

Albertus Robertson was a sensitive-looking boy, around ten years old, with light brown eyes. His hair was a long, straggly mess, clearly not brushed for weeks. Like all spectrums, he was slightly short for his age, with the usual abstracted gaze. In all other ways Albertus resembled any other child, except for one extraordinary feature: his ears. They were unnaturally wide and thin, several sizes too large, almost comical. Hinged on a specialized joint no child had ever possessed before, the ear could turn flexibly in all directions. As Rachel watched Albertus Robertson, she perceived a tiny rotation; his head moved. The motion was so small that only her spells detected it, not her eyes. It was a precise movement – a single degree of arc – as he scanned a pre-selected segment of the sky.

Rachel murmured, 'Seems as if Albertus hasn't bothered to wash or take care of himself lately.'

'He's probably got better things to do.'

'Like what?' Rachel hoped Albertus could not hear her. 'What's he looking for out here?'

'I don't know, Rach. Albertus doesn't either. That's what's so interesting about the spectrums. None of them has a clue what they're doing it for. There're dozens of them around the world, just gazing all day at the sky.'

For a while Rachel watched Albertus Robertson, but there was no change in his unnerving stillness. Even in a world now filled with unusual children, the spectrums were different. They were the only ones who had changed physically. Before the Awakening they had looked and behaved like anyone else. Following it, their ears developed within days, along with their silence and lack of movement.

'They can't fly or do the simplest spells,' Eric told Rachel.

'I've heard they don't even talk.'

'I think you're wrong about that. Everyone is. They might not talk to us, but they talk to each other – or they're going to.'

Rachel glanced sharply at Eric. 'How do you know that?'

'I'm not sure, it's just a hunch.' He could hardly take his eyes off Albertus Robertson.

'A hunch? No, there's something else going on between you and the spectrums,' Rachel said. 'You're always noticing things about them no one else does. Albertus has never been identified as their leader. How can you know he is?'

Eric shrugged.

'The spectrums don't even meet,' Rachel said. 'Surely they don't have a leader. They're all loners.'

'They don't meet *yet*, Rach. I think that's going to change as well.'

As Eric said this Albertus Robertson cocked his head. He stared at Eric, intrigued. A spectrum had not been known to do this before. They never reacted to another human presence. For a moment Albertus's placid brown eyes lingered on Eric, then his head whisked back to its former position.

Deeply affected by what had just happened, Eric said, 'There's something else about the spectrums, too. Thrill-seekers like to hang around them.'

'Thrill-seekers! Are you serious?' Thrill-seeker was the general term given to the most reckless children, always pushing their magic to dangerous extremes. To Rachel, the contrast between those daredevils of magic and the passive spectrums was ludicrous.

Eric said, 'Surprising, eh? I can't imagine what they've got in common, but something's going on. I'll bet there's a thrill-seeker round here somewhere. In fact, I know there is.'

Now that Eric had mentioned it, Rachel could detect another magical presence nearby, though keeping out of sight.

'Anyway, let's leave Albertus in peace,' Eric said, dragging his gaze away. 'He enjoys his peace and quiet, old Albertus.'

'How do you know that?' Rachel demanded, exasperated.

'Dunno, just do.' He prodded her. 'What about the prapsies? You promised! Have you forgotten again?'

Rachel said, 'No, I've just been putting it off. For as long as possible.'

'Ah, you know you love the boys really, Rach!'

'Mmm.' With a final glance at Albertus Robertson, she shifted.

They reappeared over southern Italy. Local children were plunging in and out of the Vesuvius volcano, but Rachel's destination was different. She alighted in bustling Naples. Eric was happy to be on the ground and, for a time, on foot, both of them simply explored the narrow twisting roads of the city. They passed a chic jewellery shop, extremely expensive.

'Look at that,' Eric said.

The heavy steel doors of the shop had been destroyed. Only bent edges remained to show where they had once been. Three children were placed at the entrance to guard the shop instead. They stood outside, looking casually menacing.

'Must be a lot of thievers about,' Eric noted. 'I wouldn't have expected that here. Not during the day, anyhow.'

Rachel nodded bleakly. Fences, walls, locks, reinforced concrete, barbed-wire – traditional defences like these could not keep out the really gifted children. 'I've seen worse,' she said. 'In Africa, especially. Cairo. Nairobi. Lagos. Terrible things are still going on.'

The emergence of magic had brought new problems as well as joys. The thiever gangs had started up in the poorest countries. After the Awakening millions of children who had never had enough to eat did not wait. They simply took what they needed. On the world of Ithrea, in one special room Rachel had created food seemingly from magic alone – but that was only the trick of a Witch. Even the most magical children could not conjure food out of nothing.

Typically the thievers came at night, raiding crops, stealing cattle. An experienced gang could take what they wanted before an adult could even spot them. For a hefty price kids might hire themselves out as anti-thievers to help guard a valuable property or chase down an attacker, but hardly any children could be bothered with such dull work unless it was their own family possessions they were protecting. And, supposing a thiever was caught, who dared punish the offender? Adults were no match physically for most children any longer. In a few countries desperate to keep some control over the thievers, children themselves had been sworn into the security forces, given special powers by the courts. But it made little difference. Children escaped detention; they evaded jail. Even if less talented children could be safely locked away, friends would soon use their magic to free them.

A sudden fluttering of wings, though, made Eric and Rachel forget altogether about thievers.

'Whoa! Here they come!' he said. 'Here come the boys!'

Hurrying into an alley where they would be less easily seen, he watched the prapsies flap jubilantly towards him. They headed directly for Eric, in perfectly straight lines, and incredibly swiftly. Not even the most agile child could catch a prapsy – though many had tried.

Devoted to Eric, the child-birds had recently taken to flying far and wide to find him gifts, each trying to outdo the other. Eric clicked his fingers – and the prapsies landed, at exactly the same time, on his head. Their rosy cheeks perspired in the spring air, dripping sweat on his scalp. Eric didn't care.

'Hey boys, what you got?'

One prapsy carried a broken comb in its toothless mouth. Without waiting for Eric's opinion, the child-bird attempted to tidy his blond curly hair. 'Oh, this will make you handsome,' the prapsy promised, ineffectually dragging the comb against his ear.

'Where did it find that comb?' Rachel asked. 'It's filthy.'

Eric shrugged. 'Who cares? I'll wash my hair later. You worry too much, Rach.' He turned to the other prapsy. 'And what've you got for me, then?'

The second prapsy held a knob of chewing gum in one claw. It offered this to Eric.

'Er,' said Eric. 'Where'd you find that? Did you nick it from someone's mouth?'

'Oh, no! No, Eric!' wailed the prapsy. 'I wouldn't give you second-hands. It's fresh. Only my gums.'

'Well, that's all right, then.' Eric opened his mouth and the prapsy dropped the thoroughly chewed gum inside.

'Go on,' the prapsy said expectantly. 'Chew it.'

Eric chewed away. 'No taste,' he said. 'I suppose it's been in your gob a while, eh?'

Rachel said, 'I think the question you should be asking is where it found the gum.'

'On a fence,' answered the prapsy cheerfully. 'There was dirt on it, and a fly, and some stink – but I licked that off.'

Eric spat the gum out. 'Blimey, boys,' he spluttered. 'What are you trying to do? Kill me?'

'Not good? You don't want my present?' The prapsy sniffed. Its face wobbled as it held back a tear. 'I'm sorry, Eric. Did you want the dirt and fly on it? I didn't think so.' It turned angrily to its companion. 'Your fault! You told me to suck the dirt off, you stupid pigeon.'

The other prapsy smiled smugly, saying nothing.

'Off you go!' Eric shooed them away. 'Find me a *proper* treat. Something really good!'

Immediately both prapsies hovered side by side, trembling with excitement.

'Whaddaya want? Whaddaya want, Eric?' they squealed.

'Something nice and *tasty*. Without stink!'

The prapsies sped off, spitting at each other. Rachel could still hear them when they were well out of sight, bickering and swearing.

4

tokyo

Rachel flicked away the comb still protruding from Eric's hair. 'Let's go,' she said. 'I still want to do some shopping.'

'Do we have to?'

'Yes.'

'Where, then? New York?'

'Japan!'

Rachel shifted them to the Far East, following the sun as it dipped down the sky: sunset in Tokyo. For a while she soared over the glass and steel skyscrapers of Shinjuko district, in the western part of the city. Rachel loved this area, especially the massive twin forty-eight-storey towers of the Metropolitan Government Building. By day thirteen thousand city bureaucrats still worked in the offices, but at night the structure belonged to the children.

'Check out the gangs,' Eric said. 'They weren't here last time we came.'

Several rival groups of children surveyed each other

from the roofs of the skyscrapers. Each group was distinctly dressed, so there could be no mistaking where their
allegiances lay.

'See the no-go zones?' Eric indicated the gaps between
the buildings, the invisible places where no children flew.
The atmosphere was uneasy, with few adults about. As
Eric watched, a baby – flying solo – cut across the various
invisible territories. The gangs jeered as he passed,
mocking the baby's jerky progress across the sky.

Eric blew on his forefinger. As if it was a smoking gun he
pointed it at the gang children, smiling thinly. 'Zap, zap,'
he said, under his breath. 'Want me to teach those gang
kids a lesson, Rach? Knock them right out of the sky?'

Rachel glanced at him as he lowered his finger resignedly.
'Are you tempted?'

'I'm *always* tempted. Especially with kids like these.'

Eric's special gift was that of a destroyer of spells. The
Wizard leader, Larpskendya, had himself been puzzled by
this ability. In all the Wizards' experience across many
worlds they had never come across a similar gift. After the
Awakening, Larpskendya had expected other children on
Earth like Eric to emerge. That had not happened.

Eric was unique.

Rachel understood how much he wanted to practise his
anti-magic, but how could he? Each time Eric focused on a
child's spell it killed that particular spell forever. It could
never be used again. Spells were precious; even the most
modest had its worth and value. No child would willingly
give one up.

'It doesn't matter,' Eric said, then added in an under-
tone, 'I'm improving anyway. Even without practising,
I'm getting better all the time.'

'Better at what?'

'I can detect distant spells. I mean really faint spells, out a long way.'

'How far away?'

'Do you know where the prapsies are?'

The magical scent of the prapsies was always hard to follow because they flew so swiftly. At last, more than a thousand miles to the north-west, Rachel's information spells tracked them down. 'They're over the Gobi desert,' she said. 'Flying south.'

'How close together are they?'

Rachel stared blankly at Eric. 'I can't tell that from this distance. I can barely trace them at all.'

'No?' Eric raised his eyebrows. 'Then I'll tell you. They're very close, no more than a foot apart. And one is flying slightly above the other, piggy-back style. They're cold, too. They must be because their speed's six percent down on normal. And,' he added jauntily, 'they're flying at over twelve thousand feet. They like being way up high like that. It reminds them of all those centuries they spent in the skies of Ithrea.'

Rachel gazed at him, shocked. 'Eric, how long have you been able to detect so accurately? You've never mentioned it before.'

He shrugged. 'It's been happening gradually.'

'We need to tell Larpskendya straightaway.'

'Sure, I suppose.'

'Eric, you can't just keep something this important to yourself. You know that. If –'

'All right, lay off, will you? I *was* going to tell Larpskendya tomorrow, actually, when he takes us to visit Yemi. And – er – talking of Yemi,' Eric said, 'here come his little Beauties.'

A shadow had spread over the Tokyo skyline. It was composed entirely of yellow Camberwell Beauty butterflies. There were billions of them, the flock so enormous that for several minutes it entirely hid the early stars as it steadily moved across the city. The sight was such a familiar occurrence that most of the children did not even bother to look up.

'I still don't understand why Yemi sends them everywhere,' Eric said.

'I think I do.' Rachel pictured Yemi, the two-year-old Nigerian boy, and smiled. Even her remarkable spells were in awe of Yemi's magic. Like her, he could shift and transform his shape, but he could do much more. And his magic was maturing all the time. No one had any idea what its limits might be.

As Rachel stared up, she said, 'These lovely butterflies. They're a gift. Yemi's trying to bring a bit of extra happiness to the world. But there's more to it than that. The animals – have you seen how interested they become when the butterflies are overhead? I've no idea what's going on, but their behaviour definitely changes.'

'It's their magic,' Eric said.

'What – the animals?'

'Yeah. They're not like us, but they've got a trace. It responds to Yemi and his butterflies.'

'Are you sure?'

'Dead sure.'

The Camberwell Beauties gradually passed beyond the city. There were hundreds of such flocks, wheeling in great endless migrations. By day and night they flew, their wings ceaselessly charting paths that would take them over every part of the world.

'Let's get away from the gangs,' Rachel said as the last of the butterflies melted inside the sunset glow. 'I still want to shop. Fancy anywhere in particular?'

'Not really, but I'm hungry.'

'Me, too.'

She shifted them to one of the world's premier shopping districts: Tokyo's Ginza-chrome crossroads. For a while, with Rachel disguising them as typical Japanese children, they strolled amongst the neon-splashed bars and sushi stalls. There was an even mixture of adults and children here running the entertainment centres and food outlets. Rachel and Eric bought some yakitari chicken and ice cream and sauntered up the wide streets. As they turned up the Chou-dori road, Eric whispered, 'Stop.'

'A holding spell,' Rachel said.

'Yeah. And whoever it's being used on isn't fighting back.'

'Must be an adult, then.'

'Do you want me to destroy the spell?'

'No,' Rachel said. 'Let's check it out, first.' She picked Eric up and flew along a network of side-streets until they reached a murky alley. Half-concealed by some bins a girl around seven years old stood over an old man. Without being touched the man's body was being held down, while the girl used a searching spell to check his pockets for money, or whatever she was after.

'Stop it!' Rachel shouted in Japanese – and then realized the girl was not Japanese at all. She switched to English. 'Leave him alone!' When the girl still showed no comprehension, Rachel's linguistic spells stated the same message in various languages.

Finally the girl understood. She spat on the ground near Rachel, defiant.

'She'll fight you if she can,' Eric said. 'She's preparing to.'

'I don't think so,' Rachel answered. 'She knows she's outmatched. This one's smart.'

'Who he?' the girl asked, in laboured English. She pressed her toe against the man's chest. 'Your dada? Your da?'

'No,' Rachel said. 'Of course not.'

'Then... why you help?' The girl seemed genuinely puzzled.

'I –' Rachel halted. If this girl couldn't understand that it was wrong to terrorize an adult, what could she say to persuade her?

The girl turned away. Calling a mangy cat from the shadows, she cradled it in her arms and swaggered to the back of the alley, her head held high.

The old man got up shakily, shuffling off in the opposite direction.

'Wait,' Rachel said to him. 'Are you all right? Are you hurt?'

The man clearly wanted to get away from her. Rachel was a child, and he was alone, and afraid of her even though she had helped him. He clung to the wall, edging past Rachel and Eric, bowing several times, but not lifting his eyes.

'You don't usually find adults on their own at night these days in the big cities,' Eric said. 'I can't believe he hasn't got his kids with him in a busy place like this.'

'Not everyone has children of their own,' Rachel said. 'Does that mean they have to stay indoors? Never go out?'

'Either that or accept the risk. You know the rule in the cities: adults indoors by ten p.m., or take the consequences.'

'That's a gang rule,' Rachel said angrily. 'You sound like one of them.'

Eric shrugged. 'Parents made up enough of their own rules before, Rach.'

'So it's time to even things up, is that what you're saying?'

'No, I'm not saying that. I don't like it any more than you, but adults have to be careful, don't they? Stay inside unless they know they've got a child escort, and –'

'That man could be *our* dad,' Rachel said.

Eric looked alarmed. 'Have you protected our house?'

'Of course. The point is that some adults haven't got any special protection. They shouldn't need it.'

She gazed up. The slot of sky between the alley walls teemed with children. To Rachel they suddenly appeared mildly sinister. The old man was still running down the alley, trying to reach safety. He seemed to belong to a different world. She kept an eye on him until he reached a side door. His hands shook as he fumbled with the lock. Perhaps he would be safe inside, perhaps not. Rachel knew that while most parts of the world were safe for adults, juveniles were taking control in the largest cities. Street gangs had always existed, but now they were armed with magic. Generally adults could go about their business freely, but in certain areas after dark menacing children strutted around, behaving unpredictably. A few specialized in taunting grown-ups just for the hell of it.

The old man's hands were shaking so much he could not undo the lock. He kept glancing at Rachel as if she might be about to do horrible things to him. Rachel could have used a spell to disengage the lock, but she knew that would only frighten the old man more. To make him feel less threatened, she moved down the alley – though staying close enough to make sure he got inside safely.

The whole world's turned upside down, she thought.

Nearly all of the changes were for the better. Parents rarely had to go to work any longer, unless they wished to. Their children, using magic, could perform routine chores, freeing most adults for the first time ever from drudgery. But it was still difficult for the adults, and not just because of the child gangs. Many parents had always judged their worth by how they brought up their children, by how much their children needed them. Children didn't need taking care of in quite the same way any longer. By and large they still shared the same loving relationships, but many children now spent more time exploring their magic than with their parents. And, of course, there was also jealousy. Some parents were envious of their own children. Why should only children have magic? Adults wanted to be masters of their own trajectories. They wanted to be able to fly, too ...

The old man had at last dealt with the door lock. He slipped inside. Rachel wondered what kind of life he led. He seemed so frail. I hope he's not alone, she thought. Alone in a city of child gangs. What could be worse? Overhead a baby chuckled, pursuing a night bird across the sky. Where is your mother? Rachel found herself silently asking. Where is she? How does she feel about you being so far from her?

Suddenly Rachel wanted to return home and make sure Mum and Dad were safe.

The Griddas are out there somewhere, she thought. Since the High Witches know where our world is, the Griddas must know as well. And I bet they don't waste time on games or joining stupid gangs, or fleecing adults. When the Griddas finally decide to come, she thought, how are we ever going to be ready?

'Let's get back, Eric,' she said. 'Let's go home.'

5

FIRE
without heat

'He's late,' Rachel said.

Mum squeezed her hand. 'He won't be much longer now, I'm sure.'

Rachel nodded tensely and hugged her knees, rocking back and forth on one of the kitchen chairs. A few sandwiches lay untouched on a plate next to her. She could never eat before she saw Larpskendya. She was too filled with anticipation.

Eric was more relaxed. He lounged nearby, flipping through a comic. The prapsies were in a tree a few gardens down, arguing with a family of crows.

'What are the boys up to?' Mum asked Eric, not really caring.

'They're telling the crows to stop messing about and grow some proper faces.'

As Mum rolled her eyes, Rachel whispered to her, 'Are *you* nervous? You know, when Larpskendya comes, do you feel like' – she pressed her heart – 'like this as well?'

'Yes, every time,' Mum replied. 'Oh, but it's a nice kind of nervous, isn't it?'

They grinned at one another.

A few minutes passed. Rachel smoothed out her skirt. Mum made some tea and nobody drank it except Eric. Bored with the crows the prapsies squashed their noses against the window, wanting to be back inside. Mum automatically checked they weren't carrying anything disgusting before letting them fly over to Eric.

'How'd you get on, boys?' he asked, as they alighted on his shoulders.

'They won't listen,' one prapsy said forlornly. 'They won't grow faces.'

'Did you tell them off?'

'We did, Eric. They just flew away. They always do.'

Eric leaned towards the prapsies. 'I'll tell you why they do that, boys. It's because they're ashamed. They're only crows, after all. You two can fly like geniuses, talk, everything. When you're beside them, the crows are embarrassed. They know they're nowhere near as good as either of you.'

Both prapsies beamed happily. This explanation had never occurred to them.

The patio door opened and Dad came in from the garage, wiping car grease from his hands. He was a tall, rangy man with greying hair.

'Nearly done it,' he said with satisfaction, going over to the sink to clean up. 'Almost fixed that engine. A couple more hours' work, that's all.'

Rachel could have fixed the car, but she knew better. Dad liked doing it.

Dad stood with his hands under the tap, methodically removing traces of oil. Then he came to sit near everyone else on one of the kitchen chairs, and in a hoarse voice said, 'He's overdue, isn't he?'

Mum nodded. No one needed to say who he meant. Dad sat forward to pour himself a cup of tea, then stopped. He forgot about the tea. Everyone in the room broke out into the same broad smile as they sensed it: a thrill in the sky, an ache. The clouds seemed to know; eagles halted their flight.

Rachel whispered, 'He's coming. He's coming.'

Dad straightened up to steady himself. The prapsies bounced up and down on the radiator. Eric, forgetting his cool, rushed into the living room, hoping to catch a glimpse of the Wizard bursting through the clouds.

But he was too late – Larpskendya had already shifted into the hallway.

The prapsies were there first. Searching for a gift, they found a bit of dirt on the carpet. After Larpskendya accepted this graciously, he turned to the girl dashing along the hall – and she did not need to ask his permission. He opened out his arms and Rachel ran into them. She pressed her face against his chest and held him.

'Oh, Larpskendya!' she cried out.

Her spells rushed crazily into her eyes, all wanting to see him first. Larpskendya threw back his head and laughed, kissing her and Eric and both parents in a completely informal way.

Dad, as always, was unable to take his gaze off the

Wizard. What was it about him? Not the Wizard's features – they were like those of any impressive man. It was the eyes: human-shaped, but more vibrantly passionate than any man's.

Rachel clung to Larpskendya's cream robe as she told him about recent magical developments. As usual he seemed to know already, though he did not interrupt her. Finally, after speaking with Mum and Dad in private, Larpskendya held hands with Rachel and Eric. The prapsies buzzed around his head like flies, knowing something was about to happen. With a movement too swift to see, Larpskendya caught them and tucked each prapsy inside Eric's shirt.

'Keep them close to you today,' Larpskendya advised Eric.

'Why?'

'In the place we're visiting, they might lose their hearts to another. Yemi has changed since the last time you saw him.' Eric shared a quizzical look with Rachel. 'Are you ready?' Larpskendya said. Eric did up the buttons of his jacket, pressing the heads of the prapsies down.

'Where's Larpy taking us?' one prapsy asked.

'Shush. Don't call him that,' Eric said.

'Why not, Eric?'

'It's just not a good idea, that's all.'

'Oh, I have been called worse names,' Larpskendya remarked. He laughed – and shifted. There was no sensation of flight or movement. Rachel's own spells could never grasp the silky ease with which Larpskendya shifted. The next instant – and thousands of miles – later, Rachel and Eric found themselves letting go of his hands, blinking in semi-darkness.

They were underground, in a cave. Once it might have

been an ordinary cave, but Yemi's magic had transformed it. Inside there were no windows, but endless views. To Rachel's right a fire raged, without heat. Over Eric's head a waterfall cascaded, without wetting him. Howler monkeys appeared from nowhere, screeched, vanished – and reappeared. And all around were the sights, sounds and fragrances Yemi treasured most, those of his old African home, Fiditi. And that meant warmth; it meant humidity; it meant smells of good home cooking, burning fuel and the noise of lonely night birds calling. One sound dominated all the others: the murmur of rainforest leaves.

That sound, beautifully rich, was everywhere.

'This is only one of Yemi's residences,' Larpskendya said, leading them further in. 'He creates new ones wherever he goes, an infinite number.'

They turned a corner, into the main part of the cave and there – bursting with life – was a small boy.

'Yemi!' Rachel cried, rushing over to him.

As soon as he heard her Yemi shifted into Rachel's arms. For a while he simply lay there, gazing at her in a way that asked nothing and everything. It had been three months since Rachel last visited him, and in outward appearance Yemi had hardly changed at all – still a toddler, with short-cropped curly hair, ebony skin and soft brown eyes. Characteristically, he chose for himself the least fussy clothes, a pair of wrinkled blue shorts and a plain orange T-shirt. But Rachel did not even notice what he wore. What she noticed were the animals. Dozens surrounded him, every kind of creature: mice, dogs, a marmoset, an elk, and cats, big cats – fully-grown Siberian tigers.

'We're not certain how Yemi brings them, or why,' Larpskendya said. 'Yet it seems no animal can resist him.'

Eric glanced at the prapsies, still inside his shirt. They stared back reassuringly.

Rachel rocked Yemi against her chest. While she did so a gibbon monkey jumped on her shoulder. It started preening her hair. She laughed at the tickling sensation and bent forward to kiss Yemi on the mouth.

He pulled back. He shouted at her. Shoving Rachel away, he flew to another part of the cave.

'Sorry,' said a voice from the shadows. 'I should have warned you.'

Yemi's sister, Fola, stepped forward. She was about Rachel's age, but taller, with braided hair and full lips that smiled readily. After greeting Rachel and Eric she knelt down and ruffled Yemi's hair. 'He no go let anyone near his mouth. He never does, not for long time.'

Yemi tottered over to his big cats for comfort. The Siberian tigers sat either side of him, their heads platforms for his hands. When his little temper ended, Yemi returned to Rachel, clearly wanting her forgiveness. As she pulled him close, she said, 'I think I know why he doesn't accept kisses. It's because of Heebra. She put her death spell into his mouth that way. He's scared, that's all.'

Yemi wriggled to be put down, then clapped loudly for everyone's attention.

'Flipping heck!' Eric gasped.

The animals they had already seen were not the only ones in the cave. The rest now arrived from the leafy areas. Mice hopped alongside cats; a cobra clung to the neck of a swan; a hawk settled near a chick, with no thought to snap it up.

With a splash, another animal emerged from a small pool. It was only a baby. Fat with blubber, it hauled itself forward. On five-clawed foreflippers it made its way across to Eric and gazed up at him.

'A Weddell seal,' Larpskendya said. 'From the Antarctic. The animals come from everywhere, drawn to Yemi wherever he goes.' He picked up the seal cub. 'This one was blue with cold when it arrived. It must have travelled over many nights across half an ocean just to be with Yemi. Can you imagine that?'

Eric stared in awe. 'How many make it to him?'

'Not many. Yemi is restless, always shifting off somewhere else. Only the most determined animals have a chance to catch him before he leaves.'

Eric bent down to one of the hawks. The prapsies took the opportunity to escape from his shirt. 'Hey, come back!' he yelled – but they were out, scrambling onto his shoulders.

Seeing them, Yemi jumped with excitement. He held out his arms. When the prapsies did not immediately fly across to him, Yemi was astonished. 'Come, come,' he said in a sing-song voice. 'Want.'

'I can see that,' Eric said stonily.

'Want.'

'I don't care what you want. You can't have.'

'Please.' Yemi tried smiling.

Placing both prapsies on the floor, Eric said, 'Free choice, boys. Go with Yemi if you like. I won't stop you.'

The prapsies flew straight back to Eric's shoulders.

'We know where we want to be,' one said.

Eric peered at Yemi. 'I think the boys have made their choice, don't you?'

Yemi had no idea how to react. This had never happened to him before. He tried everything to get the prapsies to change their minds. He frowned, stamped his feet, shook his fists. He implored them. When they continued to refuse, he finally burst into tears. One of his Siberian tigers came across, nuzzling him.

Larpskendya said, 'Eric, I want you to tell me exactly how you did that. I've never seen Yemi refused by any creature.'

'I didn't do anything,' Eric said. 'Nothing at all.'

'That's not true. Yemi hasn't been denied that way before, I'm certain.'

'Well,' Eric said coolly, 'I'm not sure it's right for little kids to get what they want all the time. It's not good for them, is it?'

He stared at Yemi and Yemi stared back – a meeting of eyes. For a moment Rachel knew the two boys were measuring each other in ways she could not understand.

'There, there,' Fola said, hugging Yemi. 'See, look at that! You cannot have everything!'

Yemi remained sorrowful until one of the Siberian tigers licked his face, making him laugh. His usual cheerfulness returned immediately. He jumped onto the tiger's back, slapping its flanks for a ride.

'Yemi's not really an ordinary child any more, is he?' Rachel said. 'He's more than that.'

'He is many things,' Larpskendya answered. 'But most of the time he still behaves typically for a child his age. He enjoys sweets and toys, and the usual kinds of games, especially hide-and-seek.'

'Oh yes!' added Fola. 'He no like if the animals hide for too long. But the animals must never find *him* when he hide, oh no! He's just a baby still, a *pikin*. He like this –' she took him from the tiger's back and bumped him up and down on her knee, sending Yemi into fits of laughter – 'and he has such moods, and must get his way! Crying for nothing!'

Rachel glanced across at the Siberian tigers. The behaviour of one of them had started to concern her. It was no common tiger, she was certain of that. Its movements were too precise, too calculated, almost too affectionate. Each time she studied it the tiger stopped what it was doing and gazed thoughtfully at her – an almost human gesture.

At one point Yemi spoke to the tiger. In response the tiger buried its wet nose in his ear and whispered something back. Rachel distinctly heard words.

'That's not an animal!' she shouted.

6

serpantha

Raising all her defensive spells, Rachel drew Eric behind her.

'Do not be alarmed,' said the tiger, transforming.

Rachel expected a Witch, but it was a Wizard who rose before her. Wearing a simple aquamarine robe, he was approximately seven feet high, equally tall as Larpskendya, with the same wild, unreadable eyes. Rachel found she could only look at him for a moment. She glanced at Eric and saw he felt the same way.

'I am Serpantha,' the Wizard said. His voice was rich and light and seemed to come from a noticeably younger age than that of Larpskendya. Was he younger? Not for the first time, Rachel wondered how old the wizards were. Bowing low to Rachel and Eric, Serpantha said, 'It is an honour to meet you at last, though I feel I already know you well. Larpskendya is right. There is a strength in both of you that will not be easily challenged on this world, or beyond it.'

Yemi tugged at Serpantha's sleeve, clearly wanting to play.

'You and Larpskendya are brothers,' Rachel said. 'I'm right, aren't I?'

Larpskendya said, 'I told you she would know. It is difficult to keep any secrets from this one.'

'But you are ... older than Larpskendya,' Eric said. 'You sound younger, but you're much older. I can sense it in your magic.'

Serpantha gave Eric a look that was almost fearful. 'How can you tell? That should not be possible.'

'Your spells are so tired, that's how,' Eric said. His eyes moistened as he felt Serpantha's spells calling desperately out to him. 'They've been fighting so long. It's hard for them to continue. Oh, and they don't want to, they don't want to.'

Serpantha reached out. With trembling hands he held Eric. 'Yes,' he said. 'I have asked too much of them these last years – and then I have asked more, and more again. The war – there has been no rest for myself or Larpskendya.' He lowered his gaze, then said, with a crooked smile, 'Can you tell how much strength my spells have left, Eric? It is difficult for me to be certain. They lie to me, you know.'

'They won't fail you soon,' Eric rasped.

'That is good to hear,' Serpantha said, his voice lightening again. He picked Yemi up, placing him on his broad shoulders. 'I have been here for a while with this little one.'

'Are you here to protect him from the Griddas?' Rachel asked.

'Partly. A typical Gridda would try to destroy Yemi at once – unless she thought she could use him. But actually

Yemi needs watching for other reasons as well. It is not that he is bad – of course not – it is just that an idle or misguided thought of his could accidentally destroy many things of value on your world.' Serpantha kissed Yemi, then whispered to him, 'Even your happiest thoughts can be dangerous, you wonder ...'

Rachel recalled the incident with the bears. On his second birthday Fola had given Yemi a brown bear cub. Yemi could not contain his joy at this surprise. He wanted each person to share it. The next morning everyone – every child *and* adult on Earth – woke to find a pretty cub cuddled up beside them.

'The same problems,' Serpantha said, 'beset all gifted youngsters.' He glanced knowingly at Larpskendya, who laughed. 'But Yemi's skills exceed anything I've seen before, even in a Wizard. I have been attempting to teach him the hardest thing of all – to realize that he cannot always have everything he wants. With great difficulty he's beginning to accept such things. And he has a beautiful, resourceful sister to help him do so.' Serpantha reached out and pulled Fola into his wide embrace. She smiled shyly, looking up at him. 'Fola cannot be the ever-adapting play companion I have been,' Serpantha said to Rachel, 'but with your help I am sure I will not be missed. And it is just as well, for I must leave.'

'Leave?' Rachel wanted to weep, but she did not know why.

'An opportunity has arisen,' Serpantha said. 'One we never expected. The High Witches have requested a meeting between us.'

'I ... I thought the Griddas had killed them all.'

'No, some are imprisoned, and a few survive in the

tunnels. One of these managed to escape from Ool and deliver a message, though she died afterwards of wounds even Larpskendya could not repair. The message was from Calen.'

'Calen? That's Heebra's daughter!' Rachel said. 'Her mother died here. How can you trust Calen? She must hate us.'

'Yes, she must,' Serpantha said, 'and normally I would not trust her at all. And who is to say I can now? I have spent many of your lifetimes distrusting the High Witches. It is difficult for me to change, too, though I must.' He tickled Yemi, making him giggle, then stared solemnly at Rachel. 'You have no idea what a pitiful state the High Witches are in. They are truly desperate, I've no doubt of that. I will meet with them.'

'Alone?' Rachel asked.

'If it is a trap,' Serpantha said, 'ten Wizards will probably be no better than one. I –'

'Don't go,' Eric said. 'Please don't.'

'Why, Eric?'

'I don't know. Just don't. I don't want you to.'

There was silence in the cave.

'I must go, Eric,' Serpantha said. 'Our war with the Witches has been an endless one. I would not wish the same on you. This may be the only opportunity to end it. The Griddas are a different species. I do not think their leader, Gultrathaca, will be so eager to negotiate. And there is something else you should know. The Griddas have nearly found Ithrea. We've tried to obscure it, but our concealments will not hold them off for long.'

Morpeth, Rachel thought, her heart leaping.

'So you see,' Serpantha said, 'there is more than the

welfare of your own world wrapped up in these matters. I know the risk I am taking, and though I'm cautioned against it, I will travel alone.' He turned sadly to Larpskendya. 'Well, brother, it is time for my leaving. Yemi is not happy, but he is being brave about it, as you must.'

Larpskendya said nothing. He could not meet his brother's eyes as they held each other.

'I wish I had the opportunity to spend more time with you,' Serpantha said to Eric and Rachel. 'However, I am confident this will not be the last time we meet.' He took Yemi's hand, leading the party in silence from the cave to the surface. The air was warm. The sun shone down on a field dappled with poppies and cornflowers. Rachel did not notice. She hardly saw the field at all. Something inside her wanted to keep Serpantha close.

'You can't leave,' she said. 'Who will protect Yemi if you go?'

'Fola – and there is another I have been training,' Serpantha said. 'I believe you know her well.'

He motioned to the sky. A girl arrived from it. She had pure blond hair, and eyes so light blue that those first meeting her could notice nothing else.

'Heiki!' Rachel cried out.

Heiki alighted next to Rachel, and they kissed like the true friends they had become.

Serpantha watched them interact, saw how easy the girls were with each other. 'Once, you two battled as if nothing else had any meaning except that battle,' he reminded them. 'But that has changed. We must all be prepared to change now.'

Heiki exchanged a few words with Eric and Rachel,

then took her place beside Yemi. Already her eyes scanned the sky, alert for danger to him.

'Brother, are you ready?' Serpantha asked. 'I need your strength now.'

The Wizards placed their heads together. Rachel sensed the beginnings of a shift so potent that she could not begin to comprehend it.

Yemi gazed adoringly at Serpantha. For once his animals had stayed behind, knowing he wanted to be on his own with Serpantha for as long as possible. Seeing that Serpantha was about to leave, he forgot his promise to be brave. He clasped Serpantha's leg and hung determinedly on.

With infinite care Serpantha loosened Yemi's fingers. He took a final look over the field and the undulating green hills beyond.

'I love this world,' he said to Eric and Rachel. 'And I love your race; the most magical of you give so much. It is not always so.' He embraced them – and they couldn't stand it. It was as if they were losing something they had longed for their whole lives. Fola clumsily touched Serpantha's face.

Eric stepped up. 'I wish I knew you better,' he blurted. 'I wish I did.'

'You will,' Serpantha told him firmly.

And shifted.

7

passion

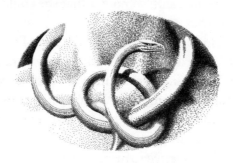

Serpantha made his way cautiously along the tunnels.

For some time he had been travelling downwards, following the magical scent of High Witches. That scent was overwhelmingly strong now – the Witches so close he could hear their stifled whisperings. The tunnels of Ool were covered in tiny luminous life-forms that emitted a murky beige light. That meant Serpantha could see, but his nails were not designed to clutch rock. Unable to find any grip at all on the smooth walls, he flew where the tunnels were steepest. At last the tunnels flattened out to become the entrance to a large cave.

Serpantha stood upright and walked boldly inside.

The Witches were waiting. There were ten of them, ten mature High Witches. Seeing Serpantha, each responded differently. Most retreated in fear to the back of the cave, their soul-snakes hissing. A few Witches held their ground, clamping their jaws to prevent them lashing out.

Serpantha had expected these reactions. Not wishing to invite an attack, he deliberately kept a discreet distance – and waited.

At first the Witches dared not approach. Then, in a swift flurry, they jumped on Serpantha and dragged him out of the cave.

Serpantha was not surprised at the roughness of the treatment. He did nothing to retaliate, though the stone cut his skin. The Witches hauled him along several corridors before throwing their burden at the feet of another Witch. If this Witch dreaded the appearance of Serpantha as much as the others, she hid it well. Her yellow soul-snake examined him with frank curiosity.

'Welcome, Serpantha,' she said.

'Welcome, Calen.'

For a considerable time Calen and Serpantha simply gazed at one another. This was the first occasion in more than two hundred thousand years that a High Witch and a Wizard had met outside of a battleground. Finally Serpantha bowed. In the nearly forgotten manner he held out his arms, offering to bond with Calen in the formal style.

Nylo, Calen's soul-snake, wanted no contact with the Wizard, but she made him fleetingly entwine with Serpantha's wrists. Neither Serpantha nor Calen expected it, but the touch sent deep surges of loss through them. Feelings arose that they had difficulty speaking through, and for a moment the original purpose of their meeting was forgotten. Raising their eyes, they looked intently at one another, saying nothing, not knowing what to say.

For much of her life Calen had wondered what it might

be like to match herself against the legendary Serpantha. Now that he stood before her, she knew how foolish that notion had been. A single glance at him showed the plenitude of his power. Even her mother, Heebra, had never possessed such ardent, lucid intelligence. His eyes held her: solemn, candid, beautiful. Beautiful? Calen caught herself. How could his eyes be beautiful? Nylo stared and stared at the Wizard, disregarding her silent command to stop. In embarrassment, Calen stepped away. She had never felt the way she felt now – unmade by the steady slow gaze of a Wizard.

Serpantha felt the same bewildering emotions. He tried to gather himself. Brushing cave dirt from his shoulder, he said bluntly, 'I expected a warmer greeting than this.'

'No doubt you did!' Calen replied. 'Check the rest of the tunnels,' she snapped at her Witches. 'Make sure there are no more Wizards.'

'I came alone,' Serpantha assured her.

'Surely you don't expect me to accept your word on that?' Calen motioned for scouts to sniff up the connecting tunnels. While waiting, she attempted to contain her emotions. What was she feeling? This was ridiculous! She had prepared so long for this negotiation. The lives of all her Witches depended on its outcome! When her scouts returned Calen, composing herself, faced Serpantha again.

'It gives me no pleasure to be here,' she said. 'Can you talk for all your kind?'

'Each Wizard speaks for all others. Always.'

'If this is some kind of Wizard trick ...'

'You requested the meeting, not I.'

Calen half-smiled. 'Heebra taught me that conversation with Wizards is pointless.'

'Did she?' Serpantha said. 'How could she have known? Heebra never asked for a meeting, though we invited her. What was your mother so afraid of?'

Calen tried to think clearly. Her attention was being diverted by Serpantha's eyes. They were smaller than hers, only slightly larger than human eyes. Absurdly, she had a strong temptation to explore the delicate brows above them. She resisted it.

Serpantha wondered: did she even know? Or had so much time passed that all memory amongst the Witches had been forgotten or removed?

'Do you realize,' he said, 'that Wizards and Witches came originally from the same world?' He watched for a reaction. 'We were once a single race, sharing all things.'

Calen's mind reeled. 'I don't believe that!' She retreated from him, staring fiercely at his body. Could it be true? Serpantha's jaws were far tinier than her own, the teeth delicate. 'We never had jaws like yours,' she said.

'No,' Serpantha replied. 'Your original jaws were smaller than ours. You altered them.'

'You're lying!'

'Am I? What advantage would I gain from it?'

While Calen absorbed this, Serpantha appraised the other Witches. Normally Highs took immense pride in their appearance. Even battle-weary Highs used magic to hide their injuries for as long as they could. These Witches were all filthy and thin, their black dresses in shreds; some had slackening jaws where the muscles no longer had the strength to support the heavy teeth.

It meant they were close to death.

Or, Serpantha realized, it could mean the Witches were pretending to be injured.

His information spells automatically performed another sweep of the Witches. Their injuries were genuine. Serpantha trusted the judgement of his spells. Not once in his ancient life had they misled him in a matter of such importance. He stroked the damaged arm of the closest Witch – a tenderness she withdrew from only slowly.

'You have suffered terribly,' he murmured. 'I see how much.'

'We are still to be feared!' Calen shouted.

'I have no doubt of that.'

Keeping Nylo close, Calen tried to determine what to do next. Instinctively she knew Serpantha was telling the truth about their origins. It both disgusted and excited her to know this, but why should it change anything between them? She could not afford to make a mistake. Already several of her Witches were lowering their guard, drawing closer to Serpantha, their fear less than it had been. One reached out to him – and Calen surprised herself by slapping the claw away herself. Strong feelings welled inside her again.

Serpantha counted the Witches in the cave. 'Is this ... all that is left of the Highs?' he asked.

'No. There are remnants hiding in other tunnels. Some are in locations I know nothing about – in case I am caught. I lead a few, where I am able.'

Serpantha nodded. 'As the daughter of Heebra, the Griddas must have a considerable bounty on your head.'

Calen laughed grimly. 'I hope so! I would be disappointed if that were not the case!'

'How have you managed to avoid them?'

'We don't avoid them,' Calen said. 'If we can smell the Griddas in time, we flee. Where that is not possible, we fight. As you can see, we have fought … many times. In any case, now that they have won the main battle, the Gridda leaders have less interest in us than you think. They are more intrigued by something else – the human child, Yemi.'

Serpantha tried to hide his concern. 'You told them about the boy?'

'Under torture even a High Witch can be made to talk, Wizard. The Griddas were curious to know why over five hundred of Heebra's best fighters returned in defeat from Earth, speaking of the spell Yemi released.'

'What do the Griddas know about him?'

'Everything we know. His scent, his skills. His innocence.' She eyed him. 'Your guard must be slacking, Serpantha. Gridda scouts study all Wizard movements to and from Earth. I am surprised you have not stationed more Wizards there to protect the boy.'

'Two are enough,' Serpantha said. 'More would have drawn greater attention.'

'Only two? Thank you,' said a new voice.

From the shadows, watcher and soldier spiders suddenly appeared. Like a tide, they swarmed from all directions across the floor of the cave. Griddas followed behind.

Serpantha reacted at once. He had never been so completely surprised by an ambush, but now was not the time to dwell on the reason. A nest of spells, some of the deadliest any creature had ever summoned, sprang to defend him. The first cluster he sent to seal off any further entrances. A second, to deflect attacks, sought to alter his body shape, scent and chemical structure. The third cluster was a battery of fast assault spells – to distract his opponents while he escaped.

But none of Serpantha's spells worked.

They lay uselessly in his mind, screaming in fear for him.

The Griddas, two full packs, ranged themselves about the Wizard. When they were in position a final Gridda dropped her bulk down from the ceiling.

She bounded across and raised herself to her full height. 'I am Gultrathaca,' she said.

'I know who you are.'

'Do you know what I am going to do to you?'

Serpantha knew. He tried to shift, but his spells could not fix the transfer points.

'An inhibiting spell,' Gultrathaca explained. 'Effective only in contact with skin. In this case, Nylo's skin. Of course, how could you have known? No High Witch ever used such a spell. When we used it on them, they were equally surprised!'

'Do as you wish,' said Serpantha, facing her. 'I will tell you nothing.'

'We shall see.'

Several Griddas trussed his arms and legs with spell-thread.

Serpantha turned to Calen. 'What have you done?' he said, his voice shuddering with regret and pity. 'Oh, Calen, what bargain do you think the Griddas will ever honour?'

With difficulty, Calen ignored him. Facing Gultrathaca, she said, 'I did what you asked. Now fulfil *your* promise. Release my High Witches.'

Gultrathaca lifted an arm and struck Calen's face. Two of her jaws were shattered. From the floor, Calen screamed, 'But...you promised! We bonded, snake and spiders! The agreement cannot be broken!'

'Do you think the niceties of your bonds and promises mean anything to me?' said Gultrathaca. She stared at Calen with contempt. 'You have betrayed all your Witches.'

Calen struggled to get up. 'But we let you maim us! We allowed it. To convince the Wizard we let you ...' Her face hardened. 'You won't find us all,' she yelled. 'There are more of us than you realize!'

'You fool,' Gultrathaca said. 'We know where all the High Witches are. Your kind make so much noise any Gridda infant can hear you approaching.'

As she was led away, Calen looked at Serpantha. A fundamental change had occurred in him. His face was blank, his eyes glazed over. All the warmth had begun to drain from his skin.

'What's happening?' asked a Gridda, prodding at Serpantha's cheek.

'It is not our doing,' Gultrathaca said. 'The Wizard is retreating inside some private realm. He thinks we cannot reach him there, but he is wrong. Eventually, he'll tell us everything we need to know about Yemi. Perhaps he'll even lead us to Larpskendya himself.'

Serpantha lay quietly in the arms of the Griddas. He no longer moved. A serene expression had spread across his features. His eyes were closed, at peace. Forcing open the lids, Gultrathaca gazed into them. The colours, once so bright, had started to fade. The Gridda pack hauled the body of Serpantha from the cave to the interrogation levels.

'Hurry!' Gultrathaca shrieked.

8

floating koalas, and other pretties

Eric strode purposefully along a winding path.

He was in an isolated wood, hundreds of miles from home. The prapsies accompanied him, taking short flights to keep up. So far they had managed not to annoy too many of the woodland animals, and normally Eric would have rewarded them by playing a game. Not today. He had a special reason for asking Rachel to bring him here.

Eric was seeking an explanation from Albertus Robertson.

Since Larpskendya left Earth to investigate Serpantha's failure to return from Ool, the behaviour of all the spectrums had altered. Until then they had been content to stay entirely still for days. Suddenly spectrums worldwide were on the move. And they were not alone. The thrill-seekers had joined them. They no longer hung back, out of sight. They had openly united with the spectrums – flying them wherever they wished to go.

Eric left the path, picking his way between scattered beech trees.

'Are we nearly there, boys?' one prapsy asked.

'Shush,' Eric replied. 'Don't want to scare him off, do we?' He tiptoed around a bush.

And there, in a small clearing, stood Albertus Robertson.

He was balanced on one bent leg. His other leg was off the ground, as though something had caught Albertus's interest in mid-step. No child in the world other than a spectrum could have held such an unnatural position for more than a few seconds. For a while Eric just hung around, trying to disentangle his feelings. What drew him to the spectrums? The things other children found creepy about them, fascinated him...

Albertus paid Eric no attention. His narrow shoulders and thin neck did not seem quite strong enough to hold his heavy head – as if, Eric thought, on a windy day an unexpected gust might snap it off.

He wanted to start a conversation with Albertus, but was put off by the presence of the thrill-seekers. There were two of them, two teenage girls. That in itself was unusual – Eric did not know of any spectrum with more than one thrill-seeker. Both girls were only inches from Albertus. Their arms were stretched out towards him, ready to lift him up at a moment's notice. One of them clearly did not welcome Eric's arrival. She glanced briefly, angrily, in his direction.

'Hi,' Eric said, feeling awkward. When there was no reply one of the prapsies screeched, 'Wake up when Eric is speaking to you!'

'It's all right, boys,' Eric said. 'Let it go.'

One of the thrill-seeker girls rotated fractionally towards him. 'Please don't interfere,' she said. 'Go away. Leave us in solitude.'

'I'm not going to bother you. I just want to ask a few questions.'

'We don't want to answer them.'

'Why?'

'If we speak to you, then some of our mindfulness will wander.'

'Wander?' Eric hesitated. 'You mean – from Albertus?'

'Of course. Please leave. You are distracting him, and there is danger.'

'What danger?' Eric stepped closer, forcing the closest girl to pay him attention. She immediately took up a defensive stance. Eric felt her attack spells being readied. At the same time the other thrill-seeker held Albertus Robertson's waist, preparing to lift him to safety.

'I'm not a danger to you!' Eric said. 'Surely you know that.'

'Go away!' the girl demanded.

The prapsies flew around her head, shouting insults she ignored.

In frustration, Eric gazed directly at Albertus Robertson. A falling leaf had come to rest on one of his upturned ears. With extraordinary speed the nearest of his thrill-seekers ripped the leaf away.

'Look, talk to me,' Eric said to Albertus. 'I'm close to Rachel and others who have our safety in mind. I sense you're part of that somehow, but you must explain your-selves. What are you all looking for? Why are you all on the move? What –'

Albertus Robertson flinched. At first Eric thought he was responding to him, but it soon became apparent that the spectrum's conduct had nothing to do with Eric. His head cocked skyward. With panic in his eyes, Albertus silently opened and closed his mouth, desperate to say something. Glancing at one another, his thrill-seekers picked him up. They flew above the trees and away.

'What is it?' Eric called after them. 'What's –'

Suddenly he gasped and fell back, understanding.

The prapsies stared at Eric. They touched the tips of their wings against his face, as they always did when they were frightened.

'Eric, what's wrong? Eric!'

'Find Rachel,' he rasped. 'Oh, boys, find her fast!'

Nine Gridda packs descended into the mild-weathered skies of Earth.

Using her spies, Gultrathaca had chosen a time when she was certain Larpskendya was absent, and there was a brief gap in the network of children patrolling the skies. The task should have been easier, but Serpantha had given Gultrathaca nothing. Throughout the interrogations he had stayed silent. Gultrathaca could hardly believe his resistance. How could he hold out for so long against the unrelenting battery of spells the packs breathed inside him? Even causing Serpantha true pain had eluded her. He had entered some kind of tranquil region where her Griddas could not reach him ...

Gultrathaca countered Serpantha's silence with numbers. On their last visit to Earth, the High Witches had helpfully left boosters to improve speeds between the two worlds. Gultrathaca used them and hundreds of

Griddas – all those who had learned to shift – streamed across the continents of Earth.

In the absence of better information, they sniffed for an individual child whose magical signature was more remarkable than all others. They should never have succeeded. Before he left Larpskendya had created a spell to camouflage Yemi's magical scent. But Yemi himself, not understanding its importance, had merely seen the spell as a challenge – and broken it.

The pack of Griddas who came across him were fortunate in another way. Heiki, charged with protecting him, had not allowed Yemi outside in recent days. This morning Yemi, in his boredom, had mischievously shifted to a summer meadow. Heiki could not persuade him back underground, and the Griddas found him in bright sunshine, playing with his animal friends.

Heiki saw the Griddas first – a sight that baffled her. She had been prepared for outstretched claws and teeth, not these oddities. Confused, she called sharply to Fola, who was talking with her brother.

'What is it?' Fola asked.

'Say the safety words to Yemi.'

'What's wrong?'

'Just say them!'

Fola turned to look. If the Griddas had come in their true form she would have known at once to whisper in Yemi's ear the words she had practised with him over and over – words Yemi had been taught meant danger, to get away.

But Gultrathaca had planned for this.

Her first instinct had been to use the tactics of terror: to scare Yemi by threatening him and those he loved. However, she had heard how easily Yemi had disposed of

Witches in the past, and sensed her Griddas would not be able to *force* this particular human child to join them.

So – to entice him instead – the Griddas came in other guises.

Having questioned the High Witches they knew what young children liked, and they came in that fashion. They came as the playthings of children. They came disguised as animals: as furry dogs and oversized kittens, floating koalas, and other pretties. They came as dolphins with merrily flicking tails. And they came as made-up things – things that were warm, that smiled at Yemi, that reached out their arms for him, that were soft and downy and pleasant to look upon. They came in bright, noisy, chuckling shapes that swept down from the clouds.

Fola reacted too slowly to Heiki's warning. Before she could open her mouth a Gridda spell sealed her lips. She tried to make Yemi understand as the Griddas closed in, but he was too mesmerized to notice.

Yemi knew that the things approaching with open paws and crazily wagging tails were not real, but that only excited him. Serpantha had assumed many animal guises when they played together; and while Yemi knew these new creatures were not disguised Wizards, they were certainly magical, powerfully so. It did not worry him that they were not real. He had himself made many objects that were not real, and those had never harmed him, after all.

Heiki seized one Gridda as it passed by. Briefly, as she fought it, the manufactured kitten-smile masking the true face of the Gridda faded. But it was too powerful for Heiki to deal with on her own. It cuffed her with a hairy blow. The blow was calculated to disable Heiki without killing her – in case Yemi noticed.

Heiki was left dazed amongst the grass and small flowers of a field.

The Griddas drifted to the ground. All Yemi's animals were joined by the new brightly-glowing companions, each given its own to play with – there were welcoming Gridda arms for them all.

An impossibly floppy puppy plucked Yemi off the ground. As the other Griddas hastily surrounded him, he did not notice that his true animal friends were left behind.

On a tide of chattering, mirth-filled magic he was carried beyond the skies of Earth.

Eric and Rachel arrived too late.

They found Heiki in the flowered field, her cheeks burning with anguish. Animals surrounded her, searching vainly in the grass for Yemi. Eric could faintly detect Yemi's dwindling scent; then even that faint smell was snuffed out as the Griddas erased it.

Rachel placed a distress call to Larpskendya while she tended to Heiki's injuries. Too distraught to speak, Heiki sat gazing at the clouds, as if they themselves had betrayed her.

Other children arrived at last from the sky, stunned by the speed of the kidnap.

For a while all Yemi's special animal friends crawled, walked or flew around the fields, searching. A few dug at the soil, thinking Yemi might be under it. Then, at the same moment, each animal stopped. They sat quite still, faces all tilted up expectantly.

'Hey, what's going on?' Eric asked. 'What are they doing?'

Rachel's information spells scanned the local area. 'I can't tell. I don't detect anything.'

'It's Yemi's butterflies,' Heiki said. 'Normally this is the time they fly overhead here.'

The skies were empty.

Rachel and Eric scanned the rest of the world. Everywhere, the flocks of yellow Camberwell Beauties had vanished – and animals all over the world were beginning to pine for them.

'At least,' Eric said huskily, 'Yemi has his sister. They took Fola, too. I wonder why they did that? She's not got much magic.'

Rachel exchanged a glance with Heiki.

'To help control him,' Heiki said.

Rachel nodded. 'Until the Griddas learn how to do it themselves.'

9

the spectrums

News of Yemi's abduction changed the world.

Virtually overnight the game-playing of older children came to a stop as Heiki, filled with an almost insane energy, turned all their talents to more serious ends. Thereafter, day and night across the Earth, children honed their defensive spells. They toiled until they were so tired they nearly dropped out of the skies.

Animals everywhere were devastated by Yemi's loss. Many refused to accept the missing butterflies. They searched everywhere: on the land, in the deep seas. Birds of many species came together in swarms so dense that their bodies blackened the skies. Those animals who had been privileged enough to have had personal contact with Yemi lost all interest in the normal rhythms of life. They ignored their food and stopped caring for themselves.

But the most dramatic reaction came from the spectrums.

Shortly after Yemi was taken they travelled from all countries to the equator. Once there, they spread out at equal intervals, forming a line to encompass the world. The thrill-seekers came with them. No longer just transporters of the spectrums, the thrill-seekers started attending to all of their needs. They clothed and fed the spectrums. They bathed them. When their throats were dry, they quenched them.

The spectrums themselves offered no explanation for any of this. They merely watched, keeping up their precise geometrical sweep of the skies. Then, one evening, there was another development: all the spectrums began to radiate pulses of energy. Some pulses they sent out into space in measured intervals; others passed between them. They were talking – a din and cross-chatter of high-speed communication that disturbed the workings of almost every item of electromagnetic equipment on the globe.

Rachel and Eric followed all these developments, but they were more concerned about the wellbeing of Larpskendya and Serpantha. Weeks passed without any further news. Eric's skill of pinpointing magic at long range outstripped that of anyone else, so every day, for hours at a stretch, Rachel carried him into the upper atmosphere, hopeful of finding the magical scent of Wizards.

Across the Earth, new defences were installed by Heiki. They were far tighter than any before; that, at least, was a lesson the Griddas had taught them all. Everyone waited. And then, one afternoon while Rachel sat at home talking quietly with Mum and Dad, Eric's face sprang to life.

'It's Larpskendya!' he cried. Then Rachel saw his face crumple.

'What's the matter, Eric?'

'Something's wrong with his flying.'

As soon as the Wizard came into range of Rachel's own information spells, she knew. 'He's hurt.'

'How badly?' Dad asked.

'Terribly.'

'Larpskendya's not even shifting,' Eric said. 'He can barely fly at all.'

All four of them stood up, rushing to the windows. Normally it was impossible to catch Larpskendya's arrival, but on this occasion there was plenty of time to see him. He flew towards the house with such difficulty that Rachel, running into the garden, had to catch him as he landed. Larpskendya's knees folded under him. He picked himself up, stumbled, tried to smile, to reassure them. Rachel placed her shoulder under the Wizard's arm and, with Dad's and Eric's help, half-dragged his large frame through the door.

'Don't let go,' Larpskendya told Rachel hoarsely.

'I won't.'

For a moment Larpskendya's whole weight leaned against her. She held out her arm to steady him. As she did so, Rachel knew that Larpskendya needed it; in that instant only a single human arm held him upright. Sensing that, her world turned upside down. It took all her self-control not to scream and scream.

'Shush, now,' Larpskendya murmured. 'There's no need for that.'

'But you're frightening me.'

'Don't be frightened. Not you. I couldn't bear that.'

Rachel's information spells found injuries everywhere. No part of Larpskendya was undamaged. He should have been dead from Gridda attacks already; only the Wizard's magic, his extraordinary spells, kept his body together.

Larpskendya tried to disentangle himself from Rachel's embrace, but she would not let him. Together they dropped down on the floor. They lay there, saying nothing, while Larpskendya recovered. At last he told them all, 'Yemi has been taken to Ool.'

Rachel's chest tightened. 'What … what will they do to him?'

Larpskendya shook his head. 'He is probably safe for now. The Griddas went to great lengths to get him. I doubt they will harm Yemi, at least not immediately. I am more concerned for Serpantha.'

Eric hardly dared ask, 'Is he alive?'

'Yes, but if the Griddas have him, it would be better if that were not so.' Larpskendya trembled, not from his wounds. 'I should have gone myself to Ool,' he said. 'Serpantha would not allow it. He was always … protecting me … He –' Suddenly Larpskendya's entire body convulsed. 'Oh my brother,' he burst out. 'What have they done to you? What are they doing now?'

Rachel reached out to touch him, and when she did Larpskendya wept.

He wept uncontrollably. Rachel and Eric were so affected that they burst out with tears of their own, without clearly understanding why. It was because Larpskendya wept, that was reason enough. They made a pile that held onto Larpskendya in the middle of the carpet. The prapsies joined them, nuzzling the Wizard's face.

Larpskendya's body was wracked by tears. Then he roused himself and stood up to his full height. 'Well,' he said solemnly, 'now it has come to this, I think it is time to explain all. I have not lied, but I have not told you everything.' He looked at Rachel.

'Larpskendya, what is it?' she asked, still holding his robe.

'The creatures you know as High Witches,' Larpskendya said, 'are not as different from Wizards as you believe. In fact, there was once almost no difference between us at all.'

Rachel let go of his robe, confused. Then she fell back as she noticed his eyes. Larpskendya no longer camouflaged the truth: tattoos, the same tattoos that had stared so mercilessly from the sockets of Dragwena and Heebra and Calen, stared out of them. Seeing Rachel's reaction, Larpskendya moved forward to console her. He stopped when she screamed.

'I know,' he said. 'It is too much.' He wanted to approach Rachel, but knew she could not accept it. 'At one time we belonged to the same species,' he explained. 'The females you know as High Witches were like us, or as similar as your own men and women are to each other, or your children. I am sorry to have concealed this truth from you, of all people, Rachel. Try to forgive me. It was not what I wanted.'

Rachel felt too appalled to answer. She felt betrayed.

While she clutched Mum and retreated, Eric gathered up the frightened prapsies. He did not recoil from the Wizard as Rachel had done.

Larpskendya stared at him. 'Did you know, Eric?'

'Not really, but I sensed something. You've occasionally used similar-patterned spells to the Witches. I wondered why. I see now.'

'Tell us the rest,' Dad demanded.

'Our species,' Larpskendya said, 'was possibly the first in which magic evolved. We discovered that we could fly, as you have done. We explored our world. We explored ourselves in ways you are only beginning to consider. And we ventured to other worlds. We travelled.' Larpskendya paused. Again, he looked at Rachel, but she was not ready to meet his eyes. 'For many ages,' Larpskendya continued, 'Witches and Wizards worked together. But as our magic developed, disputes started to arise about how to use it. A sect of powerful females decided they no longer wanted to be restricted by the jurisdiction of our magical laws. They left, and for many generations nothing was heard from them. But finally they began to leave their mark on the civilizations of other worlds, and it was always destructive. They would not reconsider or stop. The endless war began at that time.'

Dad cleared his throat. 'Why...why do the High Witches look so different from you now?'

'Partly because they simply no longer wanted to look like us,' Larpskendya answered. 'And another reason: to suit their new aggressiveness.'

'Were you there at the start?' Eric asked. 'When the war began?'

'No. I am old, but I have only been alive for a fraction of the war. It is all I have known, Eric: war, or preparations for it, or fear of it; and fear for those drawn in, such as yourselves.'

Rachel spluttered, suddenly finding her voice, 'Why didn't...why didn't you tell us, tell *me*, about this before? I could have accepted it! Why didn't you trust me?'

'I wanted to,' Larpskendya said. 'I wanted to so much. But the fate of many other worlds, perhaps all worlds, depended on this one. I was frightened, Rachel, of a second failure.'

'A second?'

'We – the Wizards – came to your Earth ages ago, but we made a mistake. The Witch Dragwena had dominated your world for a long time before we arrived. She implanted a fear of us deep within children. I didn't dare stir up that ancient memory.' He sighed. 'Try to understand. I could not risk telling you the truth because I knew there would be times when I needed to have your absolute trust.'

'You had it!' Rachel said. 'Of course you did!'

'Did I?' As he moved towards her, Rachel shrank back. 'You can barely accept the truth now, Rachel, as well as you know me. If you had known the Wizards were so closely related to the Witches, would you have really believed in me that time at the North Pole? When I said Heebra could take your life and that of Eric, would you have continued to believe in me? When I needed you to look into my eyes then – these tattooed eyes – and completely trust me with all your heart, would you have done so?'

Rachel searched herself. 'No, yes, I … I don't know! I might not have done. But' – her body shook with emotion – 'it's too much, too much. Truths and lies … how do I know you're telling the truth now?' She glared at him. 'You sent Serpantha to Ool. Why? You sent a Wizard who knew all about Yemi and the defences about him. If you've been fighting a war for so long, how could you make such a stupid mistake?'

'I cannot tell you that. I may never be able to do so.'

'More secrets?' Rachel blasted. 'How many others are there?'

Larpskendya was silent. Eric could sense his immense weariness.

'I could *force* you to believe anything I want,' Larpskendya said at last. 'I have a spell for that. I will not use it, but I am tempted to do so because more depends on me now than I can convey.' He passed his fingers over his face and robe. 'This is what I am like,' he said. 'I have come back to Earth, leaving those I care deeply about, to discuss what can be done to rescue Yemi. If –'

'Wait,' Eric said. 'Something's heading this way. Griddas.'

'I'm aware of them,' Larpskendya said calmly. 'A few only, near your moon, probably the remnants of those who ambushed me on my way here.'

'No, not those ones. There are several more packs, much further out – between Saturn and Jupiter.'

Larpskendya glanced up, startled. 'Even my spells can't detect that far. Are you sure, Eric?'

'Yes. Absolutely.'

'Then I must leave at once.'

Rachel half-lurched towards him. 'Larpskendya, what are you saying? You can't do that! I've measured your strength. You can still shift, but in your weakened state if you meet any Griddas …'

'If I stay I will endanger you all,' Larpskendya said. He touched her arm. 'I won't do that.'

Through his fingertips, Rachel felt something reaching out to her. It was Larpskendya's spells, half-insane with weariness, trying to hold the Wizard together. They needed more rest; it was too soon; they had not recovered enough. As Rachel tried to comfort them, they begged her to stay with Larpskendya and help strengthen him.

Rachel forgot all her uncertainty and rushed the short space into Larpskendya's arms. 'You can't leave,' she said, trying to think. 'You *mustn't* leave. I'll contact Heiki and the kids she's training. We'll protect you here. We'll all protect you.'

'No,' he replied firmly. 'You are not yet ready to confront the Griddas. If I die I may yet serve a purpose in giving you more time to prepare for them.' Rachel pleaded for him to reconsider, but Larpskendya would not be moved. Then, as he was about to depart, a sound filtered through the windows.

It was a rising note, a sound of urgency and terror.

'What – what's happening?' Mum put her hands over her ears.

Rachel's information spells radiated out of the house. All around, she sensed children everywhere listening.

'It's the spectrums,' Eric murmured. 'They're speaking.'

Across the world the spectrums had risen skyward. Carried by their thrill-seekers they scattered, taking up positions where every child would be able to hear their message. The message was not composed of syllables or words, but it was a message nevertheless – a clear and articulate call. The voices of the spectrums swelled, rising to an almost unbearable pitch. Each one sang until he or she had no breath left, but there was always one left to sustain the note, so at no point was there an end to it.

No child had ever heard such a message before – but their magic instantly understood. In the living room only Dad and Mum did not understand. They gazed helplessly at Eric.

'Our world is in jeopardy,' Eric told them. 'It's a warning, the first of the spectrums: *There is danger. Stay alert and defend your homes.* That's all it says.' He and Rachel listened as the note altered slightly.

Rachel looked wildly at Larpskendya. 'It's you,' she said. '*You* are in danger!'

Larpskendya nodded. 'Do you understand what the spectrums are now?'

Rachel had no doubt; nor, suddenly, with that first utterance, did any other child on Earth. 'They're protectors of some kind, aren't they?'

'A special type,' replied Larpskendya. 'I have seen their kind develop only once before. They are *species protectors*. With the emergence of magic in children, they've evolved to serve you all. You will find that their own safety or comfort are irrelevant to them. Their purpose is to listen, to warn, to raise a call to arms, to advise brilliantly, to fight if they must; to do anything in their power to safeguard the children of Earth.' Larpskendya paused. 'It seems the danger to me has brought them out. They believe your world will be in peril if I am killed. We shall see. Whatever happens, I am grateful to have witnessed the coming of age of the spectrums. That gives me more hope than I had for you. Well, there is no more time ...'

Gathering himself, Larpskendya hurriedly said his goodbyes to them all.

Rachel could not bear it. Events were happening too fast.

Larpskendya held her hands.

'Find Yemi,' he told her. 'Find him.'

'How can I?' Rachel asked. 'Without you ...'

'Don't you know how strong you are?' Larpskendya almost shouted at her. 'I have never seen a child face a Witch with more courage than you!' He held her tightly and she shook in his embrace. 'You must understand, I may not be able to return,' he said. 'I have cheated the Griddas on enough occasions, but this time...Listen: Yemi's magic is beyond anything the Wizards have ever known. He's so young...the Griddas might be able to influence him. You *must* get to Yemi somehow. Find a way.' Releasing Rachel, Larpskendya turned to Eric. 'Eric, more may now depend on your decisions than in the past. Everything may do so. Everything. Trust your instinct. You have powers beyond comprehension within you.'

Kissing them all, fighting a vast weariness, Larpskendya took a last look round. The prapsies stared up at him. Rachel tried to find some words to express how she felt, but her mind was in pieces. Larpskendya smiled at her. 'Who will comfort my spells now?' he whispered.

Closing his eyes, the Wizard called on his exhausted magic for one last great effort – and shifted.

10

the gratitude of spiders

Soon after Yemi's arrival on Ool, Gultrathaca ordered Jarius to visit her.

Jarius did not want to go. She had already disgraced herself again by refusing to jump out of Heebra's eye-window. Gultrathaca had been forced to push her. How humiliating! Even the fearful newborns had been amused by that!

This time Gultrathaca had invited her to an even worse location: the Assessment Chamber. It was an appalling place. The spell-quality of all Griddas was ruthlessly tested within the Chamber from time to time. Jarius had only just survived her last trial inside.

How could a human baby, she wondered, survive there?

As she travelled towards it, Jarius noticed an unusual number of tunnel creatures heading the same way. There were rodents, skittering insects, even shy burrowers normally far too timid to come near a Gridda tunnel. All the creatures seemed heedless of her – as if there was something below they could not bear to miss.

The traps caught them, of course. They snapped into life, passing the scampering creatures into the food processors. Little mouths waited for them: infants. Jarius heard a wail of anticipation through the walls of her tunnel.

Vast numbers of new Griddas were being raised now. If Jarius listened closely she could hear the distant sound of a newborn biting through her egg, followed by her first scream of hunger. Like all Griddas she arrived starving, desperate to inflate her muscles to a size that would impress her pack.

Jarius resumed the journey. At the Assessment Chamber entrance she quieted all her spiders. The soldiers were especially tense. They perched in the corners of her mouths, readying themselves. Scratching at the seals of the doorway, her watchers tried to peep inside without opening it.

'Welcome,' came Gultrathaca's voice from within.

Jarius warily opened the door a crack.

Instead of the usual dimness, the Chamber was flooded in brilliant sunshine – an intensity of light Jarius had not experienced before. 'No!' she wailed, withdrawing.

Gultrathaca caught her arm, pulling her inside the Chamber. 'Bear it! Bear it!' she raged.

Jarius tried to construct a darkening spell, but she had never needed one before, and she was too frightened to think. If her eye-shields had not automatically clamped shut she would have been blinded. But her loyal watcher spiders had no shields to cover their eyes. The light scorched them. Despite this, believing that Jarius was under attack, they kept scanning the Chamber, shouting out what they saw.

The bright light faded to gloom.

Jarius partially re-opened her eye-shields. 'What ... what happened?'

'Yemi responded to your fear,' Gultrathaca told her, 'and to that of your spiders.'

Jarius looked anxiously up at the child. Her pack had told her of the smallness of human children, but she was still unprepared for the size of Yemi. He appeared so frail, so vulnerable, no larger than a newborn Gridda – like a thing she might accidentally fracture.

Yemi held out his arms to her, his face full of complex worry.

Jarius backed away. 'What is he doing?'

'Apologizing. For wounding you.'

'Apologizing?' Jarius blinked in astonishment. 'Doesn't the boy realize what this place is? What harm we can do to him here?'

'No. Let him approach you.'

Yemi toddled over to Jarius. His shorts and shirt brushed against her skin. Not naked, Jarius realized. This was clothing – like the dresses of the Highs. He smiled at her, showing his teeth. Curious, Jarius ran a claw over the edges, searching for sharpness. Yemi laughed, seeing the puzzled expression on her face. Then he made his way up her torso, babbling amiably. Mountaineer-style he scrambled over one jaw, planted his toe on another and reached around to get a purchase on her bony cheeks. Swaying slightly, he pursed his lips and kissed each of her eyes.

A delicious balm settled over them.

'Oh!' Jarius glanced at him. She could not read Yemi's

expression – the architecture of his face was too different – but there was no mistaking his good intentions. His magical greeting showed that he hoped to become her friend. It was shocking: a genuine offer.

When Jarius did not respond Yemi patted her arm reassuringly, as if used to such confusion in the Griddas he met. Shimmying back down her body, he wandered to the rear of the Chamber. Jarius noticed another of his species there, reaching out a hand.

'Fola,' Yemi announced proudly.

Jarius saw an older, larger human: presumably the female. It had more hair, and a long red garment covering all the flesh down from the neck.

Fola gazed in dismay at Jarius. 'Another one!' she groaned. 'Always another one is coming! You want to be hurt like the others? Is that what you want?' She pointed at Gultrathaca. 'While she watches!'

Jarius could not understand Fola's words, but she sensed the anger. It helped her relax. This was behaviour Jarius could better understand. 'The human girl is wary at least,' she said with satisfaction to Gultrathaca. 'She fears us, I see. What does the boy fear?'

Gultrathaca smiled. 'The dark.'

This concept was too perverse for Jarius to understand.

'Humans crave light,' Gultrathaca explained. 'They need it.'

'Then – then why did he remove it when I entered?'

'Yemi wants you to be happy, Jarius,' Gultrathaca said, without amusement. 'He wants you to be his friend. He wants to play with you.'

'But – he's our prisoner! Doesn't he understand that?'

Gultrathaca laughed grimly. 'No, he doesn't. He

doesn't understand at all.' She walked over to Jarius and examined her eyes. 'What little damage was done, Yemi has repaired with his kiss. You are luckier than the first Griddas. When they entered the Chamber, Yemi thought there was something wrong with their eyes. He created a spell to redesign them. It took the shrieks of several Griddas to make him realize his error.'

'But he looks so...so harmless.'

'Yes, doesn't he,' Gultrathaca agreed. 'Perhaps that is the reason Heebra underestimated him. I will not make the same mistake.'

Jarius studied Fola, fascinated by the way she held Yemi, the way she ran her clawless fingers through his hair. Yemi giggled, half-fighting Fola off. 'I don't understand their gestures,' Jarius said, 'but clearly the female possesses little magic. Does Yemi keep her as live food?'

'No. They share a kind of pack-relationship. He protects her.'

'But she is so weak!'

'Nevertheless, he cares for her. And she cares for him. That is the meaning of the clutching motions.'

Staring at Fola, Jarius felt disgust. It dismayed her to see attention lavished on a puny creature of any species. Enfeebled Griddas were strangled at birth. It was simply the way, and she had never questioned it. How else could the pack be kept strong?

'Don't underestimate the girl,' Gultrathaca told her. 'I started off by thinking she would be easy to manipulate, but she has never co-operated, and made it far more difficult for me to obtain Yemi's trust.'

'If Fola hinders us, why not kill her and work directly on the boy?'

'We tried that. Yemi's reaction was intriguing. When we attacked Fola, for the first time he became angry.'

'Did he retaliate?'

'Yes. And that was even more intriguing. He punished not only the Gridda who attacked Fola. He punished her pack-members as well. Over the three cities they were scattered, thousands of miles apart, yet somehow his spell found them all. They felt only a fraction of the agony intended for Fola, but I believe it was a real warning that he will not tolerate any harm against his sister.'

'Then – what progress has been made?'

'None,' Gultrathaca muttered, frustration edging her voice. 'By now I had hoped to have Yemi's trust, or at least get him to perform spells that might be useful to us. But he does not react in any of the usual ways. When I threaten him he treats it as an amusement. He does what he likes.'

'What he *likes*? Something must affect him!'

'If so, I've yet to find it.'

Yemi was staring at Jarius's feet. He chuckled, crooked his fingers, beckoning.

The next moment Jarius's spiders began to desert her.

She shrieked in terror because this only happened to dying Griddas. Until death arrived a Gridda's spiders, who had cherished her through all dramas, would stay with her. Only when the healer spiders confirmed that her last breath had expired did they leave. If their owner had been killed by another Gridda, the spiders would offer themselves to the newcomer, hoping she might take a few. But if their owner died by accident, or was killed by a tunnel predator, the spiders were held equally responsible for that failure. Those spiders were never taken by other Griddas.

Left alone in the tunnels to fend for themselves, they could not survive long. There were plenty of creatures adapted specifically to hunt them down.

As her spiders ran from her to Yemi, Jarius could not speak. She explored her limbs for unknown injuries, frantically questioned her healers. Was she dying?

'No!' she pleaded, staring wildly at Gultrathaca. 'Look at me! I am healthy! Young!'

Her spiders continued to leave. Only the oldest soldiers, those whose loyalty was absolute and who would stay guarding her body even after her death, held back. The rest crept from her mouths and face-pits, hurrying across the floor to be with Yemi.

He giggled, welcoming them.

'You are not dying,' Gultrathaca told Jarius. 'My spiders also sneak off to him.'

'But – why?'

'I'm not certain,' Gultrathaca said. 'They're attracted by the boy's magic, but it's more than that.' She glanced at Jarius. 'I doubt you noticed, but several of your watchers were blinded when you entered the Chamber. Yemi is repairing them.'

'Repairing? You mean he actually cares for them?' The idea of looking after her spiders had never occurred to Jarius. Spiders were constantly being born inside her body to replace those old or ill.

Yemi attended diligently to all the injured watchers, cooling and reconstructing their eyes. The other spiders clustered on his knees. When the watchers were fixed, Yemi sent all the spiders back to Jarius. They did not want to leave him, but he insisted, sweeping them along the floor with the flat of his hand.

'They like him,' said Gultrathaca. 'And they are not the only ones.' She indicated dozens of other creatures that had started to emerge as soon as the spiders left. From the shadows they wriggled, swarmed and oozed around Yemi's feet. Jarius recognized animals and insects from all parts of Ool. There were even a few brainless slime mosses that lived in the deep silence below the Gridda caves. How could they be here? She watched as the mosses found a snug place along the pocket-linings of Yemi's shorts.

And then, in their silent way, came a pair of huraks.

Involuntarily Jarius shrank back, preparing to defend herself.

Of all the native animals that dwelled in the tunnels under the world of Ool, only this one was truly feared by the Griddas. The hurak was a huge animal, the same size as Jarius herself, feline-shaped, but with a heavy jaw capable of severing even Gridda skull-bone. What made a hurak really dangerous, however, was that its breath contained an anaesthetic to lull the watcher spiders. It could approach a Gridda completely undetected.

The two huraks settled in front of Yemi and Fola. They allowed Yemi to stroke their dark blue fur.

With a trace of awe in her tone, Gultrathaca said, 'Yemi draws them somehow, keeps them docile. If any Gridda approaches him too quickly they also guard him. These two arrived this morning.'

'From where?'

'I don't know.'

Jarius stared at Yemi. He smiled back. 'Does he ever try to get out of the Chamber?' she asked.

'All the time. He obviously wants to leave, and it is becoming harder to stop him. He keeps breaking through the holding spells. Over a dozen Griddas encircle the Chamber at all times, devising new ones just to keep him imprisoned.'

'There has to be a way to threaten him, Gultrathaca!'

'No. He is happy.'

'Happy? Happy *here*, in the Chamber? What tests have you tried?'

'Every kind. He enjoys them, like a game. I have yet to find a test he cannot pass with ease. In fact, he's becoming bored. I can't devise them fast enough for him.'

'I find that hard to believe.'

'Do you?' Gultrathaca stepped away from Jarius, and said lightly, 'The Chamber is yours to use against the boy as you wish. Perhaps you will have more success than those who tried previously.'

Fola saw what was about to happen. She had seen it many times before with the other Griddas Gultrathaca invited. '*Iro!* No!' she warned Jarius. 'Don't attack Yemi, you must not!' But, of course, it was pointless. All the Griddas who came here were too afraid of Gultrathaca to disobey her. 'Yemi will hurt you!' she shouted at Jarius. 'He no mean to, but he will! Don't make him!'

Jarius listened to the sounds of the ranting girl – and glanced warily at Gultrathaca. She had moved away, entirely across the Chamber. Not for the first time Jarius wondered why she had been called here. There were higher-ranking members of her pack who had not yet seen Yemi. Why had Gultrathaca requested her?

Because she was expendable?

Yes, Jarius thought, unable to think of another reason. This was obviously a final chance to prove her pack-worthiness. There would be no opportunity to refuse this time. Gliding shakily across the Chamber, she located the area where the main attack spells were hidden. The spells could be triggered singly or in clusters. The main advantage of the Chamber was that far more could be launched simultaneously than a single Gridda could summon on her own. When Yemi saw which way Jarius was heading he started jumping up and down.

'*Sere! Sere! Sere!*' he called out excitedly.

'I believe it is his word for play,' said Gultrathaca.

Yemi clapped his hands over and over. He could not wait to start.

Jarius twisted away, trying to hide her nervousness. How could she possibly intimidate the boy if Gultrathaca had failed? There was one chance, perhaps – a speciality spell she had made her own: a panic spell. It was intended to disable an opponent, unseat its mind, before the real attack. In one so young as Yemi it might be effective… She composed herself and faced him. Yemi backed away dramatically. He put his hands over his eyes.

He *is* frightened, Jarius thought in triumph. Then she saw him peeping between his fingers. Pretending to be frightened, she realized – to make the game more entertaining.

She glanced once more at Gultrathaca – and knew that she would kill her if there was any hesitation.

Opening her jaws, Jarius unleashed the panic.

In the fraction of a second it took the spell to reach him, Yemi reacted. He plucked the spell out of the air. He examined it. Gultrathaca bent forward avidly to watch. Eventually Yemi blew on the spell, offering it back to Jarius.

'Better!' he told her.

Jarius reached out a claw.

'No!' yelled Fola. 'Don't take it!'

Too late. As soon as Jarius's old spell made contact with her skin it gripped her heart. It was not the same panic spell she knew so well. Yemi had improved it. An immeasurable terror blazed across her mind. She collapsed on the floor. She curled up, stuffing her claws into her mouths to stifle the screams.

Seeing this, Yemi ran across to her, understanding his mistake. He removed the spell and hastily ordered all Jarius's spiders to console her.

Gultrathaca sighed. She stepped over Jarius, ignoring her agony.

Another failure, she thought. Another lost Gridda – and a member of her own pack this time. Well, there were many brighter stars than Jarius … She stared at Fola, who stared back with unsuppressed fury. 'Why did you do that? Why?' Fola shouted.

Gultrathaca disregarded her. She walked to another part of the Chamber where Jarius's unseemly writhing would not be a distraction. What else could she do to affect the boy? Hadn't she tried everything to influence him? Every spell, threat, enticement or attempt at persuasion led to nothing! These human children as a whole, Gultrathaca thought. What are they really like? A few High Witches knew their language and customs well, those who had returned from Earth as part of Heebra's failed army. When questioned, they had called Yemi an aberration: a remarkable child, tantalizing but untypical. Fola was more typical; less magical than many children, but capable of being frightened.

I've persisted too long with my challenges on the boy, Gultrathaca realized. I need a new approach. The longer Yemi withstands the Assessment Chamber the more wary the Griddas become. If a baby human can do this, what of the older children? Every day he makes me appear weaker...

While Gultrathaca made her way to the prison levels to question the remaining High Witches, Jarius lay shuddering on the Chamber floor. When she did not respond to his kind words, Yemi wanted to help her more, but he hesitated. He was frightened to put his lips near her jaws, though it was the only way he knew. He knelt beside her. He bent across her face. Placing his lips gently against her mouths, he sent soothing spells inside.

Jarius's panic ceased instantly. It was replaced by a new feeling, one she had never experienced. An indescribable peacefulness worked its way through, gathering into her heart. Jarius forgot where she was. There was no panic. There was only the breath of Yemi.

She allowed him to put his arms half-round her massive head, and rock it.

11

INVITATION

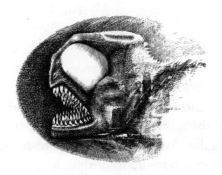

Rachel sat in the garden, staring at the empty skies. It had been three weeks since they last saw Larpskendya.

'I don't like it,' she said to Eric. 'No kids about. This exclusion zone of Heiki's feels wrong.'

'I think it's great,' Eric said. 'Peace and quiet for a flipping change. Plus Heiki's right to protect you.' He eyed her meaningfully. 'Before Yemi, the last time a Witch came to Earth was to get you, Rach.'

Heiki's surveillance teams were positioned around the house and nearby streets. They were efficient, the best available. Only the most determined fans still tried to sneak through the cordon; they never got close.

Rachel squinted up, where Albertus Robertson, as usual, hovered near the chimney. He had appeared the moment Larpskendya left. A fixture over the roof of the house ever since, he rarely moved. Rachel welcomed his presence. She trusted him without truly understanding why. It was a feeling about the spectrums all children now shared.

'Brilliant, isn't he,' Eric said. 'I could watch Albertus all day.'

'You usually *do*,' Rachel said, grinning. 'I've been out here all morning, and I swear Albertus hasn't moved. Not an eyelash.'

'Why should he?' Eric replied. 'He will, if something interests him. Those ears of his are amazing, you know. They don't just hear things; they can also pick up x-rays, gamma rays, radio emissions, all the wavelengths.'

'Mmm, but why doesn't he tell us what he's *thinking*? It's unnerving, the way the spectrums are so quiet all the time. We've heard nothing since their first message.'

'When we need their advice, they'll tell us soon enough,' Eric said.

Clinging to Albertus were his two female thrill-seekers. They took turns to hold him aloft. On windy days they held his hair to keep it out of his eyes. Occasionally they bathed his ears, keeping the surfaces free from dust or other particles.

'I wonder,' Rachel mused, 'why a spectrum's companion is always a thrill-seeker?'

'Don't you know?' Eric said. 'I thought you understood. It's because of the danger. Only the thrill-seekers are crazy enough to take the spectrums to the places they expect to go, Rach.' He gazed earnestly at her. 'Threats and more threats. The spectrums expect them; they're thinking about them all the time. That's why they're so hopeless about ordinary stuff like eating. They can't spare a second for humdrum things like that.'

Rachel realized that this was not just a guess. Eric knew. 'Are you … are you in communication with them?'

'Yes.' Eric's voice trembled. 'Only glimpses. But I'll tell you something. The spectrums care deeply about us. They're all that way, afraid all the time. They can't bear the thought of harm coming to any of us. But Albertus – well, he cares especially about you, Rach.'

'Me?'

'Yes. You personally.'

Rachel glanced up, astonished. 'Really? Why?'

'I don't know, Rach. I've no idea, but I can feel his concern.'

As Rachel gazed up at Albertus, a group of children passed over his head. It was a routine fly-over by a team of sentinels. The sentinel units were Heiki's special new guardians, the most magical children. Within a few weeks she had succeeded in turning them into a force of considerable resolve. They trained chiefly at night, knowing that the tunnel-dwelling Griddas were more likely to attack then.

Rachel stared at them, filled with doubts. 'The sentinels,' she said. 'I don't care how disciplined or brave they are. Do you think children, any children, stand a chance against Griddas? We've seen what they did to Larpskendya – *Larpskendya*, Eric, a Wizard. I don't –'

'Shush a minute.'

Above them Albertus Robertson had moved. His thrillseekers spun him in tight circles, a frenzied motion. Eric pressed his hands to his head as communications between spectrums worldwide reached an instantly feverish level. The nearest sentinel unit changed course. It descended to surround Rachel and Eric. From another part of the world Heiki arrived, shifting crazily. She hurtled towards them, her face terrified.

Eric looked at Rachel. 'It's the Griddas.'

'I know,' she said. 'They're here.'

Heiki flew straight to Rachel. 'This is it,' she murmured. 'Oh, Rachel, this is it.'

Rachel steadied her. 'Come on, now. The sentinels need you. Remember all that training? You'll be fine. I'm with you. I'm here.'

Heiki nodded, regaining her poise sufficiently to instruct the sentinel unit. The sentinels adopted tactical positions best suited to a surprise raid. Albertus Robertson stayed aloft. His head shook as he was bombarded by dozens of frantic messages from spectrums around the world.

Eric sighed – a gloriously relieved sigh. 'Three! Only three Griddas!'

'Are you sure?' Rachel asked. 'There aren't more further out?'

'I'm sure.'

'I can't believe it's an attack, then. Not if there's so few.'

Eric called the prapsies over, tucking them into the usual place inside his shirt. Heiki deployed the sentinels around Rachel and Eric, then soared off to gather more forces.

'The Griddas are travelling slowly,' Eric said. 'Hey, Rach, *really* slow. Giving us plenty of chance to notice them.'

'Maybe they want us to know they're coming,' Rachel said. She hurried back inside the house to tell Mum and Dad what was happening, imploring them to stay indoors.

When she returned, Eric said, 'The Griddas are coming in this direction.'

'I know. Toward *us*. Let's get away from the house, at least.'

Taking Eric's arm she flew to an area of barren fields several miles south. Four more sentinel units, led by Heiki, joined them on the way. A handful of spectrums also arrived, their thrill-seekers flying at breathtaking speed to make it in time.

'I wonder if the Griddas have come to talk,' Eric said. 'They aren't exactly sneaking up on us.'

'Don't assume that,' said a voice they had never heard before.

It belonged to Albertus Robertson.

He had appeared at Rachel's shoulder, held by both his thrill-seekers. Everyone gazed at him in shock. Rachel had often imagined that if Albertus ever spoke his voice would be flat or mechanical, like his movements. Not so. Albertus spoke as if all his life he had been devoted to her.

'What – what do you mean?' she asked him.

'I –' Albertus's throat dried up from such long disuse, the words becoming a whisper. Furiously his thrill-seekers massaged his windpipe until the sounds were more coherent. When Albertus started speaking again it was in a great stream of words, at breakneck speed. 'If I was a Gridda,' he said, 'and I wanted to invade Earth with minimum loss of life to my own kind, I would start by eliminating the most dangerous children. In priority sequence, given the absence of Yemi, these children are Rachel and Eric, followed by Heiki, followed by all the spectrums, followed by the deepers, the sentinels, the –'

One of the thrill-seekers put her fingers over Albertus's mouth, forcing him to take a breath. She said to Rachel, 'Is he speaking too quickly for you? Tell me.'

'No, it's ... it's all right.'

'To kill you,' Albertus continued, 'that is, to kill you, Rachel, and you, Eric, the Griddas have to get close enough. How? How do you put humans at ease? By approaching like these Griddas, not as a large threatening force, but a small group; not hiding, but coming openly; not rapid, but slowly. To seem to be a delegation. To arrive peaceably. To draw you both out.' He took another fast breath.

Rachel said, 'What do you suggest we do?'

'I am seeking strategies.' For a few seconds Albertus's head twitched as he took advice from all the other spectrums. 'Too many unknown factors,' he said. 'The majority view is that the three Griddas are either a murder party or an advance group to test our readiness.'

'Our readiness for what?' Eric asked.

'To defend. To attack. To fight.'

'So we should bring as many kids as possible,' Eric said. 'Show them we're not scared.'

'Not necessarily,' Albertus answered. 'Why big numbers of children against only three Griddas? Will they be impressed? Why bring so many if we are confident?'

'We can't just ignore them!' Heiki argued.

'Actually, we *could* just ignore them,' Albertus said. 'However, the Griddas might regard that as demonstrating weakness. Or they may be insulted. Either reaction might precipitate conflict. We could destroy the Griddas, but being too aggressive might also precipitate conflict. I suggest this,' Albertus went on immediately. 'Eric and Rachel do not meet with the Griddas. I will go, flanked by a minimum of sentinels. That way we will *invite* combat. This will give us more time to determine the Griddas' true intentions. It will also enable us to protect both Eric and Rachel. And it will endanger as few children as possible – in case this is a trap.'

'Do you think everything's a trap?' Eric asked.

'Yes.' Albertus Robertson's expression did not alter. 'Or that it may be.'

Rachel looked around at all the children. 'No,' she said. 'I won't put anyone else in danger to protect me.'

'You must do what is best for us all!' Albertus shouted at her, with sudden ferocity. Then he laid a hand against Rachel's cheek. 'The sentinel children are more steadfast than they realize,' he said. 'Let us do this.'

'Too late,' Heiki said. 'The Griddas have speeded up. We'll meet them in the sky. Sentinels! Stay close to Rachel and Eric.'

There was no time for further debate. Albertus remained by Rachel's shoulder, giving her last-minute advice. 'Say nothing about Serpantha,' he warned. 'The Griddas may know nothing about him.'

'Here they come,' Eric said.

The three Griddas dipped unhurriedly in and out of the cumulus clouds. When their orange heads and brown-furred bodies could be clearly seen, most children reacted with disbelief.

'Flipping heck!' Eric clutched the prapsies.

'Do not react to their appearance,' Albertus Robertson said.

Only the other spectrums were able to follow his advice. The rest of the children quailed at the bulk of the Griddas, their excessive muscularity, the bone-encrusted heads. Like a devil or dragon, Rachel thought. A demon, she decided. There was a vague similarity with the High Witches, but while even Dragwena had possessed some scrap of female-ness, these creatures did not even have a truly identifiable face. They seemed deformed, every part of their skull an angle, tooth or slash of bone. Only the eyes were recognizable, and how could such eyes be real? They covered too much of the head for humans to accept.

Rachel squeezed Eric's hand as the Griddas stopped nearby.

For a few moments the children of Earth and the Griddas assessed one another. Then one of the Griddas, the largest, addressed Rachel. 'As leader of all the Gridda packs of Ool, I have the honour. I am Gultrathaca. I greet you.'

Gultrathaca's voice astonished the children. Not the harshness everyone expected from that face, but the opposite: a female voice, perfectly modulated, human. All around her Rachel sensed children relaxing slightly.

'It's a lie,' Albertus Robertson said quietly to Rachel. 'No creature of this shape would naturally speak like a woman. There's only one reason for such an imitation: to put us at ease. Stay alert. Allow no physical contact.'

Gultrathaca held out a claw for Rachel to take. 'Shall we?'

A handshake? It was such a disarming gesture, such a human thing to do, that Rachel almost put her hand into Gultrathaca's giant claw. These Griddas already know who I am, she thought. They know all about us, can talk like us. Even the greeting had been appropriate: civil, complimentary. What do we know about the Griddas? Rachel asked herself. What had even Larpskendya known? Virtually nothing.

The children furthest away from the Griddas were

becoming visibly less tense. That mustn't happen, Rachel realized. Take control.

'Why did you kidnap Yemi?' she demanded.

'To protect ourselves. What other reason could there be?' Gultrathaca's tone was reserved, quiet. 'We have no doubt that Larpskendya intends to train the boy as a killer. We couldn't allow that.'

'Do you really expect us to believe you?' Rachel said.

'No, I do not. Larpskendya has already influenced you against us. Apparently you believe everything the Wizard says, though he is mistaken about us.'

Rachel hesitated. Gultrathaca was not what she had expected.

'Where is Larpskendya?' Eric asked. 'Is he ...'

'Alive. Is that what you are asking? Yes. He escaped.'

Rachel and the other children did not try to hide their relief.

Gultrathaca said, 'Yes, you love Larpskendya, don't you. He comes making promises that appeal. You believe them because you are actually a relatively simple species that judges largely on appearances. He tells you we Griddas are without conscience, but that is not true. We have honour. We look brutal to you, so you think we must be.'

Rachel was unsure what to say next. She felt Albertus's hand on her shoulder, strengthening her.

'It is we who have taken a risk in coming here,' Gultrathaca continued. 'Do you think it is easy for us to fly to this world, knowing how many of Larpskendya's Wizards protect it?'

'Don't tell her anything about the Wizards, especially numbers,' Albertus murmured in Rachel's ear. 'Neither agree nor disagree.'

'Larpskendya doesn't frighten anyone,' Eric said.

'Doesn't he?' Gultrathaca faced him. 'If you saw a Wizard fight you would think differently! There is nothing to match that ferocity! What do you really know about the Wizards?'

'We know we can trust them!'

'Yes, trust; you place a lot of trust in Larpskendya. But where is he now, when you need him?'

'You chased him off!' Eric said angrily.

'And we had good reason. But let me ask this: why didn't Larpskendya return with other Wizards? There has been time for him to do so. If he truly cared for you, wouldn't he or other Wizards be here now? On Orin Fen there are millions of Wizards, yet none are here. Not one Wizard spared to guard you while Larpskendya goes about his mysterious business. Doesn't that strike you as wrong?'

Rachel glanced at Eric, saw his brow creased thoughtfully.

Gultrathaca wriggled her face. All her spiders, which until now had been hiding inside the pits, crept out. Many children swore, backing away. With difficulty, Rachel held her ground.

'This is what we look like,' Gultrathaca said. 'We were bred to be defenders. That is why we have these appalling features. But now that we have defeated the High Witches, there is no more reason to fight. The war between the Wizards and the Highs was *their* endless war, not ours. The Griddas are ready for peace.' Gultrathaca's enormous eyes stared unblinkingly at Rachel. 'We even want peace with the Wizards, if they will allow it. We are not interested in conquest. We will stay on Ool.' She paused, studying them all. 'I see none of you believe me. You do not believe me because your understanding of the Griddas comes from Larpskendya. Let me tell you: he knows nothing about us. His judgement has been poisoned by centuries of war against the Highs. But I am here, and he is not. I am ready to extend friendship to your world, Rachel. Are you prepared to do the same?'

Rachel glanced at Albertus Robertson.

'Conclude the discussion as soon as possible,' he told her.

'All this peace talk,' Heiki said, 'but you kidnapped Yemi!'

'Yemi is safe,' Gultrathaca replied. 'We haven't harmed him, or his sister. I invite you to come and see for yourself. I invite you to Ool.' She gazed at Rachel. 'Will you come back with us? You will be honoured there, I promise.'

'What proof do we have that you are telling the truth?' Rachel said. 'Why should I believe you?'

'Why shouldn't you?' Gultrathaca replied. 'You trusted the word of Larpskendya, without any proof. What more do you expect from me? I will leave the other Griddas here as your hostages, and send more if you wish. If you travel back with me I will also be revealing the location of Ool itself. Once you know that you could send an army there. I will take that great risk, if you will take a smaller one. I doubt Larpskendya ever offered you that, did he? I'm sure he never offered to take you to Orin Fen.' Gultrathaca studied the children's expressions closely.

'Why not bring Yemi and Fola back to Earth?' Albertus Robertson said. 'If you are sincere in wanting accord, return them.'

'I cannot,' Gultrathaca said. 'I daren't take the risk that the Wizards will snatch Yemi back. And, as you must know, Yemi will not be parted from Fola.'

'If we agree, who goes to Ool?' Eric asked.

'Everyone is invited. Anyone who can shift, that is. The journey is too far otherwise.'

Was that a lie? Rachel wondered. She almost said, 'Only Heiki and I can shift,' but an alarmed look from Albertus Robertson stopped her in time. It was just the sort of accidental slippage that might prove so costly. Staring at Gultrathaca, Rachel had the feeling she never made such elementary mistakes. 'What happens if none of us go back with you?'

'Most Gridda pack-leaders are already convinced you are enslaved by the Wizards,' Gultrathaca answered. 'If no one returns with me, how will I convince them that is not the case? Especially if you, Rachel, do not return. You helped rid us of Heebra. There are Griddas who hold you in awe. I, personally, feel a debt of gratitude towards you.'

Before Rachel could reply, Albertus Robertson said, 'Thank you. We will consider what you have told us.'

'That is all I ask,' Gultrathaca said. Lowering her head, she made an almost perfect bow. For a creature with so many bunched muscles around her chest, it was not easy. She had clearly practised.

12

trust

Leaving most of the sentinels guarding the Griddas, Heiki flew to Rachel's home with Eric and Albertus Robertson to decide what to do.

Dad drew them inside and Mum shut the door, while Rachel explained what had happened. 'Well,' she said at last, taking a deep breath. 'These Griddas – what does everyone think?'

Heiki shook her head. 'Grotesque, aren't they? I liked one thing, though – the way the Griddas can't stand the High Witches. And Gultrathaca – she's interesting. But can we trust her? I don't think so. Forget the words Gultrathaca used. That's no way to tell if she's lying. I was more interested in something else. Rachel, you must have noticed: Gultrathaca talked about peace, but all I felt were her death spells rising and rising.'

'Yes,' Rachel said thoughtfully. 'I did notice. But how many of us were up there threatening her? I'm not sure we should judge the Griddas in the same way as High Witches. They're only distantly related to the Highs.'

'Are you crazy?' Heiki said. 'Witches are Witches. They don't change!'

'Don't they?' Rachel looked at her. '*You* did.'

Heiki cast her eyes down. 'Even so …'

Rachel crossed the room. 'Look, I know they're frightening, and I don't want to believe them either, but has anyone given the Griddas a chance? Has even Larpskendya? Gultrathaca had a couple of interesting things to say about the Wizards, too …'

Eric said, 'Hey, I'd sooner wait here to get Larpskendya's answers than run off to Ool.'

'I agree,' Mum said, with finality. 'It would be madness to trust the Griddas. None of you can even think about going.'

'What do the spectrums think?' Rachel asked Albertus Robertson.

For a while Albertus did not speak. The silence in the room was broken only by the noise of his two thrill-seekers breaking up biscuits that had been left on the dining table earlier that day. After making sure the pieces were manageable, the girls softened the biscuit in their mouths before placing it between Albertus's lips. Dad watched with uneasy fascination. Albertus seemed barely aware of the food. That's why they soften it, Dad realized. Otherwise, he might choke.

'We are undecided,' Albertus said. 'During the conversation with Gultrathaca spectrums monitored fluctuations in her temperature, heart rate and respiratory system. Amongst humans it is easy for us to know from these if someone is telling a lie, even a half-lie. But the Griddas can't be read that way. Their bodies are permanently hot, their hearts erratic, racing all the time.'

'That definitely wasn't her real voice, though,' Eric said.

'True,' Albertus replied. 'However, Gultrathaca may have been using a womanly voice for our benefit. Perhaps she did not want to frighten us. Perhaps her natural voice is so different from ours that we could not have understood it at all if she had not changed it.'

Mum restlessly paced the room. 'So we can't be sure of anything. Except the size of those claws, of course. And those teeth!' She pointed at Rachel. 'I've seen that look on your face before. Already made up your mind, haven't you? Well, unmake it; I won't allow you to go. Are you listening to me?'

'Yes, I'm listening, Mum,' Rachel answered. 'I'm also remembering the last thing Larpskendya told us. He said get to Yemi. He said find a way, before the Griddas do something terrible to him. This is the way, the *only* way. We can't help Yemi from here.' As Mum tried to interrupt, Rachel added, 'I won't leave Yemi and Fola on Ool. We didn't know how to find them before. There was no chance to help. Now there is.' She felt all the spells inside her shiver as she made her decision. 'I'll go on my own if I have to.'

'Whoa!' Eric said, as Mum exploded and Dad stood up.

'Now listen,' Dad said. 'I want all of you to calm down. Especially you, Rachel. No one wants any harm to come to Yemi or Fola. Everyone in this room wants to do the right thing by them.'

Rachel nodded. 'Yes … sorry … I know, Dad. Of course they do.'

'All right, then. So the question is how to judge whether to believe Gultrathaca or not. I can't see a way to be sure.'

'There's another thing, Rach,' Eric said. 'Once you're off Earth nobody can protect you. The Griddas probably know that. What's to stop them murdering you quietly in space?'

'Nothing,' Rachel said. 'I know. But why come all this way just to do that? It doesn't make sense.'

Mum came across to Rachel, held her hands, met her eyes. 'Please don't go,' she murmured.

Through her tears, Rachel said, 'I don't *want* to go, Mum! It's just... how can I leave Yemi there? I can't do that! I can't!'

Albertus rose. Without the aid of his thrill-seekers he walked the short distance across to Rachel and knelt beside her. 'I know what you are thinking,' he said. 'There is a picture, Rachel. It is in your head. A picture of Yemi and Fola, and also Serpantha, being mistreated in some awful place with no one to help them. You can't endure it. You're thinking that by charging to Ool you might be able to help. Perhaps you can, perhaps not. But think of this: what if Gultrathaca has come to Earth just to get *you*. Perhaps she can't get Yemi to do what she wants. She intends to get you to help her. Or she needs you for other reasons we could never calculate or guess.'

Mum jumped up and hugged Albertus. 'Exactly, exactly,' she said to Rachel. 'That settles it. I'm prepared to accept the advice of Albertus. Are you?'

Rachel did not want to commit herself.

'Well?' Mum pressed.

Rachel finally assented.

Albertus stared at Mum, his expression grave. 'I think you have misunderstood. The danger to Rachel is real, but there are important reasons why her presence on Ool is required. Our judgement – the combined view of the spectrums – is that Rachel should go.'

Mum flinched, her face blank.

'Here are the major reasons,' Albertus said. 'If you, Rachel, are killed, that loss would be terrible. But the loss of Yemi would be catastrophic for the world, especially if the Griddas find a way to use him against us. Thus, if there is a small chance you can prevent that, the risk to your life is worthwhile. It is difficult for me to say this, because I am your spectrum, and you are precious to me. So long as I live and so long as you live I am devoted to your welfare, but my first priority must be the welfare of all children. By going to Ool, Rachel, you may avoid war. The spectrums' view is that children could not win a war against the Griddas. You *may*, after all, discover that Gultrathaca is telling the truth. Even if she lied, and your visit only delays war, it will have served a purpose. It may give us adequate time to prepare for an invasion, should it come.'

Mum stared bitterly at Albertus Robertson. 'Tell me,' she said, 'what is the likelihood that Rachel will be killed by the Griddas?'

Albertus Robertson looked directly at Rachel, a personal look full of candour. 'It is doubtful you will ever return.'

'But you still think I should go?'

'I would request it, yes.'

'Then I'm going,' Rachel said, rushing across to Mum.

For a while Mum tried desperately to make Rachel change her mind. Eric knew it would hurt too much if he told her his own decision later. He would have to tell her now. 'I'm going, too,' he said.

'What? No, you're not!' Dad blasted. 'You are *not* going, Eric!'

'Dad, Mum, you don't understand. I can actually fight these Griddas. I don't think they've any idea what my anti-magic can do.'

Rachel shook her head. 'No, Eric, I'm not risking you as well.'

'Let Albertus decide,' Eric insisted.

Albertus stared at Eric. His thrill-seekers also stared at Eric. One of the girls' faces, for the first time, betrayed strong emotion.

'You are the fatal gift,' she said, her face white with fear.

'What? What's that supposed to mean?'

'The fatal gift is the name the spectrums have given you, Eric,' Albertus said. 'You have the ability to destroy magic. Our task on Earth is to value and honour the magic of children. You frighten us, because of what you can do. As to whether you should stay on Earth or go with Rachel, I cannot say.'

There was a period of silence while everyone absorbed this.

'The fatal gift …' Eric said to the girl. 'The way you say it … it's … you make me sound like some kind of monster.'

'No,' Albertus replied firmly. 'You are not that, and you must make up your own mind about what to do. You must choose yourself.'

The girl thrill-seeker who had spoken suddenly put her face close to Eric, so close that her long dark hair fell on his knees. No one had ever looked at Eric the way she looked at him now – as if she wanted to kiss him, or to bite him, or both. The other girl pulled her back.

Eric sat still, stroking the prapsies to calm himself down. Then he said, 'Larpskendya suggested more might depend on me than before. He said trust my instinct. My instinct tells me to go.'

Mum's face was ashen. Dad held her, fighting his own dread.

'I'll also go with you,' said Heiki. 'If you –'

'No, please stay, please,' Rachel asked, clutching Heiki's wrist. 'I need someone strong here. I need *you* working with the sentinels.'

Heiki nodded. Everyone gazed at Albertus Robertson.

'I would be of little use to you,' Albertus said matter-of-factly. 'It is the connected intelligence of the spectrums that serves the Earth. Once I am isolated from the others, I will be just like any other child. And remember, I have no magic of my own. Unless I am mistaken – and I am not mistaken – even you, Rachel, will not be able to shift large distances with more than one companion.'

Rachel could not look at Mum or Dad. 'Then it's only us,' she said to Eric.

The Griddas were escorted to a safer location, and Rachel and Eric spent most of the next hours with their parents. The painful run-through of arguments over the decision to leave never quite came to an end, but there were also preparations for Ool to be made. Rachel knew she should be able to fashion whatever clothing they needed with her spells – but what if her magic didn't work on Ool? She decided on practical light-weight body suits, comfortable to move around in but fur-lined, waterproof and well insulated. Eric's suit had extra large pockets because, of course, the prapsies refused to stay behind.

Before she left, Rachel offered a few final words of advice to Albertus Robertson, but they were not needed –

the spectrums had already commenced defensive strategies far more apt than anything Rachel could have devised. She said goodbye to Albertus and he kissed her.

There were other goodbyes, many.

And then there was no more reason to delay.

As Rachel zipped up her white body-suit, Dad slowly re-fastened one of the collar straps. Mum smoothed Eric's hair under his hood. Her children gazed back at her; only their eyes and part of their foreheads were exposed. Everyone was too distraught to speak.

'I'll take care of them,' Heiki whispered to Rachel.

'I know you will.' She looked at Heiki. 'Will you follow us up?'

'Of course.'

They departed into a warm blue morning sky. Rachel could not believe how beautiful that ordinary sky looked to her today. Millions of children had come to see them off. They flew into the air until their magic could take them no higher, then waved and called out their hopes until Rachel and Eric were out of sight.

Some spectrums ordered their thrill-seekers to escort Rachel as far as they could. It was a terrible parting for the thrill-seekers. They were bereft without their spectrums, and Rachel was glad to see them return to the ground as she rose into the stratosphere. Here, in the thinnest air, where no birds could fly, only the most magical children could still follow. Paul and Marshall were amongst them, close friends from another time of impossible decisions. The smiles of the boys were strained as they tried to hearten her. Finally Rachel, wrapping Eric in a protective blanket of warmth and oxygen, outflew even those two special children.

Only one child remained with them now.

'Oh, Rachel,' murmured Heiki. 'Are you doing the right thing? Are you sure?'

Rachel did not reply. Instead she turned away from all she knew, and said to Gultrathaca, 'Which way?' Rachel thought she saw a smile, then. Was it a smile? Even in that busted face of shattered angles, Rachel thought she recognized the expression.

'Follow me,' Gultrathaca said.

13

homage

Rachel had shifted many times before, sometimes stretching it out gloriously for hours, but never for this long – and never through the vacuum of space.

Yet instead of tiring, her shifting spells wanted more. After half a day carrying Eric without rest, they were lean, trimmed and ready for new velocities. Sensing this, Gultrathaca increased the pace. She shifted at greater and greater intervals.

Testing me, Rachel realized. I can test you too, Gultrathaca, she thought. If you've spent most of your life underground, there must be limitations to your flying skills. So each time Gultrathaca accelerated, Rachel nudged the speed on. They flew side by side, studying each other intently: for frailties, for infirmity, for the slightest defect.

Suns streaked by, beautiful constellations, barely noticed by either of them.

The talkative version of Gultrathaca vanished as soon as they left Earth. Throughout the journey she seemed self-absorbed. 'Ool is near,' she repeated distractedly every hour or so. Otherwise she hardly responded to their questions.

Eric said privately to Rachel, 'Where's the charm gone now? I thought Gultrathaca would use this time to tell us more about Ool. She's not bothering. Why?'

'I don't know. What do you reckon to those spiders?'

Gultrathaca's watchers perched on every edge of her face. Not once had they taken their eyes off Rachel.

Eric whispered, 'Do you think Gultrathaca's just going to kill us? Is that why she's so quiet?'

'If that was all Gultrathaca intended, we'd probably be dead already.'

'Maybe she's waiting for help, waiting until we get to Ool.'

Rachel wished she could answer that.

There were no stopping places on the journey. They ate while they flew. Gultrathaca's meals were tucked inside the crevices of her skin: light snacks, small live creatures. It was repulsive to watch her eat, but Rachel made herself do so – there might be far worse to come on Ool. Was Gultrathaca a typical Gridda? she wondered. Were they all so intimidating?

'The prapsies are getting hungry,' Eric complained after a few hours. 'I didn't bring much food because you told us not to bother. How far is there to go?'

'Not far at all.' Allowing all her anxieties to flow away, Gultrathaca said, 'Welcome to Ool. Welcome to the world of the Griddas!'

Ool appeared before them suddenly. It was a shade of

red, though so deep it was almost black. Rachel tried to pick out details on the surface, but there were none. A sun shone adamantly down, but gigantic cloud-formations gathered against it, like a fortress against the warmth and brightness.

Before Rachel's information spells could investigate further, Gultrathaca pointed below. 'Here come the youngsters,' she said.

Countless Gridda infants rose in long thrashing lines from the surface of Ool. Flight was awkward for them, but with jerky, frog-like kicks of their legs they clawed at the space ahead. They bit their own pack-members, desperate to be the first to arrive.

Dread trickled through Rachel. Was this a welcome? How could it be? More likely a killing party. Would it end here, before they even knew if Yemi was alive or dead?

The prapsies were frantic under Eric's body-suit. With an effort he kept them inside. 'Better get ready to defend ourselves,' he said to Rachel.

Too many, and too late for that, she thought.

Gultrathaca seemed confused by Eric's reaction. 'The infants will not intentionally damage you,' she assured him. 'Let them feel your bodies. Touch is the way they learn to identify each another in the birthing tunnels.'

Rachel tried not to flinch as the first infants arrived.

Exploratory claws reached out, almost shyly at first. Rachel's lack of angularity intrigued the infants. They circled her, looking for edges. Such woeful eyes, such clawlessness! And where were her jaws? Marvelling at her pale skin, they wanted to taste her hair, confused by its long loose texture. Eric closed his eyes as the infants sniffed up and down his body. Where were his spiders hiding? they wondered. They poked his clothes – as if the strange garments might poke back.

'Get away!' Eric warned, as one infant reached for a prapsy.

Hearing Eric's raised voice the nearest infants backed off – only to be pushed aside by others. Once it was obvious they would not be harmed, more infants braved an approach. They brushed up against Rachel and Eric: jabbering, rubbing up against them, insatiable.

One dropped a batch of spiders onto Rachel's legs.

'A gift,' Gultrathaca told her. 'From an admirer.'

'An admirer?' Rachel gazed at the infant in bewilderment, striving to see beyond the bony face to the expressions beneath.

'Get them off now!' Eric screamed, suddenly no longer able to bear it. 'Get them off! Get them off!'

Gultrathaca uttered a guttural click, and all the infants started kicking back to the surface of Ool. The one who had offered her spiders to Rachel sucked them back into her mouths, reluctantly leaving with the other infants.

Rachel tried to steady herself as Gultrathaca led them down towards the planet. How big was Ool? Her information spells measured its circumference: over thirty times the size of Earth.

They entered the atmosphere – and a sky the colour of dull metal.

For dozens of miles, Gultrathaca guided them through snow-clouds. Even on Ithrea, Rachel had never seen snowfall so heavy. At another time she might have thought the flakes had a beauty all of their own, but she was too conscious of danger. The snows themselves felt dangerous. They were not light and scattered, with gaps to see the world through. These snows were so dense it was like the weight of a person pressed on all parts of her. She drew Eric close, wiping the flakes from his eyes. The prapsies huddled against his breast, where they could watch his face and feel the reassuring thump of his heart.

At last the clouds thinned, and they burst through into clearer air.

'The Detaclyver,' Gultrathaca said tonelessly, pointing below. 'The place of death. No Gridda survives for long here.'

Rachel gasped as she saw mountains: a colossal range. Peak after peak extended over the entire southern and western continents of Ool.

'It's moving!' Eric cried out. 'Rachel, it's... living!'

The Detaclyver's body was like a vast buckling and heaving tide, trying to extend over the world. At its northerly extremity, the peaks were not turned towards the sky. They were sharper, modified for ramming into the ground ahead.

'Do you recognize what's holding it back?' Rachel called out. 'Storm-whirls!'

On Ithrea the Witch Dragwena had used her magic to create similar immense hurricanes. Those lifeless objects, however, bore no resemblance to the true sentient storm-whirls of Ool. Hundreds of them stood massively between ground and sky. Rooted against the outer border of the Detaclyver, they kept it in check.

'A ceaseless, patient battle,' Gultrathaca explained. 'Both species were part of Ool long before Witches came. The High Witches could never control the Detaclyver, but eventually were able to gain a hold on the minds of the storm-whirls. Now they obey us.'

'I don't understand,' Rachel said. 'Why do you need the storm-whirls?'

'To keep our homes safe from the Detaclyver,' Gultrathaca answered. 'The Detaclyver tries to destroy the cities. Naturally it does. It hates us.'

As they flew over the summits of the Detaclyver, Rachel looked between her feet. It seemed that nothing should be able to live among the desolate peaks but she was wrong. Her information spells discovered life and spells. Creatures were everywhere below her, in the endlessly falling snow itself, or under it, within the flesh of the Detaclyver. Amongst them were magical signatures that throbbed as powerfully as any Witch, though the creatures were not Witches – or anything like them.

While Rachel pondered this, Eric murmured to her, 'Yemi's here. Still a long way off and deep underground. Fola's with him, too.' He grinned. 'She's alive. They both are!'

Gultrathaca gazed at Eric, shocked. 'You can detect Fola's minute scent from this distance? What else can you detect?'

'Nothing,' growled Eric. He peered down at the prapsies. They peered back, fearful for him. So quiet, Eric thought. They hadn't said a thing since they arrived on Ool. He stroked their heads, feeling them shiver.

'Eric,' one said nervously. 'Look out for the snow.'

'I know,' Eric said. 'It's everywhere. Just keep your heads down, boys. I'll watch out for you.'

'No, Eric. The snow's wrong. It's going the wrong way.'

Great plumes of snow had burst from the Detaclyver's peaks. They rose, then changed direction, sweeping towards Gultrathaca. This was no ordinary snow, Rachel saw. The flakes were not blown by the wind. They were *fighting* the wind to get to her.

The snow was alive.

'What are they?' Rachel cried.

'Essa,' Gultrathaca said. 'Servants of the Detaclyver. Protect yourselves.'

Rachel held Eric close and raised her defensive spells.

Gultrathaca moved upward into fiercer winds. The Essa followed, millions of tons of tiny life wheeling in a great arc to cut her off.

'What – what should I do?' Eric asked. 'Use my anti-magic on them?'

'No, not yet,' Rachel whispered.

'But they're coming!'

'Wait, Eric!'

A small number of the Essa reached her. They hovered, quivering with interest. Who was she? Rachel felt them in her mind, all hope and expectation, their thoughts chasing into her.

They meant her no harm. Rachel knew that at once. Their target was Gultrathaca.

Gultrathaca raced through the thickest clouds, trying to throw the Essa off. But they caught her. Landing on her jaws, they overpowered the soldier spiders, and crept inside her throat. For a while Gultrathaca was slowed down; then she coughed the Essa from her body. She flew on, crossing the boundary of the Detaclyver.

A few Essa remained with Rachel. They were as light and insubstantial as the snow itself. Briefly their warm bodies clung to her face, curious and full of questions. Then they had no choice; they departed, returning to their homes in the summits of the Detaclyver. Rachel held out her hands, not wishing them to go.

'I see the Essa have taken a liking to you,' Gultrathaca said, amused. She guided Eric and Rachel northwards, leaving the Detaclyver behind. They reached the storm-whirls. When Gultrathaca ordered one to move aside, it did so at once.

Behind the storm-whirls was an area of smooth ice. 'The Prag Sea,' Gultrathaca informed them. 'Good hunting grounds for the brave.' Rachel sent her information spells under the frozen waters. There was life here, fish in their millions. Each was armoured, their blood kept at boiling temperatures to burn a path through the solid ice.

Finally they traversed the Prag Sea and entered a vast region of featureless snow plains. At their margin mountains rose starkly, and Rachel saw a line of smashed eye-towers that had once marked the edge of a city.

Eric bent towards Rachel. 'There are High Witches under us. Not many.'

'The others are dead,' Gultrathaca told him. 'We keep a few to entertain the infants.' As they soared over the remains of the towers, Rachel tried to take in the scale of the devastation. 'Thûn,' Gultrathaca declared. 'The ruined city. During Heebra's reign the greatest Highs lived here, though Gaffilex and Tamretis are larger. We tore those cities down as well.'

There were no eye-towers left standing, but as they dropped lower Eric saw that the Gridda infants occupied the ruins. Some lurked amidst the debris of stones. Others dived in and out of underground entrances, yelling with fear or excitement – Eric couldn't tell which. Many flew – with greater or lesser ability – about the sky.

At the heart of Thûn a single storm-whirl turned. It was smaller than the others Rachel had seen. 'A juvenile whirl,' Gultrathaca told her. 'It makes a playground for our infants.' She indicated the base, where the winds were light and infants vaulted and tumbled. 'A place they can learn how to fly without fear,' Gultrathaca said.

Higher up in the whirl Rachel spotted older Griddas. They fought in small groups, supervised by trainers. Occasionally one would fall, to be caught by the infants below, gathering around and howling their scorn.

'The true battles take place at the top, where the winds are hardest,' Gultrathaca said. Rachel saw one of the Griddas in the upper whirl fall. As she hit the ground her spiders were scattered across the snow. Before she could gather them up, the infants trampled them.

Rachel tried to keep her voice steady. 'Why did they do that?'

'Why not? Poor quality magic must be punished.' Gultrathaca gazed at Rachel, genuinely puzzled by her reaction.

Such casual cruelty means nothing here, Rachel realized. She thought of Yemi and Fola, wondering what the Griddas might have done to them.

From the edge of the juvenile whirl a group of young Griddas emerged. One flew over to Gultrathaca and said something.

Gultrathaca laughed – Rachel could half-recognize such expressions now.

'These ones are in awe of you, defeater of Heebra,' Gultrathaca told Rachel. 'They have waited a long time for this privilege.'

The eyes of the youngsters lingered over every detail of

Rachel's body. Then they bowed to her. There was no doubting the sincerity of the gesture. After a last look, each of the youngsters flew eastwards, calling noisily to others.

'Please take us to see Yemi now,' Rachel said.

'One thing first.' Gultrathaca halted in the sky. Several adult Griddas, considerably larger than the infants, approached Rachel and Eric. They arrived in an elegant line, unhurried. Rachel noticed that Gultrathaca acknowledged each of them individually – these Griddas were obviously important. The adults stared in an uninhibited way at Rachel. Then each in turn, starting with Gultrathaca, lowered their head. They exposed the entire length of their necks.

What did it mean? This is a warrior race, Rachel's information spells told her. They are exposing their most vulnerable areas as a way of honouring you.

The Gridda pack-leaders left their necks laid bare a long while. Finally they raised their heads and Gultrathaca said, sincerely, 'We hope you enjoyed the affections of the infants. That was why we asked them to greet you. The Griddas alongside me are the highest ranking leaders of the packs of Ool. They have gathered to acclaim you both. We esteem you, Rachel, and you, Eric. The death of Heebra means more to us than you can know.' All the pack-leaders bowed. The members of their packs close enough to witness also bowed, enormous swells of movement crossing the city.

Rachel could not believe this. A genuine tribute. Not killed in space, she thought. Not killed on arrival. Her spells jumped into her eyes, filled with hope.

'And now it is the turn of the youngsters to honour you in their own fashion,' said Gultrathaca. She led the way towards the easternmost perimeter of Thûn. Ool's pack-leaders fell in deferentially behind. As they flew remnants of the eye-towers flashed past, fewer and fewer until they left the city altogether. Infant Griddas followed. Most flew. Those not yet able to fly bounded or trampled over each other in the same direction.

Beyond the city the snows flattened out. Gultrathaca slowed down and all the Griddas became utterly silent, even the infants.

Rachel saw it before she understood: a great oval structure on the surface. It was hundreds of feet high and wide. The group of youngsters who had earlier studied Rachel were fussing over it, finishing just as she arrived.

'Oh, my –' Rachel started.

It was her face: a snow sculpture.

There was a thoughtful expression on the sculpture – a measured look, the same one Rachel had given the youngsters, captured perfectly. A strand of hair fell over one eye. Her nostrils were caves large enough to hibernate inside. Scuffed snow formed the eyebrows. A spider, tiny, sat in one of them.

Rachel lifted her hand to her real face. The spider was there, motionless. She flicked it off.

For a moment there was quiet as all the Griddas humbly waited to see whether Rachel approved of their efforts. Then Rachel heard the voices. She had heard nothing like it. Gultrathaca had arranged for all the Griddas of the city to be here. They filled the sky and ground, as numerous as the falling snow.

While Rachel and Eric stared, all the Griddas opened their jaws and roared their homage.

14

PARTING

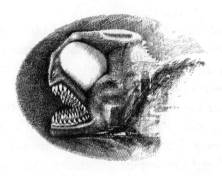

The homage of the Griddas was so deafening that Rachel and Eric had to cover their ears until it subsided. Each time that happened, Gultrathaca renewed it. Finally the pack-leaders raised their claws and there was silence.

Gultrathaca turned her attention back to Rachel. 'Now we will honour you in another way,' she said. 'Every Gridda wishes to be the first to fight you. Choose a suitable contestant.'

'Fight ... me?'

'Of course. What did you expect?'

'I don't understand. We don't need to fight. We came here for ... for peace.'

Gultrathaca regarded her contemptuously. 'Did you really believe I wanted peace?'

'But I don't ... want to fight,' Rachel said.

A look of disgust passed across the faces of the pack-leaders. Gultrathaca, with difficulty, calmed them. 'Don't dishonour yourself, Rachel,' she said menacingly.

'I *won't* fight!'

'You have no choice. There is no going back now.'

Rachel glanced in dismay at Eric, preparing to shift evasively.

Gultrathaca's eyes shone. 'Yes, why not try? By now, however, you must realize that you can never shift fast enough to escape from me if you're carrying Eric. Discard him. Give yourself a chance …'

'We should have killed you on Earth!' Eric thundered.

'That was a mistake,' Gultrathaca agreed. 'I realized you were weak, then. But how to convince my Griddas? They know you faced down Heebra, Rachel. You make them anxious. I must cut you down to size. When they see how readily you can be dispatched, the invasion of your world will be more easily accomplished.'

'Please,' Rachel began, then stopped. She knew, seeing Gultrathaca's expression, that no argument would change her mind. 'What about Eric?' she said. 'If I co-operate, agree to fight, will you –'

'Spare him? No. I plan to give him to the infants as entertainment.'

'You mustn't … I –'

'Don't plead,' Gultrathaca said. She gestured for Eric to be removed. Eric freed his hands, prepared to use his spell-killing. The prapsies sprang onto his shoulders.

'Wait,' Rachel said to Gultrathaca. 'Leave Eric. I'll … I'll do it. I'll entertain the infants for you instead of him.'

'Very well,' Gultrathaca said indifferently. 'I promised the youngsters something, after all. In that case, the first contest for you will start tomorrow.' While Rachel tried to take in what this might mean, Gultrathaca added, 'Make your parting. This is the last time you will see Eric.'

'No!' Rachel reached out for him, but her arm was knocked away.

'Quick! Should I use my anti-spells?' Eric asked. 'Should I use them now?'

Rachel agonized. 'Yes. No – not yet, Eric.'

Gultrathaca separated them. Before Rachel had time to say anything else two young Griddas flew across the sky. Knocking the prapsies off, they clasped Eric's shoulders in their foot-claws and headed out over the city. The prapsies followed, shrieking insults at them.

'Please –' Rachel begged, as she was dragged away. 'Let me –'

'You are a warrior,' Gultrathaca said. 'There is no need for goodbyes.'

'No. I –' Rachel craned her head, trying to see what was happening to Eric.

'Pathetic!' Gultrathaca hissed. 'Hold your head erect!'

'Let me talk to Eric!'

'No.'

Eric was carried southwards across the darkening skies, already too far for his voice or that of the prapsies to reach her.

As Gultrathaca picked her up, Rachel tried to shift. It did not work.

'At least you've tried something!' Gultrathaca sneered.

Rachel felt all her spells quail inside her. She trembled. 'What have you done to me?'

'I've used a skin-contact spell,' Gultrathaca said. 'It reduces your abilities. I must give the infants a chance against you tonight, after all. You cannot shift. You cannot fly. Oh, and you will not be able to shape-change either. None of your other spells are affected.'

'You've left me nothing!'

'Nothing? Hardly nothing. Your death spells are still intact. You will need your deaths tonight.'

Rachel shuddered. The deaths had always been part of her magic – the part she hid from, ignored, detested – yet they were there. Grasping her arm, Gultrathaca flew to a western part of Thûn Rachel had not seen. Here Heebra's eye-tower still stood, piercing the sky. 'A fitting place for you to stay,' Gultrathaca said. 'If you were a High Witch there could have been no greater glory – to rest in Heebra's tower, above all others! You see, I honour you still.'

'I don't care about your code of honour!'

'Do you care what happens to the children of your world?'

'Of course!'

'In that case kill yourself now. A Gridda would, the least of them. The longer you are alive, the more we'll learn from you. We'll see your spells, recognize how to counter them. We'll know what to expect when we face the children of Earth. Is that what you want?'

Rachel had no reply. 'What will you do to Eric?' she asked shakily.

'Whatever I like.' Gultrathaca flew Rachel through the cracked eye-window, depositing her on the chamber floor. 'Actually, there may be a use for Eric. I'd heard from the High Witches how he could destroy spells, but perhaps they missed something more important.' Gultrathaca left. Outside, in the gathering dark, Rachel saw the silhouettes of infants.

They scrambled over the snow, heading for the tower.

15

the long night of ool

Rachel stood next to the shattered eye-window, watching the infants.

While daylight lasted they remained at the base of Heebra's tower, content to observe her with half-shut eyes. The arrival of night changed everything. There was no dusk, no gentle sunset. One moment there was enough meagre light by which to see; the next there was nothing. Instinctively, Rachel strained to find the last of the sun. Like someone who would perish without light, who was starved and whose only food was light, she sought the disappearing patch low in the east. Ool's sun made a final stand against the dark. Then it was extinguished – and a vast shadow came hurtling across the world.

And then there was no light at all.

There was only the unbelievable cold and the sound of

breathing – Rachel's own ragged breaths mixed with new ones, the noise of infants labouring up the walls of the tower.

Rachel blinked over and over, assuming her eyes would adjust. But they did not adjust. Her pupils enlarged to feed on what light they could find, but there was nothing to find. Ool had no moon. Stars had never winked through the clouds. Rachel was so frightened that she would have welcomed even the emerald-green light that once shone from Heebra's tower – but the Griddas had forever removed that colour from the world.

Her magic came to her aid at once. First it created a candle-brightness. Seeing the Griddas outside the window cower, Rachel intensified the light, driving them back. If she could not fly, if she could not leave the eye-tower, where was the safest place to be? She chose the middle of the floor – close enough to see what might come in through the window, and close enough to react to what might enter from the doorway. In the darkness her night eyes opened, a brilliant silver.

The night of Ool had never known such gleams.

Despite this, the braver infants edged forward. Soon they became used to the glare of Rachel's eyes, and after that they did not give her any peace at all. Stimulated by her strange looks, and the stories they had heard, and daring each other, they gathered wherever there was a space: in the eye-chamber, in the stairway leading up to it, in the snows outside. They clung to the steeps of the eye-tower walls; they peered in from the darkness.

The first infants were too frightened to enter the eye-chamber. But they soon forgot their fears when Rachel made the mistake of not punishing those who came nearest. They wanted a closer look at her. She was so deformed. Why hadn't she been killed at birth?

Rachel didn't dare take her eyes off them for a second. She was hungry, thirsty, cold, needing to think, needing to rest, to sleep, most of all to sleep – but there was no opportunity for that. All through the night her spells built dams and shields and small illusions to confuse the infants. She had never needed to call on her magic so continuously before.

But the Griddas had their eye-shields, and there was plenty of time. They started finding ways around Rachel's barriers. Unable to fly away or shape-change, Rachel had to constantly rebuild and repair her defences. And, she knew, this was just a few curious infants. Her first real trial hadn't even started...

As the hours passed Rachel believed that dawn would never come. The dark deepened; the infants seemed tireless. Then, in the middle of the night, one of them punctured her shield. When that happened Rachel did something she had promised herself she would never do: she summoned her death spells. For the first time in her life Rachel invited the deaths forward, and momentarily her eyes turned black with their power.

The deaths were something the infants understood, feared. For a while they left Rachel in peace. She felt like crying, realizing how frail she was. She had always made noble resolutions about never using the deaths – yet as soon as a single infant threatened her, all those noble resolutions had evaporated.

She thought about Eric – but there was barely time even for that. The infants returned, and there were more than ever. They no longer feared her silver eyes, or the incandescence of the eye-chamber. They knew her defences were beginning to fail. Rachel found herself shaking. Several of her finest spells rose to inspire her. The deaths did what they did best: they imagined deaths. They could devise so many for the inexperienced infants – a nearly infinite number – and Rachel felt dirty as she selected amongst them. But she selected nonetheless.

Finally there came a point when Rachel could think of no other way to hold the infants back except with the deaths. She stood in the eye-tower, surrounded by Griddas. Some had started to rake her thighs. Her deaths clamoured to be set free. Rachel withheld them with difficulty.

Give me another choice, she demanded.

Her magic had never failed her before, not when her life was threatened. It looked out into the night and snow and cold and knew what to do. Rachel forced her way to a corner of the chamber. She initiated the spell.

The infants had not witnessed anything like this before. Rachel raised her arms, warning them back. Then a new light shot from her eyes, raising its blaze from the walls, from the floor, from the shards of glass, from the air itself, sucking out everything a Gridda could breathe. The chamber flickered orange the remainder of the night.

For the first time in its long history, a fire burned in Heebra's eye.

Eric sagged against a stone wall. The prapsies were either side of his face. He could feel their eyes on him, and the racy pitter-patter of their hearts.

His prison cell was a rough circular hole gouged from the rock beneath Thûn. No magic held him there. The rock was enough; none of the sophisticated spells needed to contain Yemi or Rachel were needed for Eric.

For a long time he had been sitting against the wall, trying to stay awake. He didn't dare fall asleep. This was the first break in the night Gultrathaca had given him. Why? To tease him? To lull him before the next attack? He wanted to sleep. He wanted more than anything to blank out everything that had happened to him here, but how could he forget all those Witches he had hurt?

Gultrathaca's experiments had started the moment Eric entered the cell.

The first test involved a native magical animal he had never seen before – some kind of dog. Gultrathaca herself let it in. By the time it saw Eric the animal had been deliberately whipped into a frenzy. As soon as Gultrathaca opened the door, the dog attacked.

Eric had no time to think. Without considering the consequences of his actions, he turned the entire scope of his anti-magic on the dog. He had not done this before. He had never even thought to do it. Normally he only cancelled single spells. This time, in his panic, he went much further. The dog was a simple predator – using spells only to increase its bite.

It was no match for Eric.

In his terror he reached for all the spells. He stripped away the sum of the dog's magic. He took everything. What occurred next shocked him and intrigued Gultrathaca. The dog's body, in mid-lunge, seemed to lose all potency. It flopped to the floor, no longer able to lift its head. Without magic, the dog lay panting in weak confusion.

Next came other magical animals, too many to count.

Then Gultrathaca sent against him something altogether grander: a Witch; a High Witch, one of those imprisoned. Eric had no idea what made that first one fly at him with such recklessness. The prapsies were ready, and tried their usual distractions.

'Come after us!' one squealed, flying around the cell.

'Come for us, beast!'

'*Come for us!*'

Against animals, this tactic sometimes worked. They became uncertain about the target, giving Eric enough time to disable their magic without harming them too much.

Against a High Witch it could never work.

She ignored the prapsies and went straight for Eric.

Like all High Witches, this one abounded with magic. Magic suffused her body. It riddled her mind and ensnared her heart. It was the dazzling foundation of her strength and the catalyst for her formidable intellect. The one who flew at Eric had been alive seven centuries. All that time she had lived intimately with her spells. She had used them for so long that she could do nothing without their affections.

Eric shuddered, recalling what happened next. Why had she flown at him with such insane energy? Why couldn't she have paused, just for a moment? There had been no time to argue or think. In self-preservation Eric reached deep inside her and scooped out all of her magic. In dismay he watched as her powerful body slowly unravelled in front of him.

More High Witches had followed, often several at a time, as Gultrathaca attempted to discover Eric's limitations. All the Witches came flying wildly into his cell, but after his initial panic Eric adjusted to what Gultrathaca threw his way. He stopped needing to kill the Highs. He found adroit ways of selecting certain spells to disarm them without serious injury.

For over an hour there had been a stalemate, while Gultrathaca wondered what to try next.

Eric lay down, his face against the stone floor. It was cold, but not so cold that he shivered – clearly Gultrathaca wanted him alive.

The prapsies pressed close to Eric's heart, consoling themselves in its beat. The contact was wonderful for Eric, too, but he wouldn't tell them so. He wanted them to leave. He wanted them to escape. It would have been easy enough. The roof of the cell was open, ten feet or so away. Eric could not climb the sheer walls, but the prapsies could be out and past any number of guards in a second. It was only their love for him that kept them in the cell.

Eric lay quietly, feeling their little hearts thud against his chest. Another hour passed and their rhythmic beat lulled him.

'We'll keep lookout,' one prapsy whispered. 'You sleep, boys.'

'You need to sleep as well,' Eric murmured.

'We will. We are. Each at a time.' One of the prapsies lay on Eric's chest and closed its eyes; the other walked in circles around him.

'All right,' Eric said. 'We'll take turns. One hour, that's enough. Then wake me and I'll keep watch.'

'Yes.'

Eric fell into an exhausted slumber almost at once. When he was breathing deeply, the prapsy pretending to sleep on him rose and stared at the doorway. For the remainder of the night both prapsies stayed silent and vigilant, leaving Eric to rest.

While Eric slept and the prapsies kept watch, the snow-like Essa brooded in the south of Ool. What had happened today, what wonderful thing? They had intercepted the most extraordinary beings. Not Griddas, not those bony spider-lovers. Not even the uncatchable High Witches, long gone from the skies. New things. Unfurred, small, lithe things. Without armour! Frail, keen to love, yet ... travellers with Griddas. What were they? Friend or enemy? Friend! Friend! The Essa thought so, but they were always hopeful. How could they find out more?

Poor Detaclyver – so old and tired, so beaten back. So loving. If they asked him he would not let them go to the strangers. He would say they are too expectant. He would say they do not heed their own lives enough. 'Send us out! Send us out!' they would beg. 'It is too far,' he would say. 'You cannot make the distance to Thûn.' He would withhold his mighty breath and not let them go. 'We can! We can!' they would say. He would say – 'No!'

But how long had it been since there was any hope at all for Detaclyver?

No one else could make such a long trip. The Essa shivered in the summits of the Detaclyver, convincing themselves. They did not know if they could travel so far and still have the strength to return. But still – the strangers!

One whole night away. A terrible journey. Could they do it?

Without the breath of the Detaclyver, the Essa left.

They floated northwards, in small bunches so that they did not attract attention. The winds were against them, but they were determined. Quietly, hiding in the night snow, they passed by the storm-whirls. They travelled high over the Prag Sea and the cold plains beyond. As they neared Thûn many of the Essa were too tired to carry on, and returned home to the Detaclyver, but others continued their journey.

They passed over millions of infant Griddas bedded down together in the tunnels under Thûn. They passed over the imprisoned High Witches, where Calen lay in the filth of her cell, wondering about the choices she had made. They passed over Fola and Yemi. Griddas were in constant attendance at the Assessment Chamber – even now, in the night, casting and recasting their spells to keep him from escaping.

Yemi was held too deep for the Essa to help, so they rode the winds instead over Heebra's tower. They could not miss it, that orange lustre in the night. As the Essa approached they saw the taller stranger with long hair standing her ground, wide-eyed, guarding herself against the infants. Many of the Essa were almost frozen when they hurried towards the fire. The first to arrive nearly flew into the flames. Just in time they held back and stared into that wonder, warming their tiny wings. To be so close, yet unable to help! The Essa could not wait to tell the Detaclyver, but aspired to greater things first.

They searched for the second stranger.

Where was he? No way to tell, since he had no magical scent. So the Essa crept into all the Gridda caves, passing the sleepy tunnel sentries. A few Essa became lost and could not find their way out at all. Even fewer found the hole where the boy sat guarded by two strange flighted creatures. They drifted warily next to the prapsies.

The prapsies hopped from foot to foot, wondering what to do.

The Essa touched their baby faces and felt for their minds. 'Can you carry him?' they asked.

'He is too heavy,' whimpered one prapsy.

The Essa landed on Eric and tested his weight. 'Yes, too much,' they said.

It was nearly dawn. Snowflakes so deep down in the world would be seen in the light. They wanted to stay with the second stranger and comfort him, but there was no time. They must get back to tell Detaclyver. He would know what to do.

Were they too tired? Nearly day – and they were so tired. If the wind had changed direction they would never be able to battle back.

Kissing the prapsies, kissing Eric and each other, the Essa rose up the cell walls.

16

storm-whirls

With the arrival of daybreak the infants surrounding Heebra's tower drifted back to their underground tunnels to rest. Rachel was almost too weary to notice. Left alone in the chamber at last she extinguished the fire, found a place to relieve herself and massaged her aching legs. A few spiders ran about the floor, left to perish by their negligent young owners. Rachel crawled away from them and lay down. Somehow, she slept.

Shortly afterwards, Gultrathaca entered the eye-tower. She watched Rachel for a while, watched her chest rise and fall. Finally she dropped some food on one of her hands. The food was alive: a rodent.

Waking, Rachel swiped it away.

Gultrathaca picked the rodent up by its tail. She offered it again. 'Squeamish? Disgusted? It is the same food my Griddas are eating.'

'I don't want it.'

'But you *need* it. How can you fight effectively if you have no strength?'

Rachel looked at the rodent. She was intensely hungry, but she knew that even if the rat-like animal was dead she could only eat it if she was starving. A Gridda wouldn't hesitate, she realized. She'd eat anything. To have any chance against them, I need to be like that, Rachel thought. I need to be capable of eating this rat-thing.

She reached out her hand – then dropped it. She could not eat the rodent. As soon as she knew for certain, Rachel felt all her precarious courage failing her.

I'm not going to be able to live through this day, she thought. An image of Eric came into her mind and she nearly screamed. What had Gultrathaca said yesterday? Kill yourself, before we discover anything … Rachel asked her spells. She asked for those who would help her end her life. They retreated. Even her deaths retreated. None of the spells were willing; they loved her too much.

Gultrathaca dropped the rodent and let it run off to a corner. 'You survived a night with the infants,' she said. 'Many of the pack-leaders did not expect that. *I* did not expect it.'

A compliment? Rachel ignored her. Standing upright, she straightened her body-suit. She thought of Heiki, of the spectrums, of Mum and Dad and everyone else on Earth whose existence might somehow depend on how she behaved today. She made herself look at Gultrathaca. 'When will the trial start?'

'Immediately. Unless you require a rest first.'

Yes, thought Rachel, that *is* what I need. Instead of that, she said, 'If I survive the trial, what then?'

'I think you know the answer.'

'There'll just be another trial, won't there? And another. Until I'm dead.'

'I'm glad you understand. I will give you a few moments to prepare yourself.' Gultrathaca's spiders followed her out of the eye-chamber.

When the last one skittered out, Rachel collapsed on the floor.

Could she escape? No. Not without being able to shift or fly or shape-change. In that case what should she do? Beg for mercy? How could an appeal to compassion work with Gultrathaca?

The best of Rachel's spells tried to encourage her. They told her how proud they were of her, that they were ready, that they would not fail her. As Rachel listened to their words she wondered how she had ever survived without them, in the time before she knew of her magic.

Her deaths, however, spoke in a different fashion. After all, they said, she *was* being watched. Her trial was an opportunity for the Griddas to judge the capability of all children, not just her. Fight! they argued. There'll probably be only one chance to impress. Call on all our resourcefulness!

Should she? The moment Rachel gave the deaths a fraction of her attention they rose into her mind like the killers they were. Perhaps, they said, if you fight ferociously, with enough flair and imagination and brutal directness, the Griddas might think again about challenging the children of Earth. Or at least they might delay, giving Heiki, the spectrums and sentinels longer to prepare. Isn't that why you're here? they said. Isn't that why Albertus Robertson let you go, when it was the last thing he wanted?

Rachel listened. She wondered how many Griddas she would need to kill to impress Gultrathaca. Could she do it? Should she make friends with her deaths for a day? Rachel pushed hunger and weariness and excuses aside. She probed her heart. She tried to summon mercilessness there.

A group of watchers preceded the reappearance of Gultrathaca. 'Are you ready?'

'Yes.'

'Then follow me.'

As they descended the staircase Gultrathaca said, 'I intend to make your first trial against a youngster.'

'Not an infant,' Rachel replied at once. 'I want to face an adult.'

Gultrathaca nodded appreciatively.

As Rachel emerged from Heebra's tower she saw that Griddas of all ages had assembled to observe the trial. Could Griddas recognize a human expression of fear? Rachel could not entirely hide it, but she did her best. Lifting her chin, holding herself erect, she strode across the snow.

Gultrathaca swept her arms wide. 'Select an opponent.'

Rachel gazed around. To her all the Gridda faces were the same: massive, hard-edged, frightening. 'Any opponent?'

'Any.'

'Then I select *you*, Gultrathaca.'

As soon as Rachel said the name her deaths rose like crude shadows in her eyes. She did not shut them out. She wanted Gultrathaca to see the deaths. She needed everything against this Gridda, the best and worst of her magic.

'Well,' Gultrathaca said. 'An unexpected honour. I see your deaths are ready, even if you are not.'

Making sure as many Griddas heard as possible, Rachel said, 'You have all the advantages, Gultrathaca. I've heard your talk about honour. If it means anything, let me choose the trial. I'll fight you where the Detaclyver lives. I'll fight you there.'

Gultrathaca hesitated, then saw the expectant eyes of the other Gridda pack-leaders on her. They understood the challenge Rachel had set.

'I agree,' Gultrathaca said. 'A private contest, then. But I warn you, Rachel: you may think you have found a friend in the Essa, but they are no match for an experienced Gridda.' Gultrathaca stepped back. A tight, exalted smile spread across her face. Across her jaws, her spiders ran in frenzy.

'Give me my other spells back!' Rachel demanded.

Gultrathaca touched her just under the eye. 'Not everything,' she said. 'You can now fly again, but no shifting is possible, nor any shape-changing. I won't have you escape that way. And if you try to fly anywhere except towards the Detaclyver you will be killed. We will both be escorted, watched.' Gultrathaca chose a dozen adult Griddas to fly with them. Half surrounded Rachel. 'Only one of us will be allowed to leave the Detaclyver alive. If you use any spells before we are within the Detaclyver the escorts will kill you. Are you ready?'

No, Rachel thought.

'Yes!' she shouted.

Gultrathaca sucked in all her spiders and lurched into the brightening sky.

Thrusting their powerful haunches southwards, the Gridda escort led the way. They crossed the city border. Flying in rhythm, they entered the hinterlands of the snow plains of Ool. For a while some infants thrashed behind, trying to keep up, but their immature magic was no match for the older Griddas, and they soon fell behind, their anguished cries piercing the clouds for miles.

After this there was only one sound – the wind pulsing from the thighs of the Gridda escort.

Gultrathaca's motion was assured, her speed dazzling. Not knowing what else to do, Rachel tucked in behind her, saving her strength for what was to come. They headed out over the Prag Sea, and somewhere in that unchanging region Rachel wished with all her heart to feel the touch of real sunshine. Ool's dawn offered little. There was no true warmth, no comfort of colour, nothing to repel the murk of the sky.

She tried not to look at the Griddas. They were a forbidding presence: arms sleekly out in front, brown fur flattened by the wind, their bodies supple and flexed – physiques of daunting strength.

Finally Rachel saw the bulking promontories of the Detaclyver.

And before it, like a bulwark across the world, rotated the mighty storm-whirls.

The Griddas headed straight for them. There was no gap between the whirls. Then Gultrathaca bellowed an order and they moved aside.

As Rachel approached she was merely a jangling speck. Deafening gusts blasted her hair, her clothes, her eyes. Instinctively, she turned her face towards her chest and lifted her hands to protect herself. As she did so, the uproar ceased. It became tranquil, peaceful, without wind, without cold. Rachel glanced around. The Griddas had all passed through the storm-whirls. Only she remained.

The storm-whirls had gently closed together around her.

Rachel gasped, hearing – oh, what was it? She put out her hands, dipped her fingers into the whirls. The sensation was not wind, not like wind at all. The storm-whirls enfolded her. And in that enfoldment Rachel felt their intelligence. She felt their anxiety about injuring her, and their fear of the Griddas whose spells enslaved them. But most of all Rachel felt their love: their magnificent, pounding, grave, reckless love for their ancient partner, the Detaclyver. For all the time they could remember the High Witches and Griddas had kept them apart. Whole families of storm-whirls were rooted to the Earth, forced to hold the Detaclyver back. The endless, painful creeping forward of the Detaclyver was nothing more than a desire to be closer to its companions.

Rachel bathed her face in the storm-whirls, wanting to stay there forever. She turned to gaze upwards, as if human eyes might be gazing back at her.

'Help me,' she said. 'Help me. I'm frightened.'

A terrible sadness groaned through the storm-whirls, and their winds held her head, but they said, 'We cannot. The spell-bonds are too numerous to break. We must pass you on. We cannot hold you.'

Rachel clung to the winds, trying to stay inside – and how the storm-whirls wished for that as well – but the thrall of the spells was too powerful. With a final departing sigh the whirls sent her through. For a few moments Rachel lay beyond, trembling.

Then she saw the Detaclyver.

The Detaclyver had never been mastered by the spells of any creature. It understood exactly what the Griddas had done to its beloved storm-whirls, and as Gultrathaca and the escort approached, its summits elongated into stabbing barbs.

The Griddas reacted at once. Trying to confuse the Detaclyver, they flew in several directions across the sky, giving it many targets. Gultrathaca dropped lower, searching for an entry point in the Detaclyver's skin. Finding one, she dived straight down, bit her way through and squirmed inside.

As soon as she disappeared great swarms rose into the sky: Essa.

In long surges they pushed back the remaining Griddas, keeping them away from Rachel. Another group of Essa surrounded Rachel herself. They carried her towards the Detaclyver, their tiny wings beating in welcome. 'Go in! Go in!' they cried.

'But Gultrathaca, she's –'

'No! No! Believe in us! Go in, up and away!'

When they saw Rachel hesitate, the Essa tried to calm themselves down. Couldn't she understand? Beautiful storm-friend, don't you know Detaclyver will keep you safe? Aren't we full of anxious hopes for you? Go in!

Rachel felt the Essa trying to will her into believing them. She felt their concern for everything: for her, the Detaclyver, for Eric, for the prapsies. Tiny lives, driven by hope, Rachel realized. How could the Essa survive on such a harsh world? Then she explored their magic, and knew at once that no other creatures needed it more. The Essa were held together only by magic. They navigated using magic, found each other with it; in the absolute bleakness and frost of Ool's night there was no other way for beings so frail.

Rachel stopped resisting them. She allowed the Essa to carry her body towards the opening in the Detaclyver.

'Take care! Take care!' the Essa called.

'Aren't you … aren't you coming with me?'

'No! No!' The Essa placed their bodies across the entrance, blocking the way in to the other Griddas. 'Detaclyver will look after you now. Go! Go to him! Go in!'

Rachel flew cautiously inside. There was no sign of Gultrathaca. Half-expecting to be pushing through skin and gristle, Rachel instead found herself in a kind of tunnel. Fresh air whooshed over her face, almost knocking her down. Then warm, staler air washed into her back.

Not a tunnel, her information spells explained. A capillary: a tube carrying breath around the Detaclyver's body.

Rachel put a foot forward – one step. As she did so, soft light on the capillary floor lit the way ahead. Another step. More light. Another. She walked up the capillary, reaching a fork. Left or right? The light glowed left.

I'm being shown where to go, she realized. The Detaclyver knows I'm here. Can it feel me? What if I run? I'll run!

Rachel picked up her feet and ran. Putting all her trust in the Detaclyver, she would have become completely lost except that the light guided her. Gradually the capillaries widened, until Rachel found herself rushing down broad lanes, all lit brightly. Then, as she turned a corner, a figure blocked her way.

Gultrathaca.

But at first Rachel could not tell. A light shone on

Gultrathaca so brightly that even Rachel could hardly stand it. Gultrathaca's eye-shields were half shut. Several of her watchers floundered blindly about the floor. 'The Detaclyver has done its best to stop me,' Gultrathaca rasped. 'But I see you. I still see you!'

Rachel looked for a way past. She could not go forward – Gultrathaca filled the exit. But there were smaller paths. They led off the main capillary, though none were lit. When Gultrathaca ran at her, Rachel picked the first.

Immediately, beneath her feet, the floor sprouted with spikes.

A trap.

Rachel fell to the ground. When she attempted to stand up her legs only twitched. She looked at her ankles. The spikes were already withdrawing. They left tiny holes. What was happening? Rachel felt no pain. She felt nothing – a lack of sensation.

Her information spells tried to explore her ankles, but for some reason they could not find the way. They felt ill, fatigued, vague. Lacking all clarity, they took an age to tell her:

Poison.

Healing spells drained into Rachel's veins at once, but her mind was hazy and so, therefore, were her spells. They went to the wrong places. With enormous effort Rachel managed to sit up.

Gultrathaca stood above her. 'Goodbye, Rachel,' she said. 'Enjoy the bliss. I left that for you.' She loped away.

For a while Rachel could hear Gultrathaca's heavy tread. Then she forgot about Gultrathaca entirely. A strange sensation suffused her body. It was one of profound contentment. Had she ever felt this happy? Her spells understood something was wrong, but they could not remember what. Rachel knew that she must be feeling the effects of the poison, but she had no desire to fight it, not any longer.

The poison entered her heart, and she did not mind.

Finally, she stopped caring altogether. And when that happened her spells also gave in. The finest of them, the spells that all Rachel's life had cared so much for her, even in the time she did not know they existed, stopped caring as well. All their beautiful light left her eyes.

Rachel lay down on her side. She placed her hands under her head. Her eyes wanted to close. She let them. She could no longer move. She didn't question why, not any more. It didn't matter. Her lips parted, falling slack as her jaw muscles relaxed under the final killing influence of the toxins.

She was dying.

Gultrathaca was forgotten. Yemi was forgotten. Mum, Dad, Eric. Everything.

17

the prison world

Eric sat cross-legged on the floor of his cell. The prapsies hadn't spoken for a long time.

'How are you, boys?' he murmured. 'You're very quiet.'

'We are well, Eric,' they said together. 'We are perfect.'

'You should have woken me earlier. I told you to.'

'We weren't tired. We aren't tired. Look.'

The prapsies spread their wings to show him how fit they still were. Not once had they complained while they were in the cell. Eric stroked their nape feathers the way they preferred it, thinking about the Essa. Little flakes. Snow-like beings. He would have thought the prapsies' minds had flipped, if he hadn't seen the Essa himself on the journey to Thûn.

Could he expect help from them?

No, he thought. Don't do that. Stop clinging onto the hope that something or someone else is going to rescue you. He couldn't even depend on Rachel this time. He knew that because he could sense her, a distant magical scent barely clinging to life. What was happening to her? He could also pick out another scent, a life even more precariously in balance than Rachel's. It belonged to Serpantha.

Well? Eric asked himself. What are you going to do about it? What are *you* going to do?

All morning he had been absorbed, thinking about Larpskendya. What had the Wizard meant when he said everything might depend on him now? What am I, after all? Eric thought. Just an ordinary boy, without any magic. I can't even climb out of this pathetically shallow little cell. Any kid nowadays can manage a basic heating spell, but not me. So the prapsies have to put up with being cold...

Could he do anything to affect the Griddas? The scraps of a plan were forming in Eric's mind, but it was too far-fetched for him to take seriously.

At least the experiments had stopped for a while. There had been peace all morning until a severely bruised Gultrathaca returned. Whatever had happened to her, she resumed the experiments again at once. This time, Eric noticed, she used Griddas, though they didn't come close to him. In fact, the opposite; for some reason the Griddas fired their spells at him from ridiculous distances, way beyond Ool.

There were grim shadows under the prapsies' eyes. Despite Eric's protests they had not slept at all, their eyes never leaving the doorway or open roof. 'I'll bet you want to fly, don't you?' he said, trying to cheer them. 'You must be bored, stuck here, not able to fly. Go on! Have a fly round!'

Briefly they flashed around the cell, though clearly only because Eric wanted them to. They quickly returned to him. One watched the cell doorway while the other bent its round head towards Eric.

'You must be hungry,' he said.

'No,' lied the prapsy. 'Are you?'

'Nah, I'm all right.' They both looked away from each other.

'Are you coldish, Eric?'

'No. Not a bit.'

'I could squash next to you if you want.'

'OK, but not because I'm cold, mind.'

The prapsy nuzzled up against Eric's cheek. It kept one eye on him; the other watched the empty ceiling. 'She's coming again,' the prapsy whispered, seeing movement there. 'Gultrathaca.'

'I know,' Eric answered. 'Don't worry. I'm ready for her.'

Gultrathaca approached Eric's cell. No sudden movements. No startling him. She knew how quickly his antimagic could demolish a body filled with magic.

While she walked healer spiders continued to perform repairs on her. The fury of the Detaclyver! She had been lucky to escape from its body at all, and the Essa had hounded her halfway across the Prag Sea.

She reached the opening above the cell and stood there, leaning down.

Eric! She almost liked the boy. The way he challenged her! Unlike Yemi, Eric did not smile or want to play. He mocked her gloriously. As she gazed at him now, a marvellous anger and bitterness enlivened his features.

'Are you coming down then, you hag!' he bellowed.

'In a moment,' Gultrathaca replied, composing herself.

She thought about Eric's special gift. She had seen it maturing in front of her eyes. Not his ability to destroy magic. That was remarkable enough, but more remarkable still was *how far away* he could detect magic. No Witch or

Wizard could come close to matching it. To fully test him she had unleashed magic from immense range, stretching her Griddas' spell-making in ways she had never asked of them before.

No matter how far-flung the distances, Eric knew each spell was coming.

Gultrathaca's ambitions grew larger with every new test, but how would she obtain his co-operation? Well, perhaps she could. Eric was not like Yemi. Yemi was impossible to manipulate, but Eric could be frightened. Hadn't she already placed him in a world of fear? It was time to free him unexpectedly from that fear. If I offer him hope for his sister, Gultrathaca thought, he'll want to believe it. If I promise him safety, especially for the prapsies, he'll be grateful to accept it.

Even so, at the edge of the cell, Gultrathaca hesitated. It would be so easy to misjudge this situation. It required of her a gentleness that did not come readily.

There would be lies amongst the things she would tell him. Amongst all the other lies would be one important one. Would Eric realize?

Controlling her anxiety, Gultrathaca bent over the lip of the cell and looked down.

Eric looked defiantly back. 'What now?' he sneered. 'Who are you sacrificing this time? Coward! Why don't *you* try attacking me? Do you think you're safe up there, out of my range?'

'I know you can reach me,' Gultrathaca said in the softest voice she could manage. 'But please ... don't. There will be no more things sent to hurt you. I promise. Whether you agree to help me or not, there will be no more attacks of any kind.'

'You *promise,* eh! Guess what? I don't believe you!'

'I am coming down.'

'I'll kill you if you do! I mean it.'

'When you hear my offer you will not want to kill me. I intend to release you, Eric.' Seeing that she had his attention, Gultrathaca floated into a corner of the cell, keeping her watchers in their pits to avoid alarming him.

Eric folded his arms. 'Well?'

'I will set you free,' Gultrathaca said. 'And I will deliver Rachel back to you.'

'Delivered dead, you mean.'

'No. Alive, Eric, and unharmed. I guarantee it.'

'Oh, I'll bet you do!'

Eric's voice was filled with sarcasm, but inside, inside, hope burst wildly through. He fought against it. He knew Gultrathaca was just playing some new game. How dare she! he thought. How dare she! As he gazed at her, he suddenly hated Gultrathaca with more intensity than he had hated anything in his life. Let her throw more Witches against him! That way he could at least stay mad, insulting, half-crazy. But this sudden new kindly version of Gultrathaca – if he listened to it, if he allowed himself even for one second to believe that there might truly be a way out of this, a happy ending – he would not have the nerve to follow through with his own half-plan.

That plan had been the only thing keeping him from falling to pieces already.

'I won't hurt you any longer,' Gultrathaca said. 'I will let you go, Eric. And I will free Yemi and Fola, too. I will free everyone. You can return to Earth. The Griddas will not bother you again. We – I – it is my fault – have made a terrible mistake in the treatment of your entire race. Forgive me.'

Eric nodded as if listening, but actually he was picturing how satisfying it would be see Gultrathaca's body deflate like a bag. He was picturing her as a smear on the floor. And this was no idle image. Eric could do it. Gridda magic was similar to the High Witches'. Gultrathaca had tried to shield her spells from him, but he saw through her.

She had no idea what torment Eric could place her in.

Uncertain how to proceed, Gultrathaca tried complimenting him. 'You never used your full gifts before, Eric, did you? See how deadly you've become! No more primitive finger-jabbing. You don't need to point your fingers any longer to destroy spells.'

Eric realized Gultrathaca was right – and he also realized how much he missed the finger-pointing part of him. It belonged to an older version of himself he wanted back.

'In return for freeing you,' Gultrathaca said, 'I'm not asking you to betray the Wizards or your own species. I'm asking for a simple thing, almost nothing. I want you to help me find the prison world of the Griddas.'

'What?'

Gultrathaca spread her claws over the rock floor. 'I placed you here for a reason. This cell is in one of the original tunnels. The early generations of Griddas lived here. They were just the same as High Witches then, with the same yearning for flight. They were crammed in here, in the dark, to make their eyes grow or wither, while the Highs experimented with them – us – in many ways.'

Eric knew Gultrathaca was telling a version of the truth at least. He could feel the imprint of the ancient Gridda spells. They were graven into the rocks from which they had tried to escape.

'Most Griddas have always lived on the prison world,'

Gultrathaca went on. 'The Highs did not want too many of us spoiling Ool itself.' She lowered her voice, looked away from him in the way she had seen humans do when expressing deep feeling. 'The prison world is a terrible place,' she said. 'Griddas are chained up. A few High Witches used to guard and feed them, but now we have taken over Ool I doubt that is taking place. Our Griddas will be dying there.'

Eric, observing Gultrathaca closely, said nothing.

'I know you can scent magic at considerable distances, Eric. All I ask is that you help us find this prison world. There are spells concealing it. The Highs did that to hide it from the Wizards, but they also kept the planet's location a secret from us. Do you know where it is?'

Gultrathaca asked the question in such a casual, offhand way, that Eric understood its importance at once. He tried to read Gultrathaca's expression. Was that a look of sadness? He couldn't tell if the sadness was real or manufactured for his benefit. But he could see Gultrathaca trembling. There was no doubting that.

He kept her waiting. Then he said, 'Yes, I know where it is.'

Gultrathaca held back her elation with difficulty. She had hoped – but not really believed – his gift could discover a place so distant. It had to be Orin Fen! No other world had such spells guarding it. Could the location of the Wizards' planet actually be in her grasp?

'How far is it … the … the prison world?' she asked, her voice cracking with the effort to keep steady.

'Why should I tell you?'

'Will you … will you not tell me?'

'No. Because if I do that you'll kill me. You'll just send in some animal with no magic to tear me to pieces.'

'No, Eric, I won't do that. I –'

'Shut up!' Eric said. 'Let me think.' He paced up and down the cell floor. He murmured to the prapsies. He lay down, put his hands behind his head, pretended to relax. Then he stood up, walked up to Gultrathaca and shouted at the top of his voice: 'I won't tell you, but I'll *show* you where it is if you absolutely promise to keep your word about Rachel, Yemi, Fola and Serpantha!'

'I will.' Gultrathaca's chest heaved.

Eric glared at her. He could see how much she would give him now, anything he asked for. 'Or maybe I won't show you,' he said. 'I tell you what: I'll agree to think about it, instead. That's all. And while I do I want a better place to stay than this. I want somewhere nicer.'

'Of course … of course, Eric. Whatever you want.'

'I'll tell you what I want, you ugly hag! I want you to warm this place up and give me and the prapsies a decent meal!'

Gultrathaca nodded vigorously. 'Will you help us then?'

'I'll give you my answer when I'm ready. Get out.'

Gultrathaca had never been so insultingly treated. Her jaws ached to kill Eric, but that pleasure would have to be delayed. Not wanting to irritate him or give him any reason to change his mind, she held out her claw awkwardly in the human way of parting.

'Just go away and leave me in peace,' Eric said, turning away.

Burning with rage, Gultrathaca held back her jaws and hurried from the cell.

As soon as she left, Eric started to shake. The way he had spoken! He saw how much she wanted to kill him! How could he have done something so dangerous? But it proved how important he was to her. Eric walked around his cell for a while, his mind distracted, trying to calm down.

The prapsies followed him.

'We'll be fed soon,' Eric told them. 'Good stuff. Get this place warmed up, too.'

'Don't trust Gultrathaca,' one of the prapsies said, running to keep up with him.

'Griddas, don't believe them biters,' the other whispered.

'Shush,' Eric said. 'Shush now. I know.' He stared at the walls, his mind far away. His plan might not be so impossible, after all. Gultrathaca had her own extensive hopes, but Eric's were just as ambitious. He remained still for a considerable time, watched by the agitated prapsies.

'What are you thinking about?' one enquired. 'What are you craftily thinking?'

'Nothing,' Eric said. 'Nothing at all.'

It broke his heart not to tell the prapsies what he was planning, but how could he?

'Eric, don't do anything to make the Griddas angry,' begged one. 'We're better now, better guarders. We will guard you better than before.'

'I know you will,' Eric whispered, gathering them up. 'It's all right. Gultrathaca won't hurt me any more. She won't hurt us at all.'

As he stood there, staring at the walls, not for a moment did Eric believe anything Gultrathaca had said. He knew she wouldn't free Yemi. And even if she freed Rachel, it would just be to murder her when she was no longer useful.

But was Gultrathaca telling the truth about the planet of imprisoned Griddas?

Possibly. As soon as she mentioned it, he had reached out for the magic of that distant world, and found it. There were protections around it, and invisibility spells. The magnificence of those spells! What else could they be concealing except Orin Fen? Eric penetrated the invisibility spells. Knowing that the Wizards had always hidden Orin Fen, he fully expected to find not Griddas but the magic of millions of Wizards on the world beneath. Surprisingly, there were none. Of course, the Wizards would probably hide their scent. But Eric knew with absolute certainty: if there were any Wizards he would be able to detect them – no matter what they did to try to hide themselves.

The planet had no Wizards on it at all.

So perhaps Gultrathaca really intended to take him to a world full of other Griddas.

Eric hoped so. It was exactly what he wanted.

18

tunnels

Wreathed in the final snarl of the poison, Rachel did not notice. Only her information spells, clinging on and listening out for her still, heard the sound. It seemed to well up from the bottom of the world: a warm, scented, fierce wind.

The breath of the Detaclyver.

And on that breath, riding it, came the Essa.

They did not need to beat their wings. The Detaclyver gave them all the speed they needed, boosting their little bodies along the capillaries. Would they be on time? Would they? They had helped before when Griddas tried to hurt the Detaclyver with such poisons, but this new being was far more delicate.

Through the capillaries. Beyond the lungs, up, up, up.

The Essa found Rachel lying on her side, the veins of her face turned black by the poison.

Without considering the danger to themselves, they leaped inside her half-open mouth. 'Quickly! Quickly!

Only the youngest!' Down her throat the smaller Essa flew, squeezing into her arteries. Their absorbent bodies took in the poisons. When they were filled nearly to bursting, the youngsters tottered unsteadily up Rachel's windpipe. Flopping onto her suit, they spewed out the poison – and returned for more. Long waves of them went continuously in and out until the most harmful effects of the toxins were removed.

Then, tired and woozy, and held proudly by their elders, the young Essa hovered a few feet from Rachel. They did not want to startle her.

Gradually Rachel's skin regained a healthier pallor. Her cold face twitched as the nerve-endings came back to life. When she was ready, the Essa helped her eyelids open. She blinked, and the Essa – diffidently – blinked back.

Rachel recognized them. She half-lifted a hand – and that was all the invitation the Essa needed. All their lively voices crowded into her thoughts at once: greeting her, naming themselves, tenderly touching her face, inquisitive and anxious.

'Hey, slow down, slow down!' Rachel said, half-laughing. 'Tell me – tell me what you are. About yourselves.'

The Essa would not do so. They only wanted to speak about the Detaclyver. Rachel learned it had once roamed freely across all the world. Ool had been warmer then, and the Detaclyver had wandered wherever the fancy took him, his edges billowing, accompanied by the majestic storm-whirls and his constant companions, the Essa. The arrival of the High Witches changed all of that. Over centuries, they beat the Detaclyver back to the south of the world. They enslaved the storm-whirls, encased the fish in ice oceans, and set about building the eye-towered cities.

But if the Witches expected the Detaclyver to forsake the storm-whirls, they were mistaken. The Detaclyver fought back. He heaved towards the cities, grappling with the foundations. The Witches tried to starve him. They tried to freeze him, ridding Ool of the warming sun altogether – replacing it with endless winter snow.

Even that did not stop the Detaclyver. Or his wilful Essa. Against his wishes, against all his wishes, they had decided on a way to fight back: to become like the snow themselves. The Essa did so, modified their bodies. For longer than they could remember they had hidden within the snow, defended and loved – defended the Detaclyver where they could, and loved the storm-whirls – whispering words of comfort through the long dark years, so the whirls knew the Detaclyver had never abandoned them.

Briefly, when the Griddas toppled the High Witches, the Essa had hope. But nothing changed. The Griddas simply continued the agonies inflicted by the High Witches.

While Rachel listened to the Essa, she remained still, allowing her healing spells to deal with the last of the poison. As soon as she felt capable she stood up – swaying.

'You are not ready,' the Essa said, holding her arm.

'I have to be. My brother, Eric … I have to find him.'

'Eric?' The Essa made a shape with their bodies – an outline of Eric lying down, the little heads of the prapsies close by him.

'You know where he is?' Rachel asked. 'You – you can find him?'

'Yes, but not yet, not yet!'

'We can't wait,' Rachel said. 'We've got to find Eric straight away. He hasn't got any magic. He won't survive if –'

'No! No!' The Essa, caught between wanting to reassure Rachel and another purpose, became agitated.

'What is it?' Rachel asked.

The Essa formed a new shape. The darker-hued ones gathered in places where brown would have dusted the wings. A few lined up as antennae: a butterfly.

'Yemi!' she gasped.

The Essa milled excitedly in the air, telling her what they knew.

'We'll find him, of course we will,' Rachel said. 'But if Yemi's survived this long against the Griddas, he can take care of himself. Eric needs –'

'No, Yemi first! Yemi!' the Essa insisted. 'Whispers. We hear them all. Whispers in the tunnels, don't you understand? He won't live. He can't. The Griddas won't let him!'

Rachel thought rapidly. Eric and Yemi were both captives under Thûn. How could she get there? 'I can't change shape, or shift,' she told the Essa. 'But I can fly. If I travel outside, in the air, could you hide me? Surround me, somehow?'

The Essa pondered. 'Yes,' they said. 'For a while.' Several fluttered deep into the Detaclyver to convey their decision. When they returned all the Essa clung to Rachel's body. 'Whoosh!' they told her. 'Detaclyver will start us!'

From the subterranean depths, many miles away, an immense diaphragm clenched and unclenched. Rachel felt her feet lift. Her magic steadied her, resisting. The Essa asked her not to, dancing ecstatically in the new wind.

Rachel let go – and the mighty breath took her.

Sideways she and the Essa travelled, gathering speed,

then up and away, into the summits. A peak shattered and ice particles showered down. Rachel went to cover her face, but the Essa laughed as none of the particles touched her. Up, up, still further up. Finally: the pallid light of sky. Just before the Detaclyver propelled Rachel into it, she had a moment of direct contact with its mind.

It offered her everything: passion, all its ardent wishes.

Then she was in the sky. Trembling with feelings – and hidden by the packed, determined bodies of the Essa – Rachel streamed northwards towards Thûn.

She passed over the storm-whirls. In their great stately way the whirls turned, giving no indication to the Griddas of what was coming. She skirted the edge of the Prag Sea, where fish peered up through the ice. When the breath of the Detaclyver petered out, Rachel's flying spells took over. Enveloped by the Essa, she travelled in the highest skies where enemy eyes were least likely to look. It was not until she entered the clouds over the snow plains leading towards Thûn that the first Griddas started to appear. The wind also veered, so the Essa were flying in a contrary direction to the real snow.

'Not safe to fly any more,' warned the Essa.

'But we're still so far from Thûn! We must get closer than this.'

'There is …' The Essa stopped. Rachel felt them shiver. 'Go down, go down,' they said. Copying the natural motion of the falling snow, Rachel drifted to the ground. As she landed, she could tell the Essa were striving to lower their voices. They were worried for her. They had braved the tunnels of the huraks many times, but Rachel was too big to hide. The blue cats would surely find her. Their breaths would put her to sleep, like the Griddas' spiders …

Reluctantly, the Essa told Rachel about the hurak tunnels under the plains. Some of those tunnels led to Thûn itself.

'Is there any other way?' Rachel asked, seeing how anxious the Essa were.

'No, but we will accompany you,' they told her without hesitation.

Rachel wanted to hold them when they said that, but how to hold something so small without injuring it?

Rachel's information spells searched beneath the snow. In one place a tunnel almost broke the surface. She hurried over the top. 'Stay close to me,' she said, using her magic to delve under the snow and grind through the rock beneath.

When the first chink of tunnel-light struck her eyes, Rachel drew back. The tunnel was a dazzling ultramarine blue. 'Why is it so bright?'

'Griddas don't like it,' the Essa explained. 'That is why.' They floated in little bunches ahead of Rachel, to meet the dangers first.

'No, you don't,' Rachel said. 'Get behind me. I'll use my spells.'

Determined to look ahead, a few clambered onto her forehead. The remaining Essa guarded her back, or positioned themselves on her arms to see what might be coming from any side tunnels. Rachel's body-suit felt strangely silky to them. They dug into the stitches, testing that their minute legs could pivot and turn on the material. When they were satisfied, Rachel used a spell to hush her footfall – and took her first step.

She travelled roughly northwards, but the hurak tunnels never kept a single direction for long. They were full of traps intended for Griddas: snares, blind spots, innumerable pitfalls, kinks, silences. Sometimes there were dark patches – perfect places to lie in ambush. Rachel's information spells guided her through. At every twist the Essa expected her to be put to sleep by sneaky hurak breaths, but there was no sign of the blue cats.

Rachel crept forward, occasionally flying in straighter parts where she could see ahead. The Essa became increasingly perplexed as they approached the perimeter of the city. Where were the huraks? They never left their tunnels so unprotected! A group of the Essa flitted down a tributary connecting to the tunnels of the Griddas. 'Empty! Empty, too!' they reported back. 'No Griddas!'

They left the hurak tunnels behind and entered new spaces, the residential networks of the Griddas. There were wide tunnels here, and spacious caves. All of them were vacant. Rachel flew at will through cave after cave. Recent Gridda tracks led from them. All the tracks – hundreds of thousands of claw marks – headed in one direction, towards the heart of Thûn.

'Listen,' said an Essa. Rachel heard nothing. 'Food traps,' the Essa explained. 'We should be able to hear them. Never silent, never quiet, always snapping creatures up for the infants. What does it mean?'

Rachel sent out her information spells. For miles ahead and all around there was no living creature of any kind. 'All the animals are gone, too,' she said. 'Everything.'

'Many have no feet or wings,' the Essa told her. 'How can they be gone?'

'Where do all these tracks lead?'

'Deep, into the deep,' the Essa said. 'The Assessment Levels. Yemi is there!'

'Hold on to me. As tightly as you can.'

'What are you going to do?'

'Trust me.'

The Essa anchored their feet to Rachel's clothes. They crept into her hair. Once they were firmly set, her eyes flashed blue. The colour was so intense it outshone even the hurak tunnels. Almost fearfully, the Essa stared at her.

Giving total freedom to her flying spells, putting all her faith in her magic, Rachel followed the Gridda tracks into the depths.

19

plans

While Gultrathaca awaited Eric's decision, she paid a visit to a former pack-member: the disowned and disgraced, the tainted Jarius.

What had happened to her in that brief time alone with Yemi? At first, when Jarius was dragged from the Assessment Chamber, Gultrathaca thought that Yemi must have passed on some kind of human infection. In fact, Jarius had never been healthier. The old Jarius had been a wreck of fears. The latest version was more poised; she unsettled the guards; a few had even started to listen to her talk of concord and an end to war.

As Gultrathaca arrived at her isolated cell, Jarius emerged with all her new-found serenity from the shadows.

'Welcome, sister,' she said.

'You are no sister of mine.' Gultrathaca circled her in frustration, humiliated by her continued existence.

Naturally she had tried several times to kill Jarius, but it was impossible. Yemi – even from the distance of the Assessment Chamber – shielded her with the same fervour as Fola.

Jarius shook her head sadly. 'The mighty Gultrathaca! I see it shames you to see me standing here, defying you, companion to a boy whose happiness you cannot even dent. But think differently: I am not your enemy, sister.'

'Oh, you are.'

'No. Look around you. There's open talk amongst the guards. Too many infants. The tunnels are overflowing. Skirmishes breaking out everywhere. Pack against pack scrambling for room. It's unbearable. I've heard the infants myself. They fly about the tunnels, restless, jeering at the adults, trying to provoke a reaction. What happens when you lose control, Gultrathaca? What then?'

Gultrathaca smiled. 'Do not concern yourself for me. I still have control.'

'Do you? You can hardly even control yourself. I know what you feel, Gultrathaca. It is the need for combat, for the violence of blood. You've been inactive too long. Like the rest of the Griddas, you can't wait to fight. That is what is driving your ambitions against the Wizards and the children, nothing else. I understand, because I feel it, too. It was bred into us by the High Witches, after all, this longing. But we can escape its pull. Yemi has shown me another way to live.'

'Don't prattle your peace to me,' Gultrathaca said. 'Fight me instead! Without the boy's assistance! I will remove the guards.'

'Why can't you understand?' Jarius said. 'Stop thinking continually in terms of conflict – you against me, the packs against Yemi, Griddas versus children. See beyond the tunnels! It is not merely the Wizards set against the Griddas. The whole simmering anger of Ool is turning on us. The Detaclyver has never been so active. There are Essa in the deeps. Huraks menace the home tunnels. While there is still time, find Rachel. Do everything you can to find her.'

'Rachel is dead.'

'No, she is alive, sister, alive.'

Gultrathaca tried to hide her shock.

'Yemi knows more than your own scouts,' Jarius said. 'Find Rachel. Free her, and make a truce with Earth's children and the Wizards. They want it, genuinely. There is no other way.'

'I would rather die,' Gultrathaca hissed.

'I know. That is what is so terrible.'

'No.' Gultrathaca approached closer. 'What is terrible, Jarius, is that you have forgotten the gloriousness of war. I have already sent an invasion force to Earth. It will kill all the children and adults on that world.'

'Kill them to what end? War for what purpose? And even if you succeed, what will be next for the Griddas? Will they simply go on finding new enemies, killing forever? Is that the great destiny Gultrathaca offers the packs?'

'A lifetime of fighting is all any Gridda seeks,' Gultrathaca replied. 'There is no higher honour. Once you understood that.'

'Do you think the Wizards will allow it? They will never do so. All Griddas may be killed. Are you prepared to be the cause of that? What gives you the right to make such a decision?'

Gultrathaca stared at Jarius, saw her concern to convince her, her anxiety for everyone and everything. It was the same expression Gultrathaca had seen in Fola, Rachel and the other children of Earth. It disgusted her. 'Even if we are all killed, there will be a magnificent fight first,' she said to Jarius. 'Following that, what does it matter? Why look beyond the next battle?'

'Those are not your own thoughts. That is what the Highs taught us.'

'In that regard they taught us well.' As Gultrathaca prepared to leave, Jarius beseeched her, 'Don't lead the packs against Earth. It will be a horrible slaughter.'

'Horrible? Horrible! Oh, Jarius, I pity you. Are you so sterilized that you no longer tremble with joy at the prospect of battle? War is what I want, what we all want. And not only war against the Earth. You're right about the infants: they *are* restless. To occupy them, I'll need to offer something special, and I intend to. I'll give them the Wizards as well. I'll give them the world of Orin Fen.'

'You won't find it. The Highs never did.'

'The Highs didn't have Eric.'

At last – at last! – Gultrathaca saw a quiver of uncertainty cross Jarius's face.

Eric lay back on his new bed, deciding.

His second cell was nicer than the old one had been, much nicer. Gultrathaca had fashioned him comfy chairs and warm blankets. Eric had no doubt she would have given him a cuddly toy if he'd asked. He even had pillows, frilly ones. He couldn't get over it. Did Gultrathaca really think he would be impressed with frilly pillows? Yes, he thought, she did. She didn't understand him at all.

Good. It meant his plan had a chance.

His hands rested lightly on the prapsies. They each had a little cushion of their own on the bed. At home, they would probably have been bickering over who got which cushion, but not here. They weren't even interested in the cushions. They just wanted to stay close to him. Normally they followed him everywhere, but in recent hours they had become inseparable. If Eric got up to stretch in the cell, they stretched with him. If he paced, they paced. If he decided to settle back on the bed, as now, they lay alongside, silent, never taking their blue eyes off him.

'You all right, boys?' he said, wedged between them.

'Yes, Eric,' replied one prapsy. 'But you are not. You are not all right, are you?'

'Oh, I'm fine.'

'No Eric, you are not fine.'

'That's enough. Be quiet now,' Eric murmured – and they were.

'Is there anything you want, Eric?' one asked, after a while.

'Just your company. Get some rest, now. I keep telling you that. Don't you two listen to a single word I say any more?'

The prapsies stayed silent. Eventually one said, 'We will do what you want.'

'Yes, we'll do anything for you, Eric,' the other said.

'I know. I know you will, boys,' Eric replied, his voice almost breaking. And he thought: you will have to; I'm going to have to ask everything of you now.

His fingers curling and uncurling in the prapsies' feathers, Eric forced himself to go over the plan again. As he did so fear pounded through him. He tried to ignore it. He tried, instead, to cultivate his hatred of the Griddas. He was able think more clearly when he shut out everything except that hatred.

Could he carry out the plan? Every time Eric thought about it, his mind moved sideways in terror. To reassure himself, he sent his spell-detecting talents out again. There it was: that big strange world so tantalizing to Gultrathaca. Was it truly a prison planet, full of Griddas? Maybe. Mixed signals like Griddas and High Witches leaked from it, but no Wizards; not once did he detect a Wizard.

The plan, the plan. He practised over and over what he must do.

Griddas lived beneath Thûn. They also lived beneath the other two immense cities of Ool, spread over a wide distance. Eric didn't know anything about those other places, but that didn't stop him reaching out to the Griddas who lived there, into every sinew of their magic. Gultrathaca thought they were safe. She thought that if the Griddas kept their distance from Eric he could not harm them. When he was in his old cell that had been the hardest part of all – waiting until the last possible moment to act against each attack, waiting until they reached his cell. His range was actually far greater than Gultrathaca knew. If she hadn't tested him from such distances, he would never have discovered it. His reach was vast. He could wrap his destruction around every Gridda on Ool. Now, lying here, on this bed, with his head resting on the pillow, he could kill them all.

It intoxicated and repelled him to think of it!

But while destroying all the Griddas on Ool was something, Eric's plan was more enterprising than that. He planned to destroy all those on the prison world, too. He would persuade Gultrathaca to bring as many Griddas as possible, and when they were close enough to the prison world, he would bring all the additional Griddas into his range as well. And, he thought, even if I can't kill them all, at least I'll damage them, hurt them badly. They'll be a long way from home, too far to make it back to Ool.

He realized how terrible these thoughts were. They were outrageous. He knew that. It was an awful thing he planned to do but, Eric reminded himself, he *had* to think like this. Hadn't Larpskendya said it might all depend on him now? Who else was going to deal with these appalling Griddas? There was nobody else. The Essa had not returned; Serpantha was only a wisp of life in a far-off dungeon. As for Rachel – Eric felt her racing towards Thûn, and no one knew better than he what she could do – but against a world of Griddas what chance did she have?

Better to act himself, before she died trying to save him.

There is no one else, he told himself. You have to do it. You.

What upset him most of all was that there was no chance of saving the prapsies. If his plan succeeded, if he killed all the Griddas, he and the prapsies would have to die in space with them. Eric didn't share this information with the prapsies. He didn't want to scare them any more than he had already done. There they were beside him – he never had to look for them – twitching, still in look-out mode, watching the door. How often had their vigilance already kept him safe? How often had their simple belief in him kept him from losing his spirit?

'It doesn't matter,' he said, with tears in his eyes. 'I *can* do it. I must.' He had spoken out loud, without meaning to. Gazing down at the prapsies, he found them gazing back at him with tremulous eyes.

'Do what? Eric, will you tell us?'

'I can't.'

'Eric, tell us!'

'Oh, I can't. I can't!' Unable to stand it any longer, Eric jumped off the bed. 'I'm ready!' he shouted. 'I've made my decision. Tell Gultrathaca I want to speak to her!'

The message was conveyed. When Gultrathaca entered his cell, she appeared as kind and considerate and thoughtful as he'd ever seen her before.

'We still haven't been able to find Rachel,' she started apologetically.

Eric cut her off. 'I assume you'll keep your word. I can't stand being here any more. If we're going to go to this prison world, let's do it now.'

'The Griddas are ready,' Gultrathaca said. 'I will protect you myself. Nothing will happen to you, I promise.'

Eric did not even look at her. 'I hope you have a large army.'

'I will be bringing most of the Griddas. How far is it?'

'A long way.'

Gultrathaca nodded. 'It is a good thing you are doing, Eric.'

'Yes,' Eric replied thickly. 'I know.'

Gultrathaca left Eric, trembling with excitement and apprehension. Had she succeeded? She hardly dared ask herself. After instructing the pack-leaders to make final preparations to depart, she retired to the solitude of her own tunnel for a while. One army was already dispatched, on its way towards Earth. It would menace the children, and occupy the attention of at least some of the Wizards.

But could she control the remaining packs? Would they really follow her all the way to Orin Fen?

While she waited for the main army to gather itself, Gultrathaca went to see Yemi one last time. To reach the Assessment Chamber, she had to thrust her way past hundreds of tunnel creatures. The trickle of animals that had always found their way to him now clogged nearly all the entrances. Amongst them, increasingly, were the lethal huraks. It seemed that all the blue cats for many miles around must be haunting the tunnels.

Dozens of tired Griddas met her eyes as Gultrathaca entered the doorway. Just keeping Yemi inside the Chamber was exhausting work. No Gridda pack could last longer than a few hours if he really wanted to test them. They always left dispirited, the containment spells they had spent years perfecting lying in pieces.

As this shift trudged out, Yemi followed the Griddas to the doorway, chatting good-naturedly. When he saw Gultrathaca he sauntered across the floor, offering her his usual guileless smile.

That infuriating smile! How Gultrathaca had come to detest it!

'*Sere*,' he said.

'No,' she replied. 'No more games.' You've won them all, she thought. We've nothing left to attack you with.

Yemi called over one of his ever-present hurak companions. Hopping onto its back, he used its ears as steering handles. The towering beast, all meekness, swayed dreamily at his touch.

Gultrathaca hated everything about Yemi now. She was

afraid of him, too. Only a fool did not fear what it could not threaten. She gazed at his delicate, frail skull, wanting to bite it – except, of course, the huraks would prevent her. Or, if they failed, his magic would prevent her.

And Yemi's magic *never* failed him.

Gultrathaca had already given up any hope of using Yemi as a weapon. It was only a matter of time, she knew, before he escaped. Then what would happen? No doubt he would return to Earth. Eventually the children or Wizards would find a way to tap into his immeasurable power. That could not be allowed. The only choice left was to kill him – before he prevented the possibility of even doing that.

Could she do it? The resources of the Assessment Chamber itself were formidable. To that she could add a combined assault by her most proficient Griddas. Based on her observations of Yemi, and all she had learned in a lifetime of fighting, Gultrathaca calculated that if a huge number attacked him at once even Yemi could not survive. She had already given the packs an advantage against him. Yemi could no longer shift. She had secretly used his own contact with Jarius to limit him. Did he even realize yet? Probably not. But he would soon. Fresh packs were waiting for him outside the Chamber.

Fola was near Yemi, watching over her brother as always. She picked him up. 'Why you no let us go? Why?' she said angrily to Gultrathaca. 'I wish Yemi would hurt you! I told him, but he no understand what you are!'

'I think he may soon,' Gultrathaca said. 'When he sees how many Griddas I am gathering against him.'

'What do you mean?'

Fola glanced at Yemi. His usual smile had faded. With

quick gestures, he motioned to his animals. All those within the Chamber rushed to surround him.

With immense satisfaction, Gultrathaca stared at Yemi. To wipe the smile finally from his face! His animals were frantic. As Gultrathaca left the Chamber, and saw Yemi's faltering expression, she no longer felt afraid of him at all.

In the afternoon the packs started to assemble at the designated departure points. An orange-brown haze suffused the skies over Tamretis and Gaffilex as the Griddas left in their millions. To watch the Thûn packs go, Gultrathaca flew to the top of Heebra's eye-tower. For hour after hour the packs emerged from the tunnels and swept into the clouds. It made Gultrathaca's heart leap to see the infants. They were taking orders again. Now that they faced the prospect of space, and had a reason to be frightened, they stayed without complaint next to the older Griddas. Real discipline had returned at last to the packs.

With great pride Gultrathaca raised her claws. A passing group acknowledged her with a harsh cry. Other Griddas joined in with them, their uncertainty forgotten, turning in majestic arcs to honour Gultrathaca before they left. She would join them, but not immediately. There was one thing to do first.

Gultrathaca forced her way through the animals to the Assessment Chamber. As she entered, Yemi looked up at her, no longer smiling.

Thousands of Griddas had encircled the Chamber, all with one purpose.

'As soon as the packs are gone,' Gultrathaca said to them, 'kill him.'

20

FREEDOM

Rachel flew at tremendous speed, barely staying in control as she navigated along the Gridda tunnels deep under Thûn.

Some of the tunnels were so cramped she had to flip her body on its side to pass through; others, those reserved for high-ranking pack-leaders, were like caverns. All were empty. More than empty. Rachel sensed events she needed to understand taking place above her – an enormous departure of lives and magic.

As she flew over a hole in one tunnel floor, she halted.

'No!' the Essa told her. 'Yemi is further.'

'Wait.' Rachel knelt down. A familiar scent wafted up from the hole. Normally her information spells would have picked it up much earlier. But it was weak, terribly diminished. 'Serpantha,' she whispered.

The Essa all fell silent. When Serpantha had first secretly arrived in Ool's skies they had wanted to follow the winds to him, but he moved too swiftly to keep up. They looked over Rachel's shoulder, blinking into the gloom.

'I know Yemi needs us,' she said, 'but I won't leave Serpantha. We have to go to him.'

The Essa briefly consulted, fluttering part-way down the hole. 'He is not alone. There are Griddas, too.'

'I know.' Rachel peered down the hole. It dropped vertically for over a mile. Moist smells drifted up.

'Newborns,' the Essa said. 'That is their smell, the smell of birthing levels. Why is Serpantha with them?'

'I don't know,' Rachel said. 'We'll go down.' She shimmied to the edge of the hole, letting her feet dangle while she calmed herself. 'Feet first,' she said. The Essa took stances on her shoelaces, or leaned forward on the toe caps, ready to confront whatever was out there. Once they were set, they squeezed her tightly. 'Go ahead, go ahead,' they said.

'Don't let go of me.'

'We won't,' they promised her.

Slowly – using her magic as a brake – Rachel slid down the hole. After a long descent a chute dumped them out. The Essa sprang from her at once, fanning out protectively. Before them lay the humid levels of the birthing chambers.

Rachel threw the entrances open.

Normally there would have been thousands of boisterous young Griddas to greet her, all the unrestrained cries of new life. Instead, there were only a small number of newborns. These gazed up with open curiosity when they saw the strangers, too young to know any fear. A few were actually biting a path out of their eggs, or, freshly hatched, tottering uncertainly about on the slippery floor. In a corner a tangle of sisters appeared to be playing a game.

Not a game, Rachel suddenly realized. The scent of Serpantha was on these infants.

She rushed over with the Essa. The closest newborn hissed – and another, liking that sound, copied her.

With fury, Rachel screamed, 'Get away from him!' She raised about herself a sheath of power even the newborns could not mistake, and they fled into a tributary tunnel.

Rachel and the Essa were alone with Serpantha.

The lips of the Wizard were bound with spell-thread. The Essa helped Rachel remove it. They did so delicately, to avoid cutting into him any more than the thread had already done. Inside his mouth there was more thread. As the last thread was removed from his tongue, Rachel felt all Serpantha's ancient spells sigh with relief.

Alive, Rachel realized. Alive!

The Essa flew joyfully around Serpantha, wanting to go into his body, but afraid that he was so fragile they might hurt him in doing so.

All the lovely inner radiance had left Serpantha's features. His face, petrified by the poisons and spells of the Griddas, was grey. His eyes were shut; his hands were clenched, the fingers bound many times over with spell-thread. As Rachel removed the thread, she caught the scent of the latest attacks on the Wizard. They came from the infants she had just chased off. In the end, Gultrathaca had simply laid Serpantha out on a platform of stone for the newborns to practise on.

Rachel wondered: did she dare lift him? She placed her ear against his chest, against his heart. Slow and uneven, it still murmured. And something else was alive within him – as soon as they felt Rachel's touch, Serpantha's spells knew she was there. In their elation, they called out, 'Heal him! Help us! Help us!'

The Essa did not wait for Rachel. They fluttered inside Serpantha's mouth. There was so much damage they had no idea where to start. Quietly, listening, they started work, letting Serpantha's spells advise them. Eventually they re-emerged. 'He can be moved now,' they told Rachel. 'But carefully.'

Serpantha's aquamarine robe was covered in filth. Rachel placed her left arm under his body, preparing to lift him. She gasped as she felt how light he was – virtually no weight at all. It was as if the only thing that had held the Wizard together all this time was the grandeur of his magic.

How should she carry him? It seemed wrong to do anything except hold him in both her arms, but Rachel needed to be more practical. In the end, she pulled him to her waist, clasping him there easily with one hand.

'You need both arms,' the Essa said. 'We will carry him. Allow us!'

Rachel started to hand Serpantha to them. The Essa stopped her. They started jerking in the air, holding each other up. 'What is it? What is it?' they cried.

Never in her life had Rachel felt anything like this: spells; thousands of them; spells everywhere, a deadly Gridda assault. She staggered, barely able to take in the scope. This was not an attack by one Gridda on another, or pack against pack. It was a concentration of spells on an unimaginable scale.

All the spells were focused on a single being.

Yemi.

Rachel felt him. The greatness of his magic, brought to sudden desperateness, pulsed like a generator amid the lesser scents of the Griddas. But there were thousands of Griddas; there were too many. Rachel pulled Serpantha close and flew out of the birthing caves. She did not need to use her magic to trace Yemi; the battle-cries of the Griddas were enough. They led her upwards – Yemi was trying to escape.

'Hold onto me!' Rachel told the Essa.

Her flying spells gave her all their speed up the winding tunnels. As she rose, she swerved past Griddas aching to get to the land above. Higher still, the tunnels breaching the surface were so full of Griddas that even Rachel's magic could not plot a way around. She had to slow down – enough for the Griddas to sense her, and turn.

'Don't try to fly past them,' her information spells advised. 'The quickest way is not through the tunnels.'

'Which way, then?'

'Directly up.'

The rock overhead was hard, but not hard enough to withstand Rachel's magic. She smashed through. Shielding Serpantha's head with her hands, she broke out to the surface. The Essa followed. For a few moments they shut their eyes against the suddenness of light.

Then they saw the number of Griddas.

'Quickly! Quickly!' Some of the Essa hammered at Rachel's lips. They wanted to be inside her now, where they could assist her best if she became injured. Rachel let them in her mouth, hardly noticing the light tickles on her throat. The remaining Essa formed a defence in front of her, calling out fierce words of encouragement.

At a lower pitch, Rachel heard another voice. It was faint, muffled, a human voice: Yemi's.

The Essa looked frantically for him. Rachel knew where

he was. High up in the metal-grey sky. Yemi could not be seen because he was engulfed by Griddas. Hundreds of them, in well-organized packs, were attacking him.

There were noises from the ground. When Rachel stared down she could not believe what she was seeing. Wherever a Gridda tried to leave a tunnel, it was under siege. Animals that were feline and immense had taken up positions around each tunnel exit: the huraks. Wherever Griddas emerged, the blue cats fought them, cutting great swathes through their ranks.

Then a separate movement caught Rachel's eye, and another.

She shook her head, striving to understand.

It was not only the huraks who had come to Yemi's aid. Standing alongside them were rodents. Biting the clawed feet of the Griddas were insects. Trying to confuse them were burrowers. Even the slime mosses had dragged themselves from the depths. These shy creatures, who never normally left the darkness of the tunnels, in their devotion to Yemi came now. Facing the agony of the light, they threw their little bodies at the Griddas. The creatures of Ool wriggled through cracks; they slid from the snows; and they came from the air. From the south, Essa had arrived, fanned by the breath of the Detaclyver.

Despite this punishment, the Griddas continued to harry Yemi. With Essa clinging to their jaws, time after time they smashed into him, varying their spells, attacking in long persistent waves without respite.

Rachel soared towards them. When the Griddas detected her, two packs – over a hundred Griddas – detached themselves from the main group to confront her.

Understanding at once what they must do, the Essa took Serpantha from Rachel – and carried him to safety across the sky.

Rachel did not stop to think. As soon as Serpantha was out of her arms she dived towards the main group surrounding Yemi. She struck with unwavering force and all the capability of her magic. She could not break through – but she caused a moment of uncertainty.

And that was enough. Yemi took his chance. He broke free.

Magnificently, he rose above the Griddas.

Rachel's heart leapt as first she saw his head, then his bright orange T-shirt and baggy shorts. With a bent arm he fended off several infants; with the other he held onto Fola. The Griddas dwarfed Yemi, following him up, trying to separate him from his sister. At first Rachel thought Yemi might get away. The next moment her information spells reported back how little strength he had left. After so many attacks, even Yemi's extraordinary magic was faltering.

'Yemi, shift! Why don't you shift?' she shouted. Then she understood – he couldn't. 'Come to me!' she called out, racing towards him. 'Oh, Yemi, come towards me!'

He heard her. Even amidst the shrieking Griddas, Yemi heard her voice. He turned his imperturbable eyes towards her, and as he did so Rachel sensed new spells. Protection spells. Yemi was sending them. Thinking that Rachel needed his assistance, he was using the last of his strength to guard her.

'No! No!' Rachel screamed at him. 'I didn't … stop it! I didn't mean that!'

Yemi was confused. Rachel was coming too close to the

Griddas. Why? Why didn't she fly away? He held her back, while continuing to send out magic to shield her.

'No, don't do this! Don't!' Rachel wailed. 'Yemi!' A pack of Griddas launched a massive combination of spells against her. Rachel was thrown back, and would never have survived without Yemi's assistance.

But the attack drained him. Yemi could not sustain his shield. Finally he had to choose between protecting Rachel or Fola. He could not make this choice. It was too much.

He wavered – and the Griddas broke him.

Roaring in triumph, they tugged and jarred Yemi across the sky. Two infants took their chance. They snatched Fola, dragging her to the Griddas on the surface.

Yemi cried out – a feeble, lost voice. In disbelief he stared at the hand that had held Fola. Then he came after his sister. Still keeping his protections around Rachel, he entered the Gridda packs on the ground. The huraks tried to reach him, but could not. Rachel was held back by the Griddas. It took all her strength to simply survive their attacks. On the horizon the tiring Essa who carried Serpantha had almost been caught by a group of infants.

Then Yemi re-emerged. Clutching Fola, Griddas scraping at his legs, he rose into the sky. But it had cost him everything to retrieve his sister. One more ripple of attacks, a minor one, was all it took to shatter his last defence. And when that happened the protection around Rachel crumbled. Yemi gazed forlornly at her. He whispered an apology. He stared at Fola, letting out a moan. He kissed her, slow despair creeping over his face.

And then Yemi's features suddenly hardened. Facing the Griddas, he thundered: '*Iro!*'

He turned. He looked southwards. He looked in the direction of the Detaclyver.

And a sound came from there. No Gridda living under the cities of Ool had ever heard it before.

In Yemi's final desperation he had called the storm-whirls.

And they came. First they were a shadow on the southern horizon; then a great scouring of wind that obliterated all in its path. Freed at last from their long servitude, the whirls burst the ice over the Prag Sea. Snow plains became turmoil; defences were shattered; Griddas ran and could not escape; the last shards of the eye-towers were annihilated. Nothing could slow the storm-whirls down. A group of infant Griddas, urged on by their pack-leader, flew to confront them, and were swallowed like scraps.

As the storm-whirls approached the heart of Thûn, the disarrayed Griddas broke off their attacks on Rachel and Yemi. Where it was possible, they fled to tunnels.

A single immense storm-whirl was the first to reach Yemi. As it neared him it slowed down. Its winds calmed. Yemi put out his arms, and he and Fola were drawn inside. Once they saw he was safe, the remaining storm-whirls took up new positions to hunt down any Griddas they could find. Yemi, without a word, drew their attention to him. He shook his head, no.

The storm-whirls stopped.

Yemi's concerned gaze took in everything. He understood the danger. He knew that in his damaged condition, with thousands of Griddas still wanting to kill him, he could not risk staying. But that meant leaving all his friends behind. Tearfully he glanced over them: the majestic storm-whirls, the timid rodents, the magicless insects, the slime mosses no one else cared about at all. He thought of Jarius, and wondered what more he might have done for her. On the ground, his loyal and bloodied huraks raised their muzzles. Wreathed in frost, they bayed at him, over and over.

Wanting to let him know she was not badly harmed, Rachel lifted a hand. He smiled, waved to her. Fola took her brother's other hand. She raised it for them all to see. A silence followed as every creature knew what would happen next.

With a long sob, Yemi pressed his face against Fola's dress. His storm-whirl ascended, thrusting beyond the outer rust-tinted clouds. At the edge of space it could go no further. It waited. Yemi blinked at the darkness beyond Ool. The anti-shifting spell of Gultrathaca still lay on him. He did not know how to conquer it yet, but he would soon. Until then he could fly. No one understood how fast Yemi could fly. Even he did not fully understand. Holding Fola's hand, he pushed out into the coldness of stars.

For a while everyone watched the mighty storm-whirl as it returned to the ground. Then the Essa, who had kept Serpantha safe, asked Rachel to take him while they tended to their own battered companions.

'Is there still hope for us? For Detaclyver?' they questioned timidly.

'Yes. While Yemi's alive, there will always be hope,' Rachel said.

She turned to look out over the world. In the aftermath of the battle, Thûn lay desolate. The last standing eye-tower, Heebra's, had been atomized by the storm-whirls. Uncanny winds stirred the skies. So much snow had been lifted into the air by the passage of the storm-whirls that clouds of Essa wheeled in great aimless swarms, having difficulty finding their way back over the Prag Sea. On the surface, huraks roamed in small groups; they pawed the snow longingly. The storm-whirl that had transported Yemi to the refuge of space turned solemnly on one spot, not wishing to leave.

Griddas were scattered everywhere. Still stunned by the impact of the storm-whirls, they flew raggedly about the sky or wandered in a daze amongst the snows, searching for missing pack-members.

Gazing at them, Rachel sensed something was wrong. She sent her information spells beyond Thûn, to the cities of Gaffilex and Tamretis. 'They've left,' she said. 'All the Griddas have gone. That feeling I had earlier...the Griddas here are the only ones still on Ool.' Eric? She trembled, searching for his scent, not a magical one, but his real human scent, or the tell-tale rhythm of his heart. They were missing. Without her needing to ask them, Rachel's information spells sought with all their skilful brilliance for any trace of the magical signals of the prapsies. Nothing. They tried to disguise this knowledge from Rachel, but she knew them too well. Tears poured down her face, wetting the Essa.

'Where...where have the Griddas gone?' she murmured.

'Your world,' the Essa said, catching the tears. 'We think so. A few Essa heard in the tunnels. The Griddas spoke of it.'

Rachel stared at the sky. 'I've got to get back home,' she said. 'I've got to warn them what's coming.'

'We will accompany you,' the Essa said. 'Detaclyver has asked us, and we wish it even if he did not. We are resolute.'

'No,' Rachel said. 'You've done enough already. I –'

'It is not enough! Not enough!' The Essa's voices were fierce. 'Take us!' They dug themselves into her clothes, and feeling their conviction Rachel did not argue.

The Griddas had begun to reconvene their packs. Rachel wasted no more time. She flew with the Essa into the clouds. But before she left her breath caught in her throat, for a beautiful thing was taking place in the south: the storm-whirls were on the move. Travelling at great speed Rachel saw the first ones reach the Detaclyver and wander in half-crazed joy across its body.

Whatever happens, Rachel realized, Ool will never be the same again. She turned away, tears of happiness mingled with sorrow in her eyes and heart.

'Oh Eric,' she whispered. 'Where are you?'

21

Departure

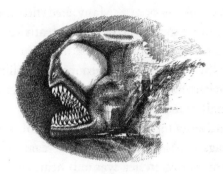

With Eric indicating the way, Gultrathaca led the main army towards Orin Fen. It was the largest force of Griddas ever assembled. Gultrathaca could not see the extent of it: wave after wave, pack upon pack, millions of Griddas making their way across the permanent nightfall of space.

Only a limited number of Griddas could shift, so Gultrathaca had to be content with the lesser speed of flight spells. But the pace was not too slow, because the weakest flyers who could not keep up were left behind. There were Griddas who lost their minds amid the maze of stars. These were also abandoned. Such minor losses meant nothing given the size of the army.

And it showed all the packs there was no going back to Ool – no slinking back to the comfort of tunnels.

There was constant friction between the younger and older Griddas. As soon as they became familiar with the peculiarities of space, the infants again started flouting the authority of the pack-leaders. They were loud, excitable, full of aggression. Gultrathaca tolerated such indiscipline, knowing that she would need all their energy to have any chance of defeating the Wizards. The pack-leaders kept a rough order. Often it was the adult Griddas who needed most support. Many had never learned to enjoy flight. And the flight demanded of them now was without respite, into emptiness.

One Gridda, however, seemed calm enough: a guest who had invited herself – Jarius. At first Gultrathaca had refused her last-minute request, but just before they set off she changed her mind. There was no more unforgivable crime amongst Griddas than to turn against your own pack-members. Gultrathaca wanted Jarius in the first line of assault troops. If she refused to fight, or fought ineffec-tually, her pack-sisters would kill her. It was fitting. Gultrathaca noticed that Jarius did not seem concerned for her own welfare. She paid no attention to the nearest Griddas, even when they bit her. She appeared more con-cerned about someone else: her eyes were always on Eric.

Eric! The enigmatic Eric!

What, Gultrathaca wondered, was she to make of him? He showed the way to Orin Fen without complaint, yet he gave her as little information as possible. On the journey she kept up the lie about the Gridda prison world, and Eric seemed satisfied, but he asked no more questions about it. Perhaps he did not really believe her. Gultrathaca was troubled about that, though she had little enough time to worry about it. Keeping the army on the move required all of her effort. There were no rests, no rocky places to hide in. The Griddas fed on the move. By threatening and coaxing the pack-leaders somehow kept them in motion between the constellations.

Finally, Eric said, 'We're getting close.'

'How much further?' Gultrathaca asked.

He looked up at her. 'You can't tell yet?'

'No. I do not have your gifts, Eric.'

His gaze held her for a moment; then he turned back to the prapsies, resuming his customary silence.

Gultrathaca passed the new information to the pack-leaders. Her heart pounded as she thought about the great train of events she had started. What opposition would they find on the Wizards' world? Larpskendya was awesomely powerful, and there were others of similar strength, such as Serpantha. It was remarkable how that Wizard had held out for so long against her; no Gridda could have done it.

How many more like Serpantha would there be on Orin Fen?

Yet there was no choice other than to go on. Nothing less than a quest of this greatness would keep the fragmenting Gridda packs together. And there was a personal reason, too. Jarius was right about her; Gultrathaca felt born for this time. All her instincts drove her towards blood and the clarity of battle.

But everything, everything depended on Eric.

How best to make him comfortable? Gultrathaca encircled him in her arms, in the same odd way she had seen Fola encircle Yemi. She let him rest. He did not seem to want to talk at all, so she rarely spoke, either. She could not properly imitate the parent-figures of Earth, but occasionally she whispered nonsense into Eric's ear in that private way she had seen Fola do with Yemi.

The journey was a long one, and during it Gultrathaca tried to make Eric feel safe. She let him lean against her body. She made no threats. She spoke kindly. Sometimes she ruffled his blond hair. It was a peculiar gesture, difficult to achieve without injuring his scalp, but Eric seemed to like it – or, anyway, he did not tell her to stop. She even tolerated the prapsies. Each time their small round faces popped out of Eric's shirt, she wanted to bite them. She restrained herself. When they spat at her, she laughed.

Eric's eating habits required special attention. When she fed him it was not with the live or raw food her Griddas consumed, but prepared the way he preferred: heated and stripped into nondescript pieces, so he could not tell what animals it came from.

How much that alone said about these humans!

Even so, as the army swerved to avoid the massive gravitational pull of a red giant sun, Gultrathaca wished she could enter Eric's mind and read his thoughts. He did not appear to have any special worries. He asked about his sister from time to time, understandably anxious. Otherwise, he just pointed the way. Such behaviour was co-operative enough, but could she trust him? No. Because he hid things from her. He would not explain the way, only lead her. He also tried to stop the prapsies' insults. That showed he did not really trust her not to harm them. None of this mattered. She would continue to raise his spirits and keep him close. He could not breathe without her knowing.

'How far now?' she questioned from time to time as they flew.

'Nearly there,' was his usual reply.

She tried to smile as if she cared for him.

Possibly, Gultrathaca realized, Eric had a plan of his own – something simple. She did not underestimate him. She knew just how devastating his power could be at close range. When they reached Orin Fen, and he discovered that it was the Wizard world, who knew what he might try? Perhaps he would try to kill her. As long as the Wizards were destroyed and part of her pack survived, Gultrathaca could accept that – though it would be a pity to miss the battle. However, she did not intend to hand her life away easily. If he planned to give her any trouble, she was ready. When the army arrived at their destination, she had her own plan to deal with little Eric.

Eric nestled against Gultrathaca, pretending he could stand her touch.

She cradled him with all the subtlety of a mechanical press. So what: he endured it. He endured the spiky way she ran her claws over his head. He leant close against her, pretending that was nice, and in a way it was because it meant he could withdraw from the hideous spectacle of the Gridda army. He moaned a little about the journey – not too much, just enough to prove he wasn't hiding his feelings. He sometimes even asked her questions about Rachel. It was painful, but surely it would seem weird if he didn't ask. He did it to show Gultrathaca that he was still clinging to her promises, like a scared kid.

Am I a scared kid? he asked himself.

Yes, he thought. I am. And that was all right, as well. It was all right to be frightened as long as he didn't become too frightened to do what he must do.

As he passed another cluster of stars, one of the prapsies said, 'Eric, your face is wrong. It's twisted. What's the matter?'

'Nothing,' Eric said, holding them both to his chest. 'Nothing at all.'

'Are you cold, Eric?'

'I thought I told you both not to talk to me. You know I'm busy. I'm thinking hard, boys. Don't interrupt me.'

'We know, but are you cold, Eric?'

'No.' They were silent again.

'Are *you*?' Eric asked.

'Yes, we are.'

Eric bent towards them, and realized that neither prapsy was cold. They had only said that to get him to look at them.

'What are you imagining in your brain?' one whispered.

'Nothing at all,' Eric said. 'Don't ask any more questions, now.'

'Why, Eric? Why can't we?'

'Shush. Just be quiet, boys. I'm thinking.'

'What are you thinking?'

I wish I could tell you, Eric thought. Oh, I wish I could share it all with you! The prapsies could be trusted with his secret, of course, but if Gultrathaca overheard or suspected, who knew what she would do to them.

Finding it impossible to look at the prapsies without it making him crazy, Eric did not look at them. Instead, he tried to harden his heart. When the time came to act, he had to be able to do it clinically. So he practised ignoring the prapsies. The silent anxiousness that followed only made things worse. All he could feel was their puzzled eyes eternally focused on him. Once, after a particularly long stretch of quietness, he couldn't bear it any longer.

'That was a stupid thing the two of you did,' he said.

'What, Eric? What was stupid?'

'Back in the cell. Trying to get all those animals and Witches to attack you instead of me. And staying there.

Staying there instead of flying off, when you had the chance. I told you to go. Stupid, really stupid. You could be free now, hiding somewhere safe with the Essa.'

'We did it for you, Eric.'

'It was stupid, that's all. You could have escaped, you know.'

'We didn't want to. Not without you.'

Eric said nothing for a while. Then, in the softest of voices, he said, 'I'm so proud of you both.' Both child-birds nuzzled him and Eric found himself adding something he didn't mean to say. He had to keep his distance from them, because of what he must do soon. 'Don't ever leave me again,' he said.

'We won't, Eric. We'll stay with you always.'

Eric turned away from them. He closed his eyes, attempting unsuccessfully to put the prapsies from his mind. To help with that, he focused again on Gultrathaca. She was obviously suspicious about his behaviour. What if she became too suspicious and decided not to go with him all the way? What if she decided to kill him before they arrived?

The madness of it! Trying to fathom what would keep Gultrathaca satisfied!

However, Gultrathaca became easier to deal with the longer the journey continued. It gradually became clear to Eric that his good-boy act was wasted on her. All she really cared about was getting to the new world. So he kept her happy about that, showing the way, more and more certain he was safe at least until they got there.

No mistakes now, he thought, not this close. They had almost reached the prison world, or whatever it was. The same odd traces like those of Griddas and High Witches seeped from it, but nothing distinctive. He didn't tell Gultrathaca. To anyone except him the traces would have been entirely hidden. Sometimes he sent his deft detections towards the Earth. He knew all about the second Gridda army heading that way, of course – how could he miss such a stench of magic! But there was another scent as well, a marvellous surprise, one he knew well: the scent of Yemi, heading home at some kind of miraculous speed.

Eric felt better, knowing that.

When he could no longer endure to lie against Gultrathaca, or look at the prapsies, or think about what lay ahead, Eric would gaze out over the Gridda army. Strangely, he seemed to have a friend amongst this wilderness of bodies. He did not know who she was, but whenever he glanced over in the direction of one Gridda, she glanced back. As he studied her now, he saw a curious expression. If what there was of a Gridda's face was capable of showing affection, he might have been seeing it.

Eric turned away from her. It was probably not an expression of affection at all – just his own wishful thinking! Anyway, he had to put this perplexing Gridda out of his mind as well. When he launched his anti-magic spell on all the Griddas, he could not exclude her. As a Gridda, she would have to suffer the same fate as all the others.

In his mind, Eric encompassed the entire Gridda army with his destruction.

The destroyer of spells, he said to himself. That's what I am. The spell-destroyer. He tried to feel at ease with that. He couldn't, but this didn't stop him rehearsing over and over what he would do.

At some point Gultrathaca broke into his thoughts. 'Are we nearly there?' she asked again.

'Nearly,' Eric told her.

'Then we can free our Griddas,' she said. 'It has been many generations since we spoke with them. I will ask nothing more of you, Eric. And I will keep my other promises. I will deliver Rachel safely, if I can. I'll take you back to Earth. You will have a place of honour in our memories, and there will be no fighting with the children of your world. There will be an end to fighting.' She paused. 'I am grateful for everything you are doing. We all are.'

'Thank you,' Eric rasped.

22

the preparation of the sentinels

With Serpantha secure in her arms, Rachel set out to catch the Griddas heading towards Earth. Already weary after the battle for Yemi, she had never needed to put so much faith in her flying spells. Gradually she closed on the Gridda army. Taking a long arc around, she overtook them, and for a while pulled far enough ahead to imagine that she, Serpantha and the Essa were the only ones soaring through the bleakness between stars. At last, however, her flying spells began to falter. Transporting Serpantha had drained them more than they were willing to admit.

'Nearly home,' Rachel murmured, urging them on.

'Yes,' they said, offering her what they did not have.

While Rachel laboured, Serpantha lay quietly in her arms. None of the Wizard's great strength had returned, but the Essa had worked tirelessly inside him, and he could think again. He thought about Rachel. Sensing her exhaustion, he secretly questioned the Essa, and judged the distance to Earth.

Too far. The Griddas would catch Rachel before she could make it back – unless he helped her.

The Wizard opened his many-coloured eyes. 'Hello, courageous one.'

A huge happiness spread through Rachel. 'You're… you're awake!' she cried, hugging him, then loosened her grip in case it hurt. 'Oh, Serpantha!'

His gaze held her tenderly. 'How ungracious of me to have held you back,' he said. 'With nothing to offer in return.'

'That doesn't matter!' Rachel said. 'Don't be silly! Of course it doesn't! All that matters is that you're getting well again! Do you want anything? Do you need something?'

'You've already given so much,' Serpantha answered. 'Yet I do have one more request to ask of you.'

'Anything!'

'I need you to let go, Rachel. You cannot make it back to Earth in time unless you leave me behind.'

'What? No, that's not right,' Rachel said.

'It's true, Rachel. You know it is. Your own spells have been saying so for some time. You have been ignoring them.'

Steadfastly Rachel stared ahead, aside, anywhere except at Serpantha. She could feel his eyes burying into her. 'I can't!' she wailed. 'I can't leave you! I won't!'

'You must!' This time, at the top of his voice, Serpantha bellowed it. 'Rachel, everything might depend on you reaching Earth in time to give a warning. Do you want the Griddas arriving at your house to kill your mother and father? Because that will happen! Is that what you want? Is it?'

'The spectrums will realize we're coming,' Rachel said, convincing herself instantly. 'Of course they will. Heiki will know. They'll be prepared.'

'We can't be certain of that,' Serpantha said. 'You can't risk everything for me, Rachel. I won't allow it.'

Rachel twisted her head away, flying at renewed speed away from the Gridda army. 'I still can't shift!' she said, over and over. 'Why can't I shift, why can't I!'

'Please, Rachel,' Serpantha said. 'You can come back for me.'

Rachel knew there would be no going back for Serpantha. He knew it, too. The Griddas would tear him to pieces as soon as they found him. It would be better to kill him swiftly, now.

Rachel looked at him, and felt her death spells rise up.

Serpantha sensed it too – and he did not object.

'Use them,' he said.

Rachel thought of Mum and Dad. She thought of everyone else on the vulnerable Earth. She knew that unless she was to put the balance of all their lives in danger there was only one thing to do.

It was the right thing to do. Serpantha knew it, and so did she.

'It's all right,' Serpantha whispered. 'You can do it. It's all right, Rachel. It's all right.'

Rachel's deaths were like savages, banging on her mind.

She looked at Serpantha. 'I have an answer for you and my deaths.' Tightening her grip on Serpantha, she continued flying towards home.

'Rachel, let me go!'

'No,' she said lightly, stroking his face. 'Not that way.' She ignored her deaths. She held Serpantha even more tightly. He tried to fight her, but she fought him back. Putting all her trust in her flying spells, she headed for the Earth.

Gradually the army of Griddas closed on them. The vanguard became visible, and they saw her. Rachel no longer had the strength to outrun them.

'Help me!' she cried to the Essa.

'We are! We are! Fly on, Rachel! Fly on!' Without Rachel noticing it, the Essa had long been bolstering her magic, plundering all their strength to give her a little more.

Rachel continued to stay barely ahead of the Griddas. An hour went by, more. The rim of the solar system swam in view. Rachel passed Pluto. She crossed the orbit of Neptune. Were her flying spells still carrying her, or was she dragging them half-dead between the worlds? Jupiter fell behind. Saturn's rings. Mars.

There. Earth was a beautiful creamy-blue, though she could not make it in time.

The Essa realized that. All the journey they had stayed quiet, their efforts put into supporting her magic. Now, encouraging each other, they swivelled to face the leading Griddas. If this was the end for Rachel, they would be with her as she exhaled her last breath, whispering their devotion into her ears still.

It was the end, but then a low voice said that it was not.

Rachel felt new spells fortifying her own.

'I'm here,' the voice said. 'I'm here. Rachel, I'm here.'

Rachel felt a shift, followed by the sun on her back – a warm sun. Real breezes tugged at her, the scents of children on them. And clasping her waist, her fine white hair tossed by the breeze, was a girl her own age.

'Heiki!' Rachel whispered.

For a while Rachel leaned against her friend while still clinging onto Serpantha. Finally Heiki managed to prize one of her hands away. 'I've got him,' she said. 'Rachel, it's OK. Let go. Open your fingers. You can let go.'

Rachel had held Serpantha for so long that it felt wrong not having his life in her arms. She allowed Heiki to take him, crying with relief.

'Yemi has returned,' Heiki told her. 'Now you're back, too! I think we really have a chance. Oh, we must have! We must!'

'The Griddas –' Rachel began.

'I know. They'll be here soon. Albertus and the other spectrums have been following them.'

Rachel tried to get her bearings. Heiki had shifted her and Serpantha to a foreign sky over rolling fields. A team of sentinel children was on guard above them, bathed in late afternoon sunshine. Frightened by the brightness, the Essa clustered under Rachel's ears. She swept her hair over them to give them time to adjust.

'Hey!' Heiki said, jerking back. 'What are *those*?'

Rachel had become so used to the Essa that she hardly noticed their touch against her skin. 'They're my guards,' she said. 'And my advisors, and extra eyes.' She laughed. 'A sort of hospital. And my companions. My friends.'

Heiki studied them in fascination, but when she reached out the Essa shrank back.

'You'll have to earn their respect first,' Rachel said.

'With the Griddas coming, it looks like I'll have a chance to do that,' Heiki answered.

Serpantha had regained enough strength to hold his own position in the sky without needing assistance. 'Larpskendya?' he asked.

Heiki shook her head. 'We've heard nothing. And … Eric?'

'We're not sure. We believe he's with an even larger army,' Serpantha said. 'The number of Griddas arriving on Earth is alarming, but if Gultrathaca truly wanted to destroy you all, the numbers would be greater still. It must be a decoy. She must have loftier ambitions elsewhere.' He paused. 'In fact, if Gultrathaca has taken Eric I can only think of one place the remaining Griddas would have gone.'

'Where?'

'Orin Fen.'

A boy was carried down to them: Albertus Robertson. His face broke with relief when he saw Rachel, but only for a moment. 'Griddas are deploying in orbit over all the world's major populations,' he reported. His head quivered as the spectrums updated him. 'Beijing, Cairo, New York, Calcutta, São Paulo … As anticipated, the Griddas intend to catch as many children as possible in a single overwhelming attack.'

'Wherever they are, we'll meet them and fight,' Heiki said.

Rachel stared at her. 'What? You can't send children against Griddas.'

'We're not just going to let the Griddas tear us to pieces, Rachel. We have to defend ourselves! What else can we do?'

'Heiki, you haven't seen how many are coming.'

'Well, they haven't seen all of us, either,' Heiki said. 'Take a look for yourself.'

643

Children were approaching from all directions. The elite teams, Rachel realized: the sentinels, all expert flyers. Several units of them aligned in formation, awaiting new orders.

'These won't be enough,' Rachel said. 'Surely you realize –'

'There are more,' Heiki told her.

Behind the sentinels other children had started to arrive. Thievers flew alongside lightning-finders. Ocean-diving deepers approached, still dripping from the seas. Rival gangs from the cities came together. There were avalanchers and other daredevils. Toddlers tagged along in their larger groups. Some had been caught unexpectedly, and were still rubbing sleep out of their eyes, or helping each other pull on coats or other clothes.

And behind these children were more breathless bunches: brothers and sisters, small family parties, clutching each other. From all the towns and villages across this part of the world they came. None were such slick flyers as the sentinels, but that didn't stop them. If they could make it into the air at all, one way or another they did so.

One type of child seemed less fearful than the others – or perhaps they only masked it better. These children were far too precious to be together. The largest sentinel units had one attached if they were lucky – a spectrum.

Rachel watched them all arrive, and noticed something: whenever the children saw her or Serpantha their frightened faces lit up, transformed.

'They think … they think *we're* going to make all the difference,' she said.

'They're wrong,' Serpantha told her. 'Only one person can make a decisive difference now. We must get to Yemi as swiftly as we can. Rachel – fly me there. I am still not strong enough.'

'Wait!' Heiki held Rachel back. 'We've tried that! Yemi won't listen. He's acting weird, ignoring everyone, just hovering in the sky surrounded by animals. Don't leave, Rachel – please! We need to know what you've managed to find out about the Griddas. Tactics. Deployment. How do they battle? What kinds of spell do they favour? What –'

'Don't you understand?' Rachel gripped Heiki's arm. 'Children can't defeat these Griddas! Even their infants never stop fighting. I've seen them. They don't give up, and they won't care how many they lose to the sentinels!'

'We have to try at least!' Heiki said. 'Won't they kill us anyway? Should we make it easy for them? I won't just sit back and let them! Rachel, I'm depending on you. If you could join that team over there, they need –'

'No,' interrupted Albertus Robertson. 'The spectrums agree with Rachel. We've now been able to scan the Griddas at close range. A few of the sentinels will hold their own for a while. All other children will be immediately overwhelmed. Wait…' His head twitched. 'The first Griddas have entered our atmosphere.'

'Where?' Heiki asked.

'Everywhere.'

The sentinel units above Heiki wanted clear instructions, having been told the same news by their own spectrums.

'The largest concentration is over the Asian peninsula,' Albertus said. 'Over the Huang Hai, the Yellow Sea between eastern China and Korea. The same place,' he added, 'where Yemi is located.'

'The Griddas realize that Yemi is still their greatest threat,' Serpantha said.

Rachel picked Serpantha up, her information spells plotting the fastest path to Yemi.

'One moment,' Albertus said to her. 'Since we cannot win this battle, we should negotiate. We have many materials to bargain with: animals and other foodstuffs; base and refined metals; our loyalty, or at least a pretence of that, and –'

'The Griddas won't be interested in any of those things,' Rachel said. 'They'll only want to fight.'

Albertus Robertson blinked, seeking alternatives from the other spectrums. 'There is no better option at present,' he said. 'Therefore, we *will* attempt to negotiate.'

'It won't work, Albertus. Don't go. These Griddas haven't come to talk!'

'Even so, we could distract them briefly. That may delay the main assault, giving you and Serpantha time to devise a new strategy with Yemi.' Albertus smiled, his lips brushing hers. Then, before Rachel could say anything, his thrill-seekers carried him skyward to meet the Griddas. Seeing those two girls so unflinchingly take him up, Rachel at last understood why, of all children, the spectrums chose the thrill-seekers as their companions – only the most fearless children could ever have flown without question into those clouds.

The Essa had stayed quiet all this time. Now they braved the light and tugged Rachel forward. 'Find Yemi!' they burst out. 'Take us to him! Take us!'

Serpantha held Rachel's hand. With their combined strength they flew across the world.

23

the three layers

Gultrathaca slowed the army down as they neared Orin Fen.

To report on the disposition of Wizard sentries she deployed stealth teams, holding the bulk of the Griddas well back. 'We need to make sure there are no High Witches keeping watch,' she told Eric, to allay his suspicions. 'We don't want them knowing we're here.'

Eric half-nodded, barely hearing her.

Gultrathaca ached for combat. Her pack-sisters had already started inflating their muscles, readying themselves. She wanted more than anything to join them, but still needed to be mindful of Eric. What would he make of the battle-wail of the infants when it started?

As for the Wizards, no doubt they would be prepared. Such a large Gridda army could not have gone unnoticed. Even so, Gultrathaca could not wait for the conflict to begin. Win or lose, she thought, win or lose, did it really matter? Her Griddas were not empire builders. Unlike the Highs, they had no patience for the gradual accumulations of power and status. What Griddas demanded was war, or the prospect of war, or the promise. They were built for its mayhem, designed for its fulfilment. What else could have carried the Gridda packs so far across the insanity of space?

For all those centuries, Gultrathaca thought, Heebra lived in the heights of her eye-tower, fantasizing about this special moment. But the Griddas, not the Highs, would enjoy it. Feeling her heart race, Gultrathaca calmed herself. She quietened her soldier spiders. She told the healers busy dropping painkillers into her veins to wait a while longer. She kept the watchers focused on Eric. This is a glorious day for all spiders, too, she realized; everywhere around her, they were alert and active.

All, that is, except the spiders of Jarius.

Gultrathaca hardly recognized her any longer. There was the same expression on Jarius's face she had seen linger on Fola's so many times in the Assessment Chamber: fear. Only the dumbest animals were without fear entirely, but humans and those they affect are full of fear, Gultrathaca thought. It hovers about their eyes, like a trap. What was wrong with them? What were they afraid of?

She gazed at Jarius, suddenly pitying her.

When Eric and Gultrathaca stopped, the pack-leaders could no longer contain the infants. 'Orin Fen! Orin Fen!' they hissed amongst themselves.

Everyone sensed the planet now. It was so near that Gultrathaca could almost reach out for it. She sniffed, testing the quality of the invisibility spells. They were beyond her understanding. And under the invisibility layer were fortification spells. Gultrathaca probed them, realizing at once that they were virtually impregnable. It would take her Griddas centuries to smash through, or forever.

How long would it take Eric?

Gultrathaca squeezed him lightly. Had she miscalculated? If Eric could not break through the Wizards' protections, most of the Griddas would perish – the infants were too weary to make the return trip to Ool unless they could recuperate on the world below.

Gradually the stealth teams brought in their news. There was nothing to report, no sign of Wizards. Where were they? Snug behind their protections? Waiting for the Griddas to wear themselves out before showing themselves?

'Eric,' she asked. 'Can you … can you deal with the spells around this world?'

'I'll see.'

Eric stared at the empty space where he knew the planet to be. Its protections were intricate, labyrinthine, marvellously engineered; too sturdy for any number of Griddas to breach – and that shocked him. This was Wizard magic; Eric had no doubt. But where were the Wizards? A couple of old trails marked that they had been here, nothing more. What was going on? Why would Wizards so carefully shield a world of imprisoned Griddas?

There could be many reasons, he thought. He didn't have time now to worry about those reasons. The important thing was that there were Witches on this world. Now that he was closer, Eric realized the leaking scent traces were more similar to High Witches than Griddas, and that made sense. If High Witches supervised this world, he would expect them to be flashing around in the skies below.

He gripped the feathers of the prapsies, deciding.

Beneath the invisibility spells, there were three layers of protection. He had to act as soon as he cut through the last one. Gultrathaca would only keep him alive for as long as she needed him. He might only have moments to wrap his destruction around all the Griddas and Highs on the planet.

Good, he thought. Less time to think about it, to think about what I'm doing.

The prapsies were entirely quiet beside him. They had stopped asking questions, stopped insulting Gultrathaca, stopped fidgeting. They no longer even talked to each other. They simply pressed against him. He didn't dare look at them, not now.

Eric felt, suddenly, like a Gridda himself, or what they represented: the consummate murder weapon. It chilled him, this destructiveness. He felt as if he had become a skilful rolling into one of all death spells, like Rachel's deaths improved on, with no nobler spells to hold them back. All the journey he had been perfecting this deadliness. He knew exactly how to unstitch Gridda bodies. It was a terrible task, and inhuman, not human at all, but he was capable of it. He had to be.

All around him the infants were screaming to each other, almost hysterical. Eric made himself watch. He let the horror of them settle in his mind. He reminded himself what these same Griddas had done to Rachel and Larpskendya, to Serpantha, to Yemi.

To carry out his plan Eric needed to distract Gultrathaca. She was not behaving with the same abandon as the others. 'The planet has several different protective layers,' he told her.

'Can you break through them?'

'If I get help. The defences are too strong for me on my own.'

'What do you need?'

'I'll get rid of the invisibility mask. When I've done that all the Griddas should fire their spells into the protection layers. That will weaken them enough, I think, for me to finish the job. We'll have to rest between layers.'

'Rest?'

'There are several to get through.'

Gultrathaca looked quizzically at Eric. His expression was blank. Was he plotting something? Did he already know what lay beneath? It didn't matter. As long as he ruptured the defences, nothing else mattered. Her claw was waiting for him after that.

She gave the orders to deploy the Griddas around Orin Fen. 'Eric, please hurry,' she said, once they were positioned. 'The Griddas below must be suffering terribly.'

'I'm ready,' Eric said – and he was. All the Gridda army and Witches on the planet were within his range. He also had a surprise. To keep Gultrathaca off guard, he had pre-pared all the anti-magic he needed. With one silky motion of his mind he would remove *all* three protection layers at the same time.

'Are you afraid, Eric?' Gultrathaca asked, seeing him shake.

He ignored her. He removed the invisibility mask. A huge yellow-brown world was revealed. Gultrathaca signalled for the Griddas to set about breaching the protections. They barely scratched the first layer.

Eric steadied himself. He clutched the prapsies. 'I'm sorry, boys,' he whispered. Encompassing the first protection-layer girdling the planet, he destroyed it. Immediately he smashed the second layer – so rapidly that even Gultrathaca did not have time to notice. Before Eric tackled the third layer he could not help himself. He stared at the prapsies. And they stared back. On the entire voyage, had they ever stopped watching him?

'We don't understand, Eric,' one murmured.

'Oh boys,' he said. 'Forgive me.'

'Forgive what?' Gultrathaca glanced sharply at Eric. She realized that serious damage had been done to the protections without any need for rest. Eric had not required the Griddas.

He was lying.

Eric felt her claw on his spine, and knew he had delayed too long. He should already have broken through the third layer! What are you delaying for? he asked himself.

But he knew, he knew. He was frightened of dying. Now the moment had come, he clung to Gultrathaca, as if *she* would save him. He was afraid of dying and he was afraid of killing. He was afraid of everything.

He couldn't do it – but he had to.

He raised his hands. They were primitive directors of anti-magic, but they had never let him down. He pointed one of them. He pointed the index finger of his right hand at the southern rim of the planet below, and began to trace the tip around the edge.

No more delays. He cancelled the third layer of protection. He closed his eyes.

He was ready.

And so was Gultrathaca. She sensed a dreadful undoing start to work on her, but there was still time. Her nail lay over Eric's heart.

But she did not use it. She wavered. Eric also wavered.

He held back. Gultrathaca had expected to see legions of Wizards pouring from Orin Fen. Eric had expected a flood of Griddas and Highs.

The creatures actually rising up from that world were ones neither of them could believe.

24

huang hai

Rachel, Serpantha and the Essa flew across four seas and two continents, following Yemi's scent.

Finally, where the grey waters of the Huang Hai lap up against Shindao, on the Chinese shore, they found him. Yemi was surrounded by birds. They circled him in protective silence: flock after flock, local birds and birds that had never been seen before over Chinese skies.

And, beneath them, on the shore, there was an even more remarkable sight: animals, pressed up against the surf. The scale of the gathering was so great that even Rachel's information spells could not count the number. All the animals were quiet. Predators stood alongside prey and there was none of the usual noise or panic that occurs when animals are crowded tightly together. Each animal stood motionless, with shut eyes. Their mouths were open, as if inhaling something blissful. Their heads were inclined contemplatively to one place in the sky.

In that place, slightly above them, was a boy in a bright orange T-shirt.

'Yemi!' cried the Essa. There was no path to him, except through the birds. As the Essa tried to make a pathway to Yemi, the flocks turned their beaks on them. Then Yemi's yellow butterflies pushed between the birds. They made a gap for the Essa, guiding them. Rachel and Serpantha followed.

As the Camberwell Beauties led Rachel towards Yemi, she could hear her own heart booming over the quietude of the scene. Yemi's eyes were closed. He appeared to be asleep, his chin pointing towards the animals.

'Have you ... have you ever seen anything like this?' she asked Serpantha.

'No, nor any Wizard,' he whispered.

'What are they doing?'

'I do not know, but can you feel the magic linking Yemi and the animals together? Can you feel the tranquillity of their minds?'

Rachel felt it: the calmness. And it was not merely the minds of the animals and Yemi that were calm. The sea itself was calm. The winds had gentled. A shark, straying under the waters below, beat its fins away again. Even the sunshine, as it filtered through the clouds, cast the same pallid light evenly across Yemi and the animals on the shore. There was no dappling; there was no place where the sun was brighter or darker against his face or that of the animals – as though the natural differences of shade and light should not be allowed to intrude on their meditation.

Rachel felt as if any words would be an interruption of whatever was taking place here, but she had to speak. The peacefulness of this scene would soon be shattered by the Griddas.

Fola hung wide-awake and suspended in mid-air next to Yemi.

'What's – what's happening?' Rachel asked her.

'I can't tell,' Fola said. 'Yemi came here, I don't know why. The animals followed him. They have been just like this for so long.' She shook Yemi. 'I tried to wake him. It's not possible!'

'It is some kind of trance-state,' Serpantha said. 'All the animals are with Yemi inside it. I can't tell if they are aware of the Gridda threat.'

The Essa pulled at Yemi's eyelids, trying to rouse him. Rachel united her magic with Serpantha, attempting every kind of waking spell.

'What can we do?' the Essa cried. 'Make him listen!'

Above them, a shriek levelled across the sky. The noise was not human. It came from the lungs of a Gridda pack. If anything could have broken the quiet reflection of Yemi, this would have done so. His expression did not alter.

High in the clouds overhead, one sentinel unit waited. As in so many other skies across Earth, it stood alone guarding an enormous area. The leader of the unit, a boy Rachel did not know, flew amongst his team, shouting instructions. His voice was hoarse. A small girl with long red hair was by his side, following him wherever he went: a spectrum.

Seeing their courage, Rachel felt anger welling up inside her. Gultrathaca had lied about most things, but what about her accusations concerning Larpskendya? Rachel had not wanted to consider these before. She faced Serpantha.

'Where are the other Wizards?' she demanded.

Serpantha's expression was anguished. 'Whoever could come, has done so.'

'What does that mean?' Rachel said angrily. 'Don't you have a whole world of Wizards? Larpskendya told me that often enough. Even he's not here this time. If I hadn't risked my life to save you, there would be no Wizard on Earth at all. What are we supposed to think of that?'

'There is no time for this, Rachel.'

'Is it because your own precious world's threatened? Is that why no one's here?'

'I will explain, but not now. You must help me to reach Yemi.'

'Help *you*!' Rachel shouted the words, pointing up. 'These children are offering everything because of Larpskendya, because of things he's told them! Where are the other Wizards?'

'I offer myself,' Serpantha said, his gaze steadily on her. 'I have nothing more to give than that.'

Rachel felt like screaming. 'Is this all we're worth to you? The life of one Wizard? After all that's happened, is that all we were ever worth to you?'

'No. You deserve far more.'

'Yes. We do!' Rachel turned her back on Serpantha. 'We do!'

The pack of Griddas had appeared overhead, their angular heads lowered. The mere sight of them appalled the sentinels, but they somehow kept their discipline, spreading out to shield Yemi on all sides. Rachel felt sharp nips on her flesh. It was the Essa: agitated, wondering what to do. They pulled at her cheeks. 'Look!' they cried.

The spectrum girl with red hair had left the sentinel unit. Carried by her thrill-seeker, she had set off to confront the Griddas.

'She's gone to negotiate,' Rachel said hollowly. 'That was Albertus Robertson's last instruction to the spectrums. It must be happening everywhere.'

The girl rose into the clouds. The Griddas did not slow down. They headed straight for her. Rachel shook with the effort to control her anger, barely able to choke out the words. 'See what that girl's prepared to do!' she yelled at Serpantha. 'Where are the Wizards? Gultrathaca said you couldn't care less about us. Have you just been using us all this time? Using us to expose the High Witches, then lure the Griddas to Orin Fen? I suppose the Wizards have set a trap there, so you can get rid of your last enemy.'

Serpantha looked intently at her. 'Do you really believe that, Rachel?'

'What else can I believe?'

'There is no trap,' Serpantha said. 'The Griddas won't find any Wizards on Orin Fen, or perhaps one, if my brother made it back. There have never been many Wizards, Rachel. Of those few born most died during the endless war against the Highs. The remainder were killed when Heebra unleashed the Griddas. Larpskendya hid that from you. I hid it from you. We had to. Only fear of us kept the Witches in check. If they had ever discovered the truth about how few Wizards there are, no world would have been safe.' He put his hand against Rachel's hot cheek. 'That is why Larpskendya has been absent so often from Earth. Do you think he would ever have left your world exposed if he had any choice? Do you think I would have done? Rachel, the reason we are the only two who have visited your world is that there are no others. Larpskendya and I are the last of the Wizards.'

In the sky above, the red-haired girl waited for the Griddas. While she did so, she attempted to hold the nerve of her thrill-seeker by looking into his eyes. Finally, however, even he turned and fled. He knew that only by doing so could he save her life. He fled to the only place there was a chance of keeping her safe – back to the sentinel unit.

As the Gridda pack closed in they divided, approaching from several directions, choosing specific targets among the children. The sentinel unit's leader flew along the line, keeping them steady.

Serpantha, with a sweep of his mind, tried to take in everyone. Rachel felt the start of an immense spell to shield the children – but the Wizard was still too weak to sustain it. Even if Serpantha possessed all his strength, Rachel realized, he could not have held back so many Griddas single-handedly. She prepared to use her own spells, knowing they were not adequate, either.

An initial ripple of attack spells came from the Griddas. The sentinels hastily erected a barrier, withstanding it – just.

'Awake! Awake!' murmured the Essa.

Yemi was rubbing his eyes, wiping away the sleepiness. The animals on the shore were also shaking themselves, stretching, flexing their limbs. Then, with a great clamour of wings, the bird flocks scattered.

Rachel gathered Yemi up in her arms. 'Can you understand what's happening?' She tilted his face toward the Griddas.

Yemi saw them, gazed back at Rachel, showing no concern.

Fola shook his arm hard. 'Stupid boy! *Odé!* Don't you see?' She peered up. 'Look at the monsters there!'

Yemi smiled at his sister, kissed her.

'We need to protect the children everywhere,' Rachel said. 'Yemi, try to understand. Please.'

The Essa raced over to a nearby seagull. They surrounded the bird and brought it back to Yemi. Rachel spread her hands to show they meant to protect everything. How could she make him understand?

'Yemi,' she said. 'I can't shift us. But we have to get everyone away from here.'

Overhead there was a groan – the sentinel unit's defence had been breached.

Then more children arrived. From the west they came, firing spells: three more sentinel units, led by Heiki. The flank of the Gridda pack recoiled. They drew back, trying to recover. But Heiki had no intention of giving the Griddas time to recover. At her signal, the eyes of the sentinel children all turned black. Simultaneously they launched their death spells.

Rachel had never felt anything like the power of the combined deaths. Even the Gridda pack-leader quavered when she felt what was seeking her out. Just before the deaths reached the Griddas, Yemi glanced up. He placed a cordon around the Griddas. He protected them. The deaths struck uselessly against it.

'What are you doing?' Rachel screamed. 'Yemi! Yemi! The children! Protect the children, not the Griddas!'

Yemi looked at her: an indescribable look. He closed his eyes. The animals on the shore did the same. And suddenly everyone – even the Griddas – felt themselves seized.

Yemi chuckled. He threw out his arms.

25

the touch of witches

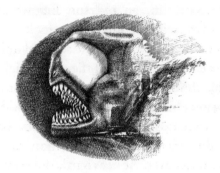

Witches. Skies of Witches. Witches everywhere. Millions upon millions, rising through the lucid air of Orin Fen.

As Eric cancelled the final layer of protection, that was what he saw.

But not High Witches – and not Griddas.

He squinted at the brightness of the planet, trying to understand. Beyond the Witches he saw oceans; he saw radiant cities; he saw mountains without snow.

Was this some kind of trick of Gultrathaca's?

One glance at her shocked face showed otherwise. Eric probed into the magic of the new Witches. He realized they were related to the Highs. The fearsome Griddas were in some way also their more distant descendants.

How could that be?

As the Witches arrived, Eric tried to understand what

faced him. The first thing he noticed was that the Witches were beautiful. They were beautiful in the same way that Larpskendya and Serpantha were beautiful. It was the colours. Eric thought he had seen all the shades of a Wizard's eyes, but he was wrong. It took the light of a wilder sun to bring out every hue. Looking at these Witches, Eric saw them all.

It was a warm sun, an old sun, but these Witches seemed older. Eric could hardly bear to look at them, or to look away.

The Orin Fen Witches shared the same height and proportions as High Witches, though they were more slender, and clawless, with human faces – a single, modest jaw.

The true Witches, Eric realized. When a group of the females left all those millions of years ago, not all had left. The original Witches – these Witches – had stayed with the Wizards.

Slowly the Witches took up a position until they girdled the planet. They confronted the Gridda army. Then, together, they opened their arms.

An invitation? Gultrathaca reeled, baffled. She had expected a battering of Wizards, not this. Confused questions were being raised by her commanders. Where were the Wizards? Disguised? Had the Wizards sneaked behind somehow, while these creatures provided a distraction?

The Witches did nothing to alarm the Griddas. They were patient, waiting until the Griddas overcame their surprise. They made no sudden movements. They merely held out their arms.

Those imploring arms!

Gultrathaca shook herself, feeling an unaccountable urge. Part of her wanted to accept those arms, to be led towards the surface – away from the horror of the sun. Was a spell at work? No. It was something else, something extraordinary about the Witches themselves.

Gultrathaca fought a yearning to go towards them.

All around her, the Gridda army felt similar emotions. The packs were primed for Wizards and death, not this welcome! Should they attack the strangers? Their bodies were ready to fight, but there was no aggression in the Witches to set them off. On the contrary, the Witches were all anxiousness of gaze – and not for themselves. They gazed at the Griddas, as if seeing torture and mutilation beyond belief in their features.

The infant Griddas responded first. For all their noisy bravado, the journey had been long, and they were tired; they wanted the refuge of a tunnel; they wanted these Witches. They started to drift towards them. Touching seemed the most natural thing. The infants touched, breathlessly exploring. Seeing the infants were discomforted by the light, the Witches diminished it. They darkened their own skies, until the cities fell into shade and the big eyes of the infants opened fully.

Pack-leaders restrained some of the infants, but they could not stop them all. Then a few of the maturer Griddas joined them. They slipped tentatively across the divide between themselves and the Witches. The lines began to merge. A leader glanced desperately at Gultrathaca for assistance as her entire pack deserted her. Witches and Griddas intermingled, touching and not touching, curious about their physical differences, repelled and attracted.

But not fighting! Not fighting! All around Gultrathaca could see the blood-lust of her Griddas cracking. Warlike instincts were being replaced by something she could not understand.

'No! No!' she raged. 'It is a trick!' She raced along the lines of her Griddas. 'The Wizards are hiding! They are cowards! Find them on the world below! Find them!'

A few Griddas followed her order, but as soon as they reached the Witches their resolve faded. They slowed, came to a stop, joined the infants.

Gultrathaca saw that even her staunchest pack-leaders would no longer obey her.

She had almost forgotten Eric. He lay in her arms, staring with open mouth at what was happening. The prapsies stood on Eric's shoulders, twitching excitedly.

Gultrathaca stared out over her forces. They were no longer an army. Griddas and Witches were flying openly together. Gultrathaca heard talk between them. She heard laughter. Even her own pack-sisters had left their defensive posts.

This was not a Wizard trick; Gultrathaca knew that. The Witches meant no harm. Indeed, Gultrathaca wanted nothing more than to be amongst them. How she wanted to! But the sight of something held her back. Jarius was no longer guarded. She flew freely with her sisters, her dishonour forgotten.

Gultrathaca could not allow that.

She summoned a death spell. Like all deaths, it gave her simple advice. It made choices easier. One of the Orin Fen Witches hovered close to her. Her smile was concerned, shy even.

Gultrathaca looked at her and loosed the death. It killed the Witch instantly. Seeing this, for the first time the nearest Witches raised their defences.

And that was enough. The Griddas reacted instinctively. More than instinctively: they reacted the way the High Witches had bred them to react. Their bodies pumped with blood; their claws enlarged. Gultrathaca rushed between the packs, instilling confidence. Contact between Griddas and Witches was broken.

Gultrathaca launched another death spell – or tried.

Eric prevented it – and Gultrathaca knew she had lost that favourite killer forever. It hardly mattered. Other Griddas had begun firing death spells. The Witches fell back, defending themselves. They started to fly away – towards the surface.

A chase!

It was a mistake. Gridda pursuit reflexes flickered alive at once. Suddenly pack on pack were descending the skies to get at the Witches.

'Please don't,' whispered Eric. 'Gultrathaca, you can still stop this.'

'I could,' Gultrathaca agreed.

She kicked him away.

Eric fell gasping, in explosive pain. There was no chance to collect his thoughts for any kind of anti-spell. The prapsies tumbled beside him, trying to stop his fall.

Jarius came for Eric. Griddas from her own pack tried to stop her, but she fought through them. Sweeping Eric and the prapsies up, she breathed life-giving oxygen back inside their lungs. They lay in her claws, only half-conscious.

The Orin Fen Witches were retreating to their cities. The Griddas followed. Now that a true fight had started, Jarius could tell that the Witches were not able to adequately defend themselves. They were more magical than the Griddas, but inferior fighters.

Jarius fled with all her speed, but there was no escaping the packs. Carrying Eric and the prapsies made her easy to catch, and several members of her own pack went after her.

Jarius had no choice any longer. With a final gasp of effort, wriggling from the grasp of an infant, she flew towards the planet. Where else could she go now? Where else?

Larpskendya watched it all, concealed by the corona of Orin Fen's sun.

His spells were still recovering. For weeks he had been hounded across all space, never able to get away from the Gridda packs for long. Finally, his shifting spells had made a last great effort. They brought him home.

As Larpskendya saw what was taking place, he almost wished they had not.

He had deliberately hidden, knowing that if the Griddas glimpsed him they would attack without question.

And then he had seen the beautiful, open-souled Witches of Orin Fen try. Those arms! How could it work? Against the violence of the Griddas, it could never work – but it nearly had.

Larpskendya felt tears on his face. What use were they? What use were tears now? Over the centuries all the efforts of the last Wizards had gone into shrouding Orin Fen. Had they been wrong? How could they have anticipated Eric's extraordinary talent? There had never been anything like him. If we had allowed the Witches to join in the endless war, Larpskendya realized, they might now be better prepared. The Witches had wished it. Always they had asked for it. We loved them too much, Larpskendya thought. We kept them apart from war – a terrible mistake.

And then Larpskendya had seen Jarius, and for a moment he had hope again. Here was a Gridda, defending Eric with all her heart.

When Jarius failed as well, rushing with Eric towards Orin Fen, Larpskendya knew it was time to show himself. There was no way to save the Witches, not against so many Griddas. Well, he would do what he could. He would at least give the Witches a chance to reach the cities, where they could defend themselves more effectively.

He flew towards the Griddas.

Gultrathaca recognized him before she saw him: how could she mistake that singular, awesome scent! She approached with the rest of her pack. As she did so, Larpskendya gave her a signal she thought only the Griddas knew.

'No,' she said, laughing. 'Not a personal challenge. I won't give you the satisfaction of that. I will decide the method of your death, Wizard.'

She ordered three packs forward.

On Orin Fen thousands of Witches turned around and started despairingly flying towards Larpskendya. The Griddas held them back.

'There will be no help for you, Wizard,' Gultrathaca said.

Larpskendya raised his defences. Even the three large Gridda packs sent against him wavered when they felt the authority of the spells. But not for long. The Wizard was alone, and they were many, and the battle-blood the Highs had bred in the Griddas would have driven them on now even if they had no chance of victory. Gultrathaca knew Larpskendya might slay all three packs. He could not, however, slay all the packs. Even the great Larpskendya lacked that strength.

As the packs closed in, Larpskendya was a solitary figure against the backdrop of space.

But the Griddas stopped before they reached him.

They stopped to look in amazement at butterflies and children.

26

the fatal gift

Every child of Earth was over Orin Fen.

Yemi had brought them all: the deepers, the thievers, the gangs; the gifted and ungifted; flyers, and those who could never fly; everyone. Many sentinels had been shifted in mid-battle. Spectrums joined them, held by their thrill-seekers. Yellow butterflies flapped, their wings in sunlight.

The youngest children congregated near Yemi. Their eyes followed his, wherever he gazed. Everywhere children were blinking, adjusting to the glory of Orin Fen's sun.

'What's happening? What's happening?' the Essa asked, clutching Rachel. The dazzling world of Orin Fen beckoned to them, and Rachel felt it, too. Like them, for reasons she could not explain, she was transfixed. She wanted to fly towards the surface.

'I've got to find Eric,' she told Serpantha.

'I know,' he said. 'And I must find my brother.'

Eric was not far. Jarius still held him. Rachel approached her warily.

'I'm all right,' Eric said. 'Don't be afraid of this Gridda, Rach. I don't know her name, but she kept me and the prapsies safe. She kept us alive.'

Rachel gazed at Jarius's harsh face. The Essa did so too, not trusting it. Jarius understood and turned instead to Rachel. 'I will take care of Eric,' she said. 'It is Yemi you must go to. He may ... he may try to do too much.'

'Go on, Rach,' Eric said. 'Get to Yemi, but stay away from Gultrathaca. Watch out for her.'

Gultrathaca stared in disbelief at the reunion of Serpantha and Larpskendya taking place nearby. What had happened here? A Wizard who should be dead; children who could never have made such a journey; even the presence of Griddas, the ones sent to invade Earth. Surprised, jolted out of the glow of battle, those Griddas could not wait to continue – but who should they attack now?

Gultrathaca reassessed the balance of power. It had altered. She no longer had numerical superiority, not with all the children to aid the Orin Fen Witches.

If the Griddas fought, she realized, they would lose everything.

Floating close to Yemi, she expected the old infuriating smile. This time, however, Yemi had no smile for her – as if realizing at last that she could not stand it. As she turned away, Larpskendya and Serpantha approached.

'End it here,' Larpskendya said to her. 'You can stop it now, Gultrathaca. A simple command to the packs.'

'What?' Gultrathaca said. 'Before the fight has even begun?'

'How many Griddas would you have die first?' This time it was Serpantha who had spoken.

Gultrathaca stared at him. 'Are you still alive? What do I have to do to kill you?'

'You should be asking a different question,' Serpantha said. 'How can you hold the Griddas back? They will fight, unless you order otherwise.'

'Why should I?'

'There is no way you can win a battle. All the Griddas will be killed.'

'Do you really think a Gridda values life more than battle, whatever the outcome? I'll kill you, Serpantha, before I die. I swear that.'

Larpskendya assessed her. 'We offer an alternative.'

'Let me guess,' Gultrathaca said. 'Some sort of peace. How meek that sounds. Do you believe the Griddas will settle for co-operation with anyone? We'll have war instead, Wizard. It is all we know.'

'That is not true.' Larpskendya's view took in all the packs. 'Most of the Griddas have only known peace. The majority here are infants. I doubt any of them have experienced battle outside the playfulness of the birthing tunnels. If you made them fight, this would be their first battle.'

'I remember my first battle as the best.'

'Do you have the courage to lead them in another way?'

Gultrathaca smiled thinly. 'What would you have us do, Wizard? Relinquish our death spells to play with the children of Earth?'

'What do you think is happening here?' Larpskendya said earnestly. 'You sound like a High Witch, seeing enemies in all places. There *are* no enemies. The children have no quarrel with the Griddas. Nor the Wizards. Only the Highs wanted the endless war. And look at what they did to all Griddas, Gultrathaca, while they waged that war. They put you underground, mutilated you, despised you, denied you everything.'

'We revenged that,' Gultrathaca said. 'This is our fight now, our choice to fight.'

'No,' Larpskendya said. 'You are still following the aims of the High Witches. They manufactured the Griddas for war, but you deserve more than they made you for.'

Gultrathaca glanced at the distant Jarius. 'I have seen the alternative to war. I would rather be dead than like her.'

'Are you sure?' Larpskendya came closer. 'War is not all the Griddas want. I think you know that. You felt it as well. I saw the reaction the Griddas had when they first saw the Witches. Even you felt something, Gultrathaca. I watched you.'

'It was not what I *wanted*!'

'It can be.' Larpskendya paused, seeking a way to make her understand. 'The High Witches constructed you, but the call of blood is just a reflex, nothing more. If Heebra could be here now, see from her grave, she would expect you to fight, Gultrathaca. But she was wrong about the Griddas. You can be more than her machines. You already chose a different destiny when you left the tunnels. And you can again.'

Gultrathaca hesitated. Were her instincts mistaken? Everything inside her shrieked for battle. The pack-leaders were ready, of course. Like her they had trained for it all their lives. She glared at Yemi, aching to see that smile again so that she could smash it. His face remained stony.

672

She studied the Gridda infants. If she raised a battle-cry, no doubt they would respond. But if they spent more time with the Witches, would they still go with her so lightly into battle? Would they?

Yet to accept terms from a Wizard – any terms – how was that acceptable? Anything but war now was not a victory at all. Not *her* victory anyway, or that of the Griddas. Instead, it would be the victory of Larpskendya and Serpantha. It would be the victory of the Orin Fen Witches. In some way it would also be the victory of Eric and Yemi – and perhaps even Jarius.

Gultrathaca could not bear that thought.

She prepared a death spell, one of her favourites. Not for Yemi. That would have been her preferred target, but a waste. She aimed it at Serpantha.

'Do not do this!' Larpskendya roared.

Gultrathaca raised the battle-cry. It had the intended effect. The infants instantly lost any uncertainty. Ordering her own pack forward, Gultrathaca signalled towards Serpantha. She expected Larpskendya to protect his brother, but he did not do so. Instead, he moved aside. He left Serpantha alone.

Eric called out, 'What are you doing?'

'Don't interfere,' Larpskendya told him.

'You've no idea what skills I've got now,' Eric said.

'I do know, Eric. Stay back.'

Rachel glanced nervously towards Serpantha. 'Don't you want any help at all? We'll all help. You know that, don't you?'

Serpantha smiled at her. 'Yes, I do. Stay a safe distance.' Serpantha said nothing more. He waited.

The Griddas could not understand. They glanced at

Gultrathaca. At her gesture, the entire pack initiated their death spells at once against Serpantha.

Yemi immediately shifted in front of the Wizard.

The deaths withered against his shield.

As Gultrathaca ordered the packs to fire more spells, Heiki exchanged a frightened look with Albertus Robertson. 'Shouldn't we do something?' she asked. 'We have to!'

'No,' Albertus answered. 'This war has gone on an eternity. Let the Wizards and Griddas play it out between themselves, if we can.'

'But I can't stand doing nothing!'

'Can't you?' Albertus turned to her. 'Neither can the Griddas. They have to fight. Part of them can't accept anything else. The Wizards realize that.'

Gultrathaca brought more of the Griddas into the assault, until immense numbers of packs were discharging every kind of spell at Serpantha. None affected him. He did not even have to defend himself. Yemi held the attacks off.

'The boy's power is not infinite,' Gultrathaca told the packs.

'You can't reach me,' Serpantha told her. 'Don't you understand? Even if you overpower Yemi, every child here will defend me – or any other target you choose.'

Like a procession, the packs continued to send their finest spells against Serpantha without any impact. Eventually, the heart went out of them. Gultrathaca gave no order, but the attacks gradually petered out. Then they ceased altogether.

Serpantha was unharmed. Yemi was unharmed. Many Griddas were exhausted.

'You think it is over?' Gultrathaca said to Larpskendya. Scarcely moving her claw, she sent a quiet assault Eric's way. It was so unexpected that he did not destroy it in time. One of the prapsies jumped in front of him. The spell struck the edge of its wing, breaking it. 'Oh, Eric,' the prapsy said. 'Oh.' It flapped the useless wing. The other prapsy ran across Eric's shoulder to hold the wing in place.

'Well?' Gultrathaca screamed at Eric, seeing his fury. 'If you have the power, use it! Finish me!' She looked at her army, and knew it was already defeated. 'Finish us all off!'

Eric listened to the prapsy's mild whimpers of pain.

'Don't!' Rachel snapped, flying towards him.

'Stay out of this!' Eric said – though he wavered, hearing her voice.

Seeing his indecision, Gultrathaca fired another spell, this time aimed directly at the prapsies. Yemi stopped it, but the intention was obvious.

'How dare you! How *dare* you!' Eric did not even need to think. He had long ago perfected his killing technique for the Griddas. He knew how to unravel their magic. He could kill them at once, or he could play out their ruination forever.

Yemi threw a shield around the Griddas. He looked at Eric. Rachel had never seen the look of fear on Yemi's face she saw now.

'Get away, Yemi!' Eric warned. 'I've made my decision.'

Yemi shook his head.

Eric probed the shield. It contained an almost limitless number of spells to guard the Griddas, but Eric had more ways to penetrate it. He started the dismantlement. As Yemi felt the shield failing, he squealed. He called on his butterflies. They surrounded him. They gave him all their strength. It was not enough.

And then Yemi put his little fingers over his eyes and spoke through his tears.

'Stop, please!' he begged. 'Eric, stop it! Eric! Eric! Eric!'

Eric heard him. He heard everyone. He heard Larpskendya and Rachel and Serpantha and Albertus, all those who loved him, all shouting, all striving to reach him. No, he thought. I'm going to finish it. He avoided Yemi's defences. Suddenly he realized that he did not even need to destroy Yemi's spells. He could side-step them; he could alter them. He did so. He removed Yemi's shield and gripped the hearts of the Griddas. He was the spell-destroyer. His was the fatal gift. He knew it; finally he knew what had frightened the spectrums so much.

There was no magic in the universe that could stop him.

The Griddas were disintegrating. Some were alone. Others were held by the Orin Fen Witches. Where they could, the Witches had gone to the Griddas, trying to keep them intact. Eric saw Gultrathaca. She shook as all the magic was loosened from her cells. Larpskendya was making his way unsteadily towards her. He reached her. She shuddered in his arms, like a child. He held her, in tears tried to hold her together.

Eric felt warmth near his ear. 'Eric,' the prapsy whose wing had been broken said to him. 'Don't, boys.' It kissed his eyes. It made him look down. Eric looked. Jarius was under him, still clutching him, her face jolting.

Eric gazed at her, and beyond her. He saw Fola, unable to comfort Yemi. He saw Witches crying. He saw Serpantha crying.

He ended it.

The Griddas breathed again.

All except one. She did not want to breathe. Gultrathaca wanted to die, but Larpskendya held her tightly. He held onto her life.

27

the wizard's promise

Eric had only just withdrawn his destruction in time.

The Griddas, strewn across space, barely seemed to know where they were. Drifting aimlessly, the infants gathered in small groups, not sure why. Older Griddas felt their bodies; they felt wrong.

The prapsies held tightly to Eric, helping him to recover from what he had almost done. He shook as he peered between the warmth of their feathers. And wherever he peered spiders were on the move. Soldiers were searching for enemies they could not find. Healer spiders called to one another, understanding how ill their owners were, without understanding what to do.

But there was healing of a kind on Orin Fen the spiders had not dreamed of.

In graceful lines, the Witches ascended. Each took a

Gridda into her private care, into her arms. Part of Orin Fen had been put in deep shade. The Witches carried the Griddas there, towards the consolation of the dark.

Gultrathaca was one of the last to be taken. There was a Witch waiting for her as well, but Larpskendya carried her himself. He held her wordlessly, because she was not yet ready for words – and Larpskendya was not ready, either. As they gazed at each other a mystery of feelings made them both weep. Larpskendya found a place where there were other Griddas, ones Gultrathaca knew. Should he leave her now, or should he stay? He did not want to leave her.

Above him, Jarius still held Eric. As one of the Orin Fen Witches embraced her, ready to take her to the surface, Eric said, 'No. Wait. I – what is your name? I don't even know your name.'

'I am Jarius,' she said.

'Thank you,' Eric murmured, touching her face. 'Thank you, Jarius.'

As she gave Eric and the prapsies back to Rachel, and was being led away, Jarius turned to the Witch who held her. 'I wish to be taken to my own pack,' she said. 'They need me now.'

Rachel spent a moment repairing a broken wing. Then she, Eric and the prapsies followed Jarius as she was gradually taken down to the shadowed part of Orin Fen. And then, while Larpskendya stayed below with Gultrathaca, everyone else suddenly seemed to arrive beside them at once. For a few moments no one said anything, but the prapsies soon broke the silence. They were hungry, and sick of being quiet all the time. Eric took an ear-bashing, and knew it was not the only one he would get.

Everyone watched until the last of the Griddas had disappeared below. 'What will happen?' Rachel asked Serpantha at last. 'What will happen to the Griddas now?'

'Until they recover, their needs will be taken care of,' he answered. 'After that, they will have some choices to make. We will all have choices.'

'Will they still want to fight?'

Serpantha smiled. 'Perhaps, but I am hopeful. If anything can persuade them otherwise, the devotion of the Witches will do so.'

'And you?' Rachel stared up into Serpantha's eyes. 'What about the Wizards? If there are only two of you left, when you die, will there …'

'No.' He kissed her. 'Each generation a few Wizards are born. If the endless war is finally over, Larpskendya and I will soon have company. I look forward to that. I look forward to many things.'

Eric started to shake again. The prapsies quietened down at once, steadying him. 'I nearly killed them all,' he whispered, raising his hands. 'How could I have done that? Oh, I nearly did.'

'But you held back,' Serpantha said. 'That was harder. That required more strength.' He lifted Eric's chin. 'There is greatness in you. Don't you know that yet?'

Eric stared at his hands. 'I'm frightened. What … what am I, Serpantha?'

'You are a forerunner, Eric. A beginning of something. There has been nothing like you before. I suspect there will be a different destiny for all of us, because of you – and those you lead.'

'Those I lead?'

'Don't you realize?' said a voice. 'Even now?' It was

Albertus Robertson. He and a few other spectrums were close beside Eric, observing him intently.

'Realize what?' Eric said.

Both of Albertus's girl thrill-seekers laughed. They glanced briefly at each other, held hands, smiled – a parting smile. Then one of the girls held Albertus's face in her hands and kissed him. Afterwards she breathed deeply and turned to Eric. She waited, her expression full of yearning.

'What's happening?' Eric asked.

'I am not the natural leader of the spectrums,' Albertus said.

'You're not?'

'No, Eric. You are.'

'What?' Eric said. 'But the ears ...'

Albertus shook his head. 'Are you still measuring those you meet by how they appear? Surely you've learned that lesson by now ... besides, the spectrums may soon be altering again. I'm not certain in what way.'

'But – how do you know I'm your leader?'

'We've always known,' Albertus said. 'However something told us not to reveal it to you until now. And there was another reason we did not tell you, Eric. We were frightened of what you can do.'

The thrill-seeker girl who had left Albertus stared at Eric. She wanted to go to him, but she needed his permission first.

'Are you still frightened?' Eric asked Albertus.

'No.' A complex expression crossed Albertus's face, and suddenly Eric could hear thousands of voices. It was the voices of all the spectrums opening up to him. The thoughts were not chaos; he heard each one clearly, personally.

The girl could wait no longer. 'I was always your thrill-seeker,' she said. 'If you wish it, I will be. Say that you do. I have waited so long.'

'I don't need –' Eric began – but she would not let him say no. She took him in her arms and, as soon as he felt her touch, Eric knew it was right. He did not feel embarrassed.

The prapsies watched. They saw the look Eric gave the girl – the same private one he shared with them. Upset, but not wanting to spoil this special moment for him, they stayed still. They tried to pretend they did not exist at all.

'What's up with you two?' Eric said loudly.

'Nothing,' one prapsy said. 'We're fine, boys.'

'Thought I'd forgotten you, eh?' Eric said. 'Get up here, you flipping idiots. Introduce yourselves. She's going to have to get used to you, so help her.' The prapsies sprang from his shoulders, hovering beside the girl. 'Say hello,' Eric ordered them.

While the girl introduced herself, a flash of sunshine lit up Orin Fen.

Drawn by the intricacies of light, and encouraged by the Witches, most of the children had already started heading towards the planet. Deepers plunged into the golden oceans to discover what wondrous life swam there. Others went further out across Orin Fen, to the exalted mountain heights. There was no snow, but surely there would be something else … As for the thrill-seekers, they seemed to have gone completely wild. They whirled and soared across Orin Fen, and for a brief time, as Rachel watched, it appeared that even the spectrums had almost forgotten themselves as they took in the beauty of the yellow-brown skies. Rachel saw other children. Some were escorting more timid youngsters, or those with little magic, helping them to explore the strangeness without fear. Rachel looked for those she knew: Marshall, Paul, more than she could name, brave children.

'I want to go there,' Eric said, pinching her. 'Hey, Rach, you coming?'

She hesitated.

'What's up?' he asked. 'You want to go somewhere else?'

'Home,' she said. 'I want to go home.' Then she laughed. 'But I want to go to Ool as well! I've got to take these ones back' – she squinted at the Essa dancing with happiness around her head – 'and I want to see the storm-whirls, and talk with the Detaclyver. And most of all I want to go to Ithrea. I have to be sure that Morpeth's safe.'

'Well,' Eric said, 'I can't take you to any of those places. But I can do one thing.'

Rachel felt shouts of joy. They came from inside her. Eric had freed her shifting spells. Her eyes turned blue as they crept up to be alongside the flyers and see what they had missed.

'Bright skies! Bright skies!' the Essa cried, staring at the colours.

'Oh, so that's what you like,' Heiki said to the Essa. She made her own eyes dazzling, trying to persuade a few of the Essa to join her.

Serpantha had been peering beyond Orin Fen, into the emptiness of space. Rachel noticed his uncertainty. 'What is it?' she said.

'Oh, many things,' he answered. 'I will not delay your return home, or any of the other places you wish to go, but it would honour me if you could find another reason in your heart to join me on Ool. Calen and the last of the

High Witches are still imprisoned. I would like you to be there with me when they are released.'

'Didn't they… betray the Wizards?' Heiki said. 'Especially you.'

'Betrayed? Yes, I suppose they did. There have been so many betrayals. But whose was the first? Who is to say what set the High Witches down their terrible path? Were the Wizards entirely blameless? In those ancient days, when there was no threat to our supremacy, did the Wizards do everything they could to persuade those first Witches? When they wanted to leave Orin Fen, who asked them to stay? Larpskendya and I made a promise to each other: that no matter what happened, we would never lose faith, not in you, nor in the Witches, wherever their hatred had taken them.' Serpantha smiled sadly. 'In any case, does one betrayal deserve another? Would you have me leave the Highs in their chains?'

'No,' Heiki answered. No. I … I wouldn't.'

'I'll come with you,' Rachel said. 'Of course I will.'

She held Serpantha's robe, for a while lost in its silken feel. Then she looked up. Strangely, while almost all the other children were now on Orin Fen, Yemi had stayed behind. He stared longingly down at the surface, but he did not fly towards it. Instead, he clung to Fola while looking at Rachel, waiting for her.

'What's wrong?' she asked, flying over. 'Yemi, what's the matter?'

'He doesn't want to leave you,' Fola said. 'I told him you no mind, but he never listens to me, you know that.' She half-laughed. 'He says he's always leaving you, and he doesn't want to, but –'

'I know. It's all right.' Rachel brought Yemi into her

arms and held him tightly. Several of the Essa naturally crossed over to him; they couldn't help themselves. 'You've got something you have to do, haven't you?' Rachel whispered to him.

Fola smiled. 'Yes! He tried before, but it was too hard. No more. Oh, no!'

Forests flashed in Yemi's eyes: the plants of a purple-skied world: Trin.

'Yes, go now,' Rachel said. 'Don't wait for me. I'll come when I can. Go to them.'

Yemi's gaze took in the miraculous colours of Orin Fen lighting up the children below him. There was no need for him to say anything. Rachel understood exactly how he felt. He glanced at her one more time. Then, amid a flutter of wings and a giggle of wonder, he, Fola and all the Camberwell Beauty butterflies vanished. They left behind a trail of yellow sparks that faded only slowly.

Rachel's eyes were moist. Below her, Witches beckoned with their elegant arms, inviting her down. 'If we're going to Ool, we should go now,' she said to Serpantha. 'But I wish I knew Morpeth was safe.'

'He is,' murmured a voice. 'He is.'

Larpskendya had returned from the shadows of Orin Fen. 'I heard you planned to leave, and I thought you might do so before saying goodbye. My spells would not allow that!' He held her shoulders, his eyes shining. 'Ithrea is safe, Rachel. The Griddas never discovered it, but even if they had I wonder how they would have conquered it. Trimak, Fenagel, Leifrim, Morpeth – there is a dedication amongst them, as amongst you all, that I cherish.' He stared at her. 'Before you leave for Ool with my brother, may I ask you to accompany me on a short journey? I would like to show you my world. It seems only fair, as I have had the privilege of knowing yours.'

'Orin Fen is ... so beautiful,' Rachel said, gazing down.

'Yes, but no more so than your own world,' Larpskendya replied. 'There is beauty everywhere. On Earth I have seen such wonders, and not only from the most magical. I have never seen tenderness or resolve greater than that shown by the parents of your world. Nor have I seen more courage than that shown by children, or should I say one child: you, Rachel.'

Rachel lowered her face. 'Oh, I ... I didn't do so much,' she said. 'I haven't got as much magic as Yemi. I can't do what Eric can do. They were more important in the end.'

Larpskendya gazed at her. 'No. That is not true. And even if it were, do you think I would love you any the less for it?'

Rachel buried her face in his robe.

Larpskendya lifted her face and kissed her. He laughed. 'Will you follow me, or do you want to lead?'

Before she could answer the prapsies started chasing the Essa. They had wanted to do so ever since they first saw them, and even the Essa could not out-dodge a prapsy. 'Behave, boys,' Eric said, winking at them. He stared down at Orin Fen. 'Where shall we look first, then, Rach? Those cities look good.'

The Essa whispered in Rachel's ear. She laughed.

'Well?' Eric said. 'Decided yet?' He waited. Heiki waited. Serpantha and Larpskendya, all of them.

Grinning, Rachel flew towards Orin Fen, not towards the cities, but the quieter places, higher up, the mountain peaks of that lovely world.

Also by Cliff McNish

the silver child

Six children leave the comfort of their homes for Coldharbour, an eerie wasteland of wind, rats, seagulls and rubbish tips. Emily and Freda, the insect-like twins, find Thomas half-starving on a food tip. They discover Walter, the giant boy, his hands buried in the ashes of a fire. Helen reaches Coldharbour at the height of a furious storm. Together they seek out Milo – the sixth child – whose skin is hot and bright with silver.

Unique gifts have drawn them to one another, but will they be in time to save themselves? The Roar, a vast and terrifying creature from worlds away, is drawing closer and is intent on their destruction.

Book I in Cliff McNish's heart-stopping *Silver Sequence* will sweep you into a fantasy full of richly imagined, breathtaking adventure.

'An intriguing and sinister tale'   *Dreamwatch*

'a genuinely original piece of writing, strongly imagined and well written.'   *Book for Keeps*

'A beguiling story'   Joanne Owen, *The Bookseller*

silver city

The Roar, devourer of worlds, is drawing closer. From the desolate reaches of space she has *smelled* the children of Earth, and her hunger knows no bounds.

Children from all over the world are rushing to Coldharbour. Here, Milo, a silver boy the size of cities, has emerged as the first great defender against the Roar. But where will the second generation come from? Six special children hold the key, but their strength is dwindling. Thomas is shocked by his discovery of the eerie Unearthers. The twins are drawn irresistibly to the ocean, compelled to dive deep. Walter, the giant, must face a terrifying trial of strength, while Helen, searching for the secret of the strange little girl, Jenny, enters the mind of Roar itself. The lines for battle are drawn.

In book II of *The Silver Sequence*, Cliff McNish immerses his readers in a spectacular, unforgettable fantasy adventure, full of the imagination and inventive touches that are the hallmark of his writing.